# STARJUMPER LEGACY
# THE PLAGUE OF DAWN

# BY CHRISTOPHER BAILEY

Published by Phase Publishing, LLC

*Starjumper Legacy:*

The Crystal Key

The Vanishing Sun

The Plague of Dawn

*Others:*

Without Chance

# STARJUMPER LEGACY

## BOOK THREE
## THE PLAGUE OF DAWN

### CHRISTOPHER BAILEY

Phase Publishing, LLC
Seattle

Phase Publishing, LLC first paperback edition
October 2015



ISBN 978-1-943048-92-2
Library of Congress Control Number 2015952509
Cataloging-in-Publication Data on file.

To Carter, for always asking me how my latest book is coming. To Chantelle and Shane, Jeff and Brandy, Jo and Adam, and Ferrell and Ron for your valued support, encouragement, and feedback.

And to my Angel. For you, even the stars will never be enough.

# CONTENTS

# CONTENTS

# PROLOGUE

# PIRATES

Allie woke slowly, and easily. She'd slept better than she had for weeks, her mind at ease for the first time since opening the box containing the crystal. Lying quietly for a long moment after waking, she smiled softly. Her mother and all her friends were safe. The Highlord was defeated, and the galaxy would be able to return to what she supposed was normal. Not that she had any idea what normal for the galaxy was, but she was excited to find out.

She would contact Katharine as soon as they made it to Sy'hloran, maybe even Jumping back to Earth to tell her the news in person. Definitely, Allie thought. That would be perfect. She would Jump herself and her mother back to Earth and surprise Katharine. Allie tried not to think about what she would do if Katharine refused to come with them to Sy'hloran.

Tic trilled softly and nuzzled her neck. Allie giggled

and gently stroked the little jicund's purple fur. Her relief at not having to take Tic back to Ayaran was immense, though part of her still wondered if perhaps Tic would prefer it. Maybe Ayaran could be a stop on the way back to Earth, and Allie could see if that's what Tic really wanted. After all, it wouldn't be fair to her little friend to just keep her without asking her what she wanted.

She stretched and sat up, Tic moving nimbly to the side, then leaping easily up to Allie's shoulder with a chirp. Allie idly scratched the jicund's neck again as she yawned and stood. Glancing at the bunk below, she noticed Imber was already up and gone. Imber was an early riser, something Allie never had been, and if she had her way, never would be.

Allie hopped down from the bunk and moved to her locker, pulling out her flight suit. She had never guessed she'd be comfortable wearing the same outfit every day, but this one was freshly cleaned by the systems inside the locker each night. Besides that, it was incredibly comfortable, and when she wore it she actually felt really cool, like a real space adventurer.

Something to the side caught her eye. A faint glow coming from inside Imber's locker. That's weird, she thought to herself. It didn't even occur to her to leave the locker alone. She knew Imber wouldn't mind her taking a look, none of them had anything very personal here, just their flight suits and weapons really. Well, and Dav's lucky pocketknife, she knew. She had no idea how he'd held onto it through this ordeal. Maybe Dav was right, and the knife really was lucky.

Opening the door to the locker, she glanced around.

Nothing was glowing, there was nothing unusual inside the locker at all. She could see Imber's rifle on its rack, and a small gun belt with a shatter gun in the holster, and the soft clothing Imber slept in. That was all. Imber's flight suit was gone of course, since Imber would be wearing it.

Closing the locker, she looked at it for a long moment, but the glow she'd seen wasn't there. It had been extremely faint, she thought. Maybe that was what the lockers did when cleaning the clothes? She'd never watched the locker perform the process, since it wouldn't work when the door was open. Allie turned away and headed out into the hallway of the Peacekeeper.

She heard voices in the cockpit, the relaxed and comfortable voices of her friends. Moving that direction, Tic chirped a greeting as they entered the cockpit, giving away her presence before she could speak.

Dav, Raith, and Imber sat at their respective stations, but the chairs were all rotated around to face one another as they talked. They all smiled at her.

"Good morning, sleepyhead," Dav teased, his grin bright and slightly playful, just like it always had been back on Earth before the mess had started. As always, she couldn't help but grin back at him. She viciously shoved down the slight fluttering in her stomach at his smile.

"Oh come on, it's not that late," she protested.

"That's what you think. We were beginning to wonder if you'd been abducted by aliens," Raith quipped with a smirk. She laughed lightly and glanced at Dav and Imber pointedly.

"I'm pretty sure I have been, actually," she replied.

Dav laughed. "Hey, we reach Sy'hloran tonight, right?"

"Shortly after dinner," Raith replied.

"Which is a pity," Dav interrupted, "I'd love to have dinner on Sy'hloran. Treat you all to some real food, not this ship's galley rubbish."

"Hey!" Imber protested, since she did most of the cooking.

"Not that you don't work wonders with the poor quality of food we have, but even your magic can't cure some of the pre-packaged survival food we've been living on," Dav backpedaled smoothly. Imber smiled warmly at him and Allie bit back a flare of jealousy. No need for that, she reminded herself.

Allie glanced at her holographic display as she sat in her own chair. She could see a couple of the Sy'hli ships that had been escorting them still in formation around the Peacekeeper, but many were gone.

"Where did the others go?" she asked curiously.

"Side mission," Dav replied. "A couple of Maruck ships came in during the night, but the Sy'hli chased them off before they got close enough to start shooting."

"I could have hit them," Raith pointed out.

"Yeah, but they couldn't have hit us," Dav answered. "Besides, the Sy'hli guard wasn't about to give us the chance. Anyway, our babysitters went after them. It isn't a good idea to leave them roaming free. With Tyren defeated…"

"The Highlord," Allie corrected. Dav still didn't fully believe her when she had repeatedly tried to explain that Tyren was a good man, it was the parasites inside him that were evil and cruel. Dav sighed. They'd been over this a hundred times. He was taking it on faith because she said that's how it was, but he had thirteen years of bitterness and resentment, betrayal and anger working against him on this subject.

"The Highlord," he conceded. "With him defeated, the Maruck have no clear direction and are likely to begin marauding on their own. The Sy'hli, or those still around and on our side, are fighting hard to deal with that threat before it can become a huge issue."

Yet another consequence of removing the man in charge that Allie hadn't considered. She was glad that Dav was so sharp, and was on top of all of this. Politics was definitely not her strong suit. Neither was math, but she felt more comfortable even with word problems than with political intrigue and its far-reaching consequences.

"My uncle and father have my people working hard to keep the lawlessness from getting out of control as well," Imber added. "We need the people of the galaxy to understand that while the galaxy is now under new management, that management won't allow things to run rampant. Too much harm has been done since the Highlord took control, we don't need more being done while we're trying to fix the current damage."

"Definitely," Allie agreed, slightly distracted and still watching her monitor. Something odd was going on, and she wasn't sure if it was odd enough to comment on. One of the Sy'hli ships had stopped. Just stopped, completely. The Peacekeeper and the other Sy'hli warship were still holding steady on course, but the other one was now falling well behind. No, she corrected, the other warship was now turning around and heading back to the first one.

"Dav?" she called. "Is something wrong with our escort?" Dav spun his chair around and looked at the sensor display Allie tossed easily onto his screen with a thought and a touch of the control bar. Dav's brow furrowed slightly and he activated the com channel.

"Peacekeeper to the Firestorm, this is Davrelan. Come in, Firestorm." His frown deepened when there was no response from the still ship. "Peacekeeper to the Skyjammer, come in."

"Skyjammer here, this is Commander Brynn. No response from the Firestorm. She's just dead in the water. Anything unusual on your sensors?" came the woman's reply over the com. Dav glanced at Allie, one brow raised in question. She had been looking intently, but saw nothing. She shook her head at Dav.

"Negative, Commander," Dav said into the com again, "Clear as far out as we can read."

Silence greeted this reply.

"Commander?" Dav asked when there was no response. No response came. The Skyjammer had pulled alongside the Firestorm and now both ships sat still and silent.

"There's an odd frequency humming below the com channel, Dav," Imber said from her station, her sharp eyes watching the frequency readouts. "I can't identify it, but I've never seen anything like this frequency. Its modulation is intense. Seems to be getting louder. What do you think, Raith?" She asked, looking his way. There was no reply. The other two turned to look his way as well. He was almost perfectly still, with just one of his hands twitching slightly, mechanically, staring at seemingly nothing.

"Raith?" Allie called, standing and moving toward him. The twitching stilled. There was a flicker in the lights, then everything went dark, and the hum of the ship's engines went silent.

"Allie? Imber?" Dav called. "You two okay?"

"She can't hear you, Dav. I'm okay, though," Allie reminded him, frustrated at the sound of the tremor in her voice. *Be strong,* she told herself.

The only light in the cockpit came from the big front windows, from which distant stars twinkled. They were very distant however, and they shed almost no light on anything. Allie could see her hand in front of her face, but only barely. Out of nowhere, a soft flicker of light appeared, and Imber's face was illuminated.

Her heirlines were giving off a soft, colorful glow. Imber had chosen white for the light, probably for brightness, but subtle pulses of other colors moved along her heirlines periodically as well. It was beautiful.

Imber took several steps toward Allie and stood beside her with a comforting smile. Imber's heirlines didn't put off enough light to really move around or navigate with, but it was plenty to give them a small circle of comfort in the darkness. Allie gave her an appreciative smile and reached out to take her hand.

"Don't worry," Dav reassured them, stepping close enough that Imber could read his lips. "I can see clearly, and there's nothing else here, nothing to be afraid of. Tic can see in this too, so you're well protected. Just an odd power surge, I think. Maybe an anomaly we flew through. Or that flew through us, it hit the ship in back first. Raith, you still with us?" Allie could hear Dav moving to Raith's side. Tic chirped softly, comfortingly.

"Raith's down too, whatever it was it must have shorted his systems as well. Hopefully it's only temporary," he said under his breath. Allie heard it anyway. "I'm going to go check the engines," he called, more loudly.

"Dav?" Allie called, trying to keep the fear from her voice as he vanished from sight into the shadows.

"It's okay, I'll keep talking so you know where I am and that I'm still all right."

"Okay," she said, unconvinced.

"I'm in the hallway. I don't see any damage anywhere yet." Dav's voice came from further away than she'd expected. She hadn't heard him move at all, it was a little creepy. She was glad he was on her side. Allie squeezed Imber's hand and nodded to let her know Dav was reporting he was okay. Imber watched Allie's lips move as she spoke back to Dav.

"Galley is clear," Dav said, voice coming from further away than before, his footsteps making less noise than that of a cat. "So is the bedroom." Allie heard the sound of a big panel being opened in the back of the ship as she repeated Dav's words to Imber.

"I'm at the engines," Dav called. "Panel control is down, had to use the manual release."

"Engines look fine," Dav called back. "No shorted circuits that I can find, no damage, nothing. I can't find any reason that the system is down."

"Great," Allie grumbled. Imber squeezed her hand

reassuringly. Tic suddenly looked up from her perch on Allie's shoulder and hissed softly, menacingly.

"Dav!" Allie called in warning. There was a thud from the back of the ship, sounding alarmingly like a limp body hitting the floor. "Dav!" Allie cried again, this time in fear.

A sound reached her ears, growing rapidly. It wasn't a bad sound, in fact it was very pleasant, soothing. *So soothing*, Allie thought.

It got louder rapidly, to the point that it overwhelmed everything else like a heavy woolen blanket on an icy winter's night. Tic dropped off her shoulder. Allie suddenly felt sleepy, so tired that she felt like she hadn't slept in days. She wasn't sure exactly when the floor rose up to meet her, but she didn't mind. The floor felt nice. Imber's light faded as Allie watched her friend lie down beside her. As the light faded, so did Allie's consciousness.

# CHAPTER ONE

# UNCONSCIOUS... AGAIN

Allie woke slowly, but not easily this time. She felt she had to claw her way back to consciousness, each tiny bit of gained awareness a massive struggle. After several minutes, she became aware of a voice calling to her.

"Allie!" It was Dav. Allie realized she'd passed out again. Mentally, sluggishly, she cursed herself. She really was getting tired of being knocked unconscious. "Allie!" he called again.

"Mmfh," she replied eloquently.

"Allie, are you with me?" he asked.

"Yeah," she managed to mumble as she tried to open her eyes. It took a lot more effort than it should have, like her eyelids had been weighted down with bowling balls. "What happened?"

"I don't know," Dav replied, "but I do know we were knocked out and taken from our ship."

"Abducted by aliens?" she asked with a groggy

giggle.

"Allie," Dav said sternly, but she could hear Imber giggle as well on her other side. That was reassuring. Her eyes opened and she managed to focus on her surroundings. They were in a small room, one wall of which seemed to be composed of a faintly shimmering purple surface. She could see through it to a hallway beyond. Dav and Imber were with her, but Raith wasn't.

"Where's Raith?" she asked, suddenly much more alert.

"I don't know that either," Dav replied, "I just woke up."

Allie stood gingerly, easing her way up and using the wall for support. Dav stood with her, with much more stability and ease than she had, she thought with a hint of annoyance. She walked carefully to the shimmering wall. Energy field, she knew. To keep them in this lovely, metal-lined cell. It wasn't well-lit in here, with most of the light coming from a murky yellow glow from the hallway, filtered through the purple energy field.

"Don't touch it," Dav warned. Allie had been thinking about it, but wisely took his advice. Imber joined them by the energy field just as a door down the hallway opened. A woman came into view.

Allie couldn't have imagined a more intense, severe, and dangerous-looking woman if she'd tried. The woman was slender, but not thin slender, whipcord slender. The definition in the muscles of her bare arms showed almost no real bulk, but iron-hard muscle cord. Her skin was well tanned, almost weathered, and her blonde hair was cropped military-short, sticking up slightly on top like tiny little spikes. A scar ran from one ear clear down her jawline, with another halfway across her neck like someone had tried to cut her once, long ago, and was stopped mid-way through. It was counterpointed by several other visible scars on her face and arms.

The clothing and gear she wore practically screamed menacing efficiency, right down to the high, black leather boots. Probably metal-toed, Allie thought. Around her upper right arm she wore an iron band, the outside facing away from her body lined in inch-long red spikes.

The woman carried a gun. Not a little gun, the monstrous gun she carried was leaning up against one shoulder, her long-fingered hand carrying it easily with the hand on the grip, finger twitching near the trigger. It looked like it had to weigh a hundred pounds, at least. The woman carried it with no apparent strain though. It was almost big enough to refer to as a cannon, rather than a gun. It was polished, mirrored silver, and made the dark leathers and rough metal of her outfit look all the more well-used and menacing.

She stopped in front of the energy field, her shockingly intense gray eyes seeming to cut straight through Allie when they locked with hers. The woman lowered the gun to hold it across her body, cradling the barrel in her other hand almost lovingly. The woman noticed Allie's gaze on the gun and grinned. It was not a cheerful expression.

"This is my boy Shane," she said conversationally. "He doesn't like it when people give me any trouble, am

I clear?"

"Shane?" Allie couldn't help but ask.

"It's from an old movie," the woman explained conversationally. Allie didn't get the reference, though the movies this woman watched probably weren't made on Earth.

"Who are you," Dav demanded. The woman turned her raptor-like gaze his way.

"Call me Spike," she replied, her voice just as hard as the rest of her, but her tone casual and almost friendly.

"Why are we here?" Dav asked, seeming totally unintimidated.

How that could be, Allie had no idea. This woman was incredibly intimidating. She wasn't big, far from it. She was tall, true, but couldn't weigh more than a hundred and ten pounds or so. Of pure, refined muscle, Allie observed. Her muscles looked like taught, iron cables rippling under her skin.

"I'm under orders to bring you to my Captain. Don't worry, I'm also under orders not to harm you... unless you give me any trouble, then I'm allowed to have some fun." She grinned at this, for a brief moment bearing a striking resemblance to a shark.

"Where's our friend? And what have you done with the Sy'hli soldiers?"

"I assume you mean the machine?" she asked. "He's in the cargo bay. The Captain wants to download his memory before we have him recycled.

"No!" Allie shouted, moving reflexively forward. She stopped a hair's breadth before hitting the energy field. The woman looked slightly disappointed when

Allie stopped.

"Just a machine," the woman said calmly.

"He's my friend," Allie replied. Spike looked at Dav, then at Imber, then back to Allie.

"You choose odd friends," she said curiously. "The Sy'hli are fine," she continued abruptly as if she hadn't paused. "My orders said nothing about them, and Sy'hli strike troops are far too dangerous to try and keep captive. No point. And killing them would lead to more heat from their people than we care to bother with. I dumped them all on the other ship, after disabling it of course. By the time they get up and running, we'll have made it back to the Blackstar in this ship. Nobody challenges the Blackstar, unless they care to spend the rest of their existence as dust and debris." Spike glanced around the hallway. "I'll say this for them, the Sy'hli build excellent warships. The Captain will be pleased. An extra bonus for this mission."

"And Tic?" Allie asked, again barely stopping herself from going right through the energy field at the woman.

"Who?" Spike asked.

"The jicund," Dav clarified.

"In a cage," Spike replied. "Feisty little thing. I like her. I think maybe I'll keep her."

"She'd kill you the instant she got the chance," Allie stated simply.

"Makes it that much more fun," Spike replied.

"What about my Interceptor?" Dav asked.

"Jinx is flying that one right behind us. An Interceptor is far too valuable to leave lying about, wouldn't you say?"

"Why would your Captain want to have us captured?" Imber asked.

"She speaks," Spike said dryly, locking eyes with Imber. "Because we're being paid to bring you in, little girl."

"By whom?" Dav asked.

"The Highlord, of course. An Ambassador's daughter, a crystal bearer, and a Sy'hli prince? You three are worth quite a bit. If the Highlord weren't paying us so well, you'd be worth capturing anyway, just for the ransom."

"The Highlord has fallen," Dav said, his voice dripping with satisfaction and a definite hint of smugness.

"Uh huh," Spike replied, looking unconvinced.

"He was captured days ago, his power and his new weapon destroyed. Your contract is void."

"He paid in advance," Spike said, "the contract will be completed whether he was defeated, destroyed, killed, or magically turned into a fluffy white rabbit."

"Why are you even bothering to talk to us?" Dav asked.

"Because it's fun to play with my prey," Spike said with a toothy grin.

However tough this woman looked and acted, Allie wasn't about to be anyone's prey. Faintly, when she focused, she could feel the energies swirling around her. Grabbing hold, she Jumped. It was much harder Jumping without the crystal, but it was a lot easier doing it without a rogellium-laced ship in tow. Compared to that, this felt surprisingly easy. She made a mental note to ask Dav about Jumping without a crystal later. He likely wouldn't have an answer. She seemed to be able to do a lot of things that the other Jumpers never could.

In a blink, she was behind the woman. Reaching for the woman's handgun strapped to one hip, Allie intended to turn the tables. Without so much as a glance over her shoulder, Spike snapped one elbow back, square into the side of Allie's head, dropping her cold.

Dav winced as he watched Allie go down. He wished she hadn't done that, the woman already knew she was a Jumper. Spike probably even had things in place to keep Allie from Jumping off the ship with Dav and Imber, and obviously had finely-tuned battle reflexes. Although come to think of it, Dav thought, the usual blocks for Jumping might not even slow Allie down. Allie might possibly have been able to Jump to safety. The woman shook her head with a smile, almost pityingly.

"Girl's got guts," Spike said. "I can respect that. Not too bright though."

"She's plenty bright," Dav defended his friend, "just inexperienced."

"Well, we all start somewhere, right kid?" she said to Dav with another friendly-ish smile.

"What will your Captain do with us?" Dav asked, eyes on Allie, lying still on the ground behind the mercenary.

"Hold you until the Highlord's agent comes for you. I expect that won't be too long."

"Spike, we're nearing the Blackstar," a voice came over the ship's com.

"Roger that," she replied to the voice, then looked back to Dav. "Well, duty calls. Got to bring a present to the boss."

With that, she reached down with one hand, picked up Allie, and tossed her straight through the energy field and back into the cell.

Dav was surprised to see that nothing seemed to happen to Allie as she passed through the shimmering field. He considered the meaning of that as he caught Allie smoothly, easing her back down. He quickly looked at her head. She'd have a nasty bruise if they didn't get their hands on a dermal regenerator soon, and she'd have a headache for a while, but she'd be okay. He touched her cheek gently, then realized Imber was probably watching. He stood and looked her way. She had a look in her eyes he couldn't identify, and didn't care to ask about.

"She'll be all right," he told her, trying to sound confident and in control.

"What do we do?" Imber asked.

"I'm not sure," Dav replied. "I think we're stuck here until we are taken to meet the Captain tho..." he was interrupted by a buzzing jolt that shook the whole ship.

"Wow, rough dock?" Imber asked in surprise, looking around.

"No," Dav said, at once hopeful and concerned, "arc cannons."

"Who in their right mind would be attacking a Sy'hli warship?" Imber asked. "And why?"

"Maruck, maybe? Could be Imperial Guard, too. This ship isn't part of the Coalition."

"Going to be an ugly fight then," Imber pointed out. "We probably won't survive, stuck in here."

"We'd better get out, then."

"How?"

"Experiment. Quickly," Dav added with a grin.

He stepped toward the energy field and unclipped one of the nutrient cells from his belt pack. Spike had taken their guns, but nothing else. He tossed it at the energy field. There was a vicious crackle, and the nutrient cell was gone. He frowned. A one-way energy field? He'd never heard of anything like that, though he had to remind himself that he was still many years behind on the technological advancements of the galaxy.

He moved to the wall where the control panel was on the outside, placing his hand on the metal behind where it should be. No hum of machinery, and the panel felt just as secure as everything else. Sy'hli weren't exactly amateurs when it came to warfare and imprisonment. The odds of their actually getting out of this cell without someone switching off the field from the outside was slim to none, but he had to keep giving Imber hope, so he pulled out his lucky knife and started testing the edges of the metal paneling.

Another lurching jolt sent him almost to his knees. Imber stumbled, but caught herself on the wall. Whoever it was that was attacking the Sy'hli warship was likely having a seriously difficult time against the Sy'hli warship and an Interceptor, though despite the odds, the Sy'hli warship was obviously taking a beating. He hoped nobody would get seriously hurt in this mess. It was stupid to attack a pair of ships that powerful unless it was with an entire fleet, which he doubted was what had been brought against them. If it were a full fleet, they'd have been hit more than twice. Another jolt, and Dav corrected himself. Maybe it was a fleet.

Another jolt came, but this one was different. This felt like the ship had been grabbed and violently shaken for a moment. In the distance, the shrieking sound of a great deal of metal being torn apart echoed through the hallway.

Things got quiet and still for a long moment. Dav resumed testing metal panels, trying to hide his growing concern. Whatever was attacking this ship seemed likely to destroy it, and everything in it as well. The door down the hallway opened. Well here comes Spike, he thought to himself, stepping sideways to put himself in front of the field again. He couldn't decide if he preferred that their latest visitor would be Spike, or whomever had been attacking the ship. Even with his self-control, he almost leapt backwards at what suddenly appeared in front of the energy field and looked up at him.

It was a little smaller than Dav, but only in height. It was nearly twice his width and probably outweighed him by a few hundred pounds. It was covered in brown fur that looked impossibly soft, and seemed, for lack of a better word, cuddly. The soft brown face looked eager and excited, the mouth opening and closing with small grunts of happiness. It looked to have noticeably sharp teeth, but dog sharp, not jicund sharp. It wore a simple outfit of brown, textured leathers that left its lower legs and its arms completely uncovered. It also wore no shoes on its huge, clawed feet.

Only the eyes and stance gave away what it really was. Small, black, and intense, they were the eyes of a Maruck. A juvenile Maruck, no less. Dav was stunned by how cute the creature was. No mistaking, he reminded himself, even at this size it could tear the arms off a human without much trouble and could likely bite his head off in the blink of an eye, but it looked like a large pet.

No less potentially dangerous than a huge dog, but seemingly just as friendly as it grinned broadly up at him, the beginnings of tusks just visible behind its lower lip. Dav's feelings on the subject of the creature's appeal were affirmed by Imber's soft gasp of delight when she spotted it.

"Help," the little Maruck said brightly, its voice sounding less like a growl or roar, like an adult Maruck, and more like a rumbly, soft purr, like an absurdly oversized house cat.

"You are here to help us?" Imber asked in disbelief. Dav's thoughts echoed her tone of astonishment. The little Maruck nodded eagerly, excited that they'd understood it.

"That panel," Dav said, pointing to where he guessed the panel to be. "Put your hand on it and tell the computer to lower the field."

"Field?" asked the little Maruck.

"Yes," Dav replied, "think about this purple field,"

he gestured at the barrier, "going away."

"Go away," purred the little Maruck and nodded his fuzzy head. It moved to the panel and reached a long arm up, alarmingly big hand resting on what Dav assumed was the panel. The energy field vanished. Imber let out a little whoop of excitement, and Dav grinned at her.

"Maruck friendly?" Dav asked, stepping cautiously toward the little creature.

"Friend. Allie friend, Dav friend, Imber friend, Raith friend, Tic friend," it said as if repeating a memorized list. It then looked quizzically at Dav and Imber and cocked its furry head. "Who you?"

Dav was astonished. How did this young Maruck know them, let alone show up here wanting to help them? And how in the galaxy had it learned to speak basic Sy'hli? Very basic, but understandable.

"I'm Dav, this is Imber."

"Dav friend, Imber friend," it repeated. It looked to Allie on the ground, and its deep black eyes looked suddenly very sad. "Friend broken?"

Dav turned and scooped her up.

"She'll be okay. We need to go though."

"Go ship," the little Maruck agreed, its expression brightening. It turned to lope in a surprisingly quick, playfully bouncy fashion down the hallway.

"No, we have to find our friends," Dav said. The Maruck paused and turned.

"Raith friend and Tic friend?"

"Yes, Raith and Tic," Imber told him. Dav again was surprised at the obvious intelligence of the helpful little beast who had apparently deduced that the girl Dav held had been Allie, leaving only Raith and Tic from the list of 'friends'.

"Help friends," it agreed. Dav had no idea why this young Maruck was here, but he wasn't going to argue. Not yet, anyway. They moved down the hallway. When the door opened, Dav had to jump back as a burst of arc rifle fire flashed through the doorway at them.

He'd caught a glimpse of the gunmen, a pair of men in patchy gear, much like Spike's. Some of her mercenaries, he guessed. They ducked back behind a table, using it for cover as they watched the door.

Without guns of their own, it would be tricky to get through that room, but there was no access on the other direction of the hallway, just more holding cells. Allie could easily get them past, but... His thought was interrupted as the little Maruck charged full speed through the doorway.

"Wait!" Dav shouted, but the furry brute ignored him, racing into the room.

Dav looked around the corner, expecting to see the creature blasted into smoking little bits, but it ducked, rolled, and leapt around arc rifle blasts like a jicund through the trees. Before anyone could react, the little Maruck had reached the table hiding the two men, who now looked extremely worried.

The Maruck grabbed the table, long arms easily reaching both sides despite his small stature, hefted the metal table like it was made of paper, and slammed it down on top of the two men, pinning them beneath it. Then the little Maruck hopped up on top of the upside-down table and began jumping gleefully up and down atop it, to the repeated grunts and moans of the men now trapped beneath it. Dav shook his head. Definitely a dangerous ally.

"Come on," he called to the Maruck cub. 'Cub' just seemed like the right word for it, Dav thought.

He ran, Imber right behind him, to the far door. The Maruck still beat them there, opening the door and leaping through. Thank goodness the adults weren't that quick, Dav thought. They were still fast, but this juvenile was so fast it was scary. That speed in an adult Maruck's body, with the adult Maruck's strength, and the Sy'hli would have been torn apart decades ago.

It was another hallway, and the Maruck paused, sniffing the air. It hesitated only a moment, then raced to the left. Dav followed. They passed several doors, but the Maruck cub seemed to know where it was going. Suddenly turning to a door, it sniffed again, huffed in satisfaction, then opened the door.

They were immediately assaulted by the sounds of a raging jicund in a cage, and the shouts of a frantic man trying to move the cage without getting his arms or face torn off. He wasn't being very successful and kept dropping it to get out of reach of Tic's black, terrifyingly sharp claws, which could just barely fit between the energy bars of the cage. There wasn't any place that would work to grip the thing without getting close enough for those alarmingly long claws to reach. The cage was very poorly designed, Dav thought.

The man didn't even have time to turn around at the sound of the opening door before the cub was on him. The little Maruck grabbed the man and tossed him like a ragdoll into a wall. The man yelped in panic, grunted as he bounced off the wall, then tried to scramble away. The Maruck grabbed him by an ankle, dragged him back, turned him over, and pounced on his torso, pinning him down.

The little Maruck paused, looked up at Dav excitedly, and asked "Eat?" before leaning down, mouth opening frighteningly wide toward the man's face.

"No!" Dav cried, almost as horrified as the man the Maruck held down. The cub looked up at Dav curiously.

"No eat?" it asked.

"No eat!" Dav said firmly. "Let him go." The Maruck looked disappointed.

"No eat? Let go?"

"Let him go," Imber agreed, her own face pale at what had been about to happen.

The man's eyes snapped back and forth from Dav to the cub, a tiny spark of hope in his eyes. He had the look of a man who had just witnessed his own death, then been told it might not actually end that way. Which is exactly what had just happened. The little Maruck climbed sullenly off the man. The man scrambled to his feet, then looked frantically between Dav and the Maruck.

"Run," Dav said simply. The man took off like a bullet down the hallway. Dav looked back at the Maruck cub. The little beast began making an odd, rapid huffing noise, and thumping the floor with a fist with evident glee. The little rascal was laughing, Dav realized! It had been teasing the man, as well as Dav and Imber!

Dav couldn't help it, he began to laugh as well. The

Maruck seemed to appreciate that Dav got the joke. It reached over amiably and patted Dav on the back. After a moment, it pointed at the cage and looked to Imber. Dav realized she'd picked up one of the arc rifles from the men in the room behind. Mentally he kicked himself for not thinking of that.

"Tic friend?"

"Yes, can you open the cage? Gently please," Imber replied. The cub nodded and moved to the cage. Tic hissed softly, but at a reassuring word from Dav, calmed again, though Tic's eyes never left the Maruck. The cub carefully righted the tipped cage, and touched the control pad on the top. The side of the cage sprung open, and Tic shot out and leapt straight up onto Allie's belly, still in Dav's arms. The jicund trilled with concern and nuzzled Allie.

"She'll be fine," Dav assured her, "she just needs rest for now." Tic chirped acknowledgement, again as if she perfectly understood. Sometimes, that purple critter worried him, Dav thought.

Dav glanced back at Imber, who was accessing a control panel on the wall. Once again, she was a step ahead of him as he noticed she was looking for Raith. He smiled. She really was a remarkable girl. The Maruck could scent the jicund, but likely couldn't track an android by scent.

"This way," Imber said after a moment, leading the way back down the hallway. Dav grinned. She certainly was handy to have around in a pinch.

Only once did they encounter anyone else on the ship as they worked their way down the extensive hallways. The pair of mercenaries came out of a door, right in front of Imber and the little cub. Imber struck one with a quick slam of the back of the arc rifle she carried. The man was completely taken off guard and the blow was enough to drop him unconscious on the floor. The cub just swung a long arm backhand almost lazily, knocking the other man straight back into the room he'd just come from. The door slid shut. He didn't come back out again.

They neared the back cargo bay, and heard the roars and gunfire long before they reached the door. When the door opened, they were met with a truly impressive sight. Three huge, unarmed Maruck were rampaging through the room, battling close to fifty heavily armed mercenaries. And winning. Maruck were always big, but these three were immense even by Maruck standards.

One Maruck stood a half a head taller than one of the others, and a full head taller than the third, and Dav and Imber recognized him immediately. Their friend Dgehf flung a massive cargo bin toward a crowd of mercenaries, who shouted in panic and dove aside. Arc rifle blasts flashed like a strobe through the room, but whether any of them hit the huge Maruck, it didn't seem to matter. They moved deceptively fast, and were apparently so tough that the few blasts that hit them didn't seem to slow them much.

Dav grinned when he recognized Dgehf. That explained a lot. The other Maruck, including the cub, must be his family. The bigger of the two other adults must be Dgehf's son, the one he'd left Tyren's command to protect. It didn't look like he needed much protection now. He was almost as large as his father, and fought with equally terrifying strength and ferocity.

"Go ship!" the little cub said, pointing to the outside cargo bay doors. Dav looked where the cub was pointing.

The doors seemed to have been peeled back, shredded curls of metal bent back and tattered against either side of the doorway. The torn edges of metal that once held the doors was still faintly glowing with heat.

Over the opening, as though swallowing the ship whole, was Dgehf's unusual Maruck ship. His own docking bay seemed designed to attach violently to any ship he cared to board. With huge, spiked gripping claws reaching in and holding the ship in place by embedding themselves into the floor, ceiling, and walls. Dgehf's boarding bay was open and clear.

"Raith!" Dav shouted over the roars, explosions, crashing sounds, and rifle blasts, looking for his friend. This was their escape route, but also the direction Imber had led them.

"Raith friend," the little cub said, charging abruptly to one side. Dav looked, and saw Raith lying on top of a cargo bin to that side. The Maruck cub would bring him, Dav understood. He moved to run through the bay, but a pocket of the mercenaries turned and fired as they were noticed, forcing him and Imber back into the hallway again.

"Dgehf!" Dav called into the bay. "We need a path!"

A massive metal machine, Dav thought it might have been a loading tractor of some kind, came gracefully arcing through the air, smashing through the metal containers the group of mercenaries had been using for cover, causing them to be knocked aside like so many bowling pins.

"Thank you!" Dav called as he ran into the bay, now unhindered by the mercenaries as they scrambled for new cover.

With a little fancy footwork, he and Imber managed to avoid the groups of mercenaries, who seemed much more interested in keeping the terrible Maruck at bay than they did in shooting at a couple of kids running by.

Imber and Dav ran into the Maruck's ship, Dav carrying Allie with Tic perched on her stomach. The little cub was right behind, carrying a rigid Raith like a board over one shoulder.

"We're clear!" Dav called to Dgehf.

The three huge Maruck flung a few more heavy objects, then loped into the bay of Dgehf's ship. Dav and Imber had ducked around the corner of the boarding bay door for cover, but Dav kept his eyes open, and Imber had taken a knee and leveled the rifle, looking for anyone pursuing. The door leading to the rest of the Sy'hli warship slid open, and Spike stepped in. In an instant, she had taken in the scene and made her decision.

"Dgehf!" Imber shouted in alarm, firing at the woman. She aimed not to hit, but just to provide some cover. The arc rifle blast went by Spike's head close enough that the woman had to have felt singed by the heat of its passing, but the mercenary never even flinched. In a smooth, graceful motion, she brought up her hand cannon, the one she called Shane, dropped to one knee and fired just as Dgehf turned.

The gun emitted a rolling, crackling ball of angry

purple energy that hissed and shrieked as it tore through the bay, leaving the air in its wake warping and twisting as though the very space it traveled through was being singed and bent as it passed. Dgehf moved, ducking below the shot, the purple orb passing just over his head. The orb hit a towering stack of crates behind the massive Maruck. In a rippling wave expanding from the point of impact, the crates tore themselves apart, pieces of warped, twisted metal seeming to wrench inward in a violent surge.

Before anyone could react, Spike had fired again. This time, Dgehf was already crouched too low to move entirely out of the way. The purple blast of energy struck Dgehf high on the chest, near his shoulder as he tried to twist aside.. The impact sent a shower of blue and purple sparks outward, and a resonating sound like a thunderclap that Dav could feel in his own chest as the shockwave passed through him.

The massive Maruck stumbled backward, expression one of complete and total shock. Dav couldn't see the impact point from where he stood, but from the way Dgehf stumbled once, then again trying to regain his balance, he knew it was bad. Dgehf finally caught himself before going down, one huge arm going behind him to stabilize and right himself.

Spike stared in absolute awe. Clearly nothing had ever remained standing after taking a hit from her powerful, beloved Shane. Dgehf looked down at the wound on his chest, the turned his gaze slowly back up to the puny human who had injured him. His expression darkened, and he began to take a deep, angry breath in.

The other two adult Maruck leapt forward and grabbed him, yanking him into the boarding bay of the Maruck ship. Spike raised Shane once more.

The shorter of the two barked a command in the Maruck language, and the bay doors slammed shut, the huge latching hooks releasing and snapping back, and the ship dropped away from the Sy'hli warship, all in a fraction of a second. The huge windows in the boarding bay lit up brilliantly for an instant in the growing, purple light as another blast from Shane approached. It struck the boarding bay door just before the surface had moved out of firing angle.

The blast slammed into the metal surface with the sound of a bomb going off, and a jarring impact enough to make Imber and Dav stumble slightly. The corner of the door twisted back, and one of the windows exploded inward. The taller of Dgehf's companions dove for the control panel as the entire group was suddenly pulled forward by the force of the air in the boarding bay rushing to escape through the shattered window.

The Maruck reached the control panel in a heartbeat, and the moment he touched it, a hissing orange energy field snapped into place over the entire boarding bay door. Instantly the pressure pushing them toward the open window stopped, leaving Dav lying flat on the ground with his feet braced against the edge of the bay door, clinging to Allie, Tic clinging to her as well, and Imber behind Dav, using his body's position as her own leverage to brace against.

Another barked command by the shorter of the two, and Dav felt the engines burst to full capacity as the huge, unique Maruck ship raced off into space. Through the orange energy field, and the broken window, Dav watched the Sy'hli ship vanish in a matter of seconds as the Maruck cruiser left it behind.

Slowly, Dav set Allie down, checking her quickly for injury. Aside from the wound on her head, she seemed relatively unscathed. Imber and Dav himself were also unhurt. The three big Maruck all had several smaller burns and wounds, but Dgehf was in rough shape.

Dav could now see the smoking, sizzling wound in Dgehf's chest. Dgehf looked at Dav, smiled sheepishly, then stumbled and fell to one knee. Dav couldn't believe the Maruck was still alive, let alone conscious. And from his reaction after being shot, he probably would have torn Spike in half if his family hadn't pulled him back.

"Dgehf," Imber said softly, moving toward him. Dgehf gave her a smile, on one knee and one huge fist propping him upright.

"Imber," Dgehf said warmly in welcome. "Glad friends okay."

"Only thanks to you," she replied, touching his cheek gently. His smiled warmed even further, showing the broken end of his damaged tusk. His other was in prime shape, but one had been broken in the brutal fight with C.A.D.E.-16 back on Kobek, Dav remembered.

Dav looked to the female Maruck. In all honesty, he could barely tell the difference between the male and female Maruck, but he recognized the etchings on her tusks. Only the females etched designs into their tusks, and each symbol had meaning. He couldn't read all of them, but knew that two he did recognize meant she was both a warrior of a distinguished clan, and a mother.

"Do you have a medical bay or some supplies?" he asked her. She looked at him for a long moment before turning to look at Dgehf. Dgehf nodded once.

"Dav friend," he told her.

She looked back to Dav, then turned, loping through a doorway into the deeper parts of the ship, hopefully in search of medical supplies. Dav didn't know how bad the wound really was, but the fact that Dgehf still hadn't gotten up from his knees spoke volumes. In fact he still looked a little unsteady, even propped up with one huge arm.

"Allie okay?" Dgehf asked, gesturing with his other hand at her prone form. Dav nodded.

"Yeah, she'll be okay. Just a little bruised. She'll have a terrible headache when she wakes up. She tried to take out the mercenary commander to break us out of the cell." Dgehf nodded at this.

"Allie good fighter," he said.

Dav thought about this and realized Dgehf was right. Allie might not have the combat training and experience, but she never shied away from a fight, especially when her friends were in danger. When she did put up a fight, she gave it everything she had. With some solid training, she would make an excellent fighter.

"Allie is a good fighter." Dav gestured at the wound in Dgehf's chest. "So is Dgehf." Dgehf chuckled, a deep, rumbling earthquake kind of sound. Dav noticed he was slowly getting lower, his arm losing ability to support him.

"Had worse," Dgehf said simply. Dav couldn't help

but laugh.

"Liar," Imber said, but she smiled as well, though her smile was heavily tainted with concern.

Dgehf smiled back at her, reaching his hand up to touch her cheek as gently as she had touched his, just before his arm gave way and he fell to the ground, dark eyes closing slowly. He carefully watched Dgehf's breathing. It seemed shallow, but steady. Dgehf's female companion had better get here soon with a med kit, Dav thought.

He glanced up at the other big Maruck. The Maruck nodded once at him in acknowledgement.

"He might die," Dav said simply. The Maruck nodded again.

"Good battle," the big Maruck said.

Dav nodded. He knew that if Dgehf did die, the Maruck would not mourn him, they would celebrate his glory as a warrior, and his nobility as a father. There was something to be said for that kind of tradition, but it bothered him that the big Maruck was taking the potential of his own father's death, if Dav's assumption about the Maruck's identity was correct, far too casually. That, Dav supposed, was the price one paid for living in a society of hunters and warriors.

# KEEPING THE PEACE

Consciousness came to her, pulling her from odd dreams of a place both light and dark, empty and full, still and churning. She couldn't have described the images she'd seen if she tried. The place scared her though. There was someone there, waiting for her. It had almost found her.

Allie's head felt like she'd been kicked by a mule. Every little noise sent a throbbing pain shooting through her skull, sounding like it was echoing and bouncing around inside her head like a ricocheting bullet. She felt sick.

"Easy," Dav said. She tried to hold still, but whatever he was doing hurt her head like he was repeatedly punching her square in the skull. She knew he was only barely touching it with whatever fancy device he now held, but it still hurt a lot.

"Sorry," she mumbled, then instantly regretted it as

another wave of pain and nausea washed over her. Gradually, far too slowly, the pain began to subside as whatever Dav was doing began to take effect.

She realized there was a buzzing in her ear on the side he held the device that she hadn't noticed before. The little device he was using was making a soft sound. It was rather calming, she thought. As she listened to it Dav continued to work, the pain and throbbing in her head gradually subsiding.

After another few minutes, she opened her eyes. Dav smiled down at her, expression comforting and warm.

"Hi," she said to him with a smile.

"Hi," he replied, his smile showing a trace of his amused grin.

"Did we win?" she asked. Dav chuckled.

"As usual, though with a little help from our friends, also as usual."

"Which friends?" Allie asked, realizing they had quite a few allies these days.

"Big, ugly, furry ones."

"What?" she asked. "Maruck?"

"You got it," he said.

"Dgehf?"

"Two for two. You're on a roll!"

Allie smiled. Once again the big, gentle brute had shown up just in time to save them all.

"Good man," she said.

"He sure is. Brought the whole family along," he said. Allie perked up.

"Really? That's awesome! Can I meet them?"

"I'm sure you can, but right now they're patching

Dgehf up."

"What? What on earth happened to him?"

"Spike shot him."

"With that huge gun?!" she exclaimed. "Is he going to be all right?"

"Possibly. I've never seen anything quite like that gun. I think it's Tchratchi technology, though how she got them to build and give her a Tchratchi weapon, especially one sized for a human, I have no idea. Those guys don't like sharing tech. Especially weapons tech, and that thing is obviously custom made. Scary thing is, I think she had the thing on a low setting, from what I saw of the controls back in the holding cell. Almost killed him. Nearly put a hole in the hull of this battle cruiser, too."

"Wow," Allie said simply, unable to find words.

"Yeah. Everyone else is pretty much unhurt, though. Imber and Tic are fine. Raith is still inactive. I'm not sure how to fix him, though I know he can be fixed."

"How do you know that?"

"The Interceptor was up and running again, remember? Whatever the mercs did to the ships and Raith, they can reverse it pretty easily."

"Good point," she acknowledged, hopeful that it would be fairly easy for them to get Raith up and running again as well.

"I can't believe I got knocked unconscious again," she muttered as Dav set the device down and helped her sit up.

"Twice," he said. She gave his arm a thump.

"Don't remind me!"

"Sorry," he grinned.

"I'm not kidding though, if I keep spending this much time unconscious, at this rate I'll never have to sleep again." Dav laughed at this.

"Oh don't worry, I'm sure it isn't doing any permanent damage to your brain," he said with a teasing grin.

"Of course it's not, Artus," she replied matter-of-factly. His grin faltered for a moment, until she laughed.

"Don't scare me like that!" he said, face filled with mock anger.

"Sorry," she replied, letting her total lack of sincerity show through. "Where's Tic?"

"She's in the galley. Turns out Maruck actually eat almost exclusively meat..."

"No surprise there," she interrupted.

"...of a number of species, including some very large insects," he concluded as if she hadn't spoken. Allie thought about this, then realized what he was getting at.

"Tic's back there, eating a giant bug?" she giggled. Dav grinned and nodded.

"Whatever it is, Tic is absolutely loving it. She's going to need a bath after this though."

"Gross," Allie said, picturing the little jicund, chewing her way through a giant cockroach. The door slid open.

"Hi Allie," Imber said with a smile. "Glad to see you're okay."

"Well, you know me," Allie replied, "I'll survive just about anything."

"Sure seems that way. Hey, I actually came back to

ask Dav if I can borrow his pocketknife. The Maruck tools Dgehf loaned me aren't quite refined enough to try and fix Raith."

"And a pocketknife is more refined?" Dav asked with a smirk.

"It is in this case," she replied. "Advanced robotics is not a Maruck strong suit, so they don't really have much in the way of tools for this kind of work. Actually most of their tools seem designed for chopping, hacking, smashing, twisting, or burning. No wonder their ships always look patched together."

Dav pulled out his knife and handed it to her.

"Just don't damage it, okay? I need that back in one piece."

"Sure thing," she said, walking back out of the room.

"It's amazing that she knows so much about androids," Allie remarked. "If anyone can get Raith up and running again, she can."

"No doubt," Dav replied.

"Can we go see Dgehf?" Allie said after a moment.

"Maybe," Dav replied. "I'm not sure his mate will let us. She's awfully protective."

"I can't wait to meet her," Allie said sincerely. Anyone who could hold a mate like Dgehf would be a remarkable person.

"She's not crazy about us," Dav warned.

"Is she being threatening?" Allie asked, hesitating.

"No, Dgehf told her we were friends. She's not hostile, just not overly friendly. Won't let any of us get too close to her."

"She's pregnant," Allie said simply. Dav froze, then

looked sheepish.

"That'd do it," he replied. "I didn't know. You'd never guess it, the way she fights."

"She fought, while pregnant?!" Allie asked, aghast. Dav nodded.

"As well as any Maruck I've ever seen. That woman is a warrior, no question."

"Brave of her, too. She risked her baby to help us, all because Dgehf needed help rescuing us."

"I'm not sure how much risk there was to her, at least not until that Spike woman brought in that cannon."

"Still, I need to thank her."

"Come on, then," he said, resigned. Dav stood first, holding out a hand to help Allie up. She blushed slightly at the gallant gesture, turning her head to hide it from Dav. She took his hand and let him help her, suppressing a sigh when he let go once she was up. She followed him down the hallway.

"How long was I out this time?"

"Not too long," he replied, turning a corner.

"Like a day?"

"More like an hour. We're not that far from where we left the Sy'hli warship the mercs captured. This ship can move though, and one of those blasts I felt before the Maruck boarded the ship disabled the engines. They're dead in the water, so no fear of us being followed by them. They still have the Peacekeeper, but there's no way they'd come after this ship with just an Interceptor. Not nearly enough firepower. Problem is, they probably know where we're headed anyway."

"I'm sorry," she said.

"For what?" he asked curiously, looking over at her as they walked.

"For that stupid stunt on the warship, that you lost your Interceptor, for several things."

"Don't worry about it," he said. "I appreciate your trying to rescue us. Besides, the Interceptor wasn't your fault, and we can still potentially recover it later. You can probably Jump us onto it with a raiding party, once we get back to Sy'hloran."

"That's a good idea," she answered, feeling a little better.

It really was a good idea, she thought. Since losing the crystal she couldn't feel the energies without really concentrating, and it wasn't as easy or comfortable to Jump, but she could bring a team onto the Peacekeeper to recover it. She could probably Jump the whole ship back to Sy'hloran, once they had been there and she could then Jump to that world.

Once there, her mother could teach her to See where she was Jumping, too. That would help a lot, since it meant she could Jump anywhere, whether she'd been there or not.

"Here we are," Dav said, bringing her back out of her thoughts. She looked up as they rounded a corner and saw Dgehf's mate. Dav wasn't kidding, she was intimidating.

"Hello," Allie said in as friendly a manner as she could muster. The Maruck blinked at her in surprise.

"Hello," the big Maruck replied. "You are Allie."

"I am. I believe you're Dgehf's mate, though I never heard your name."

"I am. I am called Garenha," she replied. Allie was astonished at how clear the Maruck's English was, until she saw Dav's expression and realized that she and Garenha were both speaking Maruck. She giggled at him, then turned back to Garenha.

"I wanted to come and say thank you for your help," she told the Maruck.

"It was an honor to fight for an ally of my mate's. He is a Maruck of great honor and power, and I am proud to fight beside him in any cause he feels is worthy," Garenha said. Allie caught the undertone.

"But you don't feel helping humans and Sy'hli is worthy," she guessed. Garenha was still for a moment, studying Allie, then nodded.

"Maruck have been slaves to the humans and Sy'hli in recent years. I am not a slave. My mate is not a slave. My son is not a slave. And yet again, we serve humans and Sy'hli." Allie could hear the resentment in the woman's tone.

"You do not serve us. We are allies, fighting alongside, and for, one another," Allie said. "Dgehf helps us so that we can in turn help your people. You owe us no allegiance, no loyalty, no servitude. In fact, we owe you our friendship and gratitude for what you've done, and if there's any help you need from us, you only need to say the word, and we'll come to help any way we can." Garenha seemed to consider this for a long time.

"Allies are welcome. Masters are not," she said finally. "If you truly are allies, you will leave my family in peace. We do not need your weight on our ship when battle comes."

"Peace is a given. And we will leave to continue our mission as soon as we are able. We're not here to cause any inconvenience to any of you, and I assure you that if battle comes while we're aboard, we'll fight, and if need be die, alongside you and your family." Again, Garenha paused to consider. After a time, she nodded again.

"My mate is right. You, Allie, are unusual. There is honor in you, and bravery. If the virtue you hint at is truly there as well, then you are welcome with my family as long as you need. If you harm any of them, I will eat your heart." Allie smiled at that, which seemed even more to take the Maruck woman off guard.

"Agreed," she said. "I would like to see my friend Dgehf, if he is ready for a visitor."

"My son has finished tending his father's wounds. If my mate wishes it, you may see him." Allie nodded, and waited as Garenha stepped into the room. She turned to Dav, who was trying really hard to keep from laughing. Not the reaction she expected.

"What?" she asked him.

"You sound really funny when you speak Maruck," he told her, biting back a snicker. "They're so deep and gruff, and your voice is so high and soft. Seriously, it's like listening to English being spoken by a chipmunk. It's adorable!" She laughed and gave him a playful shove.

"You're just jealous you don't speak Maruck," she told him. He laughed along with her.

"Not if I sound like Alvin, Simon, or Theodore," he joked. She stuck her tongue out at him, which just made him laugh harder. After a few minutes, the door opened again and Garenha emerged.

"Dgehf will see you now," she told Allie, "and the boy, if you wish it. He will walk again soon, and fight even sooner, even if he must crawl to our enemies. He is strong, the weapon could not kill him." Garenha said that last with pride.

"Thank you," Allie told her sincerely, and took Dav's hand, leading him into the room.

# CHAPTER THREE

# BROTHERS

Artus walked out of the conference room, fighting to keep the exhaustion from his steps. Showing that kind of weakness wouldn't serve him well here. The ambassadors and leaders in the room behind him would jump on it like a pack of starving hyenas on a wounded zebra.

He was struggling to establish that he was both strong and wise enough to lead the Sy'hli Empire after Tyren's imprisonment. He suspected it would be easier after Tyren had been brought successfully to Sy'hloran. Seeing him in chains, so to speak, would reinforce Artus' position a great deal. As it was, many of the Sy'hli allies were negotiating hard before allowing control of his own people in their respective territories.

Ambassador K'tchik of the Tchratchi was the only ally he felt he had in that war room, and the Tchratchi weren't even members of the Coalition. The rest all seemed eager, in the wake of Tyren's rule, to try and seize a piece of the Sy'hli Empire for themselves.

Artus had to convince them that doing so would not only be extremely costly to their soldiers, but that he intended to be a benevolent but firm ruler for the Empire, and therefore a valuable and accepted member of the Coalition.

Tyren's violent and cruel reign had hardened many of the leaders of the other races of the Coalition, and they now considered open retaliation against the Sy'hli, now that they were no longer in fear of Artus' brother. He really did intend to solidify and strengthen the Coalition, and meant to take no more control than the leader of any single race was supposed to in the Coalition Council.

The Coalition wasn't evil, it was merely the tool that Tyren had dominated and used to do great harm. The purpose of the Coalition, the spirit that it once stood for, was still as valid as the day they had founded it.

A Coalition of peoples, members of races as diverse as the colors of the Sy'hloran evening sky, each standing firm and strong in their own right, each using their strengths to uphold the other members for the betterment of all races. Honor and trust, loyalty and justice were all once virtues of the Coalition Code.

Those virtues still lived within the people of the Coalition, but many of the once-noble leaders of the members of the Coalition had been removed from power, usually violently, by Tyren when they dared challenge his idea of how things should be run.

Artus meant only to ensure that his people, the Sy'hli, were as protected as all the rest. Unfortunately, the reputation Tyren had built for the Sy'hli people wasn't a flattering one. He sighed, wishing for the thousandth time that his little brother were here. Artus was now officially the ruler of the Sy'hli Empire, but he knew full well that Dav was better suited to it.

Dav was strong, in every way, noble, compassionate, and generous. He was brilliant and clever, well-spoken and diplomatic. The boy was a natural leader, and Artus had seen it in him from a very young age. Artus had all of those same qualities, he liked to think, but not in the measure that Dav had been granted. He shoved down a surge of jealousy, and let himself remember how much he loved his brother.

If Dav were here, he'd tell Artus to not be so down on himself, that he was doing an incredible job, and that their father would be proud.

Artus was strong, he knew that. He'd always been strong because he had to be. Strong for his brother, strong for his people, strong for his own survival, but he felt he had to work at it every moment. Artus was strong like a stone wall. Solid, well built, carefully crafted to support a great weight.

Dav was strong like a huge ocean wave. He flowed around any obstacles he couldn't push through, changing his force to suit the situation, to fill the space and circumstances he was in. Artus couldn't adapt like that. It was difficult to feel secure when watching someone else handle every situation so gracefully while you felt that you simply plodded along and stumbled your way through life.

Artus had several things he wanted to ask his

brother, but that would have to wait until he arrived. Soon, if the last report was accurate. Very soon in fact, Artus corrected himself as he glanced at the clock. It was later than he'd thought. He'd been arguing with Ambassador Oren for hours.

Despite his own hand in helping to save the man's daughter, and the ambassador himself after Allie had Jumped him out of Tyren's clutches, his time in the Highlord's prisons had done great harm. He, and therefore the Queen of the Shaian, were surprisingly hostile to the idea of "allowing" the Sy'hli to retain control or power in almost any measure beyond their own world. Once the greatest empire in the galaxy, the rest of the galaxy was now discussing whether or not to permit the Sy'hli even a seat on the Coalition Council.

Imber would help once she arrived, Artus knew. She'd smooth things over with her father and provide a voice of reason to counterpoint his anger at his imprisonment at the hands of a Sy'hli tyrant.

Morgan had already been a huge help in the matter, in the beginning, but she had been forced by her doctor to return to her room after the first few hours of debate, for her health. She looked so much better, seemed so much stronger, but she still had so little energy. Her doctor sending her back to bed a few hours into the discussions had become a normal part of the proceedings for the last few days.

She was only permitted in the Council discussions to begin with since she was one of the last two surviving members of the Order of the Silver Star, a powerful group outside of the Coalition whose sole purpose was to protect the people of the galaxy. They were something of a failsafe in case the Coalition got out of control and sought to dominate, rather than help, their neighbors.

That's exactly what had happened when Tyren took power, and he'd managed to wipe out most of the Order. This didn't give Morgan much leverage in discussion, since she was seen to have "failed" the people of the galaxy by letting Tyren gain so much power. The fact that she was no longer a crystal bearer didn't help matters either.

Morgan had apparently been in contact with Sinara, the other surviving member of the Order, who was now on her way to Sy'hloran to help with the discussion and negotiations. Her help would be invaluable, as she'd always been a remarkable negotiator and a powerful ally. Sinara wouldn't arrive for another day.

Dav would be there any minute now however, Artus noted as he climbed into a small transport vessel waiting outside the Council Hall. Many of the automated vehicles sat in wait, to transport Council members and Ambassadors around the city as needed.

"Your Highness!" the com on his wrist spoke. Artus sighed. The craft lifted off the ground and soared up into the pre-programmed travel paths assigned to bring Artus to the next location on his itinerary of the day, something the man who had just paged him set up each day. Right now, he was headed to meet with Dav, Allie, Imber, and Raith as they were scheduled to land at the Royal Docks in less than an hour.

"What is it, Miran?" Artus asked, leaning back.

Miran was a seneschal, and had become Artus' right-hand-man from the moment he'd set foot on the planet. He was a good man, though he had kept a very low profile during Tyren's reign. His complete job duties were still unclear to Artus, but they apparently included handling many of the day-to-day operations of running a planet so the Emperor of the Sy'hli didn't have to dirty himself with it.

He'd been keeping things running surprisingly well on Sy'hloran, and the people were generally well cared for and happy, despite their Emperor having been attempting to conquer and probably eventually destroy the galaxy. While Tyren was busy asserting his power aggressively in other quadrants, Miran and others like him had been working hard to make life for the Sy'hli better and more stable.

The economy was good, the quality of life was good, he'd even managed to rebuild nearly all of the infrastructure destroyed in the war while Tyren fought for complete control of the Council. Unfortunately, he was also something of a panic-prone person, and every little thing that came up was of critical importance to him.

It was probably one reason he'd done so well for the Sy'hli, but Artus found it incredibly annoying that the moment he'd set foot on the planet, Miran kept hounding him for his Imperial word on everything from Imperial law to seating arrangements at the celebratory dinner planned for that evening after Dav had arrived, and all of it treated as if it were life or death by the seneschal.

"I just received word that your brother and his honor guard were attacked," Miran replied urgently.

"What?!" Artus shouted, sitting bolt upright.

"The honor guard reports it as a band of mercenaries, using a technology we've never seen before."

"Where's my brother?" Artus demanded, his tone angry and fierce.

"Forgive me, Your Highness, but we don't know. The two warships accompanying the Peacekeeper were incapacitated almost instantly, followed immediately by their crew."

"Two ships? Where were the others?" Artus asked, knowing at last report that there was a sizeable flight of warships escorting his brother and their friends.

"Chasing a squadron of Maruck raiders," Miran replied. Artus took a slow, deep breath."

"Casualties?"

"Oddly, none," Miran replied, sounding confused. "As I said, the technology that stunned the ships and their crew is foreign to us. Commander Brynn reports that the ships simply powered down completely, then the people passed out. When they awoke, she and her crew were aboard the other ship, which was still immobilized. His Royal Highness Davrelan, the crystal bearer, and the ambassador's daughter, along with the Peacekeeper, were all gone."

"Get me a ship," Artus commanded sharply.

"But Your Highness," Miran started.

"Now!" Artus snarled.

"Of course, Your Highness."

The communicator went silent for less than a minute as Artus touched the craft's control rod and accelerated the small vessel to top speed. He had to get airborne as quickly as possible. Dav hadn't been that far out that morning, Artus could get to their last known location in less than a day and could try to track them down from there. There had to be a way.

"Your Highness," Miran interrupted.

"Yes?" Artus asked, as calmly as he could.

"Your brother has been found."

"What?" Artus asked in shock. Well that was fast.

"They have apparently been rescued by a… forgive me Your Highness… a Maruck battle cruiser." Miran sounded worried at that, but Artus just smiled.

"Did the message come directly from Dav?"

"From His Royal Highness Davrelan, yes. The Maruck let him use the communicator?" he finished, that last sounding more like a question than a statement.

"Everything is fine, Miran. That Maruck is a friend of ours. They'll be here soon, then?"

"Yes, Your Highness," Miran said, "perhaps only two hours behind schedule. That Maruck battle cruiser is very fast." He didn't sound any less confused.

"When the Maruck craft arrives, I want it met with an honor guard. Give my brother and *all* of his companions, including the Maruck, the highest honors and extend them every courtesy. They are royal guests. Am I clear?" Artus commanded. There was only a brief pause before the response.

"Of course, Your Highness."

"And Miran?" Artus added.

"Yes, Your Highness?"

"Quit calling me 'Your Highness'. It's incredibly annoying."

"Yes, Your… I mean, Artus. Forgive me sir, but this isn't proper."

"Forget propriety, Miran. At least when it's just the two of us talking, all right? You can 'Your Highness' me all you like when we're in public. Deal?"

"Very well," Miran responded. He didn't sound happy.

Artus smiled and shook his head. As the com channel switched off, Artus leaned back into his seat again. It sounded like he'd missed another adventure, he thought in disappointment. That new technology worried him, though.

A weapon that could immobilize two Sy'hli warships and an Interceptor, as well as all of the crews aboard each, theoretically including Raith, was impressive and frightening.

It was non-lethal, to his relief, but it had been used with incredible efficiency to capture a couple of the most important people in the galaxy, at least to him. Allie was important to everyone though. She was the last Starjumper, as far as anyone knew.

From the report, it sounded like there had been no casualties at all, but he needed to send some men out to try and chase down those mercenaries. That weapon needed to be taken out of their hands. They may be able to immobilize a couple of ships, but there's no way they could take down an armada of Sy'hli battle cruisers.

He sent a quick message to his top general. With General Xan in charge, Artus knew they'd have those mercenaries brought down in no time, secret weapon or not. The man was a tactical genius. He and a surprisingly large armada of Sy'hli warships and strike troops had managed to elude capture for over a decade, lying low and training intensively until their chance to return appeared.

When word reached them of the arrival of a new Jumper and the return of the other two Tyr'Arda heirs, they leapt at the chance to come help. It had taken General Xan less than a day to rid the entire sector of the Sy'hli army still loyal to Tyren once he made his move. As if that didn't hold him high enough in Artus' estimation, he was also fiercely loyal to Artus, knowing the efforts he had made to resist his brother and help the people before supposedly being killed thirteen years ago.

"Your Highn... Artus?" Miran came back on the com.

"Yes, Miran?"

"The Firestorm won't arrive for some time after Prince Davrelan. The Highl... Tyren is aboard, along with a handful of Maruck prisoners.

"Thank you, Miran." There would be time enough to talk to Tyren after Dav arrived. As long as he could go meet with him without Dav in tow, he might be able to have a rational discussion with his elder brother. Until then, he had preparations to make for Dav and Allie's arrival.

# CHAPTER FOUR

# TO SY'HLORAN

Raith's eyes opened, looking up into Imber's relieved face. In a fraction of a second, he had taken in the entire situation. He knew they were not aboard the Peacekeeper, that the ship he was on was most likely Maruck in workmanship, and that they were safe. He also knew that Imber had been working for hours. He could see the weariness on her face.

"Thank you," he told her simply. She smiled at him and stepped back so he could sit up.

"You're welcome," she replied simply.

"Dgehf's ship?" he asked her. She stared in amazement.

"How would you know that?"

"This is obviously a Maruck ship. You're obviously not distressed or upset. You don't seem scared or hopeless. You look pretty happy, actually. Either we captured a Maruck battlecruiser while I was inoperable, or Dgehf showed up and gave us a hand." He smiled at her. She smiled back and shook her head, impressed.

"Right as always," she told him. "I broke us free of the mercenaries, and captured a Maruck battle cruiser single handedly in which to make our daring escape," she said grandly, striking a playfully arrogant pose. Raith laughed, causing her mock-pride to vanish with a laugh of her own.

"Uh huh," Raith said. "I'm more impressed that you got me working again. What exactly happened?"

"We're not really sure," she replied, idly scratching at one of her heirlines.

Raith noted the gesture and filed it away. It wasn't a common one for her. Possibly nervousness, he wondered? He wasn't certain what she would be nervous about, but made a note to keep an eye on her, just in case.

"Everyone and everything just shut down. We woke up on our own, but you didn't. I don't think the ships did either, I think the mercenaries switched them back on themselves."

"Mercenaries?" he asked. That was an interesting development. He was sorry he missed it.

"Apparently," she replied. "They said the Highlord hired them. Must have done it right before he caught us on the Helios. Anyway, they were paid in advance, so didn't seem to care that he'd been captured and removed from power."

"Merc code," Raith responded with a nod. "Paid to do a job, you do the job. Period. Lucky Dgehf showed up."

"Oh okay, he may have helped in the rescue a little,"

she said with a grin. "Seriously though, we're very lucky. Dav was putting on a brave face, as always, but I doubt we'd have gotten out of there on our own." Raith nodded, but before he could reply, the door opened and a juvenile Maruck loped into the room.

"Imber friend," the little Maruck said in greeting.

Raith watched the creature curiously. He'd downloaded enough ship's databases in his time on Irifal Station to have a full record, including audio and video, of Maruck in all of their life stages. It was somewhat different staring a juvenile Maruck in the face though. It was… cute, Raith had to admit. Imber smiled at the cub.

"Hello Daghren friend," she said. The creature, Daghren, did a little happy hop as she called it friend, and looked to Raith.

"Raith friend?" it asked curiously. He, Raith corrected himself as he scanned it. The juvenile was male.

"Imber is your friend?" Raith replied with a question. He knew that Imber was apparently comfortable with the young Maruck, but he wanted the creature to recognize that his friendship was contingent upon Daghren's being friendly with Imber.

"Imber friend," Daghren agreed firmly. "Raith friend?"

"Raith friend," Raith replied with a smile. Daghren was extremely happy about this and hopped about in enthusiastic joy for a moment before moving close to Raith and sniffing.

"Raith friend not person friend," Daghren said, seeming a little confused.

"Raith is a person," Imber corrected him politely but

firmly. Daghren looked at her. "Raith is a person, but not an organic person. He's a cybernetic person."

"Cyber friend," Daghren said, seeming content with this explanation, Raith gave Imber a warm, appreciative look.

"Are you Dgehf's son?" Raith asked him.

"No," Daghren replied with a shake of his fuzzy head. "Dgehf Daghren's… Daghren's…" the little Maruck struggled to find the words in Sy'hli.

"Brother?" Raith asked.

"No," Daghren said, still obviously thinking hard, "Daghren's mother's brother?" Daghren obviously still wasn't sure he was explaining himself well, but his point was clear.

"Dgehf is your uncle," Raith clarified. Daghren grinned a toothy grin and nodded happily.

"You are about three suns old?" Raith asked, estimating by the cub's size.

"Two," Daghren corrected proudly.

"You're a big two," Raith replied. Daghren nodded happily again.

"Daghren big, Daghren strong, Daghren warrior like Dgehf," he said. Imber laughed lightly.

"You certainly are," she agreed. She looked to Raith. "Daghren helped us escape the mercenaries," she told him. Raith looked back to the Maruck and nodded.

"Thank you for helping my friends," Raith told him. Daghren shook his head.

"Daghren's friends. Dgehf say Allie friend, Dav friend, Imber friend, Raith friend, and Tic friend. Dgehf say Artus friend and Morgan friend. Daghren not see

Artus friend or Morgan friend."

"They're on Sy'hloran, where we're heading," Raith said, looking to Imber for confirmation. She nodded.

"We just entered their system. We were met by an honor guard. No hostility, but they're armed well enough to take this ship down if they decide to," Imber said, tone a little concerned. Raith shook his head.

"Don't worry," he reassured her, "Artus is in charge here. He probably knew it was Dgehf's ship and wanted to give us a royal welcome."

"You're right," she replied, but he could tell the fleet surrounding them still made her nervous. Maybe that was the cause of her scratching at her heirlines? She'd done it absently twice more since the first one.

"So everyone is okay?" Raith asked her.

Daghren looked back and forth between them. Raith got the impression he was studying their speech, trying to learn more of the language. That was disconcerting, Raith thought. Good thing this family was on their side. If all Maruck were this bright, they'd be a whole lot more dangerous as a species.

"Yes, you're the last one to recover," she answered, "Dgehf was hurt pretty badly, but his son patched him up and he's doing pretty well. Not up and walking yet, but frankly I'm amazed he's not dead. It was pretty bad."

"Maruck are impossibly tough," Raith replied. "It takes a lot of training to know just how and where to hit them for any solid effect. Dav and Artus obviously know what they're doing, they handle Maruck pretty well. Most people have no clue though, and can shoot at them all day without doing much real harm. I'm glad he's okay though. I definitely appreciate his help. Imber, can I ask how you reactivated me?"

"It took me a little while to figure it out," she said, her tone implying she was frustrated with herself for taking so long. "Whatever they did actually disrupted the wavelength of the energy coming from your power supply. Kind of like watching the ripples of a rock in a pond, then dropping another rock into the ripples. The ripples sort of overlap for a second, then totally interrupt each other's patterns. I think it's why the ships stopped working too, they disrupted the energy flow from the core. I'd love to know how they did that. As for fixing you, once I figured out the problem it was pretty easy. I removed and purged your regulator and then basically just reset your neural processors with a cross-spanner."

Raith had been growing more and more impressed the longer he listened to her. In medical terminology, she basically said she'd just unplugged his heart, rinsed it out, put it back in, then jump-started his brain with a flashlight battery, and all without damaging a single brain cell. And he knew nothing was damaged, because his system maintenance sub-routines had been scanning constantly since he woke up.

She said it so casually, but what she'd done was such a shockingly complex process that, if done incorrectly, could have left him a totally inoperable chunk of admittedly outdated machinery. He tried not to think about it this way, but with her success on the operation he was now actually just an operable chunk of outdated machinery. He and Cade were the only ones left, to his knowledge, and the technological advancements since they'd been built had been huge. Almost a pity he couldn't rebuild his body. He could do some upgrades though. He decided then and there to ask Imber to help him with that later.

"Come on," Imber said, holding a hand out to him, "let's go meet up with the others and get ready to land. I've never seen Sy'hloran in person before. I can't wait!"

Raith grinned at her enthusiasm. The faintest of glows came from the heirlines near her eyes. Human eyes couldn't have caught it, but Raith saw it easily. He briefly wondered if they always did that when she got excited about something.

"Coming?" Raith asked Daghren, who had sat still and quiet their whole conversation. The Maruck cub grinned and loped after them.

Dav stood between Allie and Raith, Imber on Raith's other side. Daghren was on the other side of Allie with Tic on her shoulder, with the three huge Maruck standing behind them. Slowly, the bay doors of Dgehf's peculiar ship opened, about to reveal the docks, and the city, beyond. How Dgehf was up and walking already, Dav had no idea, but while he did so only with the support of his mate at his side, he easily had kept pace with the others to the bay.

Dav stood calmly, but inside his emotions rolled and churned. For the first time since he was an infant, he was about to set foot on his home world. In a moment, he would lay eyes on his home for the first time in his memory. Home, he thought. Finally, at last, he was home. Back to a place with his own people, with his brother, where he belonged.

Part of him ached for Earth, the only home he'd ever known, but another part of him, the Sy'hli, yearned for nothing more than to walk his home world, speak with his people, and take his place in the royal family of an interstellar empire. The Sy'hli in him knew that was where his heart and soul was meant to be.

He glanced briefly to the girl beside him. Allie gave him an encouraging smile. He showed no outward sign of his anxiety, nervousness, or eagerness, but Allie knew him. Deeper than any other soul in the galaxy, she knew him. Somehow, she could see that he was of two minds, of two worlds, and was about to be introduced to the second half of his being, the part he was born to. He took a deep breath. With her beside him, he could handle anything. He turned his blue eyes forward again.

The sun was setting on Sy'hloran. He'd read about it, seen pictures, even watched a few videos on the Runner back on Earth. What all of those failed to capture was the depth and breadth of the colors that greeted him, rippling across the Sy'hloran sky. Like on Earth, when the sun reached a certain angle in the sky, its light hit the atmosphere and broke into individual colors.

Unlike Earth, the composition of the Sy'hloran atmosphere was subtly different, causing the colors to become more precisely spread across the sky, in sharply distinctive, shimmering bands of rolling color. It was like pouring oil paints into the gentle surf of a relatively calm ocean. The color spectrum he could see here was different as well, lending a vibrancy to the sky that the Earth in all the glory of its wildest dreams would still have envied.

The sky and setting sun, in all their stunning beauty, still didn't captivate him like the city before him did. The Royal Docks was actually a floating series of platforms, high above and overlooking the city itself. From where he stood, Dav looked out across a city that looked forged of crystal and glass, capturing and casting back the colors of the sky in a mosaic of glittering buildings.

He heard Allie and Imber both gasp on either side of him, clearly as taken as he was with the sheer majesty of the city below. Called Lan'Reya, the capital city's name meant the City of Stars. When the sun fully set, the city's lights would blend with the reflected starlight and make on overhead view of the city even more stunningly beautiful than the sky above, or so it was said.

Artus, Morgan, Ambassador Oren, and a virtual army of soldiers and emissaries stood arranged to the side of the ship, taking up the bulk of this particular platform. Cheers and shouts erupted from the crowd as Dav and his crew stepped around into view, but the cries of enthusiasm dulled somewhat when the Maruck came into view. Artus threw a dark look at the crowd, and their cheering erupted even louder than before. Artus looked somewhat satisfied by this.

He looked like an Emperor, Dav thought. Artus stood tall and proud, his clothing no longer the jeans and t-shirts, or even the tactical flight suits Dav had grown used to seeing him in. Even Dav's untrained eye could tell the material was finer than anything Artus had ever worn on Earth, the colors in vibrant blues and silver, making his piercing blue eyes all the more striking. His hair had been neatly combed and subtly styled, far more carefully than Artus had ever done himself.

This was home, Dav reminded himself, and in an hour or two, he'd be dressed similarly for the celebratory dinner arranged in honor of the last of the House of Tyr'Arda returning to Sy'hloran. Morgan and Ambassador Oren looked very much like they wanted to rush forward, but they held back and moved forward elegantly, gracefully, alongside Artus as he moved forward in a stately fashion.

"Davrelan, of the House of Tyr'Arda. I greet and welcome you home to Sy'hloran, to Lan'Reya," Artus said formally.

Dav bowed in return, deeper than Artus had as was proper by their rank. He felt very out of place, performing a formal royal greeting while wearing a tactical flight suit.

"Artus, heir to the throne of the great Sy'hli Empire, I greet and thank you. The journey is long, but home is well sought," Dav replied, using the ritualized words he'd memorized years ago in the hope of one day returning to the world of his birth. He fought the lump in his throat. He was finally here, finally home.

"May you find the warmth you seek," Artus returned, then grinned. The ritual was simple and old-fashioned, but it held great meaning for the two brothers. Moving forward in a rush, Artus covered the last few feet in a blink and grabbed his little brother in a tight hug. Dav hugged him just as tightly. The formality broken by the Imperial heir, Morgan and Ambassador Oren ran forward to embrace their children. Dav noticed none of it. He gripped his brother tightly enough to have killed a human, unable to restrain the rushing tide of emotion threatening to carry him away. He'd dreamed of this moment his whole life. Artus had already had his homecoming moment, but even so, Dav could feel his brother's tight grip and knew that Artus was feeling the rush of emotions as well. For both of the brothers, the return home wasn't complete until they were there side by side. The two brothers had fought so hard and so long to try and get to this point.

They had won, finally won. They were home, they were safe, and Tyren had been brought down. They could now settle into the even harder job of helping bring peace and prosperity back to the galaxy, and Dav looked forward to every second of it. The brothers separated and Artus smiled down at his brother. He tousled Dav's hair in the time-honored tradition of affectionate older brothers on many planets, and turned to the Maruck standing quietly behind the others.

"Dgehf," Artus said, stepping forward, "once again, I owe you our lives. You and your family are welcome here as our guests for as long as you like. Anything you need, simply ask and it shall be provided to you. For now, we go to the palace where we can all refresh ourselves before the feast!" The crowd cheered again, still sounding forced as Artus reached out to shake Dgehf's hand. Dgehf gave a broad, tusked smile and reach out, his own hand literally engulfing Artus' entire arm. "Come my friends, the time for rest and revelry is upon us!"

# CHAPTER FIVE

# JAILBREAK

Klythe was not as stupid as the Sy'hli believed him to be. Even the Highlord underestimated him. They, like so many others, believed that broken speech patterns meant they weren't smart enough to learn the complex Sy'hli language. The truth was that many of the sounds in the Sy'hli language weren't physically possible for the Maruck to pronounce, so the few Maruck who bothered to learn the language used a broken form, leaving out the words they weren't able to properly make the sounds for.

The Maruck had developed some of the most powerful weapons in the galaxy, second only to the Tchratchi and advanced space-faring battle cruisers that were strong enough to conquer huge sectors of space and leave the rest of the galaxy afraid of the Maruck. Even the phase drive in the Interceptor-class cruisers had been invented by the Maruck, though few people knew that. The Sy'hli had stolen credit for that particular invention.

Their power was limited at this time only by the fact that they'd dedicated themselves entirely to helping the Highlord with his cause and had invested little in technological research during the war. The Highlord was a great man, as he recognized the Maruck's power and had earned their loyalty in battle during the early days of the war. All save a few traitors, that is.

Klythe snarled to himself at the thought of Dgehf. He had been humiliated in battle against the traitor aboard the Helios. His men would no longer follow his orders. It didn't matter, Klythe thought to himself. He would redeem himself by continuing to help the Highlord, despite the Highlord's change in form.

A couple of the Maruck in the cell beside Klythe inched away from him at the snarl. He may have been defeated in battle by Dgehf, but every Maruck in the crew knew that they would have been beaten even more severely by the incredibly powerful warrior, and that Klythe could readily kill any one of them in battle. Only the strongest ruled the Maruck.

The former Maruck leader understood what had truly been going on with the Highlord, and recognized the change in the man who had once been his master. The Sy'hli Tyren was no longer the Highlord, and Klythe knew it. The Highlord had been defeated using deception and trickery, tactics that were very dishonorable, but he had taken shelter within another host body.

Klythe didn't yet know who, but knew the Highlord would be weakened for a while. Weakness wasn't tolerated among the Maruck, but Klythe knew his best chance at revenge against Dgehf would come from his helping the Highlord.

Unfortunately, at the moment Klythe was locked in a Sy'hli holding cell in a Sy'hli battle cruiser on the Sy'hli home world. It would be very soon that the strike troops would move Klythe and his men to a high-security facility on the planet. What that meant for Klythe was that he didn't have much time. He believed that when the strike troops attempted the transfer, it would be his best chance at escape.

He could count on help from the others as well. Not because they were still loyal to him, he knew they weren't, but because they were loyal to the cause of violence and destruction, which couldn't be brought about while they were imprisoned.

Once he made his move, the others would leap into the fray for no other reason than that they knew it was their only chance as well. Klythe turned his midnight-black eyes on his cellmates. Many averted their gazes. He knew they weren't loyal, but they were still afraid of him. He was more powerful than any Maruck alive, excepting only Dgehf. Klythe would kill him soon as well, but for now it was enough that the other Maruck still understood his strength.

He felt the gentle vibration of the craft touching down and slowly rolled his shoulders back in anticipation. Without the loyalty of his men, he knew that his only hope lay in recruiting outside help. He knew just who to contact, but he'd have to escape, first. A Maruck on the Sy'hli home world would stick out just as much as his presence on the girl's cursed planet Earth would, but he didn't plan to be on this world very long.

Waiting was something he was surprisingly good at. A good hunter had to be able to sit silently and still for long periods of time, and Klythe was an excellent hunter. He preferred the part where he got to tear his prey apart, but he could wait when needed for a very long time. This time, waiting didn't take long.

A full dozen Sy'hli came down the corridor, armed to the teeth. Klythe knew there were at least ten times that many outside the ship, waiting for them. They'd be foolish to have any fewer. A dozen men inside coming to transport the prisoners was only because the narrow pathways through this warship would make more than that fairly pointless, since they couldn't maneuver well or line up shots around too many companions.

Any other prisoners and the Sy'hli would have used the stunning shackles, but Maruck were immune to the effects of the shackles. It was one of many quirks of the Maruck that made them so dangerous a foe.

He had six of his companions standing beside him. Twelve Sy'hli strike troops were more than a match for seven Maruck, even seven of the best-trained Maruck warriors in the galaxy. Klythe had a plan however. His men wouldn't like it, but they were no longer his men so he didn't really care.

Four Sy'hli moved to either side of the doorway and raised their shatter rifles. Klythe hadn't seen those in years, and knew that these Sy'hli were part of the resistance that had disappeared into the stars many years ago. A lesser weapon, by all accounts, they were still incredibly potent and formidable. Especially if these

Sy'hli had been working on improving them rather than developing new weapons. Klythe looked the weapons over and confirmed to himself that these looked to be improved models.

The remaining four stood against the wall directly across from the force field blocking the door. The commander, standing against the wall, gestured to one of the men to move forward and open the cell.

"Resist if you like," the commander said to the Maruck, "but if you do, we will have no difficulty in killing you. I'd almost rather you resisted, it would save me a lot of paperwork signing you into the prison."

Klythe snarled deep in his throat for effect. The commander didn't even flinch. Definitely a seasoned warrior, Klythe knew. Even among the Sy'hli, Not many people could hold the gaze of a snarling Maruck. The commander would have to be taken out first, Klythe knew. Simple enough.

As the force field lowered, the commander gestured the Maruck forward. Klythe hesitated, earning him a sneer from his former second in command.

The lesser Maruck stepped forward past Klythe, exactly as Klythe had hoped he would. Another of the Maruck passed him as well before Klythe stepped into the corridor behind them.

The transition from a steady walk to explosive motion was so quick that even the Sy'hli didn't react in time. Klythe shoved one Maruck ahead of him to the left, the other to the right, and lunged forward at the commander himself. The Sy'hli opened fire, but the two Maruck Klythe had pushed took the brunt of the blasts.

Immediately entering battle frenzy, the other Maruck behind Klythe leapt at the Sy'hli, using their falling comrades as cover.

Klythe's jaws snapped forward, his arms still coming back from shoving his former comrades. Quick as a snake, he caught the Sy'hli commander in his powerful tusks. The other Maruck slammed into the Sy'hli with the force of a tsunami, tearing into the ranks on either side while Klythe flung the commander back against the wall.

Quickly immobilizing the Sy'hli, the Maruck grabbed their weapons and flung them into the cell, activating the force field. Only the first two Maruck had even been injured, and only because Klythe had sacrificed them. Knowing that they would never escape without losing most of their number, sacrificing those two had actually saved the rest of them, but the looks they now gave him showed they weren't concerned with that. The move had been treacherous and underhanded.

"Do you want to escape?" Klythe snarled in his people's language.

"Of course," snarled another.

"Then we do what we must. The Sy'hli are dangerous."

"We are dangerous," growled another. Klythe grinned darkly.

"Yes. We are. Let us show them just how dangerous," Klythe rumbled menacingly. The four Maruck before him nodded and Klythe loped down the corridor.

The main command room would be on the far side

of the craft from where the main bay was, which was doubtless where another large troop of Sy'hli was waiting, outside of which would be possibly a hundred or more Sy'hli, armed and ready.

The ship would have landed within the prison complex, which would be suspended thousands of feet in the air. It prevented prisoners who attempted escape from getting off the floating island. Only during transport was there a ship anywhere landed on the prison. Several more would be patrolling just outside. That made things harder, Klythe knew, but not impossible. So far, nobody knew that the Maruck were loose, so the element of surprise still belonged to the mighty Maruck.

In the next corridor over, more holding cells lined one wall. Klythe paused as he saw the man inside the only occupied cell. Tyren looked up from the hard cot on which he sat, surprise on his face. There was a flicker of hope on his face as he obviously thought the Maruck might, thinking he was still the Highlord, let him out.

Klythe smirked at the Sy'hli, spat at the force field, then continued on his way. Tyren being on this same ship was a definite plus, he thought. Klythe could use him as a hostage later. Most of the galaxy might be perfectly happy to see the man dead, but Klythe had witnessed the fight on the bridge of the Helios and knew that the older Tyr'Arda whelp still loved this man and understood the same thing that Klythe himself did. Tyren was not the Highlord.

Bursting into the bridge of the ship, the Maruck dropped the two-man flight crew with satisfying efficiency. Two of them hurriedly dragged the Sy'hli down to an open cell while Klythe sat down in the commander's chair in the middle of the room. He grabbed the control bar and began activating the jump drive.

So far, no alarm had been sounded, and they had perhaps another minute before the men in the bay sent a team in to investigate the delay. A quick check of the sensors showed the men in the bay were exactly as Klythe had expected. Another dozen men, armed and at the ready. Outside the ship were nearly two hundred Sy'hli, even more than Klythe had guessed there would be.

That made no difference, now that Klythe controlled the ship. As long as he could get the jump drive powered on before the Sy'hli in the bay began to get anxious and came looking to see what the trouble was, they would escape cleanly.

His Maruck companions returned from the holding cells and took battle stations at the controls. Klythe grinned. They would follow him. And as long as he continued showing cleverness and strength, they would continue to do so, he knew.

Klythe's worthiness as a leader was brought into question when Dgehf had defeated him, but he was proving himself once again. Once they were free, he'd have firm command over these four soldiers at least. Especially with the manner of his escape, his capacity for violence and command would be solidified in their minds. It was enough, for now.

The holographic display indicated jump drive

readiness. Klythe's huge jaws spread wide in a vicious and eager smile.

"Fire all arc cannons at the side of the prison," Klythe snarled.

The Maruck at the weapons station looked at him in surprise. Klythe roared at him and the foolish Maruck flinched and turned back to his controls, unleashing a massive arc cannon volley at the prison walls. He could have fired at the conveniently grouped Sy'hli around the ship, but that would result only in a number of casualties. Klythe wanted to create more chaos and problems for the Sy'hli, enough to distract them long enough that Klythe and his stolen craft could jump without being tracked. Freeing a number of prisoners would do just that.

The moment the volley slammed into the side of the prison, walls exploding inward, he pushed the ship's engines to send them over the edge of the platform, arcing easily down underneath the floating platform just as the three watching Sy'hli warships opened fire on the place where the ship had been.

Klythe triggered the jump drive and Jumped the ship not up and out, they would expect that, but straight through the planet to the other side. The moment the Sy'hli warship appeared on the other side, he banked straight out away from the planet, effectively dumping the Sy'hli in the bay straight out the back before they could react to the sound of explosions and the Jump.

Glancing at the sensor readout, he was annoyed to see they had Jumped in directly over a city docking bay, so the Sy'hli had only fallen a few dozen feet. The cursed Sy'hli were strong and agile enough to land a fall like that harmlessly on their feet. Oh well, he thought to himself, and pushed the drive into potential overload as he Jumped a second time, this time to the extent of its range, straight perpendicular to the path he'd taken to Jump through the planet.

Pushing the craft to full velocity as he closed the rear doors with a thought, he and his crew left Sy'hloran and its system behind. He changed course several times, growling orders to the others. By the time the Sy'hli had regrouped enough to try and figure out where the craft had gone, they would be nearly impossible to track. One of his crew had already disabled the tracking device on the craft. The warship wouldn't be able to activate its phase drive for some time, Jumping twice so rapidly without allowing the systems to recharge had depleted the power core, and it would take a while to recharge enough to use the jump drive or phase drive again.

Comfortably on their way to one of the many Maruck outposts he knew about, he stood. With a quickly barked order to one of the other Maruck to keep an eye on the sensors and alert him to any threat, he stood and returned to the holding cells. He came to the cell holding Tyren. The man gave him a dark look, standing and moving to just inside the force field. Close enough that he probably felt the tingle from the barrier's energy output.

"Klythe," Tyren said.

"Tyren," Klythe replied with a menacing smile.

"Highlord," Tyren corrected.

"Not anymore," Klythe rumbled. That caught Tyren off guard. He obviously had also underestimated the large Maruck. Klythe took some measure of satisfaction in that.

"What do you plan, Klythe?" Tyren asked.

"Kill Tyren, kill Tyren's family, kill Jumping girl, kill Dgehf. Help Highlord."

"The Highlord is dead," Tyren retorted coldly.

"Not dead," Klythe said smugly. Tyren's expression went from confusion, to understanding, to panic in rapid sequence. Klythe laughed cruelly.

"Who?" Tyren asked. Klythe didn't know, it could have been any of the brats or even Artus or one of the other Sy'hli soldiers, but he didn't want to give Tyren the satisfaction of knowing that Klythe was ignorant.

"In time," Klythe replied. "Now, Klythe need allies. Strong allies."

"It won't work, Klythe. My brothers will find you and stop you. They'll find the Highlord and stop him, too. They already did once, at the peak of his power. He is weak, Klythe. Broken. You would help such a weak ally?"

"Highlord rule again," Klythe assured the Sy'hli. "All Maruck enemies die. All die."

"With the help of only five Maruck?" Tyren sneered. "Against the entire Coalition?"

"Not all Coalition," Klythe said, "many will fight Sy'hli. Klythe have ally, also."

"Besides the damaged Highlord?" Tyren said condescendingly.

Tyren's face paled and Klythe watched the fear touch the Sy'hli's eyes as Klythe spoke a single name.

"Sandro."

# CHAPTER SIX

# FRUSTRATIONS

"How did this happen?" Artus shouted at the man before him.

"Forgive me, Your Highness. Nobody expected seven Maruck to even attempt to escape from two hundred watchful guards and three Sy'hli warships," the guard captain told him. Dav, standing beside his brother, had to admit the move was incredibly gutsy, and so foolish that the Maruck would have had to be nearly suicidal to even consider it.

The banquet had been a beautiful affair, right up until it had been interrupted with news of Tyren and the Maruck's escape. Dav was livid, and completely convinced that Tyren had orchestrated the entire escape in order to make contact with his old allies. He was sure that Tyren wanted to continue his plot to destroy all life in the galaxy. Neither Artus nor Allie had been able to convince him that Tyren was not the Highlord, and never had been. The timing of the escape was too convenient.

A number of other prisoners had escaped as well in the explosion and chaos, and a lot of good men had been hurt. Tyren's history of cleverness, violence, and brutality was right in line with this escape.

Artus was certain that Klythe was behind it, as he knew that the leader of the Maruck had been aboard the Firestorm as well. Dgehf and Artus had both battled him and won, and his pride was badly hurt in both instances. Dav didn't buy it.

"Allie, can you Jump a team onto the Firestorm?" he asked, turning to her. She shook her head, like he knew she would.

"I can't Jump anywhere I haven't been before, not without a programmed crystal key," she told him. He knew that already, but he'd hoped that with her unusually growing gifts, she might have found a way around that restriction.

"I might be able to help with that," Morgan interjected. "I just don't know if that would be faster than just sending the fleet out to try and find them."

"What do you mean?" Allie asked.

"I can teach you to See," Morgan clarified.

Dav looked between the two, momentarily struck by their similarity. Not necessarily in appearance, though Allie definitely had her mother's striking eyes, but they both held the same presence. Both mother and daughter stood tall and strong, with an air of calm confidence. He was certain Allie hadn't had that air of self-awareness and surety even a month ago, before she'd taken her first Jump.

"Depending on Allie," Morgan continued, "that might take very little time, or a great deal of time. It usually takes many years, but with the way her gifts are manifesting, she might take to it naturally."

"Or…?" Artus asked, curious.

"She may not be able to See at all. Some Jumpers can only see the energies, and cannot use them as a channel with which to See where they are Jumping."

Artus nodded. That made sense, Dav thought. Allie's gifts were amazing, but there were bound to be limitations. Things that many Jumpers were once able to do might be completely beyond her unusual gifts.

"Send the fleet," Artus said to General Xan. "Morgan, will you try to help her to See? I can't gamble on her being able to learn it quicker than the fleet can find them, but there's no reason you two can't try anyway. And if it works, so much the better."

The others nodded and Artus dismissed everyone but the general. Things to discuss, he said. Dav took it as a sign that Artus too believed that the war wasn't over, and that Tyren's escape was the first step in bringing the remaining loyalists together to stage a full assault on the Coalition that was still allied with the Sy'hli Empire.

Dav knew many of the Coalition races had shown outright hostility to the Sy'hli once word got out that Tyren was no longer in power. Without Tyren to intimidate, threaten, and coerce them into cooperation, the many years of oppression and violence and the resentment and fear they had bred had begun to boil over.

Artus had done incredibly well keeping things held

together, Dav knew. He could see the strain on his brother's face though. Dav was worried, but had the utmost faith in his brother. Artus wouldn't quit. Ever. He would stand strong and fight for what he knew was right until he fell over from exhaustion, and then would start again the instant he was able. Dav hoped it didn't come to that, but if full war was about to break out once more, which seemed more likely by the moment, it could last years, maybe decades.

The opposing factions now dividing the Coalition were all very powerful. Many lives would be lost. Casualties could be in the trillions. They had to prevent war, for the sake of all the innocent people in the galaxy.

"You okay?" Allie asked from beside him, walking along and keeping pace. Raith and Imber walked behind them, with Morgan taking up the rear. Artus had refused Ambassador Oren the privilege of joining them for the brief meeting.

Dav almost snapped at her, but bit it back. Apparently the strain was getting to him, too. He would never have snapped at Allie for anything even just a few days ago. They needed to resolve this whole thing before it drove everyone to the breaking point.

"Yeah," he told her, shoving down a surge of irrational anger with her. "Just tired of all of this. We can't even sit down to dinner without being interrupted with some terrible thing happening. I thought everything was all finished and done, but Tyren is still out there, and still has enough allies to be very, very dangerous."

"It's not Tyren," Allie said, a little harshly.

"Right, the Highlord," he replied fighting to keep his

cynicism out of his voice.

"It's true," she told him. "I think deep down, you know it, too. Dav, Tyren is your brother. The man I saw inside his mind is just as noble and good as you and Artus. He was a prisoner inside his own mind. Can you even imagine what that would be like?"

"No," Dav admitted. Rationally, he trusted her. He knew she spoke what she believed was the truth. But Dav had spent his entire life in hiding on a backwater planet from a man he knew only as a tyrant, a murderer, and the man who had killed his own parents. It was hard to change a lifetime of anger overnight.

"Wait until you can really sit and talk with him," Allie told him, "You'll see what I mean."

"I may not get the chance. He's escaped, remember?"

"I know, but we're going to rescue him."

"Rescue Tyren?" Dav asked with a bitter laugh. "What happened to 'capture'? Things have sure changed."

"Yes, they have," she replied.

Dav looked over at her, into those green eyes. He could get lost in those eyes, he knew. If only things there were different too. He knew they were of different worlds, though. Besides, he was firmly in the "friend zone" with her, and that was unlikely ever to change.

"Are you ready to begin? The party isn't going to resume tonight, so we might as well make the best of our free time." Morgan asked from behind them. Allie nodded, then reached over and squeezed his hand comfortingly. He greatly appreciated the gesture. She always knew exactly what he needed, from a laugh to a reassuring touch. The irrational anger faded.

"Can I come along?" Imber asked.

"It's very important that Allie be able to focus without distractions," Morgan replied, "sorry Imber." Imber nodded.

"That's okay. I do want to be on the team that Allie Jumps over though, so I'll just go get some target practice in. My father told me he would spend some time at the range with me, no time like the present." Imber smiled, and cast a glance at Raith that Dav could see a lot of meaning behind. Those two had something special, he knew.

He wasn't sure how he felt about that. Imber was attractive, but Dav was in love with Allie. Always had been. Raith was his friend, probably his best friend besides Allie, but he was a machine. How that relationship would work, he had no idea. He couldn't help being a bit jealous, though. He knew Raith liked Imber too, a return of affection that neither of them had spoken about yet, but at least it was there, and clear to everyone looking in.

He shook his head with a sigh as Imber waved and jogged away. Raith stood beside Dav for a long time before saying anything, as the pair watched the others walk down the road.

"You okay?" Raith asked finally.

"Come on, should I just start telling you guys that I'm not just for a change of pace?" Dav asked, annoyed at the repeated question. He'd been hearing that a lot today.

"We're just concerned," Raith replied. "It's pretty obvious that you're under a lot of pressure and frustration right now. Your body temperature, heart rate, and breathing patterns tell me that you're a little off, although apparently even a human can read that much."

"What's that supposed to mean?" Dav asked, irritated at his referring to Allie as human, though he knew she was. The connotation that humans were inferior bothered him, either way. Allie was every bit as important and helpful as anyone in the group. More so, in many important ways.

"Just that she can't read your vitals like I can, and even she can see that you're having a rough time. You've been getting progressively more irritable by the day."

"You don't like it, you don't have to hang around," Dav said with a glare, turning and starting to walk. Raith followed, easily moving up alongside him again.

"I don't like it," Raith replied, "but that's all the more reason to stick around. You need friends right now, Dav. Allies, if nothing else. If you keep letting things get to you like this, you're not going to be able to make the right decisions in a tight spot and could get yourself, and others, hurt. I assume you're going with the team to rescue Tyren?"

"Of course," Dav retorted.

"So is Allie," Raith pointed out.

It was an obvious point, but hearing it so clearly stated shook Dav. Raith was right, he needed to hold it together so he wouldn't be endangering his friends, especially Allie, while on this ridiculous rescue mission. Come to think of it, even if Allie didn't learn to See, she could jump him to the Interceptor and they could at least get his ship back. Either way, they'd be in the middle of a fight and he needed to be cool and focused. He took a deep breath and sighed.

"That's true," he said after a moment. "You're right."

"As always," Raith said with a wink. Dav couldn't help but smile. "Hey, can you spare a few minutes?"

"Sure," Dav said, confused by the random question. "Why?"

"I need to take some measurements from you."

"Like height, weight, that kind of thing? Going to clone me?" Dav asked. Raith laughed.

"No, like biometric measurements."

"You're starting to scare me," Dav said, giving his friend a sidelong glance.

"Not to worry, my friend," Raith said casually, "I'm building you a new toy." Dav paused, and turned to look directly at his android friend.

"Really? Why?"

"Because it's awesome," Raith laughed. "Seriously, I've been working on it for days, trying to figure out the mechanics. I'm going to build a prototype and I need someone to test it. I don't know anyone as well suited to testing this bad boy than you, but I need to key it to your biometrics. I sure don't need anyone else playing around with it."

"Wow, that's... extremely cool," Dav said with a widening grin as his excitement grew. "What is it?"

"Oh, you'll have to wait," Raith told him. "I think I'll have the prototype fully functional by tomorrow night though, if you can let me get some scans tonight."

"Sounds good," Dav said sincerely. "Let's go."

"This place is amazing," Allie said softly, looking around.

The dome-shaped building was huge and shiny, like everything else in this incredible city. Allie had been captivated by the city at first glance and was afraid she was falling in love with it. It was everything she had always thought an alien city should be.

Lan'Reya was significantly advanced technologically, it was breathtakingly beautiful, full of exotic and interesting alien people, and had broad walking streets between buildings, with all of the big vehicles traveling effortlessly through the air. Many people rode by on the ground on odd little vehicles they rode atop though, probably this world's equivalent of the bicycle.

She had made a mental note to ask Dav about that, since she remembered Ghier telling her on Ayaran than flying vehicles generally took too much power to operate than would really be worthwhile. Apparently on Sy'hloran, it was worthwhile. Allie sure thought so. It was incredibly cool, seeing the diverse flying craft cruising through the skies. There were as many varieties of flying vehicle here as there were models of car in any big city on earth.

The thought of Ghier struck Allie for a moment with a pang of sadness and regret. His betrayal had stung, but his actions had been brought on by fear for his people, and she couldn't really blame him for that. She hoped he was doing well, and that his people were happy and safe.

The inside of the building was just as incredible, and pulled Allie smoothly from her thoughts. Inside the massive building were terraced gardens lit softly by ambient lighting, but the huge glass windows the building seemed made of probably let in amazing amounts of natural light from the beautiful, slightly blueish sun of this world.

There was a smaller, red sun as well, but it didn't give off much light. It was more of a large red star floating beside the big, pale blue sun. Dav had assured her it was technically a binary star system, and the bright red star was also a sun to this world.

Beyond the terraced gardens were a number of doors, very widely spaced between each door.

"What is this place?" she asked as she walked hand in hand with her mother between gardens, enjoying the sound of a couple of small fountains, and the whistling call of some brightly-colored creatures in the trees.

They sounded a little bit like birds, their whistles musical and charming, and their bright coloring was much like tropical birds as well, but the creatures looked more like squirrels or chipmunks with oversized ears and impossibly long, slender bodies. Tic, on Allie's shoulder, chirped back at the creatures happily.

The delicate scent of flowers unlike anything she'd ever experienced seemed to brush her senses, drawing her closer to some. Her mother let her pause and smell the beautiful flowers with a laugh.

"This is our apartment," she said. Allie turned to

stare at her. "Artus set us up with an ambassador's suite. He offered to set us up in the palace itself, but I always hated the need to maintain total propriety inside that palace. I like to relax, and can't do that in the political atmosphere in the palace. Don't get me wrong, it's beautiful there as you saw, but I couldn't live there."

"Which one of those doors is our apartment?" Allie asked.

"All of them. That one is your room," she said, pointing to one door, "and the one beside it is mine. They're connected inside, with a shared living space between them. The other doors have some other useful rooms, like a gym and a small swimming pool, but those two are for the main living area."

"This one room is bigger than my entire block back home," Allie pointed out. Her mother smiled and nodded.

"It took some getting used to for me, too. There are advantages to being a political representative. Don't feel bad, I agree this seems awfully extreme, but refusing would have caused even more political issues than us requesting to set up living quarters outside the palace already will. Besides, this seems incredible to me too, after thirteen years in prison."

Allie glanced at her mother at that comment, but her mother didn't seem too bothered by it. She had sprung back with amazing resilience. After a number of days on nutrient packs, she'd begun eating normally and had been regaining her strength very rapidly. She no longer looked like a skeleton with skin, though she could still stand to gain more than a few pounds, and some muscle as well. It was nice seeing her looking so much better so quickly, though.

"Come on," her mother said, interrupting her thoughts.

Allie followed her to one of the doors, the one her mother had said was Allie's. They stepped into what looked like a very large living room, with two pairs of couches arranged to provide two relatively private areas to sit and talk.

Two doors came off this room, one was clearly to a restroom since the door sat slightly open, one closed not far from that door, and a huge archway that appeared to lead to a big dining room, with a large kitchen beyond. A hallway extended beyond the kitchen, and looked like it held the other entry door that her mother had pointed out from the indoor gardens. In every room, the decoration was beautiful and elegant. Allie suddenly felt like royalty.

"Good grief, we live here?" Allie asked in wonder.

"For now," her mother said. "Eventually, I'd like to find something permanent for the two of us. Three of us if Katharine doesn't explode when we tell her the truth and invite her along."

"Really?!" Allie practically squealed. Her mother had apparently been thinking the same thing she had been.

"Of course! She did a great job raising and caring for you when I couldn't, she raised you into a young woman strong and brave enough to come and rescue me, I owe her everything. She was my very dearest friend, and she's done more for me than I can ever repay. The least I can do is offer her a long and comfortable life on a world far safer and more comfortable than Earth. Of course, we need to resolve this nonsense with the Coalition first. Until then, she's safer on Earth."

"That makes sense. We should leave her a message though, so she doesn't worry too much."

"We will, but after we rescue Tyren. Time may be very important. Are you ready to begin?"

"Yes," Allie said seriously, and followed her mother to one of the couches.

# CHAPTER SEVEN

# WATCHERS

"The first thing I need you to do is breathe deeply and slowly," her mother said. They were seated on the incredibly comfortable couch, angled toward one another. "It's important that you be as relaxed as possible."

Allie felt pretty relaxed. That might be due to weariness, but either way her only tensions came from anxiety about whether or not she'd be able to learn this in time to help Tyren. She was determined though, and wouldn't let Dav and Artus down by letting their brother die if she could help it.

"Now, reach your mind out and feel the energies that you use when you Jump. Those energies are part of the fabric of space. They're the force that holds space together in a three dimensional form. The reason that you can Jump is because you are able to manipulate those energies. Seeing is a little bit different. Instead of using the energies to push your way between three dimensional space, you need to let those energies communicate with you."

"How does it communicate?" Allie asked softly.

Her eyes closed and she reached out for the energy she knew was all around her. It came a little easier this time, probably due to her relaxed state. The energies were there, as always, little ripples and eddies like the water in a tide pool.

"That energy isn't part of three dimensional space. It flows between physical space and someplace else. Nobody's really sure what is on the other side of it, but for our needs that doesn't matter. If you can let it into your mind, it can give you information about things, fill your senses as if you were standing there looking at, hearing, smelling, feeling those things yourself. It's tricky to control, so it's okay if your first glimpse of someplace else is erratic, maybe even dream-like. You'll probably not even get anything this first time. Or even the second. I just want you to focus on letting those energies into your mind. Don't force them, don't push or pull, just open and let them flow through."

"Okay," Allie said, attempting to do what her mother instructed.

The energies were there, swirling gently around her. They didn't enter her, though. That was interesting, she realized. If that energy was literally everywhere at once, why wasn't it inside her? The energy pushed away slightly, and she mentally forced herself to relax again. Her own thoughts influenced the flow of the energy so profoundly that even when not concentrating on it, she was manipulating it. She hadn't realized that.

"They don't want to come through me," Allie said.

"No, they don't. Part of what makes us able to Jump the way we do is that, to some extent, we exist outside of three dimensional space as well. The energies tie to three dimensional space, so they don't connect well with people like us."

Allie considered this. It made sense, as much as she understood it, anyway. To move outside of space, you had to not be part of it, at least partly. Dav had explained to her that was how the phase drive worked. It shifted the matter of the ship slightly outside of normal space so it could move faster than matter was normally able to travel. If she and the other Jumpers were already not quite part of normal space, with the focus of the crystal they could then direct their matter to another point in space without crossing the three dimensional space between.

"Why don't I need a crystal to Jump?" Allie asked suddenly.

"Focus, Allie."

"But that part doesn't make sense," Allie said, her eyes opening. "Everyone says that nobody can Jump without a crystal, but I can. Everyone says that nobody can Jump near rogellium, but I can do that too. I can even make large amounts of rogellium, like on the Helios, Jump with me. Why?"

"Honestly Allie, I have no idea," Morgan said with a sigh. "I've never heard of anything like that. You shouldn't be able to do any of those things. You shouldn't have been able to Jump a ship the size of the Helios even with a crystal, let alone with no crystal and the ship laced with rogellium."

"And what about the languages?" Allie asked.

"What about languages?"

"I can speak any language I like, without even thinking about it. Even Maruck and Sy'hli."

"I thought maybe you just had a knack for learning languages," her mother said, thoughtfully.

"Are you kidding? I was flunking English back home. There's no way I'd have been able to learn Sy'hli. It's so easy I don't even have to try though. Any language of anyone I talk to, I can speak it."

"That's a new one too, Allie. I really wish I knew the answers to those questions, but I don't. You're unique, for whatever reason. I think it's because there's something great you're meant to do."

"I already overthrew the Highlord," Allie pointed out. Her mother smiled.

"You sure did. Maybe that was it. If so though, you still have the responsibility to use your gifts to help others."

"I know," Allie replied. "I already thought about that. I thought at first I'd be going home after Tyren was stopped, but the more I thought about it the more I thought about how unfair it would be for me to have been given such great gifts and not use them to help people whenever I can." Her mother looked at her proudly.

"That's how I always saw it, too. Your father always loved that about me, that I couldn't leave a problem alone once I found out about it, until I had figured out a way to help."

Allie got quiet at the mention of her father. She'd always held out hope that her parents were alive somewhere, and just couldn't come to get her for whatever reason. She'd been half right. She closed her eyes again, determined to make this work. The energies brushed along her skin, moving gently and fluidly. They did not pass the barrier of her skin, however.

She sat quietly for some time. She wasn't sure how long it was, as she slowly lost herself in the gentle drifting of the energies. Allie didn't know when she realized it, she just sort of gradually became aware that something was watching her.

It was somewhat familiar, and it took another moment to recognize it as the same feeling she'd had when she'd Jumped the Helios. It didn't seem like a scary feeling, just sort of uncomfortable. As she tried to zero in on the direction the watching came from, she realized it wasn't coming from a direction. It seemed everywhere, and nowhere, all at the same time. Like the energy, she thought.

Like the energy, she reached out for it. As if her reaching for it made the watcher realize she was aware of it, the attention on her suddenly, almost painfully, became razor sharp. It still didn't feel hostile, but it was definitely uncomfortable.

"Think of someplace unfamiliar," her mother whispered, interrupting her thoughts. The sharpness went away. Without conscious thought, Allie thought of the Rrughn back on Kobek. Their minds had felt somewhat similar to the one watching her, bringing them to her thoughts.

Her awareness shifted, leaving her looking at a stone cliff-side, reaching high into the red and black sky above her. The ground beneath her feet was red, dry, and cracked, with a faint yellow glow rising up from some of the cracks. The stone cliff-side was pockmarked with holes, most of them not far above ground level, though high enough that she had to stand on her tiptoes to see inside one.

She wasn't really here, she knew that, but she could see everything clearly, smell the odd scent of the atmosphere on this world, feel the hot breeze. Allie was still on the couch back on Sy'hloran, she could still feel the couch beneath her, the coolness of the apartment air, and hear the gentle murmur of her mother's voice. Part of her mind was no longer there, however.

Peering into one of the holes, she saw something she didn't expect. One of the Rrughn lay curled inside a small shallow in the hole, which wasn't nearly as deep as she'd expected. Surrounding her were three wriggling Rrughn pups, looking like their eyes had opened for the first time that very day. Their fur was a mottled, patchy red and black, not like the lined and sharply-patterned fur of their mother. They yipped and squealed as they squirmed, like tiny, high-pitched versions of their parents' terrifying howls.

As though sensing her presence, the mother Rrughn lifted her head, sniffed the air, and growled low in her throat. Allie reflexively stepped back before remembering she wasn't actually there. Although she was apparently there enough for the Rrughn to sense her.

*"Be calm,"* Allie said, touching her mind to the Rrughn as she had done back on Kobek not so long ago, *"your pups are safe."*

*"Speaker,"* the mother Rrughn replied in surprise, *"and other."* At that last, the Rrughn's growl resumed. Allie could feel the mysterious entity watching her grow surprised.

Before another word could be exchanged, Allie's mind snapped back to Sy'hloran, to the couch where she sat with her mother. She blinked as she opened her eyes, slightly disoriented.

"Allie?" her mother asked, looking concerned.

"I'm okay, Mom," Allie said. "I'm fine. That was weird."

"It obviously worked to some extent. Possibly better than it should have. What did you see?"

"The Rrughn," she replied.

"What?"

"I thought of the Rrughn and was there, at their den. I've never been to their den. There's something else there, though."

"In their den?"

"No, in the Between," Allie said. Morgan laughed incredulously.

"The what?"

"That's what the Rrughn call the place we move through when we Jump. They use the energies to Jump and to speak mind to mind. I can talk to them. But that's not what was weird."

"That's not weird?"

"Mom, you know what I mean!" Allie said, laughing

in slight exasperation. "What was weird was that something was in the Between, watching me. It wasn't Jumping, or talking mind to mind like the Rrughn do. It was just there, in the Between. I don't think it knew I could really sense it until the very end. The Rrughn I was talking to sensed it, too."

"Wait, so you were talking mind to mind with this creature on Kobek while you were Seeing it?"

"Yeah," Allie replied.

"You shouldn't be able to do that, either. Your senses can experience it as if you're there, but you shouldn't be able to interact with anything when Seeing it. You're not really there."

"It makes sense though," Allie argued. "I mean, if Seeing is just sort of connecting to the energies, and the Rrughn use those same energies to communicate, I should be able to communicate with them when I'm connected like that."

"I suppose that does make sense. How'd you get to be so bright?"

"Natural talent," Allie said with a grin. Morgan smiled back.

"Obviously you have a lot of that," her mother said, "including for Seeing. That watcher you mention worries me, though. I've Jumped thousands of times, before Tyren captured me, and I never even realized that there was a Between, let alone felt something watching me in there. Thinking back, I can see the signs of there being a space between space, but it never occurred to me. I know there's something on the other side of those energies, but not that there's something between. That's incredible."

"I didn't see it either, until the Rrughn started talking about it the first time. Then it suddenly seemed really clear."

"Well, that's more than enough progress for one day. I want to start again early tomorrow, so we should probably get some sleep," Morgan told her daughter.

"Okay, Mom. Good night. And thanks, I think I'll get this figured out pretty quickly, and we can go get Tyren and Klythe. Maybe even tomorrow."

"Maybe so," her mother said.

Allie stood and went to the closed door, opening it. Despite knowing it would be a beautiful bedroom, she still had to take several moments to simply stand in the doorway and admire it. Tic chirped curiously after she'd paused several seconds. Allie scratched her friend's soft fur.

Moving to the wardrobe, a flicker of movement caught her eye at the window. It was completely dark outside, lit only by starlight since the Sy'hloran moon hadn't yet risen. Sy'hloran, like Earth, only had one.

She couldn't see anything in the courtyard outside her window, and dismissed it as a bird or something similar. Touching the control panel by the window she darkened the glass until it was completely opaque. Turning away from the window and returning to the wardrobe, she didn't see the figure clinging to the wall outside above her window like a spider. The time wasn't yet right, so C.A.D.E.-16 simply watched… and waited.

# CHAPTER EIGHT

# MIDNIGHT

The Highlord was working hard, while Dav's mind thought he was sleeping. He'd had a prototype of the device he now worked frantically to complete almost ready for testing back on the Helios. It was now more urgent than ever that he successfully complete it. It's first test would be  a trial by fire, as Allie planned to Jump them all to the Sy'hli warship Tyren and Klythe had disappeared on as soon as she learned to See it.

He knew it wouldn't take her long. Even more so now that he had seen Dav's mind, he knew how unique and unusual she was. Why, he didn't know, and neither did Dav. The fact remained that she was unique and incredibly powerful. The memory of what she'd done to him on the Helios, had almost done, made him shiver in the warm room.

From the back of Dav's mind, he had watched as Imber had begun to show signs of the virus in her system.

Faint glow was coming through her heirlines that nobody else seemed to have noticed yet.

The Highlord had theorized that due to the way the Shaian bodies had evolved to create and transmit light, Imber's body would not only be the perfect first victim for the plague he had released upon her, but would also be one of the fastest possible incubators.

She had less than a week before it would kill her, he knew. Most of its victims would linger for twice, even three times that long before death, but the Shaian would fall like dominos once it took hold on their world. That part hadn't been planned into the engineering of the virus, but it was a nice little perk.

Now that the glow had begun to travel along her heirlines, others would already be infected, though it would be a while before any of them knew it. As it grew brighter, people further away would receive strong enough doses to contract the virus. Another few days and Imber herself would be unable to contribute to the fight against him. A few days more and none of the others would either. In time, only that blasted android would remain, and for his end the Highlord planned something a lot more fun than just watching his batteries run out.

The Highlord fused another set of circuits in the small device as he thought. Once Allie Jumped the team to rescue Tyren, the Highlord would either see his device proven successfully, or he would die once and for all. Those energies were strong enough, and he was still weak enough, that a single Jump would finish him.

This device, he thought as he caressed the sleek black case he was building it into, a case smaller than a grain of rice, would protect him from the girl's agonizing energies. She'd no longer harm him by Jumping him, and could no longer push those energies through him. In theory, he could still be successfully brought along for the ride when they Jumped, the energies simply wouldn't enter him.

If it failed, the energies would flood this body and burn any traces of the colony out of it. The Highlord would be no more. He took some comfort in knowing that with his plague already released, his survival or death would have no effect on whether his vengeance on the races of the galaxy would be complete. They would all die now, one way or another, it was just a question of whether the Highlord got the chance to kill the few he truly hated with his own two hands, or if he'd have to leave the virus to finish his work.

It didn't matter in the end, but the Highlord wanted the satisfaction of killing Artus, Imber, and Raith himself. Dav, his unwitting host, would die by his own hands, some irony there, on the Highlord's own home world just before he released this body, the new atmosphere of the terraformed world destroying him instantly.

Whatever others had thought, his goal was not to rule the galaxy. He wanted it ended. All life, everywhere. Wiped clean like they had done to his own home world. He also wanted his own end to take place on the very world it began. The colony within Dav's body was growing rapidly, allowing for more and more control as time passed. As long as the girl's energies didn't kill him, he would survive to see his home world one more time, after all other life was gone.

His brilliant creation, the virus to end all viruses, would travel on light itself, consuming organic cells as it went and converting those cells into even more light on which to spread. It would take seven thousand years for it to reach all sides of the galaxy traveling on light from the point it had been released, but the Highlord had taken it a step beyond and had enabled the virus to travel and spread through wormholes as well.

With the network of wormholes shifting and moving throughout the galaxy, it would be less than a year by his calculations before every living thing in the galaxy had been infected and killed, all organic matter slowly converting to light itself. Add to that the fact that it was so small that no medical scans would reveal it, and the virus was a perfect killing machine. Undetectable, incurable, and spreading at the speed of light.

A few more finishing touches, and the device was complete. The Highlord activated the device, and nestled it securely into the tiny case with the nanogrippers he'd been using before removing the glasses he'd been wearing for visual magnification as he worked.

He'd done amazing things with nano technology since taking over Tyren all of those years ago, from this device to the very virus that even now infected everyone in this city that he'd been working on for a decade. It was much easier to work with and understand nanotechnology when you yourself were a nanospecies.

The device powered on. With a deep breath, he inhaled the device into his host body's lungs. It would bond with the inside of the lung, unremovable, undetectable by any but the most careful body scans, making him immune to any attempts by the girl to harm him.

He felt an almost instant change in the feeling of the form he inhabited, as if a constant, uncomfortable pressure had suddenly been relieved. Dav wouldn't be able to feel it, as he wasn't sensitive to the energies. Allie wouldn't either, since it didn't influence the energies anywhere except inside his own host body. For the first time since the Sy'hli had first come to destroy his world with their terraforming, he was without pain. It was almost too much, and he nearly released control of the body before he caught himself.

That would have been bad. Dav's body would have fallen, his mind asleep and the Highlord without control. Hitting the ground or the table would have awakened Dav, who would have immediately been aware of being someplace other than where he slept and he'd have begun to figure out what was really going on.

For that matter, the Highlord had to work hard to keep his anger and hatred of the girl from showing through too much when Dav was awake. Dav had already noticed the unusual responses, and while he thankfully was attributing the illogical emotional response to stress, it wouldn't take much more for Dav's incredibly sharp mind to figure out that those feelings weren't in fact his.

"Highlord to C.A.D.E.-16," he said into the com on the coded frequency.

"C.A.D.E.-16," came the reply.

"Location?"

"Watching the crystal bearer at her apartment. Can I

kill her?"

"No, the time isn't right yet. Not until I can see her face. Not until all the other pieces are in place."

"Very well."

"I need you to begin sabotaging the Sy'hli fleet."

"Quietly, or loudly?" the android asked, sounding slightly more excited than he had a moment ago.

"Quietly," the Highlord replied.

"Very well," came the reply, enthusiasm gone again. Well, the Highlord thought, might as well give him something to be excited about.

"I want you to rig the warships so that they'll work fine until we activate a trigger switch, then they can explode."

"Yes, Highlord," C.A.D.E.-16 answered, his excitement back. He liked things exploding, especially if there would be casualties involved. Somewhat disturbing for a machine to be that bloodthirsty, the Highlord thought, but it did make the android very effective. The Highlord switched off the com.

His work was complete for the time being. He would return to the bed after cleaning up all evidence of his work, and return the body to sleep. Dav would awaken in the morning unaware of any of it, while the Highlord continued to watch from within. When Dav's friends were at their weakest, he would strike. As long as he survived the next Jump.

Imber couldn't sleep. She itched slightly, the kind of

subtle itching that happens when someone starts talking about something crawling on your skin. Not strong, and probably all psychological, but itchy nonetheless. That wasn't what kept her awake however.

A faint haze of light had entered her vision. It wasn't enough to impair her sight, but it was concerning, especially when combined with the itching along her heirlines and the general achiness that was subtly, but noticeably, building in her system. She wasn't foolish enough to just brush it off, especially with so much going on at the moment. She needed to be at the top of her game to help her friends, and if there was something wrong with her she needed to address it immediately.

She rose from her bed, and changed clothes quickly, then left her room. She moved quietly so as not to wake her father in the next room, and went to the door of their ambassadorial suite in the palace. Unless something was found to be legitimately wrong with her, she didn't want her father to know about it. Unfortunately, the doctors wouldn't treat her without her parent's consent, which made sense, but it complicated things.

If her father thought there was anything even slightly wrong with her, she'd be on lockdown and would never be able to help her friends. Not that her father would be that keen on her going on the rescue mission anyway, but she would deal with that after she went on the mission and he found out she'd gone.

Imber hated sneaking around him like that, but with circumstances the way they had been recently, he was more than a little paranoid about her safety, despite her proven ability to take care of herself. The last thing she needed was to give him reason to be even more protective and worried.

Luckily, she had a way around parental consent regarding her well-being. It didn't take her too long to reach Dav's room, despite the incredible size of the Imperial Palace. They had all insisted on being fairly close together, except Allie who was staying with her mother outside the palace. Everyone had kept their mouths shut about that decision, though she could tell that Raith, Artus, and Dav were all uncomfortable with her staying out of their direct supervision.

Allie had argued that they could reach her on com any time and she could Jump right to them. While a valid point, it wasn't really the same. Imber touched the control pad by the locked door, telling the system to give a soft alert to Dav that someone was outside his door. It took much less time than she expected for him to reach the door.

"Imber?" Dav asked. He didn't look like he'd just woken up. He was wearing soft, long pants and no shirt, but his eyes looked bright and awake as if he'd been up for some time.

"Hi Dav, I'm sorry to wake you," she said, even though she didn't think she had.

"That's okay, what's going on?" he asked. He looked concerned, which was only natural to being awakened by a friend in the middle of the night.

"I don't feel very well," she told him. "I want to go talk to a doctor and get a full scan, but I can't without letting my father know."

"So why don't you want him to know?" Dav asked.

There was a look in his eye she couldn't quite place, but it bothered her slightly. He may not have been sleeping due to the stress and worry about the rescue mission as well, she thought.

"He'd put me on lockdown for sure if he found out I was sick or hurt. I need to help on the rescue mission. You can understand that, right?" Dav considered her for a moment, then nodded.

"Sure, no problem," he said. "Let me get dressed and I'll run down there with you." She nodded and he ducked back inside.

It took less than a minute, and he came out, hopping slightly as he pulled his boots on while he tried to walk. She smiled and he grinned at her. They moved at a quick walk down the hallway toward the front of the palace where the royal family had an in-house physician. Perks to being the brother of the heir, she thought.

"So you think you're sick?" Dav asked, with a sidelong glance at her.

"I don't know, maybe. Just not feeling quite right, and I want to make sure it's nothing that will cause problems for me to help you guys out."

"Makes sense. It's probably nothing. A lot of crazy things going on, you're probably just tired and stressed."

"I thought so too, but it's just… I don't know, weird I guess. It feels like more than just being tired. "

"That is weird. Well, the doctors will tell you pretty quickly, shouldn't take more than a few minutes to get you scanned once we get there."

"I really appreciate it Dav. I know that asking you to tell the doctor to take care of me without parental consent is probably a major favor, and I don't want to get you in trouble with Artus over it."

"Don't worry about it," Dav replied with a shrug. "If Artus had his way, I wouldn't have been involved in anything dangerous either. He might as well be my father, the way he treats me sometimes. Other times though, we're just partners in crime, so to speak."

"That would be hard," she replied, "for both of you." Dav shrugged again.

"We make it work," he said.

They walked in silence the rest of the way. Dav seemed a bit off himself, she thought. Maybe he should get scanned too. She shook her head. He'd know if he needed a scan, she knew. And since they were going anyway, if he needed one he'd say so while they were there. For him, it probably was just tiredness and stress. He obviously hadn't been sleeping when she had come to his door.

They walked through the doors to the office of the palace doctor. It struck her as odd, having a doctor in residence at your own home, but this was a tremendously big home, with a lot of people. Getting to medical care in an emergency could be difficult. For the royal family, having someone on staff at all times was much safer.

It looked like most small doctor's offices she'd seen in her day, with a small desk up front and a doorway leading back into the exam room. The exam door was open and the myriad of scanning and medical equipment showed both cutting-edge technology, and meticulous care and upkeep. She found that reassuring.

There was no office assistant at the desk, but the doctor herself was standing by the window holding a small techpad she was working on. She looked up as they came in, and bowed when she saw Dav.

"Your Highness," she said, "are you well?" Her note of concern was sincere and Imber liked her immediately. She was Sy'hli, and older, with a very motherly kind of face. She was likely a distant cousin to the royal family, to get a position like this one.

"I'm fine," Dav replied, sounding a little irritated, "but Ambassador Oren's daughter is feeling a bit ill. Can you look her over?" The doctor frowned.

"Where is Ambassador Oren?" she asked.

"Sleeping," Dav replied. Before the doctor could protest further, he continued. "She just needs a quick scan. You have my word that if anything of note comes up in the scan, I'll make sure he knows about it immediately."

Imber wasn't sure she wanted to let her father know even if something were wrong, but she also knew that getting checked out without his knowledge was one thing, but hiding an illness from him was quite another. The doctor hesitated, then nodded.

"And don't mention anything to anyone that we came by," Dav added, "unless of course something is wrong. We don't want to worry the ambassador unnecessarily during discussions with the Council." The doctor nodded. She didn't look entirely comfortable with this, but Dav's assurances and his direct instruction made it impossible for her to refuse without causing trouble.

"Come in then," she said to Imber, "and if Your

Highness will wait out here?" That last was directed to Dav, who simply nodded and sat in one of the luxuriously comfortable chairs near the door. Imber went inside and climbed up onto the exam table at the doctor's instruction.

"What seems to be the trouble?" the doctor asked.

"Mild itching, a bit of excess light in my vision, and general achiness," Imber replied. The doctor nodded.

"I understand you've had quite the adventure these past few days," the doctor said. "It's not hard to imagine that your body is just overtired. We'll scan you to be sure though, don't worry, but it doesn't sound like anything to get too concerned about. Lie back and relax please."

The doctor touched a control pad to the side of the table, and a holographic display lit up overlapping Imber's body as she lay down. From the feet up, a silvery bar of light climbed up her body from the scanners above, and as it passed, the holographic interface began filling in with detailed, complex information. Imber would never have been able to interpret all the data, but that's what doctors were for.

Imber waited patiently for the scan to complete, a process that took less than a minute even though it was scanning her entire body at the molecular level. She hadn't even needed to disrobe. The doctor touched a different panel once the scan was complete, and another, flat display sprang up in front of her.

"Should take me just a moment, young lady," the doctor said. Imber nodded, though the woman was looking at her display, scrolling through data, and not watching Imber.

"Cardio and respiratory all normal, tissue seems in good shape though you've definitely been working yourself hard recently, all organs functioning well, brainwave frequencies perfect for your species. No abnormal bacteria or viruses. All in all, you're in good shape young lady. Nothing to be concerned about. I suggest getting some sleep, and taking it easy the next few days. Try to find something relaxing to do."

Yeah, that's exactly what she would do, Imber thought wryly. Assaulting an enemy ship to rescue the former tyrant of the galaxy from a band of armed and trained mercenaries along with a handful of other thirteen year olds was restful and relaxing, right? Plenty of time to sleep when this was all over, if exhaustion really was all that was wrong with her.

"Okay, well that's good to hear," Imber said with a smile.

"Do you want something to help you sleep?" the doctor asked.

"No, thank you," Imber replied. "I'm tired enough to sleep, I think." The doctor nodded.

"Come back if you change your mind, okay?" Imber nodded and walked back out of the room. Dav stood immediately.

"So, what's the word?" he asked. He looked concerned, which she appreciated, though that worried her a little too.

"Clean bill of health. Like you said, I just need to rest," she told him. He smiled slowly and spoke, almost as if to himself.

"Perfect."

# CHAPTER NINE

# A SIMPLE RESCUE

Allie sat in a large, comfortable rec room with her friends, waiting for Artus and Morgan to return from the morning session of Council discussions. She was practicing her Sight, and that morning had decided to try Earth.

Her thoughts stood in her kitchen, watching Katharine preparing herself a late dinner. It was night back on Earth, Allie realized. She'd adapted more than she'd realized to the time systems used in space, it was a little disconcerting sitting in the rec room with her friends with a bright, sunny sky outside, and also standing in her old kitchen with night fully upon the world.

Katharine was moving almost automatically. Allie could see the note she'd left sitting on the kitchen counter. It was worn, as though it had been held and read a lot. Katharine turned to face Allie as she moved toward the far counter for the stove. She almost walked right through Allie, startling Allie enough to jolt her out of the vision.

Katharine had looked sad, and worried, Allie knew. Her guilt at leaving her like that was enormous, but she knew Katharine was much safer uninvolved in any of this until it had been sorted out. She resolved to go back and leave another note. She'd go talk to her directly, but Katharine would never let her leave again if she saw her. Besides, Allie wanted to return to Katharine with her mother by her side, and Morgan wasn't yet fully recovered.

Before she could plan out what to say, Dav's laughter pulled her attention. He and Raith were obviously joking around again, Raith having just made some remark that Dav had thought was hilarious. Imber was laughing too, Allie saw, and Raith with a teasing smirk on his face. Just as the surge of love and remorse had come over her at the sight of Katharine, the surge of love and appreciation flooded her as she looked at her friends.

The finest anyone could ever ask for, she knew. Every one of them had risked their lives to save her, and to save one another's. She had done the same for them, and she suspected they all would again several times before this was all over.

It was hard being away from home, away from the mother she had grown up with, but beside her friends she could endure anything, overcome anything. Her thoughts were interrupted by the door sliding open and Artus storming in, her mother right behind him.

All four of them stood right away and moved to the big table near the door, where Artus had already bee-lined. Sitting down, Dav waited until Artus had taken a few deep breaths before speaking.

"All right Artus, what is it?" Dav asked softly.

"The rescue mission has been banned by the Council," he replied angrily.

"What, why?" Allie asked.

"They say you're too unpredictable, too young to take the risk, and the rest of you are certainly too young to participate in rescue missions of any kind."

"They do know we rescued Morgan from Tyren, right? And Imber, and Ambassador Oren, need I go on?" Dav said, his own anger showing.

"Doesn't matter," Artus sighed, "They say there are trained professionals for this work, already en route to intercept."

"Intercept what?" Raith asked pointedly. "They don't even know which direction they went."

"I tried to tell them that."

"Do they know that I'm able to See my Jumps?" Allie asked proudly. "Even if I haven't been there? I've been practicing all morning and have been able to look at all sorts of places I've never been. I'm sure I can Jump someplace new."

"I knew you'd take to it like a duck to water," Morgan said, more than a little proudly herself. Allie grinned at her mother.

"Morgan told them about your rapid progress," Artus told her. "They don't care. They're concerned with putting any of you at risk."

"They're not putting us at risk," Dav argued, "we are! It's our choice."

"It's not, I'm afraid," Morgan said. "You're all still too young to be considered adults in any of your cultures. By law, decisions regarding your health and safety have to be made by your parents."

"My parents are dead," Dav growled.

"Or guardians," Morgan added, with a nod to Artus. Dav turned to regard his older brother. His expression intense and expectant.

"I'd want you beside me," Artus said slowly, "but I can't go either. The Sy'hli Empire can't risk the heir being killed, not only before the coronation, but right in the middle of the Council's discussion over what to do with the Sy'hli."

"'What to do with us'?" Dav snapped. "We're the most powerful species in the galaxy, what right do they have to decide our fate?" Allie stared at him. That didn't sound at all like Dav. She knew he was stressed and angry, but this was extreme even for him.

"That's precisely the point, Dav," Artus told his brother, his tone calming and gentle. "We are the most powerful species in the galaxy. And to their eyes, we've used that as a weapon against the civilized races of the galaxy for many years now."

"Tyren did that, not us!"

"The Highlord did that," Allie corrected him, "but used the Sy'hli Empire to do it." Dav sat back in his chair, glowering. She had a point, and he knew it.

"There's another problem," Raith added. Everyone looked at him. "What we want to find Tyren for and what the Coalition wants to find him for are very different things. If we let them take over the rescue, he won't survive long enough to go to trial. I've intercepted several communications going out from various council members to their own fleets, who are now all looking for Tyren as well."

The group stared at him.

"You've been monitoring the outgoing communications of royal ambassadors?" Artus said carefully. Raith looked sheepish.

"I'm sorry, I can't turn that function off. I'm a recon android. It's what I was built for." Artus looked like he was struggling with something internal. Finally he nodded.

"Fine, but keep that data classified."

"Of course," Raith said. "Unless it effects our safety or the safety of people we're protecting," he added.

"I could order you," Artus said with a stern look. Raith flashed a cheeky grin.

"I can ignore you," he replied, looking like he relished every word of that sentence. Allie grinned and Raith winked playfully at her. Artus looked about to snap at him, but finally sighed and nodded again.

"Fair enough," he said at last.

"In the meantime, we just have to hope that the Sy'hli fleet finds him first," Morgan said, "and try to keep the Council from completely turning on us." Artus stood and Morgan followed suit.

"We've got to grab a quick bite before returning to the council chambers. Do you kids want to join us?" Morgan asked.

"No thanks," Allie said quickly, "Still too early for us, we had breakfast two hours ago." Artus nodded and turned to leave. Morgan regarded her daughter for a long moment, then nodded once slowly, and followed Artus. The door closed, and Dav stood with a low growl. Allie stood as well.

"Come on," she said. Imber and Dav frowned. Raith grinned.

"Where are we going?" Imber asked.

"To rescue Tyren, of course," Allie said.

"The Council forbade it," Dav returned.

"All that means to me is that we won't have help," Allie said, sounding more sure than she felt. "It'll be just the four of us. And if we're going to do this we'll need to move fast, before the Council takes steps to ensure we can't go."

"Your mother will kill you Allie, and so will your father, Imber," Dav argued.

"My mother just gave me permission," Allie replied.

"And if we rescue Tyren it will be worth my father killing me," Imber added. Dav looked back and forth between them.

"You don't have to come Dav," Raith said softly. "We all know how you feel about Tyren."

"Of course I have to come," Dav snapped, "if all of you are going. What will we do with Tyren once we have him?" Allie smiled at his assumption that if they went, they would succeed. She appreciated the enthusiasm, even if his mood was so quick to change lately. In fairness, she thought, he had been a lot less happy since all of this started anyway, and mentioning Tyren was always a surefire way to get him riled up.

"Bring him back here, and put him in Artus' care. Once Artus has custody of him, the Council will have to deal with Artus diplomatically if they want to get anything from Tyren. We only have zero negotiating leverage with them about this because we don't have Tyren. He's still missing."

"Escaped," Dav grumbled.

"Dav," Allie said gently, touching his arm. Dav calmed considerably at her touch.

"Sorry," he said, frowning slightly.

"Nobody here has to come," Allie said to the rest of them. "I'm defying the Council, but some of you have more riding on their approval than others do."

"I'm not a diplomat, but this may affect my father," Imber said, "even so, I have to go. My friends are in danger, rescuing my friend's brother. If I sat back here while you all ran off after him and you got hurt because I wasn't there, I'd never forgive myself. I'm in."

"I've got no ties to anyone but you three, and I will be invaluable in getting through their systems, and fighting if it comes to that." Raith shrugged. "No reason for me not to go, and every reason for me to come with you."

"He's my brother," Dav said quietly. "Hate him or not, I want to make sure he's dealt with the way I think he should be, not the way the Council thinks he should be. Besides, if you're right Allie, he might be a prisoner of Klythe and the Maruck, not a leader of them. If Klythe knows what you know, Tyren is on borrowed time already. Tic?" Dav asked with a smile at the furry purple jicund on Allie's shoulder. Tic chirped once sharply. Allie laughed.

"She's in."

"Okay then, we're all in. Gear up and meet in my rooms in one hour," Dav said.

Allie left the rec room and headed through the corridors. She wasn't heading for her room for gear, that would take too long, leaving the palace, traveling to her apartment, then returning and navigating all the way back to Dav's room. Instead, she headed for a restroom. Glancing up and down the hallway, she made sure it was clear and nobody was in sight before she ducked inside.

Once inside, it was only an instant before she had grabbed the energies around her and pushed, Jumping to her apartment. She could feel the unseen entity watching her as she Jumped. Once she figured out who that was, she thought, she was going to poke them in the eye.

Running to her closet, she grabbed her flight suit, making sure all the nutrient packs were full before changing. She grabbed the two shatter pistols and their holsters from the shelf and strapped them on.

Picking up her helmet, she held it in her hand as she looked around and thought about the mission and what she'd need. That was all she really needed, she decided, then nodded to Tic, who jumped back up onto Allie's shoulder, gripping comfortably onto the ridged shoulder plate Raith had built into Allie's suit.

She looked into the helmet at the visor and watched for a few minutes. The little map in the corner of her visor display suddenly sprang up with a light gray dot some distance away. Raith had finished putting on his suit. She smiled, waiting for Dav's blue dot to activate before Jumping to his rooms. She'd Jump into his sitting room of course, not his bedroom, but she was still uncomfortable with the idea of Jumping into his rooms knowing he was changing in the bedroom.

Raith's gray dot moved quickly once it appeared, and in under a minute he was at Dav's rooms, or where she approximated them to be. The little map was great, but didn't have the palace floorplan programmed in, so couldn't tell her precisely where he was.

Imber's purple dot appeared next. Dav was ready last? That was strange, she thought. Raith was there though, they may have started discussing the plan before Dav had changed. There was still plenty of time before Dav's one hour designated meeting time. Imber was moving too, heading toward Raith.

There it was, Dav's blue dot appeared right next to Raith's. Allie gathered the energies and Jumped her and Tic to Dav's sitting room. Dav and Raith were there. Imber walked in less than five seconds after Allie's appearance. The total time passed was less than half an hour from when they left the rec room. They were all eager, it seemed.

Dav and Raith were over on one side of the room, talking conspiratorially as they leaned over something in Dav's hands. Allie grinned. This could only mean more of Raith's brand of mischief.

"Okay boys, break it up," she said playfully. Dav and Raith turned to regard her, then over her shoulder to Imber walking in. Dav's grin could only be described as eager and Raith's was plainly satisfied. "Uh oh," she said, still smiling.

"Raith made me a new toy," Dav said, sounding for all the world like a kid on Christmas who had not been given what he'd asked for, but had instead received something a thousand times cooler than anything he'd ever even thought to ask for. He held up his arms.

On his forearms were a pair of long wristbands, running from wrist to halfway up his forearm. They were metal, though a darker metal that matched the flight suit perfectly. They were obviously technological in nature, though had no flashing lights or visible buttons. They looked almost like high tech armored bracers, though with the flight suit's design, wearing armor beyond what they had was pretty pointless. Besides, the boys wouldn't be nearly so excited over armor.

"I repeat, uh-oh," Allie said. "Okay so what do they do?"

"You'll have to wait and see when he gets a chance to test them," Raith told her. "Right now we're just field testing the suit interface. With luck, after we get back he can take them for a real test drive. Won't be much need on this mission, but I do need a good chance to test the suit interface."

"Well make sure we know about it in time to not freak us out when you make them do whatever insane thing it is you've designed them to do, okay?" Allie said with a laugh. Raith and Dav laughed with her. Raith handed her a pair of gloves.

"New gloves?" she asked. Raith nodded.

"Nothing too intense or crazy," he replied, "just built strike rings into them for better close-quarters combat. I don't know why I didn't put them on the first edition suits. I have some ideas for more features on the full suits later, but haven't had time to test my prototypes, and this isn't the time for it." He handed a pair to Imber as well. She took them and both girls changed gloves, setting the old ones on an elegantly carved side table.

"Everyone ready?" Dav asked, expression having turned to one that meant all business. He was ready, and was obviously pushing his emotional reactions to the idea of rescuing Tyren aside in order to get the job done. That was something Allie admired about Dav. He was light-hearted, funny, sweet, and playful, but had proven time and again that when it was time for business, he was all focus and resolve.

Allie waited for everyone's nod, and they all put their helmets on. Allie closed her eyes and concentrated. She felt the energies a little quicker this time, which surprised her. She could also feel the watcher again. It felt curious. Once she reached her mind along the flowing current of energy and focused on Tyren, she could see him. He was being held captive, as she'd suspected, sitting in the same kind of cell on the Sy'hli battlecruiser that they'd been in when Spike and her crew had abducted them.

He was sitting calmly in the center of the room. It looked like he was asleep sitting up, until she realized he was meditating. She didn't know Sy'hli did that. There were three Maruck sitting around outside the cell, clearly on guard. They were speaking to one another in Maruck. She listened a moment, then focused again on her friends as she opened her eyes.

"He's in a cell, under guard," she told them, directing the words to Dav specifically. His expression looked uncertain, like he wasn't sure if he should be glad or angry at this news, but he nodded acknowledgement. "Three Maruck. They're almost to their destination, some kind of outpost on a Maruck colony planet. Klythe is captaining the ship. There's another ship nearby though, and closing in. They seem excited for a fight. We need to get Tyren out of there."

Allie held her hands out. Her friends moved into ready position, each facing outward from Allie, each making sure they either had a hand on her, or she had a hand on them. Dav's hand on her shoulder was shaking slightly, as though he were nervous.

"Here we go," she said by way of warning. She grabbed the energy, focusing on the place her mind had just been. Well, not exactly that place, but a place slightly down the corridor she'd seen where their appearance would put them ready for the Maruck guards. The watcher brushed her awareness, causing her to momentarily lose focus.

"Sorry, one moment," she said. Dav glanced at her, concerned.

Reaching out again, she got a firm hold of the energies, and actively ignored the watcher. She found her focus, and her destination, and Jumped.

The energy instantly tore around her in a chaotic storm she'd never seen before. The place she felt connected to, her destination, suddenly seemed to shift.

It took her a moment to realize the watcher was trying to hijack her Jump, and send her and her friends where it wanted her to go. It had a loose hold of the energies, as though they were at the edge of its reach, but was incredibly powerful. She wrapped her mind around the energies forcefully, and wrenched the energy back under her control.

Quickly resetting their destination, she completed the Jump. The watcher, brushing against the back of her mind again, felt very surprised. And eager. She shivered despite the perfect temperature of the flight suit, and realized after a long moment that she was lying on the ground and felt nauseous and disoriented.

In the distance, she heard shouts and the sound of both shatter gun fire and Maruck roars. It sounded muffled, muted. As she slowly regained her focus on her surroundings, the sounds died away. She lay on the ground, head cradled in Dav's lap. Imber was leaning over her, expression worried. Someone had been calling her name for some time.

Looking around, she spotted Raith to one side, shatter guns raised down both directions of the corridor, ready. Three Maruck lay unconscious in the cell across from her, its containment field humming. She looked up at Dav and could see a mix of emotions on his face through his visor, from frustration to concern to surprise. She sat up, slowly.

"Sorry," she mumbled.

"What happened?" Dav asked.

"I don't know," she replied honestly. "Something interfered with the Jump. I had to fight to get it back." Dav and Imber frowned at each other before looking back to her.

"You mean like in the Shift?"

"No, it felt more like… nevermind. I can't really explain it. I need to talk about it with my mother when we get back. Where's Tyren?"

"In his cell. We didn't want to bring him out until you were okay, just in case he decided to try something," Dav said.

"I'm okay. Let's get him and get out of here," she replied.

"Do you seriously want to try to Jump us all home again after that?" Imber asked.

"What choice do we have?" Allie replied.

"We can take this ship," Raith said, still watching the corridor, "I checked our coordinates, and we could be back on Sy'hloran in two days. Assuming that other ship leaves us alone."

"The one coming toward us?" Allie asked, remembering hearing the Maruck talking about it. "The Maruck were preparing for a fight."

"Maruck are always preparing for a fight," Dav retorted, "They might be peaceful, or coming to ask for help."

"They might be coming to blast a Sy'hli warship out of the sky," Allie replied.

"I vote we rescue Tyren, take over the ship completely, and try to communicate with the incoming vessel. It's not large," Raith added.

"Neither are the Tchratchi, but I don't want to tangle with them either," Allie said. "It's okay guys, I can make the Jump."

"Easy enough to take the ship," Raith said. "There

are only two more Maruck on this ship, both in the control room." All of us together, will have no trouble with two Maruck."

"What about two Maruck and one Sy'hli?" Dav asked, gesturing at Tyren's cell down the hall. "What if he takes the opportunity to turn on us."

"I'm not worried about that," Allie replied, "I saw inside his mind. Whatever monster you think he is, he's not. The man back there in that cell is your brother. The one who killed your parents is not. Same body maybe, but very different minds." Dav shook his head in frustration.

"Fine, you make the call."

Allie looked at Dav a long moment. He watched her expectantly. She glanced to Raith, who just gave her an encouraging smile. He'd back her no matter what she chose. She looked to Imber. Imber looked thoughtful.

"What if they are coming to ask for help? What if we abandon them by Jumping out of here, and the two Maruck in control room kill them?" Imber had a valid point, Allie thought.

"Okay. We grab Tyren, take the control room and lock the other two Maruck up down here. Then we try to contact the incoming ship. If they're friendly, we wait and see what they need. If they're not, we Jump the ship back to Sy'hloran."

"The whole ship?" Dav asked incredulously.

"I've done it before," Allie retorted, "and this one isn't even laced with rogellium."

"What about what just happened when you Jumped us here?" Dav asked. This time his voice was nothing but concern, and his expression showed that concern was largely for her.

"It'll be fine. I wasn't expecting it before, but I'll be ready if it happens again."

"As good a plan as any," Raith said, glancing at the readout above the control panel, guns still up and ready. "That ship is going to be in range of this ship's weapons in just a couple of minutes. If we don't take the control room from the Maruck, that ship may not have the chance to announce its intentions at all."

"Then let's go," Allie said, standing.

She was still a little dizzy, but not enough to let it show. She wanted her friends to be confident in her ability to get them out in a pinch, and her stumbling around wouldn't help that at all. The others fell into step with her, Imber beside Allie, Dav in front, Raith in the rear.

They moved in front of the cell field and Allie moved beside Dav. She looked in at the man, sitting in his meditative posture as if nothing were going on. He had to have heard the fight, but hadn't moved so much as an inch since Allie had Seen into his cell.

"Tyren," Dav said, tone cold and hard. The man's piercing blue eyes opened. Allie was astonished. Without the hatred and cruelty twisting his face, Tyren looked very much like the brother of Dav and Artus. He had the same sparkle in his eye, though Tyren's was much subdued. He had the same quirk to the edge of his lips as though about ready to burst into a smile. After a few days without the Highlord infesting his mind and body, he now looked like the man whose heart she had seen while battling the creatures within him.

"Hello Dav," Tyren replied. Allie could see the man forcibly fighting back an emotional overflow. "I wouldn't have thought you'd come for me."

"I didn't. I came for Allie." His reply was as cold as his tone. Tyren just nodded though, and smiled sadly.

"I understand. Thank you for coming anyway. And the rest of you. It is brave, though probably foolish of you to come for me."

"Not foolish," Raith said, "we have the Starjumper here with us. We can handle a few Maruck, and she can get us home. Quick, clean, and easy."

"I heard you take out the guards," Tyren replied, "that was well done. Well," he added, standing up smoothly with the same grace his people seemed born to, "we'd better get moving. Am I to be cuffed, or just to stay ahead of the group so you can shoot me if need be?"

"I'm sending you in first after Klythe. We'll handle the other Maruck in the control room," Dav said. To Allie's surprise, Tyren smiled. It was a very predatory smile.

"Good. He needs to be taught a lesson."

Allie looked to her companions. They each nodded in turn. Imber backed down the hall to have a clear shot at Tyren, and enough time to react if he charged. Dav and Raith moved Allie back and stood between her and Tyren. Both held guns at the ready. Raith touched the control panel, not taking his eyes off Tyren.

A quick glance at Tic on her shoulder showed the jicund was perfectly relaxed, which further affirmed Allie's trust in Tyren. The field dropped, leaving Tyren free. He calmly stepped forward, nodded his thanks, and turned down the passage toward the control room. The others followed behind, prepared for the next fight, whether it came from Maruck, or from Tyren.

# CHAPTER TEN

# PARTY CRASHER

Tyren stood before the door to the control room, Dav and Raith at his back. Allie was so convinced of Tyren's innocence that Dav found himself slowly slipping in his resolve to see Tyren destroyed for his crimes. Looking into his brother's eyes had shaken him, badly. Allie had been right. This man wasn't the same as the one he'd locked gazes with back on the station when he'd tried to kill Raith and destroy the crystal key.

Part of him still hated Tyren, but for some reason, he had been finding it harder and harder to deny that an entity, or group of entities, could take a person over. Despite that, he held his gun ready and wouldn't hesitate to shoot his brother if the man tried to attack any of his friends.

Tyren glanced back over his shoulder. Raith nodded, and Tyren touched the control panel, opened the door, and stepped in smoothly, proudly. Not how Dav himself would have entered, and probably a stupid entrance since Klythe and his cohort probably were armed. Tyren didn't shy away from it though. He strode into the room a few feet, just enough to give Imber a clear shot as Dav and Raith each moved to one side of the doorway inside the room. Allie stayed back, guns up and ready, though she knew she would be crazy to shoot through that doorway with all her friends so close. Her aim was nowhere near that reliable.

Dav watched his brother carefully, closely, while keeping an eye on the two Maruck who stood from their stations and turned to stare at Tyren.

"So bold, little man," Klythe rumbled. "No more Highlord, you still think you boss?"

"No Klythe, I'm no longer anyone's boss. But you and I have a score to settle." The Maruck to the side of the room watched Klythe for cues on how to handle this. Klythe snarled.

"Tyren weak. Not strong, no like Highlord."

"You're an idiot Klythe," Tyren said disdainfully. "You've been fighting on the losing side from day one, and you're too stupid to know it. I'd offer to let you surrender, but you'd just find that insulting. Frankly, so would I. You want this as much as I do."

"Yes, Klythe want," the huge Maruck said, leaning down low into a battle stance as he moved into the room.

"Come on then pup, let me show you how a real warrior fights," Tyren told him.

Dav watched and listened in fascination. His brother sounded every bit the Sy'hli warrior. The Highlord had been perfectly willing to fight, but had always seemed to find excuse not to unless he had the clear upper hand. Tyren against Klythe was admittedly leaning in Tyren's favor, after all Raith, Dgehf, and even Artus had all bested Klythe over the last month. Come to think of it, Klythe's pride was probably just as wounded as his body. Yet with this many guns backing Tyren, he wouldn't have had to fight if he didn't want to. He clearly wanted to, at least with Klythe. Dav was willing to let him.

Klythe roared and charged. Tyren turned partially sideways and set his feet. Lowering his back hand, he clenched it tightly. Allie and Imber had moved out from directly behind Tyren. Raith kept the other Maruck firmly in his sights as the others watched Tyren and Klythe.

At the last second, Tyren pivoted gracefully as any dancer right out of the charging Maruck's way fist swinging in a tight backhand directly into the side of Klythe's neck. The big beast collapsed to the floor like a marionette with his strings cut. He didn't move. Everyone stared at Tyren in astonishment. He looked down at Klythe in disgust.

"I told you that you were an idiot, Klythe," he said needlessly, since Klythe couldn't hear him. "I can't believe you charged me. Me, of all people." Turning back to the other Maruck, Tyren raised a brow.

"Well Brigon? Are you going to let these nice folks take you to a cell or shall I help them drag your crippled body down the corridor into a cell anyway?"

The Maruck, Brigon, growled low in frustration, and resignation. Tyren obviously knew that Brigon was no alpha, and having watched his leader dropped so efficiently would never be so bold as to attack while Tyren was still around. He moved toward the door.

"Oh, and take the trash with you," he told the Maruck. Brigon growled again, but grabbed Klythe by the scruff of his neck and dragged the limp Maruck leader back into the corridor, Raith, Tyren, and Dav right behind. Imber watched them walk out, then moved to the communications station. Allie sat in the sensor station.

"That other ship is close," she said. "It's in weapons range, but hasn't fired anything at us."

"This is the Sy'hli battle cruiser directly ahead. Please identify yourself immediately," Imber transmitted across the com channel. There was no reply. "Unidentified vessel, this is the Sy'hli battle cruiser you are on a direct course to intercept. Identify yourself." Imber and Allie waited a long moment, but there was no reply.

"They may not be answering, but their distress beacon is activated," Allie said, noticing the small readout alongside the ship on her display.

"They really must be in trouble," Imber said. Turning back to coms, she spoke again. "Unidentified vessel, we have registered your distress beacon and have cleared you for docking at the rear of the craft. You will be met with an armed guard. If you enter our craft with weapons, we will open fire."

"Wow, look at you being all tough," Allie whispered with a giggle. Imber laughed.

"Come on, let's get the guys back to the docking bay so we can find out what's going on."

The girls stood, setting the ship to hold steady.

Moving back into the passage, they saw the two boys and Tyren coming their way at an easy walk.

"Distress beacon on that ship is active. No response over coms. I told them they could dock and we'd meet them in the bay, and to come unarmed," Imber said.

"Bad idea," Tyren said, falling into step beside Allie and Tic as the group turned to follow Imber and Allie to the docking bay.

"Not much choice. We can't abandon someone in distress," Allie said.

"No, no you can't," Tyren said with a slight smile. "Present company included, apparently."

Tic chirped at him, and Allie realized Tic was inches from the man she'd earlier mauled. A quick glance told her there was no hostility in Tic right now. Tic was sniffing at Tyren, and seemed a little confused. After a moment, Tic reached one clawed hand up and touched Tyren. Allie watched in amazement as Tyren reached up to touch the subtle scars along his chin and right cheek that even dermal regenerators had apparently been unable to fix.

"Don't worry little one, no hard feelings huh?" Tyren said, reaching the hand over to Tic. To her satisfaction, and banishing any doubts she might have had of Tyren's virtue, Tic leaned up and nuzzled the hand. Tyren chuckled softly and scratched the little jicund. Dav pointedly looked away.

They reached the docking bay quickly, and took up positions to prepare for the mysterious guest. Imber held her rifle across her chest, but in hand such that it would be a fraction of a second to raise and fire.

Raith had his guns holstered, but she knew he could draw and fire them faster than most people could fire even if they already had the guns out and aimed at their target. Dav held one gun out in his left hand, and still seemed to be watching Tyren as much as the docking bay doors.

A mechanical whirring sound came from the door, and there was a gentle bump as the ship docked with theirs. Tyren stood to one side, in Dav's line of sight but out of all of their line of fire if they started shooting at the docking bay visitor. Slowly, the docking bay doors began to open. Allie was both excited and nervous to see who it would be. The ship had been unfamiliar, obviously to herself, Imber, and to Raith, all of whom had seen it on the scanner.

The door opened, revealing a man standing on the other side. A single individual, slightly larger than a human though not a great deal bigger. It was impossible to determine gender as it was definitely not human. While seemingly built like a large, powerful man, it wore no clothing, and had no visible gender distinction. Its night-black, glistening skin was deeply ridged all over its body, and seemed less like skin and more like narrow, tight cords all tightly packed and formed into a man-like structure. It walked forward in an odd, sinewy kind of glide.

Allie saw its face bore some resemblance to human as well, though was comprised of the same kind of tightly packed cords that the rest of its body was. As she looked, she noticed a faint rippling beneath the strange surface of the creature's cord-like skin. The face had a vaguely nose-like shape, a mouth-like opening, and indents for eyes, but there were no eyes, no real nose, and the mouth was nothing more than an opening between the odd cord-patterns. The odd mouth was curved in a smile.

She was about to open her mouth to speak as the creature took its first few steps, but was abruptly silenced when she heard Tyren whisper.

"Sandro… oh no…" Allie looked to Tyren. His face had gone white as a ghost, and he looked near to a full-on panic.

"Klythe?" the figure spoke, its voice more like the whistle of wind through willow branches than a voice.

"Run!" Tyren shouted without warning and turned, bolting back toward the docking bay doors into the ship.

Everyone hesitated a moment in surprise. Everyone except Raith. Raith turned and ran toward Allie and Imber so fast that Allie barely saw it. An instant before Raith, and then Dav, reached Allie and Imber the creature emitted a horrible, wailing roar, the sound of hurricane winds rushing across the mouth of an impossibly deep cave.

The form took two running steps forward, and then its humanoid shape evaporated as the thousands of cords that comprised what had looked like the creature's skin exploded in a writhing, roiling, grasping nest of tentacles. The nest of tentacles lunged forward like a horde of angry serpents, expanding in width and snapping into the ground and through the air where Allie and Imber had just been standing. Dav and Raith, now carrying the girls, were running full tilt back down the hallway.

Allie watched as the tentacles tore backward across the ground, leaving huge gouges in the metal docking bay floor. The mass of tentacles that was Sandro lunged forward again, gaining despite Dav and Raith's frightening speed. Raith touched the door control panel for the briefest instant as he ran past, and the inside docking bay doors slammed shut.

It was less than half a second later that the thing, whatever it was, hit the closed metal door. An ear-piercing shriek came from the door as the glistening black tentacles tore through the metal framework, ripping the door effortlessly free and sending it spinning back into the docking bay.

The tentacles poured into the corridor like a flood of water, reaching and grasping every which way. Allie tried to see where the center of the mass was, the controlling body, but all she could see was the thousands of tentacles, tearing gouges through the walls, floor, and ceiling as it went. It was definitely gaining.

"Allie!" Tyren shouted. "You have to Jump us! Leave the ship, he'll tear it apart to get to us! Now!"

Allie reached out to touch Imber's outstretched hand, and she felt Tyren move closer as they ran so he could put a hand on her arm. Her mind reached for the energies and she almost gasped in relief to find nothing else holding the swirling energies around. She pulled them in, focused on her friends and Tyren, and Jumped them all back to Dav's rooms on Sy'hloran. Allie swore she could hear the howling roar of the nightmare behind them for several seconds after the world around them had stabilized.

"What… in all the galaxy… was that?" Imber gasped out as she fought to catch her breath.

"That," Tyren replied, "was Sandro."

"Yeah, but what?" Allie asked, her own voice shaky.

"Nobody is really sure," Tyren answered. "As far as anyone knows, he's the only one of his kind. Nobody has ever seen anything else like him. Not remotely like him."

"Is he going to kill the Maruck," Allie asked.

"No, Klythe obviously hired him. Sandro must have been coming to negotiate."

"Why the distress beacon then?"

"Sandro recognized that your voices weren't Maruck, and knew Klythe wouldn't have allied with a pair of young girls. He wanted on board to find Klythe, or to kill anyone he found. He'll find Klythe, so the negotiation will begin."

"You knew about this?" Dav asked dangerously. Tyren shook his head.

"I knew only that he said he had allied with Klythe. I didn't know he was coming to negotiate, or I'd have been urging us to Jump away from the first second," Tyren said.

"Sandro is a killer," Raith added, "Pure and simple. He's a mercenary some say, but assassin is more appropriate. And not the quiet, stealthy, kill your man and escape kind of assassin. Sandro is more the type to kill the target, the target's friends, the target's family, the target's neighbors, and anyone else who just happened to be unlucky enough to be in ten square miles of the target kind of killer. If Klythe has hired him, things just got a whole lot scarier around here."

"How do we kill him?" Dav asked.

"You don't," Tyren replied. "Sandro has so far proven himself to be immune to fire, cold, acid, electricity, shatter guns, arc rifles, plasma, explosions, the vacuum of space, and all forms of cutting tools. He also can tear through any metal known in the galaxy without much effort, can swim through space if his ship is destroyed, and has been alive for at least three hundred years so far when the first reports of his destroying entire cities started cropping up. Who knows how long before that he's been around, or how long until he dies of old age, if ever. He's not a creature, he's a force of nature."

"You're kidding," Allie laughed incredulously.

"I wish he was," Raith said. "We need to tell Artus and the Council right away."

"We need to tell them about Tyren, too," Allie pointed out. Dav sighed, and Imber grimaced. Tyren just nodded in resignation.

"I'd like to see my other brother before the Council has me burned at the stake, so to speak," Tyren said dryly. "Let's go, then."

# CHAPTER ELEVEN

# COUNCIL OF WAR

Artus took a deep breath to ensure his response was a rational one. Things had gone badly over the last two hours, with the Coalition Council beginning to very clearly take sides, dividing into those who supported the Sy'hli Empire's right to continue on the Council in equal measure, and those who felt that Tyren's rule had destroyed any rights the Sy'hli had at all in the galactic Coalition.

The latter group felt that the entire Sy'hli Empire deserved punishment and close monitoring for the actions of one man. Artus couldn't deny that many in the Sy'hli Empire had gone along with Tyren's ruthless tactics willingly, but many others had resisted at all costs. Many had paid for that resistance with their lives.

It didn't help matters that many of the Resistance that stood against Tyren were of many of these representative species, but none of the Resistance leaders had come forward. It was still very soon after Tyren's fall, but many have stated that any who would come forth and be heard would at least have sent messages by now.

Absence of word could only mean that there was either no Resistance left, or that they too feared the Sy'hli's retaliation, believing that the new Sy'hli heir would be just as bad as his brother. Many in the Council here seemed to feel the same, never mind that Artus himself had been in hiding for thirteen years and had been instrumental in Tyren's downfall. Never mind his willingness to abide by Coalition Code and swear an oath to such effect. None of it seemed to matter.

The issues on the table remained narrowed down to only two. Should the Sy'hli Empire's rights in the Coalition be terminated, and should Tyren be executed when caught. Artus couldn't deny that the Highlord was responsible for staggering casualties over the years, but try as he might, he could not convince the Council that it was the actions of a parasitic entity controlling Tyren's mind that was the true source of the evil he had committed, and that Tyren himself was as much a victim of the Highlord's cruelty as any.

Cries of insanity running in the House of Tyr'Arda royal line had nearly brought Artus to violent response more than once. He knew full well that such a reaction would only validate their beliefs in their eyes. One more deep breath, Artus told himself after another ridiculous and groundless accusation against the Sy'hli Empire as a whole.

"Queen Ydrisa, the Sy'hli Empire has long been allies to the Shaian. Even during the Highlord's reign, your people retained positions of power and influence in the Coalition. Your great niece herself is a close friend of the house of Tyr'Arda and was instrumental in helping us to bring down the tyrant. Even now, she sits with my younger brother and the Starjumper, waiting to hear word of the Council's decisions. I urge you to hold fast to that alliance and not turn your backs on the Sy'hli Empire in this time of chaos for the whole galaxy," Artus pleaded with the Queen of the Shaian.

"The galaxy has been in turmoil for decades, Artus," she replied. Artus ignored the breach of protocol in using his first name so familiarly. Now was not the time to raise issue over minor details. "Why now should we be so much more concerned?"

"With Tyren removed from power, the entire galaxy is in a state of fluctuation as those still loyal to him seek to wage their own small wars against the Coalition in the less patrolled quadrants. Bandits and pirates are rising up to fill the void left by the release of pressure with Tyren's removal as well. Thousands, possibly millions could die in the next few years as the Coalition seeks to regain control and restore order. The Sy'hli Empire is powerful, and I am prepared to turn the full force of that power toward rebuilding the damage done during the Highlord's reign. Our forces, joined with the rest of the Coalition, could cut the recovery time in half, and could help to restore order with much less loss of life," Artus replied fervently.

"You threaten to not assist with this problem if we remove your rights on the Council?" Ambassador Oren asked, the beginnings of outrage in his tone.

"Certainly not," Artus turned to the ambassador. How a man whose feathers were ruffled so easily could have raised a daughter who was so calm and collected under pressure, he'd never know. "The Sy'hli Empire will do everything in its considerable power to restore peace to the galaxy, with or without Coalition Alliance."

The ambassador huffed, trying to decide if he could get away with being angry at that subtle reminder that the Sy'hli were powerful enough to not need the permission, or assistance, of the Coalition to take control. Artus hoped the reminder would also make it obvious to the ambassador that Artus was pointedly not taking that route, and was seeking not only Coalition assistance, but approval in his chosen course.

"Artus, the fact remains that the Sy'hli Empire very nearly destroyed the Coalition," the queen pointed out.

"The Highlord very nearly destroyed the Coalition," Ambassador K'tchik of the Tchratchi reminded them all.

Several of the council members had to look down at the small translator screen when he spoke. Very few spoke Tchratchi, and the Tchratchi couldn't pronounce most of the other species' vowels so couldn't use their languages.

"The Sy'hli Empire was a tool used for an end," the tiny insectoid ambassador continued. "It is a powerful tool, but a tool nonetheless. Like any tool, it can be used for great good, or great harm. The power, and the choice, lies in the hand of its wielder. Prince Artus has proven himself time and again not only recently, but before he was forced into hiding that he is a man of virtue, honor, and integrity. The Tchratchi are not of the Coalition. We are beyond the Coalition. We are here not to vote or negotiate, but to state our position. The Tchratchi stand with the Tyr'Arda heir, and will help him and the Sy'hli Empire to restore peace to the galaxy. Your Coalition squabbles have done enough damage for one era."

"Your words are nearly an act of war, Ambassador," stated Ambassador Lithri of the Hgrundewa. "You openly state you would oppose the Council's decision should we decide to restrict the Sy'hli Empire's actions."

"The Tchratchi do not concern ourselves with your politics. We concern ourselves with the galaxy. Too long did my people stand by and watch as the Highlord wrought much destruction among the Coalition worlds. Had his reach extended outside of Coalition territory and into our space we would have killed him and any who stood with him. Even so, many of my people took sides with the Resistance. Had they sought open war, something my people do not lightly engage in, even that number would have crushed the Coalition. Your outrage, Ambassador Lithri, is inconsequential. We will not wait another decade for this mess to be resolved. The Sy'hli heir has proven himself to us and seeks the same ends we do. That is enough. We do not seek war with your Coalition, Ambassador Lithri, but if you declare it, we will end you."

The entire chamber was silent. The Tchratchi Ambassador hadn't said much over the last few days, taking his time and learning everyone's positions. He had clearly made up his mind however, and everyone was painfully aware that not only had he just said his people were going to help Artus clean up his brother's mess, he had flatly stated his people would kill anyone who stood in the way of that goal. After a long moment, Councilman Tobriah of the Uhran spoke.

"We are not here to declare war on anyone, my friends. We are here to determine if the Sy'hli are still enough of a threat for us to attempt to restrict. Should we choose it, we could successfully restrict the Sy'hli. Not because we have the power to enforce it, but because the Prince is an honorable man and would allow it, should we so decide. The Sy'hli were always the most powerful among us. The Highlord's rule has solidified that without question.

"The Uhran as well have seen enough of both younger Tyr'Arda sons to have faith in their noble intentions, and we too would help them bring back the harmony our galaxy once had. We too would see the Coalition restored not only to its former power, but to its former reputation of fighting for the people, not against them," the Uhran ambassador finished, sitting back in his chair indicating he had said his peace.

"I thank Ambassador K'tchik and Councilman Tobriah for their votes of confidence and support," Artus said with a small bow to each representative. "Ambassador Lithri, Councilman Tobriah speaks truth. We would honor any restrictions placed on us by the council, if that is what the council deems best for the people of the galaxy. That being said, you and I both know that the Sy'hli Empire's help will be invaluable in the solidification of Coalition authority and the restoration of galactic peace. The Coalition rules not out of fear or force, but out of cooperation with our brothers.

This is the Coalition we seek to restore. This is the authority we wish to see in charge once more of galactic well-being. As much or more than any here, I wish to see the people once more free to pursue their lives and better their people without fear of oppression and domination from more powerful and advanced races. The Maruck are still rampaging. The Highlord's loyalists are…"

Artus stopped as the door to the council chambers opened. He stared with the rest of the Coalition Council in shock as Dav walked in, followed by Allie, Raith, Imber, and then by Tyren.

The shock lasted a full two seconds in absolute silence before the room erupted in outrage, shock, and excitement, in mixed amounts from various council members. The ruckus went on for a full minute, with Tyren standing passively in the center of the room.

Cries of outrage at the disobedience to the prohibition on Allie Jumping a rescue team to bring Tyren back were overwhelming, though they were punctuated by calls for Tyren's death, and the occasional underscore by someone calling for reason and calm.

Through it all, Dav, Allie, Raith, Imber, Tic, and Tyren stood still and calm in the center of the room, ringed by the council table. After a minute, Artus held up a hand. Surprisingly, the council members quieted down. Artus, looking at Dav, tried to hide his shock that the move had worked.

"Prince Davrelan," Artus said with a small bow. Dav returned the bow, slightly deeper than his brother's.

"Prince Artus."

"Were you, or were you not specifically told that we

had been forbidden from mounting a rescue mission?" he asked.

"Ah, yes," Dav said smoothly. "Forgive me, my brother. When you stated 'we have been forbidden', I misinterpreted this to mean the Sy'hli Empire had been forbidden from mounting a rescue mission. Since the Starjumpers are outside the Coalition, I did not realize that you meant to imply that the Coalition Council had attempted to exert authority over a power outside their realm of jurisdiction and forbid her as well."

Artus stared in shock. So did most of the council. The clever little weasel, Artus thought. He'd just blatantly defied the Council, strolled directly into the council chambers during session with evidence of his defiance, and then flatly told them that he not only had not defied any order they had the right to give, but pointedly reminded them of the limits of their authority. And he had done so in such a way that nobody could even express their anger with him over it without admitting that the Council had over-reached its authority.

Artus wished he were that quick. Dav really was a natural. He glanced at Morgan, in her seat on one side of the table. She was desperately trying to hide a smile. She had known, Artus knew. Artus himself should have known, he thought. Had he not been so frustrated by the Council, he wouldn't have missed it.

A quick glance around told him that at least a couple of the council members had been intentionally using that tactic, knowing him to be unseasoned in diplomatic and political discussion. He clenched his jaw and decided to play it as casually as Dav was.

"I see," he replied. "I can understand your confusion. Well, since it has already been done and the object of the discussion now stands before us, I think we should now turn our attention to more pressing matters." Artus turned to the Council.

"The discussion of what will happen when each of you gains custody of Prince Tyren is now moot. He is in the custody of the Sy'hli Empire. As is Sy'hli custom, he now has the chance to speak a few words before he is imprisoned, where he will await fair trial."

A few voices started to speak in protest, but Artus silenced it with a simple phrase. "Sy'hli law is not open for debate in Sy'hli territory."

This was a simple and fundamental tenet of the Coalition. Each species had votes on galactic matters and issues of major morality as carried out in individual regions of space, but the bottom line was that Coalition Law did not hold sway over species law. In Sy'hli territory, Coalition Code was to be followed, but Sy'hli law was not open for discussion or intervention without going through the proper channels of protest. Artus gestured to Tyren.

"Ladies and gentlemen of the Coalition Council. You sit here looking at me and expecting an apology. You'll not receive one from me," Gasps and angry rumbles met this statement, "because I have committed no crimes. I'm sure by now you have all been told the truth of my unfortunate circumstances. I'm equally sure that most of you do not believe it. The fact is that the Highlord you all know is a colony of parasitic creatures who infected my body and imprisoned my mind. The evil done under his rule lies on his hands, so to speak, not mine. I have come here willingly with my brother Prince Davrelan not because I believe that I deserve punishment, but because I believe that the evidence of the truth will absolve me. My brother has brought samples of the parasitic nano-species to the lab for testing and study. These samples are evidence in my case. I now go to my imprisonment peacefully to await my right of fair trial. I have faith in my brothers, faith in my people, and faith in this Coalition. The right thing will be done. That is all."

He gave a half bow to the council, and even that much was considered a great show of respect from a Prince to many individuals who were his lesser by rank. It was not required by protocol. Several murmurs of acknowledgement went through the room as four Sy'hli guards stepped in at Artus' call and escorted Tyren away.

Dav bowed to his brother and left, Raith, Imber, and Allie remaining behind. Tic turned to look over Allie's shoulder, eyed the Tchratchi longingly, then was out of sight. Artus turned back to the council, a renewed strength to his resolve. He couldn't wait to go talk with his brothers. Not until this session of the Council was over, however.

Artus cast his steely blue gaze around the ringed table. Dav had given him a stronger position to negotiate from, and he intended to use it.

"Well then, where were we?" he asked with a smile.

# CHAPTER TWELVE

# THE PLAGUE SPREADS

Raith watched Imber closely over the next day as he continued to work on the new toy he was building for Dav. The interface wasn't quite right yet, and it needed to be flawless.

Her idle scratching at her heirlines had stopped, but there was now a faint, steady glow to them, and he'd caught twice a hint of glow from within the depths of her eyes as well. He'd only seen it twice, but it was from the same angle both times. She also looked slightly too pale, and was moving noticeably slower, as if moving hurt her. The slight discoloration beneath her eyes told him she wasn't sleeping, either. It was an obvious conclusion, Imber was sick, and getting progressively worse.

"Imber, can I talk to you?" he asked her once he was certain.

"Sure Raith," she replied, immediately looking up from the datapad she was working on. He wasn't originally sure what she was doing on the pad, but from his brief glimpse he read a whole page on various Shaian illnesses. She was concerned as well.

"I know this question gets asked a lot around here, but are you okay?" he asked. She looked at him for a long moment before answering.

"No, I think I'm sick. You know that, though." Raith just nodded. "It's not really bad, just kind of annoying. It started out with a bit of itching, but that went away. Now I just ache, kind of a burning feeling in my veins and heirlines."

"Do illnesses in your people often make your heirlines glow?" he asked. He didn't know a lot about Shaian biology beyond the basics, something he decided to download the next time he passed a control panel.

"No, what?" she asked, suddenly a little confused.

"It's still below the light intensity I think most races can see, but it's getting more noticeable. I think if you went into a perfectly dark room you'd see it."

"That's definitely not normal," she told him, sounding worried.

"I think we need to get you scanned," he told her. She shook her head.

"I already did. Dav took me night before last," she admitted. Raith frowned.

"Nothing came up?"

"No," she said, shrugging. "Weird, because I definitely don't feel well. The doctor said it was probably just exhaustion and to try and rest. I think it's more than that."

"Me too," Raith agreed. "I'd like to do some tests of my own, if that's okay. If nothing came up on the scans then it isn't a virus or bacterial infection. Those would both show up bright and clear. There's obviously something wrong though. I'll download some medical databases on your species and come up with a few things to check out the scans may have missed. Is that okay?"

"Of course," she answered without hesitation. Raith smiled at the obvious trust she placed in him. "It's funny, we seem to have become each other's best medical provider." Raith laughed at this.

"And neither of us with a license. What would the medical board say?"

"I think it's a unique situation," she said solemnly.

He actually agreed with that. There weren't many people left who could do the kinds of repairs on a system like his that she could do, and none of the remaining android engineers he'd trust to so much as examine him, since most of the android engineers had been killed by their own androids during the Infection, and the few left Tyren had employed to attempt to build more androids like Cade.

Raith almost shivered at the thought. Giving an emotional subroutine to a combat android was beyond a bad idea, it was insane, and whoever had programmed Cade initially was beyond insane. Cade of course had taken it to a whole new level of psycho himself, but he'd been programmed to be homicidal to begin with.

His thoughts continued uninterrupted as part of his focus shifted to the door of the rec room opening. Multiple lines of process were simple enough for him. Ambassador Oren walked in. He looked tired too, Raith noticed. Dav and Allie looked up from the game they'd been playing across the room.

"Hi Daddy," Imber said, standing up and going to hug her father.

"Hello Imber," he replied, returning the hug.

Raith noted several fluctuations in his voice, all indicating he was exhausted. Looking him over, Raith observed a similar paleness, though not as severe as Imber's, and sure enough, a faint glow to his heirlines. Ambassador Oren was sick, too. This was a definite problem, Raith thought. Whatever it was, it was obviously contagious among the Shaian. If Ambassador Oren had it, the queen likely did as well.

He had no idea how serious it was, it could be something minor like a Shaian variation of a flu. They could get over it by morning, for all he knew. Or it could be something more serious, and the medical scans weren't detecting it. That really concerned him.

Those medical scans could detect a flu virus days before any symptoms appeared. Anything that had progressed to the level this had with full-body symptoms, should show up instantly in a detailed medical scan. He somehow doubted that the Royal Physician would have done anything less, if Dav had been the one to bring her in.

"How are things going in the Council?" she asked him. Ambassador Oren gave Dav a pointed look. Raith almost rolled his eyes. The ambassador didn't want to discuss anything openly with Dav in the room.

Those council idiots had no idea that Dav and Artus were potentially their best and greatest ally right now, and this fool was treating them like the enemy.

Apparently saving his life meant very little to him. In fairness, he considered Allie to be his sole savior on that point, and he spoke and interacted with her quite fondly. For whatever reason, he considered Dav and Artus to be a threat, though.

"Well enough. Better today," he told her.

Raith made a note to ask Artus about it later. If Ambassador Oren thought it was going better, then things probably weren't going too well for Artus.

"That's good," Imber said, though Raith could read the subtle modulation in her voice that told him she'd just had the same thought he did. He smiled again as he watched her.

Ambassador Oren gave Raith a look, and then a nod of acknowledgement. It was polite, but forced. Raith knew Ambassador Oren didn't consider him a person, and only made the effort to treat him as one because Imber insisted that he was. Dav stood and approached. This should be interesting, Raith thought.

"Ambassador Oren," Dav said with a respectful nod. The ambassador bowed slightly.

"Your Highness."

"I would like to ask if you have perhaps had the opportunity to go and speak to my brother Prince Tyren yourself. The lab results will be back tomorrow on the sample I brought back from the Helios, which should prove conclusively that my brother is innocent. It would go far for you politically if you made a point of going to speak to him before evidence was presented."

"I have not, Your Highness, but you do have a point. If he is proven innocent," Ambassador Oren put heavy emphasis on 'if', "then it would go well for me to have shown support. However, if he is proven guilty of his crimes, my visiting him would show support for the greatest tyrant our galaxy has ever known. Not something that would help my position."

"And you believe him to be guilty," Dav stated, rather than asked. "The word of two princes, the Starjumper, and your own daughter is insufficient?"

"Forgive me, Your Highness, I do not mean to imply you are untrustworthy, merely that you are all quite young, and were in a very intense situation. I admire your success in such circumstances, but cannot deny that your opinions may be heavily swayed by your youth and lack of experience." Dav, rather than getting angry, simply shrugged.

"Suit yourself, Ambassador. A lack of support at this time is noted. I simply wanted to give you the opportunity to regain some of the ground you've lost politically since taking a stand against the Sy'hli Empire in this debate."

"Dav," Imber said softly. Dav looked at her and smiled apologetically.

"I'm sorry, you're right. He's under enough pressure in the council room, he sure doesn't need any from me while trying to visit his daughter." Dav turned back to the ambassador. "If you'll forgive me, I'll leave you to your visit in peace." The ambassador nodded, and Dav walked out of the room.

Raith suppressed a sigh. Dav had gotten very confrontational the last few days. He wasn't sick, Raith thought, unless he had the same illness the Shaian were showing and it was just manifesting differently in him, but there was definitely something on his mind that was causing him to be a lot more moody. That concerned Raith, too.

Allie sat quietly across the room, watching Dav leave as she stroked Tic's soft fur. She looked concerned, too. Raith suspected it may simply be that after all the excitement of the last few weeks, Dav was now trying to adjust to a whole new lifestyle. He'd been better when they'd gone on the rescue mission.

Maybe Dav was just a man of action and didn't feel quite right unless he was busy saving the world, now that he'd had a taste of it. Raith could relate. He liked to be actively doing something. It was actually amazing he hadn't gotten into more trouble during his thirteen years between capturing Morgan and rescuing Allie.

A faint buzz ran through his com scanner. That had happened a couple of times the last few days, but he couldn't identify an actual com signal related to it. It was just an odd bit of random static. Maybe his scanners were burning out. He'd have to ask Imber to take a look later. That, at least, could be replaced. Unlike his power core.

He returned to his work on the wristbands for Dav, leaving Imber and her father to walk out of the room. He wouldn't tell his friends this, not yet anyway, but his power core had eleven months, six days, fourteen hours, thirty eight minutes, and fifty two seconds left before it burned itself out, at his average power consumption. It would barely last half that long if he kept burning energy the way he had been the last few weeks.

The power cells used for the Theta androids were

impressive, but he'd already managed to outlive what his normal lifespan would have been even without the Infection. By several years, in fact. For an android, he'd had an amazing life, long, full of excitement, and at the end, full of freedom and friends, two things he'd never experienced before in his life.

He didn't have any regrets, and was comfortable with the idea of powering down for good, but only if he knew his friends were safe and taken care of. He would do anything he could to keep operating until the day he knew they'd be safe, even if that meant strapping an old Runner battery to his chest and jump starting himself every few hours. If things kept up the way they had been for much longer, it might come to that.

Allie came over and sat beside him. He looked up at her. Speaking of remarkable young ladies, he thought with a grin. She smiled back. He reached over and scratched Tic behind the ears. The little jicund trilled happily.

"Do you think Dav is going to go talk to Tyren? All that with the ambassador, and Dav hasn't gone to see him himself," Allie asked. Raith considered a moment, then shrugged.

"I don't know. When I first met him, I'd have said absolutely not. Then a week ago, I'd have said he absolutely would. The way he's been the last few days, I'm just not sure anymore," he told her honestly.

Tyren was a sore spot for Dav to begin with. As emotionally unpredictable as he'd been lately, nobody really knew. Raith heard someone else approaching outside the door. Popular rec room today, he thought.

The door slid open and Dgehf entered, Daghren in bouncing, happy tow behind. Raith smiled. He hadn't seen Dgehf since the interrupted dinner, and was glad to see the gigantic brute.

"Hi Dgehf," Allie exclaimed. "Hi Daghren! I'm glad to see you guys. Come on over!" Dgehf and Daghren both came to the table. Dgehf sat on the ground, and still towered over them. Daghren sat in a chair and was at eye-level with Raith and Allie.

"Allie, Raith," Dgehf said with his impossibly deep rumble. While Daghren was smiling his toothy grin, Dgehf was not.

"What's wrong," Raith immediately asked.

"Something bad here," Dgehf replied.

"Of course there is," Raith retorted. "The entire Council is here. A lot of bad apples there."

"No," Dgehf shook his head. "Selfish, stupid, yes. Bad, no. Something bad here." Allie and Raith both realized Dgehf was speaking of something dangerous.

"Can you tell what it is?" Allie asked. "Is it like it was back on Kobek?"

"Yes, and no," Dgehf said, trying to find the right words.

"Use Maruck," Raith told him. Allie could speak and understand it, and Raith was fluent, just like he was in every language he'd ever taken the five minutes to study.

"Thank you," Dgehf replied in Maruck. "This is much easier. It feels the same as it did on Kobek, but there is something more."

"Do you think Cade is here?" Raith asked. Allie looked afraid. As she should, Raith knew. They'd gotten lucky on Kobek. After a moment, Dgehf nodded.

"I think he is. And I think he is not the only danger here. That android is close. Other dangers are closer."

"More than one?" Raith asked. Dgehf nodded. Daghren watched the exchange quietly, listening. He was surprisingly well behaved, Raith thought idly.

"What should we do," Allie asked, looking to Raith.

"Can't do much without knowing what the threat is. Maybe we should take a trip, get away for a while? We'll have to let Artus know about Cade either way, so the Imperial Guard can hunt for him. He may not have done anything yet, but if he's here, people are going to get hurt. Probably a lot of people. We need to get the jump on him. Maybe if we leave, he'll follow us and leave Sy'hloran alone."

"Where would we go?"

"Anywhere, really." Raith replied. "In an emergency you can always Jump us back. We could load up onto a ship and just take off. We could even go try to get the Peacekeeper back."

"From the mercenaries? I don't think that's a good idea," Allie replied. Raith grinned.

"When have we done anything that was really a good idea? You're probably right though, that's a task for a large battalion of Sy'hli strike troops. We might be able to do it, but I don't really know what we're up against so can't make a good call on that."

"I think you should go," Dgehf said after a moment. Daghren suddenly looked sad.

"Friends will go?" he asked.

"They should go," Dgehf told his nephew. "Do you

want them safe?"

"Yes, they should be safe. Okay, go. But call if you need help, good?" Daghren said. His command of Maruck showed he was still young, but it was much clearer than his Sy'hli was.

"That's a good idea, thank you Daghren," Allie told him.

"We should talk to Dav and Imber. Dav will need to come with us, he's one of Cade's targets I think, but Imber is probably safe. I don't know if she should travel anyway," Raith said.

"What? Why not?" Allie asked.

Raith had already decided that they needed to know about it, just in case. If one ally had a weakness, the rest should know about it. If she suddenly turned extremely ill in the middle of a life or death situation, it could result in all of their deaths.

"Imber is sick. So is her father. We're not sure with what, yet. She's doing okay right now, but it's getting worse," he told her. Dgehf and Daghren both frowned.

"That's one danger," Dgehf said firmly, as if hearing Raith's words had confirmed his suspicion. "Sickness is spreading here." Raith wasn't comforted to hear that Dgehf had sensed what Raith had already deduced.

"Do we all have it?" Allie asked. "I feel fine."

"I'm not sure yet," Raith admitted, "only the Shaian are showing symptoms. It might be species-specific. It might also be that they just react to it faster, or were exposed first. I don't know. Whatever it is, it doesn't show up on a full medical scan."

"That's strange," Allie said, half to herself. She had

become nearly convinced of the near-omnipotence of the Sy'hli's advanced technology and was surprised to hear that they hadn't cured all illnesses for good yet.

"It is unusual. Pretty rare, actually. Not the first time something has gotten past the medical scanners though. The scanners get better every year, but viruses are notorious for mutating at incredible rates, so there's always something new. Okay, so we should leave Sy'hloran for a little while, get away from Cade and hopefully lure him off the planet. We should also stay clear of anyone else, to keep whatever it is from spreading, in case you and Dav have been exposed. At least until we figure out what's going on."

"Okay. I'll go find Dav and tell him what's going on. I'll have to tell Imber, too. She won't be happy about all of us leaving her."

"She won't be, but she needs to be near the best medical care possible," Raith said. Dgehf rumbled his agreement.

"If you start feeling sick too," Dgehf added, "come back here right away. And stay away from other people."

Allie nodded. Her expression concerned, she stood and went to find Dav. Raith watched her go, then turned to Dgehf.

"And the other danger?" he asked pointedly. Dgehf sighed heavily, a sound like a minor rockslide.

"I do not know," the big Maruck admitted. "It's bad, but subtle. I can't smell it, see it, or hear it. It makes my fur tingle though. Something else is very wrong. Something we're all missing."

Raith nodded as he thought. His hands kept working

on the wristbands as his mind wandered.

"Thank you, Dgehf," you're confirming a lot of what I already suspected. Maybe we can go do some good while we're out and about, and maybe figure out what's really going on. I'll get a ship equipped with some good medical gear, just in case, and get a sample from Imber for testing." Dgehf stood slowly, smoothly, and Daghren hopped up beside him.

"We will leave soon too. Artus is very welcoming. The others are not. My family is not comfortable."

"I understand," Raith said with a nod. "I'll send you our com channel so you can reach us if you need anything. When I do, send me yours so we can reach you for the same reason. Thanks."

Raith gathered the wristbands and his tools and stood. He clapped Dgehf on the arm and headed out the door.

# CHAPTER THIRTEEN

# PIRATES... AGAIN

It didn't take long to convince everyone of the need to go. All Allie had to do was tell her mother and Dav about Raith and Dgehf believing C.A.D.E.-16 was on the planet, and he was ready to go. He had gone to his room to pack, while she went to talk to Imber.

Imber had been impossible to negotiate with, and in the end, she raised the point of Raith's capabilities and said she'd just have him study Shaian biology and medicine before they left, and he'd be more qualified than the Sy'hli doctors would be, as long as they stocked their ship with good medical equipment.

Imber's father had also been incredibly difficult to convince, and Allie had accidentally walked in on the pair arguing. It was disconcerting. They stood still, silent, and staring at each other angrily, while their heirlines flashed and flicker through the entire spectrum so fast it looked like a pair of strobe lights having a shoot-out.

She'd apologized, but neither had heard her enter, or heard her apology. So she backed gracefully out of the room and left them to it.

In the end, all of the adults had agreed to let them go, on two conditions. First, that Allie Jump them back to Sy'hloran the instant things got dangerous, and second, that they go with a full Sy'hli and Shaian war escort. Artus had instructed them all to keep close, but to largely leave the four alone. Artus had even given them permission to not have an adult chaperone on the ship with them.

Allie appreciated that with all they'd been through and done, Artus recognized that they didn't need to be babysat. Her mother had agreed with him. The ambassador had again been the harder sell, but with twelve Shaian gunships packed around their ship like armor, along with the six Sy'hli battle cruisers Artus sent, even C.A.D.E.-16 wasn't a threat.

She suspected his real complaint with the whole trip was that once again, the Shaian daughter was spending time around the Sy'hli heir. Their friendship really bothered the ambassador.

Allie wished she knew why he was so against the Sy'hli in general. She could understand his hostility toward Tyren, considering what the Highlord had done and tried to do to him, but the Sy'hli weren't responsible for that. Especially not the Sy'hli soldiers and nobility here on Sy'hloran, most of whom had been in hiding for quite some time, waiting for their chance to help overthrow the Highlord.

In the end, Dav, Allie, Imber, Raith, and Tic were

loaded securely onto an armored transport vessel, to Dav's disappointment, and sent off into space surrounded by heavily armed war ships.

Raith had them traveling out into empty space, rather than moving toward any place specific, so that if that combat android caught up with them they'd have ample notice. Raith was experimenting, as usual, with new technology, and had made some modifications to their sensors. They were now more accurate, and had better range and sensitivity, according to Raith.

Artus had promised to send them the data on the lab results of the sample Dav had brought back, but there was still no word on that yet.

Until then, they were cruising through space at a comfortable speed, trying to gain some distance between themselves and any potential pursuers. Allie hoped C.A.D.E.-16 was following them, both because it meant the innocent people on Sy'hloran were safe, and also because if he caught up with them out here, their bodyguard fleet would completely annihilate the combat android

Allie had caught that light in Imber's eyes again, and her father's when they hugged goodbye. Imber had explained that it was a symptom of their illness, when she asked her about it later. Both Imber and her father had undergone an intensive additional round of scans before he'd let Imber go. He insisted he was fine, but obviously could see that Imber wasn't well. Allie was made to promise to bring her straight back if it got bad. She and Imber had both agreed.

Allie woke up their first morning out in her own

room aboard the transport vessel still exhausted. She'd had nightmares of masses of black tentacles clawing at her, dragging her down under the ocean. Sandro hadn't been in the water, so she wasn't sure where the ocean in her dream came from, but the images were plenty terrifying either way.

Stretching lazily, she dragged herself out of bed. Tic yawned, showing her rows of impressively serrated teeth, and hopped up on Allie's shoulder. Walking out into the passageway, she paused as the power suddenly dropped in the ship. Almost immediately after, she heard a sound. It was subtle, but vaguely familiar. As the sound grew louder, she recognized it and immediately was struck with panic.

"Dav!" she screamed as she ran blindly toward the control room. She wasn't sure what he could do, but she felt the need to get to him as quickly as possible. She made it six steps before the blackness overcame her.

When she awoke, she found herself staring into Spike's hawk-like gaze.

"Not... you again," Allie had to force out. She felt odd, and speaking took a great deal of work. She realized she couldn't move. Spike laughed lightly.

"I told you we would get the job done. Highlord Tyren paid us too well for us to neglect our duty. Besides, you had to leave Sy'hloran sooner or later, you had to know we'd be waiting." Allie had actually completely forgotten about the mercenaries. She suspected saying so would only anger Spike, though.

Allie looked around, though only her eyes could move, and that took enough effort that it gave her a headache. This time, instead of a holding cell, she was lying on a wide table, wearing a pair of stun shackles.

"Don't worry, all your little friends are here, including your robo-boyfriend."

"What… now?"

"What are we going to do with you now? Deliver you to the Highlord, of course. I told you that last time.," Spike pointed out.

"Captain?" Allie mumbled.

"He'll be here in a moment. I signaled him when your Sy'hli friend here started to stir. He's strong, that one. Moves a lot better than he should be able to with the stun shackles on. We had to physically strap him down. Nothing like going a little old school."

"Imber?" Allie asked.

"She's right beside you. And fine, by the way."

"Escort?"

"My, aren't you chatty," Spike said with a smile. "I'm impressed you can speak so much. Your Sy'hli and Shaian escort are both fine as well, just drifting dead in the water. We left them all as is. No reason to anger two powerful empires more than we already will by taking you four."

"Five," Allie clarified. Spike looked puzzled for a moment, then laughed.

"The jicund, right. How you got one in captivity I'll never know. Even unconscious, she bites when startled, did you know that? Took a piece out of one of my men's armor. If he were any slower, she'd have taken his leg."

The sound of a door sliding open caused Spike to look back over her shoulder, than stand straight and salute sharply.

"Playing with your food again?" came a deep, heavily accented voice. Allie didn't recognize the accent, and had never heard anything quite like it. Spike grinned.

"Just saying hello to some old friends," Spike said. Heavy boot steps came closer and a man came into view.

He was built like a brick wall, wearing a tight red high-collar shirt trimmed in gold. His skin was dark, almost black, and his eyes were nearly as dark. His head was completely bald, and showed more than one scar. He looked human, though like a very well-muscled human. A gold earring hung from one ear.

Allie no longer had to wonder what a space pirate looked like. One look at this man, and she knew that's exactly what he was. Spike had identified them as mercenaries, but she suspected that more than a few transport vessels had been raided by this man and his crew.

"They're so young," the man said, voice somewhat surprised. "I can't imagine what the Highlord wants with them. Perhaps they can tell me. This one is speaking?" he asked Spike. She nodded and he moved to lean directly over her. He opened his mouth to speak, but as he made eye contact he paused.

His expression moved slowly through confusion, then surprise, then disbelief, then awe. The man, the captain Allie assumed, reached one big, dark hand up to touch her cheek almost tenderly. She was getting seriously creeped out until he spoke again, and everything flipped around in her stomach.

"Allie?" he said. She had no idea how to react. He said the name not like someone who had been told the names of his prisoners, but like someone who knew the name, and knew it fondly.

"How?" she stammered. Before answering, the man immediately reached down and deactivated the shackles. Allie's body was instantly hers again. She scrambled back away from the man and nearly fell off the table.

"Allie, Allie, wait. You're safe here," the big man said, both hands held up in a gesture pleading for calm.

"What are you doing?" Spike asked in astonishment.

"Who are you?" Allie asked, climbing down from the table carefully and inching toward Dav, still shackled and tied down, and gagged, on the table next to hers.

"I'm Captain Abram, of the Blackstar. That won't mean much to you, though. What will mean something to you is that I was your father's closest friend before he died."

"You knew my father?" she asked, stunned enough that she stopped moving toward Dav.

"Very well. We were like brothers. I was close with your mother too, though not as close as I would have liked before she married your father," he said. The big man smiled wistfully, and sadly.

Allie could see it immediately. He had been in love with her mother too. She moved closer to Dav. Captain Abram caught her movement, glanced at Dav, then to Spike. For the first time, Allie noticed that there were ten other mercenaries along the walls standing perfectly still, weapons in hand.

"Spike, let the others go," he said, his tone firm.

"But Captain," Spike said in protest.

"Now," the captain said softly. Spike gestured sharply, and two other men moved forward and let Dav and Imber free. Both of them scrambled off the tables and moved protectively toward Allie. Raith lay on the floor to one side, Tic unconscious in a cage next to him.

"And them," Allie said to Spike, gesturing to her remaining two friends.

Spike opened her mouth to snap something at the insolent girl, but one look from the captain silenced her. Allie saw Spike's look too, and knew something she didn't think the captain did. Spike was in love with him. Moving to the cage, she opened it, careful to stand to one side in case Tic was faking and came shooting out like a blender with teeth. Tic didn't move though.

Spike pulled a small device from her belt. It looked like a garage door opener remote, Allie thought. Small, rectangular, and with two buttons on the face. Spike hit one of the buttons as she pointed the device at Raith. After a few seconds, Raith blinked and sat up. Allie glanced at Imber, who was staring at the device in Spike's hand. She was thinking the same thing Allie was. They needed to get a hold of one of those.

Allie moved to Tic's cage and carefully lifted her furry friend out. Tic was breathing, which was a relief, but wasn't moving.

"Can you fix her, too?" Allie asked Spike. Spike looked at Allie for a moment, then glanced at her captain. After a moment she shook her head and looked back to Allie.

"No. Organics awaken at their own rate. She's fine,

though," Spike said.

Allie stood as Raith stood beside her, and she moved back to her friends. They all watched the captain and Spike closely. Allie wasn't sure what to do next. This captain knew her parents, knew her, and clearly intended to let them go. But she now had a million questions. First things first, she decided, as she realized her friends were all taking their cues from her.

"Are you going to let us go?"

"Of course," Captain Abram replied, which earned him another incredulous look from Spike. Spike was fondling the handle of her gun Shane, which was strapped to her back. Allie got the impression that was an absent habit Spike had when irritated or anxious.

"We were paid to do a job," she told him flatly. The captain nodded.

"Yes. And we will refund full payment to our employer. This is one job I can't do." The captain looked back to Allie and spoke to her. "I owe your parents that much, at the very least. Allie, you and your friends are free to go, but… if you would… please stay for a time. I would talk with you and your friends."

Allie considered for a long moment. A quick look to her friends told her they would follow her lead. She turned back to the captain and nodded. He smiled. It was a surprisingly warm smile.

"Thank you. Someplace more comfortable, though. Come."

With that, the Captain turned and headed for the door. The mercenaries standing in front of the doorway immediately moved out of his way. Spike stood back, and waited until Allie and her friends had gone through the door before following. Allie noticed their weapons sitting on a table by the door, and grabbed them on the way out. The other mercenaries followed behind.

It took only a minute before the captain turned through another doorway. Allie was actually surprised to see the ship was in such good condition. It wasn't shiny and silver like she kept thinking of spaceships being, and was decorated in a lot of reds, browns, and gold. It looked incredible, and clean, something she also didn't expect on a mercenary ship.

Following the captain through the doorway, she was greeted by the sight of a fairly opulent sitting room, with big, comfortable couches covered in pillows of a myriad of colors, and all of elegant-looking fabrics. She suddenly placed it. The room and décor of the ship looked Mediterranean. Come to think of it, so did the captain's outfit. She wondered if that was a coincidence.

"Sit, please," The captain said. Allie and her friends took seats. Dav and Raith sat on the outside of Imber and Allie, and Allie noticed both of them sat on the edge of the couch, ready to be up and moving in a flash. Allie appreciated that. She still didn't know what to make of Captain Abram, and she definitely wasn't comfortable with Spike, who took a somewhat menacing pose by the doorway.

"Allie, I last saw you just before your mother hid you away," the captain started. "I helped smuggle her out of the quadrant."

"She could have just Jumped," Allie pointed out. Captain Abram shook his head.

"She had already sealed the crystal so it couldn't be tracked. Using it to Jump would have given away her position to the Highlord and his trackers." The captain looked sidelong at Raith. Raith flashed him a mischievous smile.

"Why would you take the job to abduct us for the Highlord?" she asked pointedly. The captain smiled.

"You get your subtlety from your father, I see," he said. "Two reasons. He pays well, and I was not told you were children. My morals have always been a bit... flexible, but I would never willingly put children in the hands of the Highlord."

"You're saying you'd have let us go even if you didn't recognize me?" she asked doubtfully.

"No, I would have had one of my other ships stage an assault on us and we would have smuggled you away with them. I'd have claimed you must have been killed in the blast when we were shot," the captain grinned broadly, his perfectly white teeth looking impossibly bright next to the darkness of his skin.

Allie had to admit, that would have been a decent plan. Then he could have continued pretending to hunt for Allie and her friends, all the while keeping her just out of reach in his other ship. She didn't know if she believed him, though.

"I have no reason to trust you," Allie said. He nodded, smile fading.

"That's true, you don't."

"And we have a lot of reason not to trust her," Allie said, gesturing to Spike. The captain cast a fond look toward his lieutenant, then looked back to Allie.

"No more than you have to trust me. Spike is efficient. She is all business, and incredibly good at what she does. She does worry overly much about money though," the captain said, raising his voice on that last to make it clear he was directing the comment playfully at her. Spike's expression darkened, but the captain just grinned. "Don't worry, Allie. Nobody on this ship, or any other belonging to me will harm you. Your Interceptor is in the docking bay, you can take it and leave whenever you like." Dav perked up at that.

"There's war coming, Captain," Allie said. "The Highlord has fallen, the Coalition is divided, and the Maruck are rampaging in the absence of his leadership. We're being chased by combat androids and assassins, and every Coalition force still supporting the Highlord's cause. Getting involved with us at all is likely to get you killed."

"Killed? How dramatic," the captain grinned. "Most of the assassins in the circuit I know personally, and the few I don't aren't good enough to worry about. The combat android is interesting, I'd like to have a go at one of those. Or rather, I'd like Spike to have a go at one of those. I'm not the least worried about the Coalition, or about Maruck or war. War is actually good for my business, though I certainly wouldn't encourage one if I didn't have to. "

"Sandro?" Dav said simply. Captain Abram's eyes snapped to Dav, the whites showing all around. Spike had her hand on her gun so fast Allie hadn't even seen it move.

"He sent Sandro after you?" the captain asked

carefully. Allie nodded, and the captain whistled through his teeth.

"Allie, what did you do to gain the Highlord's wrath? I know why he wants his brother here, but why you?"

"I'm a Starjumper, like my mother is."

"A Starjumper? I like that," the captain said with a smile. "Well, that does explain… Wait, did you say 'is'? Allie, I don't know how to tell you this, but your mother was killed shortly after delivering you into hiding." Allie shook her head.

"No, she was taken to the Perenite Center on Niertagh. We rescued her last week." Allie said matter-of-factly.

She felt some satisfaction in the look on the captain's face. That satisfaction disappeared when she saw the look on Spike's face. She loved the captain, and the captain loved Morgan. Allie had just told the man Spike loved that the woman he loved was still alive after thirteen years of his believing her dead. No friends won with that one, Allie thought with a sigh.

"Morgan is… by the stars, I never would have dreamed…" He took a deep breath and let it out slowly. "Allie, thank you for telling me that. I can't describe to you how I felt when I heard she had been killed. You're too young to understand it anyway, even if I could."

Allie glanced at Dav sidelong. If Captain Abram had reacted to her mother's death the way Allie herself would react to Dav's, she could understand it all too well. She felt a lump growing in her throat just thinking about it. She looked quickly back to the captain.

"She is well, then?" he asked.

"Yes. Recovering from her ordeal at the Perenite Center."

"If I had known, I'd have… no matter. What's done is done. Allie, your father was my best friend, and I loved your mother dearly. I owe them everything. If I can help you, I will do so."

"If we asked you for weapons?" Allie asked.

"Done," Captain Abram said.

"Your stunning technology?" she asked. The captain hesitated.

"I can't," the captain said. He did sound legitimately sorry to say that. Allie shook her head in annoyance. "I'm sorry, but that device was given to me under only two conditions. First, that I never use it to kill, and second, that I never share it with anyone. It has the capacity to be fatal without much effort. Not only could it be terrible destructive in the wrong hands, it could be lethal accidentally by even the right hands that don't understand its use. If I gave it to you, you could kill someone accidentally, or it could be stolen from you. Neither would rest well on your conscience or mine. I'm sorry, that technology stays with me."

"Fine. We don't need it," Allie said. He had several valid points, and she didn't really want any of them playing with technology that powerful that was so easy to misuse. She couldn't deny they got captured a lot, and lost their ships a lot. It was a legitimate risk that it could be stolen.

"What else do you need?" he asked.

"Nothing, really. We have the gear and equipment

we need, we have the resources we need, and as long as you give us the Interceptor back, we're fine," Allie replied.

"You didn't strip it out or anything, did you?" Dav asked, concerned. Captain Abram laughed.

"I did not. I have… had, I mean… a buyer lined up on Irifal Station. I take it you're the pilot in this crew then?" Dav nodded. "Well, are you sure you can handle an Interceptor?" Dav glared at him, but Raith laughed.

"He's the best pilot I've ever seen, Captain," Raith said honestly. "He can outfly me, and if you know your android specs, you know what I mean when I say that." The Captain looked from Raith to Dav, then shrugged.

"Well enough, then. I just don't want you to crash that beauty. She's a remarkable piece of machinery."

"I know," Dav said, "I've been flying her for a while." Allie knew this was a stretch, they'd only had it for a very short time, but the captain didn't necessarily need to know that.

"You are all welcome to stay here as long as you like as my guests," the captain said, "but at least stay through this evening and tonight so you can leave rested and refreshed tomorrow. We'll look out for you tonight."

Allie opened her mouth to agree, but the com in the room activated as someone from the ship's control room spoke through it.

"Captain, we have an organic incoming."

"An organic?" The captain asked, confused.

"Another clump of asteroid moss?" he asked.

"No, sir. This is a solid, single organism. Coming in fast, too. We only just now detected it. It will reach us in just a few seconds."

"Potentially damaging?"

"Unsure, sir. It has a lot of mass, but seems very fluid. Scanners are having a hard time getting a read on it."

"That's strange," the captain said as he stood. His eyes suddenly snapped to Allie. "Allie, did you say Sandro?" Allie nodded, a sinking feeling in her gut.

"Wills, open fire, everything we've got!"

"Yes, sir!" came the reply.

"He came without his ship so we wouldn't detect him," the captain said. "Come on, we have to get you out of here now."

They stood and followed. Tic began to stir in Allie's arms as she began to run. Allie stroked her fur and whispered calmingly so she wouldn't be frightened when she woke.

"It's okay Tic, I've got you," she said. Tic's eyes opened, her huge irises dilating dramatically as the light hit them. Tic looked around, taking in the situation. She saw Spike running behind them and hissed warningly. Allie thought it was interesting that is was Tic's warning hiss, not her angry hiss. "No Tic, she's helping," Allie said quickly. Tic looked confused, but calmed slightly. Allie noticed she kept watching Spike, though.

At least for a moment. Suddenly, Tic's eyes snapped upward and ahead of them, her growl was definitely a hostile one this time.

"Wait!" Allie shouted. Everyone stopped. She looked down at Tic. Her companions looked to the jicund as well, understanding she was the cause of the call to halt. Tic's eyes darted around the ceiling of the passageway ahead, moving sharply from one point to another. Tic suddenly shrieked her most aggressive shriek, and began scrambling back in Allie's arms.

"We can't go that way," Allie shouted, turning to run the other way.

"What do you mean?" the captain asked in exasperation.

He was answered by the ceiling ahead of them, where they'd been about to run through, being torn back, a flood of writhing, glistening black tentacles pouring into the hallway. Some as thick as the captain's legs, some as narrow and whip-fast as a bullwhip.

"Move!" he shouted, drawing a gun from his belt, but instead of turning and firing, he stepped out of the way and flattened himself against the wall of the passage.

Allie saw why a moment later. Spike, who had been right behind them, took a knee as she swung Shane out from his holster on her back. The hand cannon came into her hands so smoothly, so perfectly, that they seemed two parts of the same body. Allie and her friends dove back against the walls as Spike fired. The pulse of rolling purple energy seemed to pull Allie forward as it passed, as if trying to drag her into itself. It passed fast enough that she just stumbled a few steps into the hallway, but the feeling was very disconcerting.

The blast from Shane struck the roiling mass of tentacles with a sickening sound. The impact shockwave shook the hallway, and Sandro, the supposedly unkillable Sandro, let out the most terrible sound Allie had ever heard. It was fingernails on a chalkboard, but a thousand times louder. All of them clapped hands over their ears as Sandro's tentacles recoiled, several of them smoking and smoldering. All of them except Spike, who fired a second shot.

Allie was prepared for the pull this time, and didn't stumble, though she felt herself drawn toward the pulse again. Once more, the ball of purple energy warped the air behind it as it traveled, leaving on odd shimmer in the air behind it for a few seconds after it passed. Again it struck Sandro, again Sandro recoiled with an ear-splitting shriek. As quickly as they had appeared, Sandro's tentacles vanished back up into the ceiling.

"Go!" Captain Abram shouted, sending them all running back down the passage the way they had come. Allie didn't need to be told twice.

A tentacle tore through the ceiling and grabbed for Dav. He rolled to one side, avoiding its touch, and the tentacle snapped back up into the ceiling before Spike could fire at it. She fired at the ceiling where the tentacle had come from, and the blast left a gaping hole where it hit. Allie could see through three floors of the ship when the blast from Shane had traveled its course.

Dav dragged on her arm encouraging her to keep running. Another tentacle came out of nowhere through one of the side walls, and grabbed Allie's arm. The burning pain that ripped through her was worse than anything she'd ever experienced. It hurt too much to react, too much to even scream.

Tic leapt on the tentacle in full purple fury, shrieking and tearing into the beast's tentacles. Her claws had been known to tear through metal, but they barely broke the black skin of the tentacle horror attacking them now. It was enough to sting the beast though, and the tentacle released Allie, swinging violently back against the wall, slamming Tic hard into the metal surface once, twice, three times before Tic let go and dropped to the ground.

The tentacle vanished back into the wall. Allie let out a whimper, all she could force past the excruciating pain in her arm. Spike cursed behind them, lowering her weapon. She hadn't had a clean shot, so had held back.

Dav scooped up Tic, and then Allie, and continued running. Another tentacle, this one bigger around than Allie's torso, burst through the wall and swung widely down the passage at them. Dav jumped the tentacle smoothly, ducking low so his feet cleared the tentacle, but his head didn't hit the ceiling.

Spike got another shot off at the base of the tentacle, hitting it squarely. The shrieking from the monster was deafening as the entire tentacle fell to the ground, torn free of its body. The tentacle writhed and thrashed for several seconds before it melted, turning to a thick, black tarry substance that immediately began eating through the floor.

The next tentacle burst out directly over Spike, who barely dodged it with a smooth and lightning-quick shoulder roll. She came up running, and the rest kept going.

"Allie!" shouted the captain as he ducked another whip-fast tentacle. "Jump yourselves free!"

"I can't," Allie sobbed, the pain flooding her thoughts.

"You can," Dav said softly, right next to her ear.

She looked at him through her tears. His eyes, which she would later swear were bluer than she'd ever seen them, reached right through her. She felt his strength, his determination, and his faith in her, and knew she could do anything he asked at that moment.

"What about you?" she called to Captain Abram.

"Don't worry, I have a plan! Go!"

Allie looked back to Dav, and reached for the energies all around them. Grabbing tightly, she pulled them in hard and fast. Imber and Raith touched them quickly as time seemed to slow around Allie.

She watched, detached, as the ceiling seemed to slowly peel back and Sandro dropped through into the hallway ahead of them. The tentacle form compressed into the humanoid form as he fell, landing on humanoid-shaped feet. Allie could see black ichor dripping from several wounds on the tentacles now pressed together to form the body. Where each drop struck, the floor hissed and bubbled.

"Captain, stop them and we can talk!" Sandro hissed in his moaning, windy voice as he realized Allie was Jumping. It was too late. They were all moving far too slowly now to reach Allie in time.

Allie Jumped. The watcher reached out in her weakness and grabbed the energy as she attempted to forge it into a link to the place she wanted to go, back to Sy'hloran. The watcher pulled hard, throwing Allie off balance mentally. The pain in her arm surged, which further distracted her. She felt their destination slipping away from her.

Before she could grab it again, it was gone. A new

destination, someplace that felt unlike anything she'd ever experienced, set itself in place. No, she thought. We do not go where you want, we go where I want!

Drawing strength from Dav, whom she felt still holding her tightly, she wrenched the energies back under her control. There was no time, she knew. She grabbed the first place she could find that felt like a planet, could See something that looked like a ship, and completed the Jump.

She landed hard on her wounded arm and screamed as the pain stole her focus away from her. For that instant, all that existed for her was pain.

# CHAPTER FOURTEEN

# A SHOW OF FORCE

"Hang on, Allie," Dav said urgently, "hang on."

Allie was lost in pain so intense she couldn't seem to gather her thoughts. She looked down at her arm where Sandro had grabbed it. That was a mistake.

Dav had used some tool from his belt to cut the sleeve of her flight suit free. She could see where it lay. Sandro's tentacle had torn through it like paper. It had torn through her arm too, leaving a thick, black tar on it that burned worse than fire. She looked away, clenching her eyes shut. Tears flowed freely as Dav worked. She could vaguely hear Raith and Imber in the background, but couldn't make out what they were saying.

"I'm sorry, this will hurt," Dav said apologetically. A different kind of pain tore through her arm. She didn't know what he was doing, and didn't really want to know. Only a few seconds later, the pain relieved so dramatically, so abruptly, that she gasped with the shock.

It was like being on fire and then being thrown into a pool of ice water.

Her breath shook, gasping and quivering, as she fought to regain her focus. It took a full minute before she could focus enough to open her eyes and realize Dav was talking to her.

"Almost done, Allie," he was saying. "Just a few more seconds."

Allie took a long, deep breath and looked down at her arm. Dav had obviously had to do some drastic work to get the acidic tar off her arm, and then to treat the wound beneath it. Even with the dermal regenerator he was even now finishing up with, her scar was severe and obvious, stretching in a three-inch-wide band across her upper arm, arcing down toward her elbow. The pale strip of scarred skin was still an angry red.

"Will it always look like that?" she asked softly. Dav shook his head.

"It will be very pale once it finishes healing in a few days. It'll never tan either, so will always be lighter than the skin around it. I'm sorry, I did the best I could."

"No, don't be sorry," she said shaking her head gently. "You probably just saved my arm."

"Your life," Raith corrected as he came closer. He had a gun in his hand and his eyes were scanning their surroundings. "That black gunk was not only acidic, it was toxic. It would have killed you."

She looked to Dav, who was focused on the last touches on her arm.

"Thank you," she said, voice barely above a whisper. He looked up at her. His eyes were so warm, so blue, they seemed to swallow her whole. She loved him, she knew. Intensely.

"Of course," he said with a casual smile. She could see it in his eyes though, the experience had shaken him, badly.

"Are we okay?" she asked, looking around. For the first time, her surroundings registered. It was loud. There were animal and insect-like sounds all around, as well as sounds she couldn't begin to identify as either animal or plant, or maybe something completely out of her realm of experience.

They were in a swampy jungle, surrounded by foliage thick enough to almost seem woven together. Heavy mist seemed to seep out from the branches of the trees and drift down on them. The ground beneath them was wet and spongy, and there was what looked like a small bog just to the other side of where Raith stood. It stank. Badly. Although she couldn't be sure a big part of it wasn't the puddle of bloody, black ichor eating through her torn sleeve.

"So far," Raith said, eyes scanning the foliage. "We've had nothing attack us yet, but there are a lot of creatures around trying to decide what to do with us. Air quality is sketchy, but should at least be breathable for a little while for all of you. Allie, you'll start to feel light-headed if you breathe too deeply, so try to keep your breaths short and shallow."

Allie noticed Imber was on one knee with her rifle aimed at the bog, and was slowly scanning it back and forth across the surface.

"Something in here," Imber said. "The ripples in this

water aren't natural current."

"Something of one form or another everywhere here," Raith responded, turning his head so Imber could read his lips. "I wish we had our helmets so you could see what I see right now."

"I'm kind of glad I can't, actually," Allie replied. Judging purely from the sounds she heard all around, she firmly decided that ignorance was bliss. Imber moved back from the edge of the bog even further, so she could spare a moment here and there to keep up with the conversation as she glanced from one face to another, then back to the water.

"Something besides animals in there," Dav said, looking at the readout on his hand scanner.

"Yeah, plants too," Allie quipped. "They would probably eat us given the chance as well."

"It's metal, pretty large, and structured. There's a power source there, too. I think it might be a ship of some kind."

"Allie, can you get us out of here?" Imber asked. Allie reached out for the energies and recoiled. The watcher was there, waiting.

"I don't know. I almost didn't get us here. Something is interfering with my Jumps. I don't know how many more times I can beat it. I almost didn't this time, and barely landed us on a planet."

"Let's see what's under the water, then," Raith said. "If it's a ship, I might be able to fix it and we can fly off this soggy rock."

"I'd rather risk Allie Jumping us than going into that water," Dav said, looking at the water with both nervousness and disgust. The smell was definitely coming from more than just the acidic slime that had gone through her sleeve and was now eating into the spongy plant material they all now sat and stood on.

"I'll go," Raith said. "I can see, or sense, better down there than you can anyway, and won't be harmed by any little animals coming for a nibble."

"What about big ones?" Allie asked.

"Well, it'd have to be pretty big to hurt me, and I don't think the water's that deep."

"So we see what's under there, and if it's usable, we try and fix that to fly out. If it's not, we have no choice but to have Allie Jump us home, if she can," Imber said. "Did I get it all?"

"Perfect," Raith said with a smile. "Okay, Dav, man the jungle line, I'm going for a swim. Imber, if anything bigger than I am decides to make an appearance heading my way, feel free to shoot at it." She winked and took a knee again, ready. Raith grinned and moved to the water.

"Allie, can you stand?" Dav asked.

He held out a hand as he himself stood. She took the hand, and he helped her up. She was unsteady for a second, but regained her equilibrium quickly. She nodded and drew her gun. Her wounded arm felt incredibly weak, and after one attempt to raise the gun, she moved it to the other hand.

With a graceful dive, Raith vanished beneath the murky, muddy surface of the bog. Allie winced.

"That's disgusting," she said. Dav chuckled. He now had guns out and aimed at the nearby wall of foliage.

Raith wasn't gone long. He reappeared only two

minutes later, dripping water, and slime. As he walked out of the water, he pulled chunks of plant matter off his suit and out of his hair. Allie winced again. Raith caught the look and grinned.

"I think somebody needs a hug," he said, holding his arms out wide. Allie grimaced.

"Touch me, and I might just have to shoot you," she told him. Raith laughed. Allie noticed he held a narrow black cord in one hand. "What's that?"

"Oh this? Just a tether cord I had, attached at the other end to the remarkably well preserved ship below."

"It is a ship?" Dav asked, excitedly. "What kind?"

"I'm not sure. It doesn't match anything in my database. It's old, but seems sealed tight. I don't think there's a drop of water on the inside. Should make it easier to haul up too. It's not big, it'll be crowded quarters for a little while, but we can probably make do."

"Well let's get it up here and take a look," Imber said, watching the conversation. Allie was watching the bog, since Imber had looked away.

"Dav, I think you and I can bring it up, if the girls keep us covered."

"Good plan. Will that cord hold it?"

"It should, it's nanofiber."

"Wow, really? You just happened to have nanofiber cord lying around?"

"Sure, it was in my handy utility belt. I told you, I may not think of everything, but pretty close." Raith grinned. "Come on then." Imber took position to watch the wall of foliage, which seemed a little louder to Allie, and she turned to watch the water.

She thought she'd Seen a ship just before they completed the Jump. With it at the bottom of a swamp, that explains why it had been so difficult to really be sure it was a ship she'd spotted. Raith tied a couple of loops in the end of the cord, and a few feet in, and he and Dav each grabbed loop.

"Count of three?" Dav asked.

"Three!" Raith shouted and pulled. Dav laughed as he leaned into the pull as well. For a long moment, nothing happened. Then slowly, inch by inch, they began to make progress. Several minutes they worked, before Dav asked for a break.

"Woah, that thing is mucked in there good!" Dav said with a tired laugh.

"Yeah, like I said, it's old. A lot of sediment and mud has settled in around it. We're getting it, though. Should only be another few minutes and it'll be free of the muck, then it should slide right up."

"Easy for you to say," Dav said.

He was breathing hard and sweating. Allie had never seen him do that. In fairness, she thought, two thirteen year old boys were singlehandedly hauling a spaceship large enough to carry four people and a jicund into space out of a bog where it has sat for who knows how long. She wondered how much force those two were actually exerting between them.

"Too bad you can't just magically lift spaceships out of swamps, right Dav?" Allie teased. Dav laughed at the reference.

"Sure I can, I just need a crazy, little, green mentor to teach me how," he replied. Allie laughed.

She found herself a lot more relaxed than Imber looked, but knew it was only due to the fact that Tic didn't seem concerned. The little jicund was happily running around the smaller brush at the edge of the little clearing, snatching up what she assumed were insects, and eating them. She was having a great time. Allie would have stopped her, but Tic knew far better than she did whether an area was safe. Allie watched Tic more than she watched the swamp.

"Okay, let's get this done," Dav said to Raith.

The pair stepped forward and grabbed the cord, and began to pull again. Inch by inch, they progressed. For several more minutes they went like that, an inch at a time, and then suddenly with a horrible sucking sound, the ship came free and burst out of the water. Raith was right. Once it was free of the muck, Raith and Dav hauled it ashore like it weighed almost nothing.

Raith was right, the ship was odd. It was admittedly filthy and dripping wet, covered in slime and swamp plants, but Allie was pretty sure the metal underneath was naturally green. The design was all sharp angles and ridges, and it was wingless. It was supposed to be, Allie figured from the look, but it was still odd seeing a space ship without something at least pretending to be wings. Almost every one she'd seen since Jumping the first time were winged in one form or another.

This one was shaped more like a bullet train engine, she thought. Very different in a lot of ways though, she recognized. That was just what the basic shape reminded her of. She couldn't see through the front window, there was too much mud and muck on it. Dav and Raith both let out a whoop as it came to a halt.

"That thing can fly?" Allie asked.

"Not only do I think it can fly, I think we can take it clear back to Sy'hloran," Raith replied.

"Are you kidding me?" Allie exclaimed. "That thing looks like an Acme road-runner trap!"

"Oh, she may not be the most stylish ship around, but as long as the engines power on, she should do just fine." Raith answered.

"Well let's see what the damage is and get out of here," Imber said. She seemed nervous.

Allie glanced at Tic, who still played happily. Tic was from the jungle, so this was not too far from the environment she had grown up in. The environment Allie knew she'd have to return her to eventually. Raith moved to the front window and wiped across the glass, leaning forward to look inside.

"Good news and bad news," he said. Allie rolled her eyes with a smile.

"Of course. Bad news first," she said.

"Bad news is, the occupants are still inside."

"Are they alive?" Allie asked, suddenly concerned that there were living creatures trapped inside the ship.

"Not for a long time," Raith replied.

"Gross," Imber said.

"What's the good news?" Dav asked.

"The good news is I was right. It's bone dry inside, and I don't see any damage. I don't know what brought this thing down to begin with, but everything inside and out looks fine, from here. Let's crack it open and take a look."

Raith moved to the side, where the door was. That was odd too, Allie thought. Every ship she'd seen you either boarding from the back or from the top.

"Primitive design," Raith said as he studied the control pad beside the door. "Definitely an old ship. From the energy signature though, it'd get a decent speed in space. Not to Dav's standard, but…" Raith flashed a teasing grin at Dav, who returned the smile. "It's a push-button system, too. As long as it has enough power left to start up, we should be fine."

Tic paused in her play and looked at the heavier brush beyond her play area. Allie stopped to watch her, nervously. Allie noticed it was suddenly getting quieter, the animals around going slowly silent.

"Can we get inside?" Allie asked quietly. "I think something is coming this way." The others turned to look at her, then followed her gaze to Tic, who was now backing slowly toward the ship.

"Definitely," Raith said, and began touching buttons on the pad. His fingers moved almost faster than Allie could follow. Seconds passed, and Allie grew more and more nervous as Tic turned and ran over to the door into the ship, sat expectantly, and looked steadily back at the swampy jungle she'd just left.

"Sooner is better," Dav said.

"Patience," Raith said as he worked.

"There will be time for patience later," Allie said, "now is the time to hurry." The swamp had gone silent. A few more seconds passed.

"Got it," Raith said. With a hiss, the door slid open. It moved smoothly, despite its age and filth. Tic bolted inside. Allie stepped toward the door, but almost gagged.

"Oh man, the smell!" she said around her cupped hand that she clapped over her mouth and nose.

"Well, you get to smell that or sit around at here and wait for whatever's coming," Dav said with a glance at the jungle. Allie ducked inside. The others followed, and the door slid shut.

"Okay, now to see if this thing still works," Raith said, moving toward the front of the craft. It was pretty dark inside, with only the muted light filtering first through the treetops above, then the heavy mist, then the muddy windshield.

Allie followed him, fighting dry heaves from the stench. Tic chittered nervously as she hopped up onto the console and watched out the front windshield. The smell was one of rot, but with a sourness she couldn't quite place.

In the cockpit of the small craft were two seats, both occupied by the dried, skeletal remains of the owners of the ship. They were humanoid, but had seven long fingers on each hand, and the rib bones seemed more like interlocking plates than narrow ribs. The skulls flared up and out, like a smaller version of a triceratops, with a paired row of holes running from more than halfway up down to where the eye sockets on the skull should be. Allie could easily imagine that all of those holes were eye sockets, giving the aliens a dozen eyes in two vertical rows.

"Gorem," Raith said.

"What?" Allie asked.

"Gorem," he repeated. "A space-faring race

hundreds of years ago. They died out due to war within their own people. I can't believe this ship is still so well preserved. The Gorem have been gone for four hundred years."

"Smells like four hundred years to me," Allie said, watching Tic nervously. "Can we go?"

Raith reached around the pilot and touched a couple of buttons on the panel. A whirring hum rising in pitch began, fading in volume as the engines warmed up.

"Now that's even more impressive," Raith said to himself. "Now if…" he tapered off as he flipped a few more switches. The hum changed pitches, dropping to a deep, smooth purr. "What do you know, she's operational."

"Good, let's go," Allie urged, nearing panic as she watched Tic's fur stand on end, the little jicund crouching low and aggressive.

Raith touched a few more buttons, and then grabbed what looked like a joystick. His position was awkward, but he made no move to touch the corpse he leaned over to reach the controls. Allie didn't care, as long as they left, and soon. There was a slight jolt as the craft lifted.

"Inertial dampeners could use some work," Raith said.

Dav watched carefully as Raith lifted the craft. He was learning to drive, Allie knew. The craft rose steadily, and Allie began to feel a little better, until a jarring impact knocked her to the ground, sending one of the two skeletons toppling to the ground.

"Well that was close," Dav said.

"What happened?" Allie asked, trying to keep the

panic out of her voice.

"I think whatever was coming to visit just tried to take a bite of us. We're well above it now, though. Nothing to worry about," Raith explained.

"I worry that if we'd been one second slower, we'd be lunch for something down there," Allie grumbled as she climbed back to her feet. She almost tripped again on a bone as it rolled across the floor. "Gross," she complained, stepping back.

"All right, we're out of atmosphere. Free and clear, folks. Now to figure out the navigation system, and where in the galaxy we are, and we can be on our way back home."

"I'll take cleanup duty," Dav offered. "Someone else should do a search of the craft, find out what we have on this thing that we can work with." Allie sighed.

"Well, that was a short escape from Sy'hloran. I hope C.A.D.E.-16 left Sy'hloran and is following us. He'll have quite the adventure trying to figure out where we went if he did. Maybe we bought some time," Allie finished hopefully.

"Maybe," Raith said doubtfully. He didn't sound like he believed it at all.

She sighed again and turned toward the back of the ship. She rubbed at her nose, but knew that smell was going to linger for some time. No help for it, she knew. Time to make the best of their ride home in a four hundred year old space ship full of dead aliens.

# CHAPTER FIFTEEN

# OUT OF COMMISSION

Raith, of course, figured out the navigation system without much trouble, and they were on their way to Sy'hloran. Allie wasn't surprised. What did surprise her was that Raith had said that even with the known wormholes, it would take five days to get back home. Dav could probably have gotten them there faster if he had his wormhole data, since he'd successfully tracked so many of their patterns, but without the data, he didn't remember enough about this specific region to risk trying them.

Raith was now working on fixing the communications system, which he said looked to have blown a few circuits, probably part of whatever had caused the ship to go down in the first place. He said it wasn't a mechanical failure in the engines, or the navigation systems, since he had done full diagnostics on both and they were both fully functional.

She didn't know what Dav had done with the bodies up front, and didn't care to ask. There was probably a storage bay someplace on this ship. He'd been cleaning aggressively for the last two hours, and she had to admit the place looked a lot better.

Allie had found a number of tools and devices that she couldn't identify in her search of the craft, and Dav was going through them to identify them, test them, and find anything useful. She noticed he was being very careful with everything he touched and wondered if he planned to preserve the items. It would make sense, she thought. They were centuries-old relics of a dead race after all, they probably had museums on Sy'hloran for things like that.

The living quarters on this ship were going to be tight indeed. There were only two cots, one above the other, and while they were wide, Allie and Imber would have to share one. Dav would get his own since Raith didn't need to sleep. Dav had tried to offer to let the girls each have one and he'd sleep on the floor, but they had put up such a protest that he'd finally given in.

Imber had started out helping Dav clean, but had been forced to sit down due to exhaustion. Allie had noticed her heirlines were glowing constantly now, and that glow in her eyes was visible from most angles. With her skin getting so pale, the heirlines and her eyes glowing, and the dark circles under her eyes, she actually looked pretty creepy, Allie thought.

Imber currently sat up front with Raith, helping him with the communications systems. Allie opened the last of the storage lockers on the ship, having to stand on tiptoe to see the back of the top shelf. Nothing there, she saw, so she lowered herself back down and closed it.

"That's it," she told Dav. He nodded from his seat on the floor amid a pile of small containers, various devices, and piles of clothing and sheets for the cots. She was about to sit down next to him, but heard Raith start talking up front.

"Sy'hloran Command, this is R.A.I.T.H.-84, accompanying Prince Davrelan. Come in, Sy'hloran Command." Static answered his call. Allie looked toward the front and watched as Imber turned a tiny screw in the open control panel the barest fraction and nodded to Raith.

"Sy'hloran Command, this is R.A.I.T.H.-84, accompanying Prince Davrelan. Come in, Sy'hloran Command." This time there was a response, though it was scratchy, broken, and faint.

"We read… I.T.H.-84, this is… loran Command. Ple… your location."

"We are in sector 47-B, quadrant 3, en route to Sy'hloran. Please reroute Shaian and Sy'hli bodyguard squadron to intercept. Velocity, twenty one point nine."

"Understoo… erouting squadron to interce… aintain course and veloc… Hold, communica… ansferred to Prince Artus."

Raith glanced back at the others. Dav and Allie had both heard and were already moving up front.

"Raith, this is Ar… ou read me?"

"You're coming in broken, Artus, but we're getting the message," Raith replied.

"Is everyo… ll right?"

"Most of us," Raith replied. "Imber is getting worse. We lost our ship and our entourage. All the medical supplies were on our transport vessel, I can't even run basic tests."

"Ambass… ren is doing ba… s well. He's been mov… ospital, they're comple… Nobody has any ideas. The queen has fa… as well. The Shaian ar… nding a specialis… ctor, but won't be here for tw… ays. They're telling me your escor… reach you for three days either."

Raith looked at Imber for a long moment, then to Allie and Dav. He shook his head very slightly, telling Allie plainly that they didn't have three days to wait, and needed to get Imber to proper medical care now.

"That's not good news, Artus," Raith told him.

"I know. Morgan wa… ow if Allie can Jump you all h… ght now."

Raith looked to Allie again. She reached for the energies tentatively, and felt the watcher there, waiting. It felt more distant though, but still close enough to be a problem if she tried another Jump. It still didn't feel malevolent necessarily, but very eager, and definitely wanted her to Jump where it wanted her to Jump. They couldn't afford that risk right now. Opening her eyes, she shook her head apologetically.

"No good, Artus. Allie is still getting major interference. Tell Morgan it's the same as before, but is getting worse."

It was quiet on the other end for a long moment before Artus came back on.

"Understood. Tell h… ep trying, and the moment she's able, to get y… ere immediately. We'll keep in cont… ll update you if they do… nd anything out."

"We read you," Raith replied. Allie nodded.

"More bad news," Artus came, slightly louder and clearer as Imber made another miniscule adjustment to the screw.

"Break it gently," Raith said with a rueful smile. Always more bad news, Allie agreed.

"Harelo has b… ocated."

"How is that bad news? That's great! Let's get him home!" Raith replied.

"He's be… isoner by Preston on a sh… ctor 31-a. We can't get any… ch him for another week."

"Preston has him?" Dav asked suddenly, expression concerned. "That's not good. If Preston has him, Harelo doesn't have a week."

"Why do you thi…" Artus replied.

"Preston is going to kill him."

"Preston might n… ven know Harelo is an agent," Artus argued.

"He knows," Dav replied. "I just have this feeling, Preston knows. If Harelo is even still alive, he won't have long. What else can we do to save him? He saved our lives. All of our lives."

"I don't kn… be we can run a few ships thr… mholes and hope they get th… in time." Dav's expression fell.

Allie agreed. They hadn't had much dealing with Harelo, but he'd saved all of their lives more than once. The idea that he was about to be killed and there was nothing they could do about it was heartbreakingly tragic.

"Understood," Raith replied, his own tone regretful.

"Keep us posted on all fronts, Artus. We'll let you know if there's any major change to Imber."

"Thank you, I'm gl…. re all okay."

"Us too. Raith out," he said, as he closed the com channel.

"Well, lovely news all around. Whatever Imber has is spreading, nobody knows what's causing it, and Harelo is in danger. We're stuck in the middle of nowhere with a four hundred year old ship with no help arriving for three days, with Imber getting worse by the day," Raith said, his tone filled with frustration.

Allie knew she could help. She could get them all home. She could get Harelo home too, if that watcher would leave her alone long enough to do it. She touched the energies again. The watcher was there, ready for her. Like she did with the Rrughn, she tried to reach out, mind to mind.

*"Are you there?"* she asked. Words didn't return, but the thought that came to her was positive, and excited.

*"We need to help our friend. I don't know what you want with me, but I can't Jump with you pulling the energies every time I try. Do you mean me harm?"*

The thought that came back to her, still wordless, was negative. Harm was not intended. She didn't know if she could believe that, but didn't have any choice right now. Harelo and Imber both depended on her ability to Jump.

*"Do you need my help?"* she asked. A strong affirmative came back to her.

*"If you let me Jump to save my friends, I promise that I'll come help you after. Deal?"* There was a long pause before

response. Another affirmative. She felt the watcher's grip on the energies relax immediately. It was still there, still watching, but it wasn't holding the energies around her anymore. She sighed in relief. Why hadn't she thought to communicate with the watcher sooner?

*"Thank you,"* she replied.

"Okay guys, we're good to go. Let's get Imber home, and then go get Harelo."

"What?" Dav asked. All three turned to look at her in surprise. Tic chirped on her shoulder.

"I think I've sorted out the interference problem for now. I can Jump this ship back home, then Jump a team to go get Harelo," she replied, a little smugly.

"When did this happen?" Imber asked with a strained smile. She really didn't look well, Allie thought.

"Just now. The energies feel clear, I think I can do a quick Jump or two."

"Check on Harelo," Dav urged.

"Now?"

"Now. I don't think he has long at all," Dav said.

"How do you know?"

"I don't have any idea, but something tells me Preston is going to kill him. Please, can you See him before we Jump back to Sy'hloran?"

Allie nodded, surprised at his urgency, and focused on Harelo. Almost immediately, smoother and faster than ever before, she was mentally right beside him. He was stun shackled on a table. Preston stood over him holding a very nasty looking piece of equipment, some electronic device with a pair of small, sharp pins on the back.

"You'll tell me Harelo, one way or another." Preston pressed the device into Harelo's arm. The blue light on the front of the device immediately lit up, and Harelo's paralyzed body began to spasm.

She looked quickly around. The room was filled with soldiers, all armed and ready. They were all looking all around, as if expecting someone to appear at any moment. Preston knew Allie could Jump in to rescue him, and had put men in place to shoot her the moment she appeared.

Her mind drifted out into the passage beyond. Several soldiers were positioned there as well. Preston had men positioned all over the ship. His paranoia, while justified, sure made her job harder. She couldn't find anywhere she could Jump them in that wouldn't get them shot before they could react. Allie's mind jerked backward, snapping back to her friends.

"You're right, we have to go now. Preston is torturing him," she said. "I don't know where we can Jump to though, he has men armed and ready all over the ship, waiting for me to Jump in."

"So we don't Jump in," Raith replied. "Do you think you can Jump this ship into their docking bay?"

"There are soldiers there, too."

"So land us in a corner someplace aiming in, and I can clear the bay with the laser cannons on this thing."

"This boat has laser cannons?" Dav asked, curiously.

"I told you it was four hundred years old."

"I thought you said laser cannons were useless," Allie asked Dav. He shrugged.

"Should work just fine if nothing in the bay is

mirrored." Allie thought about it.

"I don't think anything there looked mirrored. The men sure aren't."

"Laser cannons it is, then. I always wanted to try one of these things," Raith said with a grin.

"Okay, Allie, Jump us into the bay like Raith says. He and I will exit first, and make sure the bay is clear. You follow, ready to Jump us all out at a moment's notice if need be. Then we fight our way to Preston and Harelo. Imber…" he looked down at Imber. Her face was drawn, and she'd broken into a light sweat. "Imber, you lay down on the cot and don't move." The fact that all she did was nod told Allie all she needed to know about how badly Imber was feeling. A quick glance at her friends showed Dav mirrored her concern. Raith's concern was more than that.

"Ready?" Raith asked, bringing the Gorem ship to a halt and standing, drawing a gun, other hand still on the control panel.

Dav nodded, guns already in hand. Allie drew one of her guns, and held a hand out, placing it on the side of the craft. Her mind wrapped itself around the ship, drew in the now-peaceful energies under the watcher's attentive gaze, and sent her mind to the docking bay of Preston's ship. She found an uninhabited corner, most of the soldiers watching the two bay doors.

With almost frightening ease and speed, now that the pressure on the energies was released, she Jumped the craft and her friends. The Jump was so fast she didn't even feel the space Between. The ship appeared right where she wanted it, and Raith fired the laser cannons.

Unlike the movies, she didn't see beams of green or red light fire from the cannons. Instead, she saw the air in front of the ship suddenly superheat in a line directly out from the cannons. The big freight containers where they aimed almost instantly glowed red and exploded.

Soldiers dove for cover, and Raith and Dav left the ship so fast Allie hadn't even reached the door by the time they had run into the bay, and reached the two groups of soldiers still recovering from the unexpected blast.

"Stay here, guard Imber!" Allie shouted to Tic, who leapt off her shoulder just as she dove out the door.

The boys each dropped all four soldiers in their group before the men had even regained their feet. The soldiers, all unconscious, were quickly dumped into a cargo container that Raith then bent the edge of the lid shut.

"There we go," Dav said, dramatically dusting his hands off. "Eight soldiers in a can, and we have safely docked with Preston's lovely torture-mobile. Let's go," he said with an eager grin.

He looked like a hungry cat when he grinned like that, Allie thought with a smile. Raith flashed her his own mischievous grin as he closed and sealed their little Gorem craft's doors so nobody could get in, and the trio was off. Allie really hoped they'd be in and out again in less than five minutes, but appreciated the gesture of security.

Racing into the passageway beyond the docking bay, Dav and Raith both dove to either side, coming up shooting at the soldiers even now charging their way.

Again, by the time Allie got there, the pair had handled all soldiers in sight.

Allie found herself wondering how many of the Coalition guard that were loyal to the Highlord were of races similar in strength and speed to humans. Raith and Dav were both impressive, but she knew if those soldiers had been Sy'hli or another race with the speed or strength to really fight back, this wouldn't be going nearly as well.

It wasn't far from the docking bay to the room where Preston held Harelo. Allie had to help down this hallway, more heavily guarded as it was. She found she still couldn't hold her wounded arm up with the gun long, so was forced to stick with her other hand. Her aim was terrible, but just before they reached the hallway, she touched a control panel and shut the lights off in the hallway.

Everything went instantly black, and Allie was blind. Dav and Raith weren't, though. She heard the sounds of the boys fighting the guards, and from the speed with which it got quiet, assumed most of the guards couldn't see in the dark either. Once it was all quiet, she turned the lights back on.

"Nice move," Raith said with a grin as she poked her head around the corner. She smiled back and came jogging over to them.

"Hey, I've got to be useful somehow, right?" she said with a laugh.

The door to the room Preston and Harelo were in slid open and the blast of arc rifle fire that erupted from the opening almost tore a hole in the wall across from the doorway. Dav and Raith, both standing right in front of the door, both leapt to the side. Both got hit more than once though. Dav glanced at the charge pack on his belt as the suit redirected the energy into the pack. He looked at Raith and raised a brow in question.

"No!" Allie shouted. "That's where Harelo is!" Dav nodded, understanding that pressing the button to set the battery pack to self-destruct as a grenade wouldn't be viable without hurting Harelo as well.

"Throw down your weapons and surrender," came Preston's nasally voice from inside the room. "I know who's out there, and I know even you can't get to me through this many guns aimed at you."

"Not much motivation to come in, then," Raith muttered.

"Weapons down! Come in and surrender or I'll kill Harelo!"

"Ah, there's the motivation," Dav said, shaking his head. He poked his head around the corner and pulled it back immediately as another burst of arc rifle fire tore through the doorway, slightly melting the metal frame.

"At least two dozen men, with a couple watching the backs of the others, and several behind cover, so Allie can't Jump us in behind. All very ready for us. The room is too open, there's no cover near the doorway and too far to run before we'd be shot at but at least a dozen of them. My pack is already full," Dav said, looking again to the battery pack at his belt.

"Mine too," Raith responded. He and Dav held gazes for a minute, then took a deep breath almost in unison. Allie knew what was coming.

"No!" she shouted. They both looked her way.

"Five seconds, or Harelo dies!" Preston shouted.

"I've got this," she replied. That last Jump, the speed, the ease, the clarity of Sight, had given her an idea.

"What?" Dav asked in surprise. Raith raised a brow. She took her own deep breath.

"Fine!" shouted Preston. Allie didn't hesitate any longer. She Jumped.

# CHAPTER SIXTEEN

# LIKE A FLASH

Dav didn't even have time to react, and Allie was gone. Stunned for a fraction of a second, it took him a moment to realize she'd just Jumped into the room. Poking his head quickly around the corner of the doorway, ready to pull it back quickly if the soldiers opened fire, he witnessed something unlike anything he'd ever seen before.

Allie was in the room. All over the room. She was Jumping in and out so fast that the soldiers were literally spinning in circles trying to track her. With each Jump, she appeared behind another soldier, touched him, and vanished. The room was big, full of soldiers, and there were even soldiers up on a walkway around the perimeter of the room. None of this slowed Allie down. He'd never seen someone Jump so fast, so rapidly in succession.

In a flash, she was on the walkway, and then gone,

the soldier she touched vanishing with her. She reappeared on the ground across the room and vanished, another soldier disappearing.

The small white flash of her Jumps flickered around the room like a strobe light, each flash signaling another vanished soldier. Dav could barely track her from the doorway, the soldiers in the room had no chance. Nobody even got enough of a chance to raise a weapon her direction, let alone try shooting her. The entire process took only seconds, and she appeared behind Preston, whose weasely face had gone white, and his head whipped around in a panic trying to spot her.

She touched his hand, and Jumped once more. Dav watched in amazement as she reappeared halfway between the table Harelo was on and the doorway. Preston appeared with her, unlike any of the soldiers, and he was in his underwear, his clothes piled on the floor where he'd been standing.

Preston yelped and tried to cover himself. Dav couldn't help it, he started laughing. Stepping fully into the room, he walked calmly toward Preston, whose face was a picture of panicked bewilderment.

"Didn't see that coming, huh?" he asked. Preston stared at him in shock.

"If it makes you feel any better, neither did we." Raith laughed, a step behind him.

Dav looked to Allie, who smiled at him, somewhat smugly. She'd earned it, Dav thought as he moved to Harelo, deactivating the bracelets and removing the device from his arm. Harelo's twitching body instantly went limp.

"He's going to need medical care," Dav said. "Can you get us all out of here?"

"No problem," Allie said. She touched Preston again, and before he could yelp, she Jumped the pair of them to a spot right next to Dav. Dav had expected it this time, and clapped the stun shackles on him as Raith stepped up beside him.

He put a hand on Dav's shoulder as Dav put a hand on Harelo, and another on Allie's arm. Allie, still touching Preston, touched Dav, and Jumped again.

Dav couldn't help but notice that this time, there was no slowing of time, no odd stretching sensation of his body, no moment where you felt like you weren't actually anywhere. This time, he was in the room where Allie had just performed some kind of miracle, and the next moment he was in the Gorem ship.

He helped ease Preston down to the ground, and a little roughly shoved him aside into a corner. Preston's stiff body rolled and came to a stop facing the corner. Allie had managed to Jump them positioned in such a way that Harelo, who was lying on the table, was now lying on one of the cots. Dav had no idea how she did that.

Imber was on the other, eyes closed. Her breathing was shallow and rapid, and she didn't react at all to their appearance. Her heirlines glowed brightly, and he could see the glow from behind her eyelids. Looking a little closer, he could see a glow coming not only from her heirlines, but from the veins beneath her skin as well. She needed help immediately. Dav wasn't even sure what the Sy'hli doctors could do for her, though.

"One more," Allie said. Touching the side of the ship, they Jumped again.

Dav looked out the front window and saw they were in the Sy'hloran Palace docking bay. Sy'hli Royal Guard were already panicking, and charging forward drawing weapons. She probably could have used a less threatening entrance, Dav thought with a sigh as he moved to the door, opening it. Stepping out, he held up both hands.

"Prince Davrelan!" The first guard to reach them called, dropping into a bow. The other guards did the same as they arrived. "What in the stars are you doing in that wreck?"

"Just out for a joyride," Dav replied. "We have a sick friend of mine inside, we need her taken to the palace infirmary. Bring anyone you can that might be able to help. There is also an injured Uhran, also a friend of mine. Take him to the infirmary as well. Last, but not least, we have a prisoner inside. Have him taken someplace top security, immediately. Don't remove those shackles until he's in a cell and under constant guard, am I clear?" The guard saluted.

"Of course, Your Highness." He gestured to several of the guards, and they moved inside.

Raith and Allie moved to the side, Tic sitting once more on Allie's shoulder. Two guards came out carrying Preston, while several more ran to get a couple of gurneys. A quick message through his wrist com and Dav knew a medical team was on its way for Imber and Harelo.

Moving inside after the guards carrying Preston left,

he went to Imber and Harelo. Harelo was out cold, and looked in reasonably good shape. He definitely needed some attention, but Dav was sure Allie had Jumped them there in time. Imber was also out, her breathing still shallow and rapid, that glow eerily radiating from her body. He looked up at Allie, who had turned to watch the men carrying Preston. From this angle, he could undeniably see it. A faint glow in her eyes.

His heart sank. It wasn't exclusive to the Shaian, and Allie had contracted it as well. For all he knew, so had he, but the idea of Allie sick, especially sick with something nobody knew could be cured, or even what the long-term effects were, terrified him. She probably didn't even know she had it, he doubted she could see the glow yet.

It was less than a minute before four guards and two doctors ran into the bay. Two of the guards were pushing floating gurneys to move the sick and injured. Dav, Allie, and Raith stepped outside to give the men room as they pushed the gurneys effortless into the small craft.

They all watched as Imber and Harelo were brought out of the Gorem ship. Raith immediately fell into step beside Imber's gurney. Dav and Allie did the same, but they stopped when Artus and Morgan ran into the room.

"Seriously Dav, I can't let you out of my sight for a minute!" Artus said, only half joking. Morgan ran up and hugged Allie. The pair stepped aside to talk, leaving Dav with Artus. Dav watched as Raith left the docking bay with Imber and her escort. The doctors were already running vitals scans.

"It's not my fault we keep getting abducted by pirates," Dav replied.

"Pirates?" Artus asked. Dav realized he hadn't had the chance to tell Artus about the first time Captain Abram's crew took them captive either. They had a lot to catch up on, but Artus was always in council session. Speaking of which…

"Long story. Why aren't you speaking with the Council?"

"No point," Artus said with a sigh.

"What? Why?" Dav asked.

"The Council has been shattered. Talks escalated into arguments yesterday after you left. Arguments turned into extreme hostility, and the Council split, taking sides. Apparently some of the Highlord's loyalists among the Council have been hearing from him."

"What? That's impossible, he's in prison!"

"Well, there are two problems with that," Artus said. "First, Tyren isn't the Highlord. I've had guards on him at all times since he went in, and he hasn't spoken or communicated with anyone. He's not the one communicating with the loyalists. Second, Tyren isn't in prison anymore."

"What?" Dav asked, stunned yet again.

"Lab results came back on the sample you brought in. It's definitely a colony organism, and has capabilities we can't even begin to understand. Our biologists say they've never seen anything remotely like it."

"Now that's saying something," Dav said, astonished for several reasons.

Sy'hli biologists loved the variety of life in the galaxy, and studying alien biology was required in their preliminary studies, and most kept it up once graduated and in the field. There wasn't much they hadn't seen. Also, Tyren was loose. Dav had no idea how to feel about that. He still harbored huge amounts of anger and resentment for his eldest brother, and found that hadn't lessened despite Allie's insistence about the alien parasitic colony being proven true by the Sy'hli's top scientists.

"Yeah. Anyway, Tyren should be here any second."

"He's coming here?" Dav asked, his stomach tightening up.

"Of course. He was worried about you, too."

"Was his release part of the problem with the Council?"

"Definitely. Many still feel he should be executed, despite the evidence. He was tested as well and our scientists found traces of the dead organism in his system. He was unquestionably infected. Many others want to rejoin him now that he's free. They think Tyren should be back in power, so the strong can continue to rule the galaxy."

"Bad call. The Sy'hli and the Tchratchi are aiming for a more harmonious, participatory galactic government. The two strongest races in the galaxy. If it comes down to a battle of strength, we'll win."

"I know that," Artus said, "and so do you, but the loyalists think Tyren is going to take control of the Sy'hli again and use our strength to subjugate the galaxy once more."

"Idiots," Dav thought, though some part of him in the back of his mind actually considered that to maybe not be the worst idea. If the Sy'hli ruled the galaxy, they could enforce the peace the galaxy needed. "So how do we convince them that's not going to happen?"

"Too late for that, too. Half the Council has left, to 'solidify their positions'. That's code for 'prepare our armies'. This is going to come to war, Dav."

"Hasn't this galaxy had enough war?"

"I sure think so," Artus agreed with a sigh. The doors to the bay opened and Tyren walked in. Just Tyren, unguarded, by himself. Dav's jaw clenched slightly. "Easy, little brother. He's been proven innocent, remember?"

"Yeah," Dav said simply. He still wasn't entirely convinced.

"Artus, Dav," Tyren said as he neared, nodding to each. Dav looked at his eldest brother. He did look different, but the same in many ways. When Tyren looked at Dav though, the strength in his eyes gave way to nervousness and uncertainty. Dav had never seen that in those eyes before.

"Tyren," Dav said.

"I want very much to sit and talk with you, but I'm afraid there's something urgent that needs to be brought up first," Tyren said. Dav frowned.

"You mean besides war breaking out? Again, thanks to you?" Dav said. Tyren sighed.

"I regret that my release has caused many of the council members to pursue their foolishness, and regret further that that foolishness will devolve to violence. I will do anything I can to help, and have already sent messages to the Coalition loyal to the Highlord telling them to stand down. That's not what I have to talk to you about, however."

"Great. What is it now?" Dav asked.

Seeing his brother brought his anger flooding to the surface. There was a disdain and disgust for his elder brother there now as well that hadn't been there before, however. It felt oddly foreign. Tyren looked at him for a long moment before speaking, as though studying him.

"I have seen Ambassador Oren, and passed his daughter Imber in the halls. Word has reached me of several others, not Shaian, who are showing symptoms as well. I am afraid I know those symptoms." Dav's anger froze.

"You know what's wrong with them?"

"I do," Tyren said, expression grave. "Trapped in my own body, I spent years watching what the Highlord was up to. He had been working for many years on a project, a biological weapon called the Dawn Virus. For years, he failed. Until he changed tactics near the end, and managed to successfully test the virus. It was contained on the Helios, and I assumed it was destroyed when the Helios went nova. How Imber contracted it, I don't know, but I believe she's the first to contract it, and it spread from her."

"Imber is patient zero?" Artus asked.

"What does the virus do? How do we cure it?" Dav asked, almost frantically. If Tyren could cure Allie and Imber, Dav was willing to forgive almost anything. Tyren again sighed in resignation.

"You can't cure it," he said. "It's not technically a virus, though it behaves like one. They're nanobots, but not like anything ever developed before. They're so small that they can travel on photons, literally riding the light to new carriers. The nanobots break down organic molecules, literally burning them for light and energy, to both replicate themselves and to transmit themselves. Your friend Imber is being slowly converted to light, from the inside out. I think the Shaian biology is why they're reacting so quickly."

"There has to be a cure. Why would the Highlord develop a virus without a cure?" Artus asked.

"He had a cure, but only one dose. He intended for me to take it when he released the virus, so that this body would be the last living thing on the planet. The cure was on the Helios."

"Which exploded," Dav said, with a sinking heart. No, he thought firmly, he wouldn't give up. "But if there was a cure, then we can find it again."

"Maybe," Tyren said with a shrug. "Our doctors are good, and I've already explained what this is to several of the team leading the research on this virus. They may find something. Not in time to save the Shaian, however. Maybe not in time to save anyone here. The virus may travel on light, but it can also travel through wormholes and will spread across the entire galaxy in a remarkably short time. Nobody is immune. Except your android friend, that is. The virus only affects organic cells. That does mean that all plants, animals, bacteria, and even real viruses will all be wiped out in a matter of months."

"How can a virus travel on light?" Dav asked.

"All viruses travel on other things. Some viruses are so big they can only transmit by blood to blood contact. Some are much smaller and can travel on water particles emitted when the sick person sneezes or coughs. Some can travel on the air itself. This virus is so small that even a nanoscanner wouldn't detect it. The Highlord developed several more advanced nanoscanners of his own over the years, specifically to work on this particular project. All on the Helios."

"So the only people safe are those in complete darkness?" Dav asked.

"There's almost no such thing. And the virus has a thousand year lifespan before the individual nanobots begin to die off. If anything does survive, it would be a miracle."

"So you've killed the entire galaxy," Dav accused, anger flaring again. Tyren sadly shook his head.

"The Highlord has, yes. As I said, the Sy'hli may find a cure. Other races may as well, messages are doubtless being transmitted to other worlds with our current data, I'm sure. At the rate this virus progresses however, I suspect that even the hardiest species won't last more than two weeks once infected. If you were all infected on the Helios, then you have only another week or so before you will all die as well. And me, I am no more immune than anyone else."

"Well, there's that at least," Dav said with venom in his voice.

"Dav!" Artus snapped. "That's enough, you're behaving like a child."

Dav glared at Artus, then back at Tyren. Tyren was studying him again, looking concerned. He stormed away from the two, and out of the bay. Who was Artus to accuse him of behaving like a child? Dav had been one of the biggest contributors on every mission they'd gone on, missions that would have killed even the best trained adults of many species.

Fine, Artus and Tyren had gotten all buddy-buddy again, he would look for answers on his own. Allie would help him, at least while she still could. Raith would help too. He would help even if Imber weren't sick. With Imber sick, there wasn't much Raith wouldn't do to help.

Dav thought again about Allie dying due to this Dawn Virus and felt sick to his stomach. Didn't a virus become a plague when it reached a certain point? This virus would reach plague proportions in days, if it traveled on light.

With half the council heading back to their worlds, they were simply carrying along the virus. It was far too late to contain it. It was already a plague, Dav thought. A Plague of Dawn.

# CHAPTER SEVENTEEN

# FIRST STRIKE

Allie was sick. She knew it, could feel it in her veins. It was a faint burning sensation. It wasn't painful, but it itched like crazy. Her mother had told her what Tyren had shared about the virus. She knew what it was, and knew she didn't have long.

Her mother had insisted she go to the infirmary as well, and Allie had done so. Not because she felt that the doctors could help, but because she knew that's where her friends would gather, and there they could plan what to do. Her mother insisted that this was something the adults had to take care of, but Allie was no longer the kind of person to sit back and wait while other people tried to fix the problems all around her.

Allie sat beside Imber, who was still unconscious. She looked across the room to where Harelo lay, also still unconscious. Whatever Preston had done to him, it had shorted out some of his neural systems, and the doctors weren't sure he'd ever wake up. Not that it mattered, if they all died of this illness, Allie thought bitterly. Shaking herself, she pushed the thought away. They wouldn't die. None of them would die. Dav and Raith would help her find a cure.

Raith was already sitting at a console to one side of the room, working hard on analyzing the blood samples. Allie had watched them draw Imber's blood. It was definitely eerie, watching them withdraw a syringe of glowing liquid from Imber's veins. Even the Shaian weren't supposed to have glowing blood, she knew.

The screen on Raith's console was going through data and screens so fast that it hurt Allie's eyes to watch it. If anyone could figure this out, he would. Once he had heard it was a nanovirus, he'd gotten all excited and sat down at that computer console. He hadn't moved since. Literally, not a single part of his body had moved so much a hair's breadth since he sat down.

That was a little creepy too, but she knew it meant he wasn't devoting any of his processing power to emulating human mannerisms, including some minor fidgeting and pretending to breathe while he was sitting still like he usually did. She forgot a lot of the time that he wasn't organic, despite the silvery scar that still ran from his forehead almost to his mouth over one eye.

Watching him sitting now, perfectly still, it was obvious he wasn't organic. It was hard to remember he was alive. He wasn't, by a lot of people's standards. She considered him alive, though. He thought, he felt, he acted, that sounded alive to her.

"Allie," came a deep, rumbling voice on her wrist

com. That was odd, only her own team and a few outsiders had the frequency and code to access these coms. She recognized the voice, though.

"Dgehf?" Allie replied, curiously.

"Allie, bad things happen," he said. She wondered why he didn't speak in Maruck, but didn't ask. He sounded upset and urgent.

"What's going on?" she asked.

"Highlord's men here, Maruck here, Coalition here, both sides. Big fight. Dgehf think war start now!"

"Where are you," she asked.

"Ayaran, Dgehf's ship Ayaran. Highlord's men, bad Coalition, try to take over wormhole."

That actually made a lot of sense, Allie thought. The wormhole between Ayaran and Pahrvic was a major supply line between the two major, heavily populated quadrants of the galaxy. There were sentient species all over the galaxy of course, but like humans on Earth, people of similar technology and culture tended to group together in pockets of more dense population.

Space was a lot like that. There were huge stretches with absolutely nothing, and then a dozen solar systems right next to each other that were absolutely packed with people. The wormhole between Ayaran and Pahrvic was like the freeway between Los Angeles and New York City. Controlling that would influence a lot of supply lines and troops transport.

"Are they going to win?" she asked, nervously.

"Yes," Dgehf replied. One word, but it carried a lot of information. The good guys were outmatched at Ayaran.

"I'll get Artus. We may have people nearby that can come help."

"Yes, hurry," Dgehf replied.

The com channel switched off. She could hear it in the deep rumbling voice, Dgehf was in trouble, as was Ayaran. She thought of Ghier, and of Tic's people. Allie knew that Ayaran had a Coalition military outpost loyal to the Highlord. They must have turned on the Coalition forces nearby loyal to the true Coalition, to try and gain control of the wormhole. Allie switched on the com and opened a channel to Artus. It was funny how second-nature things like this had become. Not much different from a set of walkie-talkies though, she thought.

"Artus, we have a problem. The Highlord's loyalists have turned on the Coalition forces around the wormhole at Ayaran. Dgehf says they're going to take it. He's there, but says things are going badly."

"That's all we need," Artus said angrily through her com. "They're sure not wasting any time. If they take that wormhole it will take months to get more ships anywhere near that sector. We don't have anyone in that sector that isn't already at or around Ayaran or Pahrvic. If they're going to lose, this war just got a lot longer. I need to talk to General Xan. Thanks for the heads up. You're even faster than my information agents." Allie smiled, but she was worried.

"Artus?"

"Yeah?"

"I think I can Jump a fleet there."

"You can Jump a… what?"

"A fleet. My last several Jumps have been so easy, I

barely had to think about it. I was touching everything I Jumped, but I actually am not sure I need to. I only Jumped a small ship, but it felt really not any different than Jumping just myself. I don't think how much matter I Jump makes a difference. If we can get a fleet gathered close together and me on one ship, I think I can Jump a lot of ships. Even if I can't, I can Jump them one at a time really quickly."

"Thanks Allie, I'll mention that to the general. I may need you to do that."

"Just say the word, Your Highness," she said with a grin.

"Stop that!" Artus said, a smile in his voice. She switched off the com.

"Allie, you can't Jump a fleet," Raith said, now more focused.

"He's right," came a voice from the doorway. Her mother stood there. "You shouldn't have even tried Jumping that ship back here, the way things have been going for you. Allie, I give you a lot of leeway since you've been doing this without me so well already, but you can't keep pushing. If you keep this up, you're going to break. Maybe that's where the interference when you jump is coming from. Maybe you're damaging your gift already."

"That's not it," Allie insisted. "There's someone out there that needs my help. They can reach through the energies and interfere with my Jumps, but I guess they can't Jump themselves. They're trying to make me come to them, I think they need help."

"That's not only crazy, it's very scary," her mother

said. "Nobody can interfere with another person's Jump."

Allie thought about this. She thought about how she Jumped, and what she was able to do with the energies in the Shift, not only with the damage in the Shift, but with the strange creature that hunted Rrughn.

"I actually think I could," Allie said thoughtfully.

"That's even more frightening," her mother said, coming to sit beside her. "Allie, I don't know what your power limits are, or why your limits are so far beyond anyone else's. I've never heard of anyone being able to do the things you can do, and it scares me. I lost you once when you were so very little. To me, you're still so very little. I couldn't bear to lose you again. We might not have much time left anyway…"

Allie hugged her mother. She could see where she was coming from, but she also understood that she had a responsibility not only to herself and her family, but to anyone she could help. If you had the ability to help someone and didn't, didn't that make you nearly as guilty as the person who hurt them in the first place?

"Mom, I know. I know I'm only thirteen, I know we only just found each other again, and I know how hard it would be to lose that. But everyone is getting sick. I'm sick, you're sick, Imber is sick, and it's spreading everywhere. Maybe my trying to Jump a fleet won't matter, because we'll all die of this virus anyway. But maybe someone will find a cure. If someone finds a cure, and I don't try to help right now, maybe the loyalists will gain control of the wormhole and cut off supply across the galaxy. Maybe that means millions of people will die.

It could even be the key that kelps the loyalists win, and even without the Highlord, they take charge of the galaxy, and millions, maybe billions, of people die anyway and the rest live in fear. Could you live with that? I couldn't," Allie concluded with finality.

She knew her mother felt the same way. She knew that's why her mother had risked herself so many times before Allie was born, and after, to try and help other people. That's why her father had died, too. He was also the kind of person who couldn't stand by and watch people suffer. He had to help. So did her mother. So did Allie.

Her mother looked at her for a long moment, then embraced her daughter tightly.

"Allie, I can't believe how much I've missed. Forget what I said, you're not little at all. If we survive this, Sinara and I will induct you into the Order of the Silver Star. You're exactly the kind of person we need to rebuild the Order, to help the people who can't help themselves."

"Thanks Mom," Allie said into her mother's shirt.

"Just do me a favor and be careful, okay? Jumping even one ship is hard work, and risky. Trying a whole fleet is beyond risky. I don't entirely know what makes you different, but I'm not sure it's completely stable."

"Are you saying I'm unstable?" Allie asked with a grin.

"Maybe a little," her mother said with a smile.

Dav walked into the room. He looked angry. Her mother saw Dav's face and stood, heading for the door.

"Come see me before you go," she said before ducking out. Dav came over and sat beside her, looking at Imber.

"She doing any better?" he asked.

"No," Allie said. "We both know she won't until someone finds the cure."

"I know."

"Someone will find the cure," she said, leaning forward to encourage him to look up at her. He did so.

"Maybe," he replied with a shrug.

"They will. There's no way that some stupid nanobot is going to be the end of our galaxy."

"Will they find it in time to help us?"

"Of course. Raith will."

"Allie?"

"Yeah?"

"Where did you send those guards on Preston's ship?" he asked. Allie giggled.

"I dropped them all on one of your floating prison islands here on Sy'hloran."

"You… Jumped two dozen times in ten seconds, from Sy'hloran to Preston's ship?" he asked, staring at her. She shrugged.

"It's getting really easy, now that I sorted out the interference problem."

"Allie? Warn me before I ever get on your bad side, okay?" Allie laughed.

"I just wanted to help. Hey, speaking of helping, Dgehf is in trouble. He's at Ayaran, trying to keep the loyalists from taking control of the wormhole."

"Really?" Dav asked, suddenly very alert. He wanted to help Dgehf as well, she knew. "Smart move, though awfully bold. If they fail they've lost a lot of ground already."

"If they win, they could really win," Allie agreed. Dav nodded.

"So what's the plan?" he asked.

Allie smiled. She loved that his first reaction was the correct assumption that they weren't just going to sit idly by and let it happen. She noticed he was wearing the wristbands Raith had been working on. She hoped he'd finished them, whatever they were for. Chances were, they were going to need all the help they could get once they got out there to Ayaran. Artus and Morgan assumed that Allie would Jump the fleet and just Jump back. Allie had other ideas.

"Artus is talking to General Xan. Once they agree with my plan, I'm going to Jump a fleet to Ayaran." Dav laughed, but the laugh faded when he saw her face remain serious.

"You're kidding."

"Not even a little."

"Okay Allie, you're making me worry about you. Kind of a lot. Next thing I know you'll be Jumping planets."

"I sure hope not. They're where they are for a reason," she said with a grin. He rolled his eyes.

"Seriously Allie, are you sure you can do this? Your Jumping has been… unpredictable lately."

"I sorted it out. Though we may have to take a trip after this is over."

"Do I want to know?"

"Probably not," she said with another smile.

"Well, just let me know what weaponry to bring,

we'll get it done. For now though, we're going to Jump a fleet, then what?"

"I thought we'd find Dgehf and give him a hand."

"He's probably fighting on his ship."

"So we give him a few more gunners. That ship has so many guns there's no way that even he, his wife, his son, and his nephew can operate them all at once. And nobody is a better gunner than Raith."

"Good point," Dav agreed. "Okay, I'll get my stuff. Again. You know, it's ridiculous how many travel packs I lose hanging out with you."

"I'm worth it," she said with a smirk. He shook his head with a grin as he headed for the door.

"Yeah, we'll re-evaluate if you ever make me lose my lucky pocketknife," he said as he walked out. Just before the door closed behind him, she threw in the last word.

"Still worth it!"

# CHAPTER EIGHTEEN

# HIJACKED

General Xan wasn't about to refuse a chance to instantly move a huge squadron of battle cruisers to a critical strategic location at a time when their presence could turn the tide of a battle, especially a battle whose victory could make or break the rest of their war efforts.

He and Artus spoke for less than ten minutes before the plan was made. Artus said he was confident Allie could do it, though he wasn't entirely, and on his word, the general ordered the mobilization of a hundred Sy'hli battle cruisers. There were many in the air already, but the hundred ships he wanted to send were docked and waiting.

They had decided it would be easier for her to Jump them all if they were very close together, and totally unmoving. The docked ships had recently been upgraded as well, and carried the best the Sy'hli had to offer in the realm of weaponry, which was a lot.

Artus knew he couldn't go, however much he might want to. Leaving Sy'hloran now would seem to the remaining Coalition council members that he was abandoning his home world in their time of need. There were disadvantages to being in charge, he thought with annoyance. He really would much rather be out there in the sky, helping in the fight. With Dav as his pilot, they'd be unstoppable.

He'd told Dav he couldn't go either, though. They were sending these ships directly into a battle field. Letting his little brother off to run relatively harmless missions was one thing, letting the boy leap headlong into a war zone was entirely another. To his surprise, Dav hadn't argued the matter, but had simply said he understood and had gone back to his room. He was obviously upset, but had taken it better than Artus had thought he would.

Allie had to go of course, and it was fine if Raith went with her. Raith could keep her safe better than anyone else, besides, he'd told Raith to make Allie bring them straight back after Jumping the Sy'hli ships to Ayaran.

Artus still wished he could go. He was so tired of sitting in council, arguing with stubborn, foolish, and sometimes outright dangerous council members. He was almost glad that many of the Council had shown their colors as Highlord loyalists. It would make things much easier when the Coalition regained control, since none of those individuals would be welcomed back onto the Council.

Artus was sure that this resounding victory, and a hundreds Sy'hli battle cruisers pretty much guaranteed that since nobody else had even a tenth that many ships anywhere near Ayaran, would show the loyalists that pursuing this war was foolish.

He would be there when Allie Jumped though. He wanted to see this. Nobody in history had ever Jumped more than one ship at a time before, and certainly not anything they weren't actually touching.

If Allie could pull this off, it would be the most incredible military ambush of all time. A full hundred Sy'hli battle cruisers was enough to decimate almost any full fleet anywhere in the galaxy, excepting the Tchratchi of course. Either way, this was something Artus had to see.

He would have coms open with the fleet at all times during this fight, so he could keep apprised of the situation as it was happening. He wasn't worried, though. That much firepower appearing out of nowhere might cause the loyalists to surrender on the spot. If they chose to fight, it would be a short fight.

Allie and Raith were already there. She'd probably Jumped there Artus thought, as was Dav. Artus frowned at this, but couldn't blame his brother for wanting to see this. Artus had insisted on seeing it himself, so had no room to criticize. He nodded to his brother against one wall, and looked out over the fleet sitting under the open sky.

It was undeniably impressive. Each ship was big enough for fifty Sy'hli strike troops on extended missions, and one hundred ships, even in two rows, extended further than the human eye could see. Artus could barely see the end himself.

Allie and Raith were standing some distance out from the wall, next to General Xan. He was explaining something to Allie, because she listened attentively and nodded from time to time. Artus smiled and walked toward them. General Xan bowed when he saw the prince approach.

"Your Highness," the general said. Artus gave the man a nod.

"Hello General. You've not wasted any time."

"We don't have it to waste," the general replied. Artus nodded.

"Let's do this, then. We don't know how long our allies have before the enemy wins that skirmish."

"Are you ready, Allie?" the general asked.

She nodded, took Raith's hand, and Jumped into one of the ships near the middle, as had been the plan. She couldn't go along outside of a ship, since they were Jumping straight into space. Artus glanced at Dav.

Dav leaned against the wall, scowling. He definitely was not happy that he couldn't go along. That was how it had to be, though. Allie and Raith wouldn't be fighting either, and were coming right back. Assuming Allie actually managed this at all.

Artus didn't have long to wait. Only moments after Allie and Raith had vanished, the entire fleet shimmered for a split second, then in a blinding flash of light, was gone. Incredible, Artus thought to himself. She made it look so easy.

"That girl is remarkable," General Xan commented.

"I couldn't agree more, General," Artus replied.

"I'm glad she's on our side," the general muttered.

Artus chuckled and clapped the man on the shoulder.

"Come on, we need to get to the command center so we can monitor the situation." He glanced back to the wall. Dav was gone. He'd probably taken off the instant Allie had finished the Jump. Artus sighed. His brother would resent him for this, but at least the boy was safe.

Jumping herself and Raith to the ship had been easy. Pulling Dav from the wall where he'd been standing once she and Raith had landed was a little harder, since she wasn't right next to him when she pulled him from the wall where he'd been leaning several seconds later. She knew this next part might not be nearly as easy as she hoped it would be. She stood on the bridge of the huge Sy'hli battle cruiser, six Sy'hli soldiers at battle stations around the room, with the Captain in the center.

Allie was amazed how fast they'd gotten the crews together and aboard the ships. She actually suspected these men lived on this ship, so it was just a question of getting them onto the bridge. The Captain, a beautiful, solidly-built woman, was watching Allie closely. She seemed unconcerned by Dav or Raith's presence. The gaze made Allie a little uncomfortable, and she held more tightly to her flight suit helmet in her hand.

Her eyes closed again and her mind reached out. She could See the battle, and immediately saw how badly it was going. Less than a dozen Coalition ships were still fighting the loyalists, and debris was everywhere. Dgehf's unusual Maruck craft was still in the fight as well, holding strong against a number of loyalist ships.

Several of the ships were Hgrundewa, which didn't surprise Allie in the least. They seemed to have been Highlord supporters from the beginning. Thirty loyalist ships were slowly wearing through the Coalition trying to protect the ring supporting the wormhole.

Allie mentally locked their position behind and above the loyalist forces, giving them a surprise attack from the rear, without putting the Coalition forces in the line of fire. Now came the hard part. Her mind in the Sy'hli cruiser stretched out, her Sight now in three places at once. Ayaran, the dock yard as a whole, and her own self-awareness. When touching her companions for a Jump, she didn't have to think hard about bringing them. This was different.

Mentally, she wove a web around the ships, connecting each not physically, but by the energies she was drawing in from around her like a massive vortex. She and Dav had practiced this a few times before coming down, but only on him. She had yet to try it with more than one subject, and definitely not this many at once, let alone subjects this big.

It took her several moments to accomplish, but it felt like hours, each additional ship taking more and more of her focus and energy. There. She had it, she knew. All tied together by the energies, Allie had linked a hundred Sy'hli battle cruisers, and had locked them to a place hundreds of light years away. Now to make the Jump. Pushing hard on the energies, her focus taxed to its capacity, her energy control at its limits, she Jumped.

She felt the resistance of moving so much mass, and

knew her words to her mother were wrong. The amount of matter she was traveling with did make a difference. A big difference. Her mind and body felt stretched to their breaking point, the slowing of time and feeling of touching the Between telling her this wasn't as smooth as her last several Jumps had been.

The moment their physical being was no longer of Sy'hloran, before they could appear at Ayaran, while no physical time had passed, Allie felt the watcher. The entity pounced on her weakened state like a cat on a wounded mouse. It seized control of her Jump, changing her destination to something completely outside her understanding.

No, she thought! A hundred Sy'hli ships, each carrying fifty men, all being thrown to some unknown destination, leaving her friend Dgehf and his family to die losing a battle that could cause the Coalition to lose the war before it began? She would not allow it!

Wrestling for control, she pulled hard against the watcher. The watcher seemed surprised when she was able to tear the destination away again and began pushing it back to the space above Ayaran. The force the watcher brought to bear against her will was tremendous. She nearly buckled under the pressure.

Allie would lose this time, and she knew it. The watcher had control of the Jump. She couldn't allow this to happen. Changing tactics, she focused instead on her net of energy. The Jump was connected directly to her as the focal point, the others being towed along by her woven net of energy. In a place between space, outside of time, she began to unravel her net. Not the entire net, just the parts connecting it to her.

She had only one chance at this, and didn't even know if it would work. With a snap, she disconnected herself from the web of energy tying the ships, and her friends to her, flinging the ends of the energy back to her original destination above Ayaran.

As she herself was yanked backwards, suddenly free of the extra weight and pulled violently in the direction the watcher had chosen, she watched as one hundred Sy'hli battle cruisers, one containing two of her dearest friends in the world, vanished back into the physical world.

# CHAPTER NINETEEN

# LOST BETWEEN

Allie wasn't sure where she was. Her sense of direction was going crazy, her equilibrium was in chaos. Images, light, sound, and color all flashed past in rapid succession. She felt like she was going to be ill.

She didn't know how long it took to regain her focus, but it felt like an eternity. When she finally managed to stabilize her mind a little, she realized she was drifting. Literally drifting, as if floating in the air. Only there didn't feel like there was air. This caused her to gasp for a few seconds, until she realized that whether she had air or not didn't seem to matter.

Allie tried to look around, but had trouble making sense of her surroundings. There was nothing, all around. No light, no objects, no air, nothing. At the same time, other images and sounds seemed to be struggling to break into the place. She saw a desert, with creatures she didn't recognize in one place, then what might have been the inside of a nebula in another. A person spoke in a language she didn't recognize behind her. Looking back, there was again, nothing.

Voices and sounds seemed to come and go all around, images coming and going as well, all overlaying atop the pure, unbroken emptiness all around. She wasn't even convinced she was really seeing or hearing any of these things, that they weren't just flitting into and out of her mind.

"Help!" Allie called. Her voice sounded odd here, flat. Like it had no life to it. For a moment, she panicked, thinking she had died.

"You are not dead," came a voice.

This voice sounded firmly present, but like her, flat and dead. She turned to look. Allie wasn't sure at all how she turned, since she wasn't actually standing on anything, but the moment she thought about turning, she turned.

Before her stood a man. Sort of. He floated, like she did, but didn't flicker in and out of existence like all the other images and sounds around her. He was very tall, at least twice her height. He was also incredibly slender. He didn't look frail though, his muscles tight and corded. The skin-tight, full sleeve gray shirt he wore showed off the muscles, and accented the fact that they were attached in a strange fashion.

Allie couldn't quite explain it, but it seemed like someone had detached all of his muscles, and then reattached them in just slightly the wrong places. It made all the curves on his body look strange. His face was strange as well. It was humanoid, almost human, but similar to his muscles, everything just seemed a fraction off. A quick, casual glance might even mistake him for completely human, but any closer inspection revealed he wasn't… quite. Even his long, golden hair really looked like actual gold.

"Who are you?"

"I am Ei."

"That doesn't tell me anything."

"You ask the wrong questions," said Ei.

"What should I ask?"

"Oh, any number of things. Why am I here? Where is here? What do you want with me? What are you? Asking 'who' is simply asking me to identify myself, which without proper frame of reference, tells you nothing."

"What do you want with me?"

"Better," smiled Ei. Something about his eyes seemed wrong as well, Allie thought. They were deep, and intense, but also slightly vacant, like he wasn't entirely present. "I want you to help me."

"Are you the one who brought me here?"

"I am."

"I told you I would come help."

"Yes, you said when you were finished helping your friends. You finished, so I brought you."

"I did not finish!" Allie protested. "I was just sending help to more of my friends when you hijacked me! Where is this place?"

"This is nowhere," he replied.

"Everywhere is somewhere," Allie replied.

"You would think so, wouldn't you?" Ei replied, his

smile amused.

"If we're nowhere, what is all of this?" she asked, gesturing to the images and sounds flashing by all around in a dizzying, dreamlike progression.

"All of that is somewhere," Ei replied.

"Why can I see somewhere, but am nowhere?"

"You can actually see everywhere, if you learn to control your thoughts. But you cannot reach anywhere. What you see and hear is created by your mind as it struggles to separate from your plane of existence."

"Send me back."

"I cannot. There is no going back from here. This is the place between realities. Dimensions, if you will. Right now, you are between length and height, between depth and time, between here and there."

"This is the Between?"

"Yes," replied Ei.

"Is this where I Jump through?"

"Jump?" Ei asked, his head tilting curiously.

"Yeah, when I go from one place to another instantly."

"Jump," Ei said, sounding it out. "A charming term, though vastly inadequate."

"Whatever, is this where I travel through?"

"Yes, and no," Ei replied, "this is beyond that. This is nowhere. In this realm, you are truly between. When you… Jump… you only touch nowhere briefly, you do not come here."

"Why can't I leave?"

"You can travel from one place to another. You cannot travel from nowhere to somewhere."

Allie grit her teeth. This being was infuriating.

"What do you want with me?"

"Ah, but I have told you. I need your help."

"Why me?"

"Because you can," he replied. Well that was a simple enough answer.

"If I help you, will you send me back?" Ei sighed at this.

"I told you, you cannot go from nowhere to somewhere."

"What do you want me to help you with?"

"This place is between realities. I want you to help me move to the next reality."

"Are you from my reality?"

"Yes, but from a very long time ago, by your counting."

"Isn't going from here to the next reality going from nowhere to somewhere?"

"No, it is going from nowhere to everywhere."

"That doesn't make sense."

"Only because you do not understand."

"That's what I said," Allie said, frustrated.

"Yes," replied Ei.

"How did you get here?"

"The same way you did. I… 'Jumped'."

"You're a Starjumper?"

"In a sense. I am more. I am what you might think of as a progenitor. A source, or origin, if you will. You can Jump, because my people created you to be able to Jump." Allie noticed Ei was becoming more comfortable using the word Jump to reference traveling the way she did.

"Ghier on Ayaran told me that there was a race, a long time ago, that seeded the planets, hybridizing their genetics with the local creatures. Is that you?" Ei smiled at this.

"I am surprised anyone remembers."

"Ghier knows about it. You can't be though, he says that was tens of thousands of years ago."

"It was. Time does not exist here."

"We're having a conversation, that's taking time," she argued. He considered this before answering.

"It is difficult to explain, but no, this is not taking time. It is also taking eons. Here, time is not linear. It doesn't flow, as you think of it. Like length, depth, and width, time here is… an idea, rather than a reality."

"Why did you create the other races?" Allie asked.

"Because ours was dying. We had begun to damage space. We created the other races, not all of them were our creations, mind you, just many, to try and one day create you."

"Wait, what? Why me?"

"Because only you can help me."

"What's so special about me?"

"Among thousands of races, we created three lines. One line, where most races came from, carried none of the gene to allow them to travel between space. Another line could travel through space, but in a limited fashion. Those are your… 'Starjumpers'. They needed a key to help them travel in such a way, and so we created crystal keys to help them. The third line was special. They themselves were keys. In their line was the secret to unlocking the full potential of my people's genetics. In them was the key to creating you. One of your parents could Jump?"

"Yes, my mother."

"Then it was your father who was of this other line. It is through the combination of the two lines, tens of thousands of years to occur, that created you."

"So again, what's so special about me?" Allie asked, fascinated despite herself.

"You, Allie Bennett, exist outside of space. Entirely. You manifest within it, but your essence, your nature, is here, in the Between as you call it."

"What does that mean?"

"It means not only do you not require a key to travel, but you do not require space at all. You, and only you, have the ability to help me complete my journey. I alone among my people, survived the trip here. I alone exist. And you alone can bring me the rest of the way."

"I can't bring anyone anywhere. There's no energy here to Jump with."

"There is, but the energy here is different. It's the energy from the other side of your reality, the underside, if you will."

"I'll help you, if you help me."

"And what would you like help with?"

"The same as you. I want to leave this place. Only I want to go back to my friends."

"I told you, you can't." The constant shift of images and sounds was beyond annoying, it was going to drive her crazy if she watched much more of it. No wonder Ei was a little cracked.

"I don't believe you. If you can leave here traveling one way, I can leave traveling the other."

"You don't seem to understand," he said. "Time doesn't exist here. This state of Between touches everywhere and nowhere. Even if you could break the barrier, you would end up randomly anywhere, anywhen."

"I can Jump from anywhere in the galaxy to where I need to go," she argued.

"So narrow minded," Ei muttered. "Listen closely. Take a moment and think about this. There are more stars in your galaxy than grains of sand on every beach on your planet. There are more galaxies in your universe than there are stars in your galaxy. And there are more universes in your plane of reality than there are galaxies in your universe. Do you even begin to comprehend how big that is? No, I see that you don't. My people, in millions of years, only explored two universes before we discovered our method of travel was damaging space and we began searching for ways to move beyond space. You could end up anywhere. Not just your galaxy. Not even just your universe. Anywhere in your plane of reality. You could even wind up in the place between universes, and what would you do then? And that's not even mentioning the anywhen part of the equation. Care to appear during the origin of the universe? Or the end? Or in any of the nearly infinite time in between? The barrier cannot be broken, and even if you could, your friends would have been dead for eons, or wouldn't yet be born for eons, even assuming you survived wherever you landed for more than an instant."

"You sure are negative," Allie said. Ei took a deep, steadying breath. She was glad to see she was as frustrating for him as he was for her. "I can't help you, I have no idea how to get you to the Beyond you're talking about. I have to get back to my friends," Allie said, turning away.

"You will help!" Ei shouted.

"If I refuse?" she asked, turning back.

"I have time to wait," he said with a wicked grin. She understood what he meant. If time meant nothing here, he would simply wait. He would wait an eternity, if need be, until she gave up and helped him.

"I wouldn't even know where to start," she argued.

"Reach your mind out and explore. The energy is here, just different." Out of sheer curiosity, she reached her thoughts out. She couldn't feel anything.

"There's nothing here."

"Deeper," Ei said. Allie sighed, but pushed deeper. She still felt nothing. Ei was crazy, she decided. He probably didn't even exist. This was a bad dream she'd fallen into while lying unconscious after trying to Jump too much at once. A fraction of a second before she opened her eyes, she felt it.

The energies here were very different. What she was used to felt and moved like water in her mind. These energies felt like earth, and they didn't move. At all. She ran her mind over it, but couldn't find anything to manipulate.

"This is really weird. I can't move these energies. They don't seem to move at all."

"You can't move them, you can only ask them to

move to you."

"You're a Jumper like me, why can't you do this?"

"There was something missing in our gift. Something we couldn't figure out how to create, but something we knew would occur naturally eventually in the joining of the two lines. We just needed enough random genetics in the third line to eventually come together as it blended with the other two lines."

"You can't feel this?"

"No," he said.

"How did you know it was here, and how to work with it?"

"Our science is sound. You found it, didn't you?"

"Yeah," she had to admit he had a point. Interesting though that he'd waited an eternity for her to come along, based purely on a scientific theory that there was even an energy here to be manipulated. Couldn't fault the guy for his faith in science. And he was right, there was an energy here. Might as well try it his way.

Allie focused on the energy, and pulled her mind slightly back from it. Her thoughts made the space she'd left inviting, hoping to lure the energy out. Ei made it sound like the energy was alive. Maybe it was. Maybe the energy she Jumped with was, too. Nothing happened. Rather than talk to Ei, which irritated her, she instead pulled her thoughts all the way back in, opening herself up.

Almost instantly, the energy seemed to shift and flow, not like a liquid, but like an earthquake. A huge, spiraling pillar of it rose up and filled her body. For a brief moment, she felt like she and the energy were the same, a solid mass of something that wasn't quite space.

Like with her Jumping, she could suddenly See, but what she could See was not anything her mind was equipped to process. It was madness, different from anything that existed in her entire galaxy, universe, or realm of existence. This was Beyond. This was where he wanted to go.

"Good, good!" Ei shouted distantly.

All she had to do was grab him with the energy and basically Jump through with him. She knew instantly upon seeing that place Beyond that neither of them would survive for even the tiniest nanosecond in that reality. It simply wasn't built for anything from their dimension. She was about to release the energy and tell him that, when he grabbed her arms in an iron grip. She felt his own energies lash around hers, using hers to manipulate the energy around them. She felt him start the Jump to the Beyond.

"No!" she shouted. "We can't go there! It will kill us both!"

"It is the ultimate transcendence!" shouted Ei.

She felt him grab the destination, something that passed for a world in the Beyond. Its very nature began burning in her mind. Death would be instantaneous, and she knew it. Matter was different there. Energy was different. They were made of the wrong kind of both. His energy was so strong, she couldn't push it away. He had her, he had the energy of the Between, he had the destination Beyond. Her mind could not beat his. So she tried a different tactic.

Allie slammed a fist up into Ei's jaw. Despite his

argument that nothing was physical Between, she connected solidly. Her punch was weak, inexperienced, but the strike rings Raith had built in to the gloves worked their magic, and the explosion of energy that came from her hands blasted Ei back, forcing him to let go of her. She almost dropped her helmet from her other hand. His energy still held hers firmly, but she had a fraction of a second where he was distracted. She shoved his mind out of hers. He pulled the energy with him.

"Ei, stop!" she shouted over the vortex of power now circling them ominously.

"At last, I can transcend reality! My people's dream embodied in me!" he shouted. And then he Jumped.

The energies around them exploded with violence, wrenching, stretching, and twisting her body beyond physical possibility. At the apex of the explosion, Allie felt it. The energy of her home dimension. As she began to descend fully into the Between once more, she grabbed it and clung to it like a lifeline.

She didn't release the energies of the Between either, looking for a brief moment back at Ei. In one tragically glorious moment, a millennia-old progenitor of her species reached his heart's desire, and he moved Beyond, vanishing from her Sight. The energies of both places began to pull away, threatening to tear her in two.

Her Sight reached out along the energy she knew, the energy she controlled, and scanned the dimension. An infinite number of places and times were all around her, all at once. Flickers of others moving Between suddenly were everywhere, brushing past her as they moved instantly from one place to another. Most passed by without noticing, but not all. One reached out for her, physically and mentally.

A hand, with three long white fingers and a slender white thumb clamped onto her arm. She turned her face toward her attacker and screamed. The further from her arm the body went, the more translucent it was, as though only contact with her kept it here at all.

The face staring at hers was a shock. The long hair was completely white and straight, skin pale as ivory, with large eyes such a pale blue that they were nearly white as well. It wasn't an unkind face, but one in the throes of panic. Allie could relate.

She felt the energies pouring from the man clinging to her. The instant she touched his energies, some of his frantic thoughts reached hers. He was lost Between as well, though not all the way. He was Jumping for the first time, and didn't know how to set a destination. He didn't even know he could set a destination, or that he was traveling at all. Who he was, where he was, when he was, she didn't have any idea, she only knew that he thought he had died and his soul was lost in the spirit world. She tried to speak as the storm of energies threatened to tear them both apart.

"Focus," she said softly, voice more thought than sound.

His ghostly eyes locked with hers, pleading, and she followed his sharpening thought, tying his destination for him. With that, she shoved him away. He would land where he wanted to go. It had taken too much time, she knew. She was losing her grip on both energies. Allie had no idea what would happen then, but couldn't afford to find out.

Her own mind sharpened with laser focus on the one thing her mind, body, and soul felt tied to. Dav. As her thoughts of him clarified, she found that she could See him. He was shaky, his image bouncing back and forth erratically as if his place in space, or hers relative to him, wasn't fixed. It was enough. There was no more time. She focused on him, pulled on her helmet, and Jumped.

# CHAPTER TWENTY

# SABOTAGE

Dav felt the tearing sensation as space itself seemed to rip around him. He barely kept his scream in as the hundred ships Allie Jumped seemed to lurch in mid-Jump. He had no idea what happened, but as quickly as it started, it was over. He stood on the bridge of the Sy'hli battle cruiser, Raith beside him. But Allie was gone. Tic was on the ground, shrieking her concern as well, spinning about as she looked for Allie.

"Allie!" Dav shouted, quickly scanning the room. Raith looked where Allie was on Dav's other side as well, and quickly scanned the room himself.

"She didn't land with us!" Dav shouted.

"That's not possible," Raith replied.

"Then where is she?" Dav demanded.

"Incoming," the Captain said calmly. The ship jarred as a plasma cannon struck it. The loyalists hadn't wasted time in turning on the new arrivals in panic. A quick look at the scanner station's display over the shoulder of its operator told him that the Sy'hli outnumbered the loyalists by three to one. This would be a short battle.

"Fire at will," said the captain. "Offensive maneuvers, bring us in line with one-four and five-nine"

"Roger," came the replies from the gunner stations and the navigation station. Without warning, Sy'hli ships on the scanner began exploding.

"Captain!" shouted the man at the scanner station.

"What in the stars is going on?" she shouted, leaping to her feet and charging the poor man at the station. An explosion rocked the ship.

"Damage control!" the captain shouted, barely keeping her feet. The door to the bridge opened, and a figure walked in, calmly, casually. Dav saw the figure and his blood ran cold. C.A.D.E.-16. Tic hissed.

Cade raised his hand, weapons springing from his forearm and locking into position. He saw Dav, looked momentarily confused, and hesitated. Raith didn't. Cade was blasted backward as Raith opened fire with both enhanced shatter guns. He dove forward and touched the control panel, closing and sealing the door. Another explosion rocked the ship.

Dav glanced at the scanner station and saw that the Sy'hli battle cruisers were literally falling out of the sky, random explosions shaking them apart. The alarmingly close Ayaran's gravitational force pulling the damaged ships straight toward its surface. There would be many minutes of falling before they entered atmosphere, but none of the ships seemed able to recover.

No enemies had even fired at them, Dav saw. How

Cade had gotten onto this ship and what was going on with his and the other ships, he had no idea.

Raith grabbed Dav's arm and shoved him toward the rear bulkhead panel. Tearing the panel free like it was made of paper, Raith pushed Dav inside. Dav listened to the captain shouting commands behind as another explosion rocked the ship. This one was the bridge door being blasted off as Cade came back.

Tic shrieked and turned to leap at Cade.

"Tic!" Dav shouted.

"Go!" Raith yelled, giving Dav another shove. He followed Raith's instructions and raced in a bear-crawl down the low, narrow passage, listening to the sounds of all manner of weapons going off and Tic shrieking in her tiny, but effective, rage.

"Right!" Raith shouted. Dav turned at the intersection. Another right, a left, and a long drop down a vertical passage and Raith turned, kicking open another panel. They were in the small docking bay that housed the escape pods.

"Not again," Dav groaned.

"Move!" Raith shouted.

The sound of someone rapidly pounding along the service tunnels they had just come from urged Dav into action. He opened an escape pod door and turned in time for Raith to hit him with Dav's bag that Raith had apparently grabbed before shoving Dav into the bulkhead tunnel.

Raith came right behind in a flying tackle. The pair hit the ground inside the escape pod as a blast tore over their heads, smashing into one of the pod's control panels. Raith grabbed a control bar, reaching up from the ground, and the pod door slammed shut.

"Tic!" Dav yelled again. He didn't see the jicund anywhere.

The pod shook with another impact, but the engines fired and the pod blasted out into space. Dav scrambled to his feet, and looked out the narrow pod window. Their ship was right overhead, drifting down toward the planet, where Dav realized they were currently rocketing toward.

"Wow. I have to admit, that's determination," Raith said quietly, pointing. Dav followed his gaze. C.A.D.E.-16 was soaring through space, directly at them. He had literally jumped at them from the escape bay door.

"Can't we catch a break? Well, he can't steer out there, let's change course so he'll miss us."

"No breaks there, either," replied Raith, pointing at the smoking, sparking control panel Cade had blasted.

"Come on!" Dav shouted in anger.

"Here," Raith said, pulling Dav's helmet out of the bag.

He pulled it on, and looked back out the window. Smart move, Dav thought. Cade was going to tear his way in here, and the sudden cold vacuum of space would kill Dav almost instantly. Not that it would help much. If Cade caught them, they were dead anyway.

The pair watched as Cade drew closer, the force of his jump exceeding the force of the tiny engines in the emergency pod. Closer he came, almost painfully slowly. He would hit in less than ten seconds, Dav thought, trying to figure out his attack plan when Cade reached them. There was no need.

From the side, a huge plasma blast tore across their view, slamming straight into the falling Cade. Ablaze, C.A.D.E.-16 was hurled sideways out of control. Dav and Raith both watched him fall, then in unison turned their heads in the direction of the source of the shot. Dgehf's distinct, huge Maruck craft screamed past.

"I love that guy," Dav said, watching the craft. Raith laughed.

Leaning back, Dav caught a look at the scanner display of the small pod. Another tiny figure was also falling toward the planet. He moved over and touched the control bar, zooming the view in on that figure.

"Allie," Dav whispered. She was just above the atmosphere, falling steadily. In seconds she'd be in atmosphere falling straight to the planet's surface. "Raith, it's Allie!"

"Where?" Raith asked, moving over to look. "How did she…?"

"I don't know, but we have to help her!" Dav snapped.

Raith looked at the damaged control panel, then back to Dav, expression one of helplessness. Dav thought frantically. Suddenly, he looked down at his wrists. Raith's new wristbands were clamped firmly around his wrists. Raith had said they were ready for a test. He looked back up to Raith. His friend shrugged with his most mischievous smile.

"Why not?" Raith asked.

Turning, Raith kicked the hatch of the escape pod, tearing it free and sending it spinning off into space. The air in the pod burst outward with the sudden release of pressure. Dav held tight to the chair to keep from getting blown out. Raith had braced himself on the doorway and had no trouble.

Raith grabbed one side of the hatch frame with both hands and pulled his legs in tight. Dav realized what he was doing and slipped out the other side. Bracing his feet on Raith's, one hand holding the pod for stability, he crouched low as if standing on the soles of Raith's feet. Lining himself up toward Allie's still-falling form, he set his angle. With a nod, he and Raith both moved.

In one synchronized explosive action. Raith and Dav both uncoiled as if jumping as high and hard as they could. Raith's arms braced on the escape pod, all of their combined force went straight into Dav's bullet-like launch into space on an intercept course with Allie. If Dav's calculations had been wrong, he'd miss her. He'd have a little bit of maneuverability once in atmosphere, but not much.

He was gaining on her, and fast, but it was still a long, slow wait as Dav's heart pounded in his ears. Closer, just a little closer, he thought. Allie, facing down toward the planet, hit the outer atmosphere. Both the sound and feeling of the impact would likely have killed her without the specialized, armored flight suit. Even protected, the jolt must have awakened her. The moment she hit atmosphere, she suddenly jerked as if startled. Then Dav heard her scream through the helmet com. He had completely forgotten about the communication device in their helmets.

"Allie!" he shouted. She flailed wildly in complete

panic.

It was still a long way to catch her, Dav knew as he estimated the distance still between them. At least her wild positioning would slow her down. Dav had legs straight, toes pointed, and arms flat to his side, dropping like an arrow. A few seconds later, he hit atmosphere.

The impact was definitely jarring. He'd never done this outside a ship before. As terrifying and desperate as this situation, Dav actually decided he wanted to try this again sometime. The feel of the enormous friction on his body, building as he fell, even through the flight suit was intense.

Allie's flailing was sending her spinning through the air, and changing her trajectory slightly.

"Allie! Go flat, like you're spread out face down on a bed. Relax your legs!" Allie paused, recognized his voice and her flailing stopped. She tried to maneuver into the position he had instructed. She couldn't do it, and instead ended up on her back, unable to right herself. She saw Dav, closing fast.

"Dav!" she screamed.

"I've got you," he said confidently into the com.

He shifted position to change his angle slightly, and lined up better over her. Tucking in tight again, he dropped, straight toward her. She held her arms out, and at the last moment, Dav whipped his arms out and around her. The movement sent them both spinning through the air, but she clung to him for dear life.

"On my back!" he called into the com. He tried to move her around, but she wouldn't let go enough to move. "Allie, you have to relax your grip and move around onto my back!"

"I can't!" she shouted back.

"Allie, you can do this! Look at what you've already been through! A little relaxing is easy!" He laughed, to help her relax and show he wasn't afraid, though he was.

They were approaching the ground far too fast. The heat from the friction of their freefall was intense, and he was starting to feel it even through the suit. If he didn't get her into position soon, they would hit the ground, hard. Or rather, he corrected himself as he looked down, hit a large lake. At this velocity it wouldn't make much difference. Even in the suits, they'd be killed on impact.

He could feel her take a deep breath. She was the toughest person he knew, and he made a note to tell her that later. He didn't know anyone else who could come from her background, go through what she had, and still walk out of it in control of herself like this. Like he did, she just needed the reminder now and then that she could do it. She relaxed slightly, enough for him to guide her around to his back. She put her legs around his waist and arms around his neck.

"Raith," Dav muttered to himself, "If this thing doesn't work, I'm going to kill you." Here goes nothing, he thought.

In the movement Raith taught him, he swung both arms in a tight circle from his sides out in front of him. From the sides of the wristbands, a mechanism snapped out, swinging into his waiting, open hands. Attached to the wristbands, the two hinged control bars aligned with his grip perfectly. The instant he had hold of the bars, he sent the device the thought to activate.

For a moment, nothing happened. Dav sucked in a sharp breath, preparing for the impact seconds away. Then he felt the thrum of power from the microcells in the wristbands. From the outside of the control bars, beams of white energy shot out, curving and bending in around them.

In less than a second, the energy beams had connected in place, energy fields springing up between them. An energy field construction beyond anything any world had ever built, Dav knew. A fully functional, one-person holographic jet. The panels were invisible, the skimmer visible only along the angles and planes of the white energy lines holding it all together. Dav wished he knew how it looked, but it felt amazing. How Raith had built the propulsion system Dav had no clue, and right now didn't care in the least.

He mentally pulled up on the control bars, and a fraction of a second before hitting the water, the little holoskimmer banked sharply enough to make Dav feel sick from the g-forces, tail missing the water by inches. The thrusters roared, sending them tearing along inches above the surface of the lake fast enough that they kicked up a twenty foot plume of water in their wake.

Dav let out a yell of pure joy and exhilaration. He was vaguely aware of Allie screaming and her grip turning to one that would leave her sore for days afterward. At that moment, the pilot in him took over and he pushed the sleek energy craft to its limits. They left the lake and raced onto the fields beyond. He gained altitude until they were several hundred feet above the surface, just skimming the treetops of the jungle they now crossed.

The energy fields that formed the skimmer supported him leaning forward, like on a racing motorcycle, but was surprisingly comfortable. He could see every detail of the trees a few feet below them through the invisible panels of the holoskimmer. Or he could have if he weren't going so fast that even to his eyes they were one big, green blur.

"Dav! Dav!" Allie was shouting. He came back to the present enough to realize she'd been shouting his name for a while now.

"What?" he called into the com.

"Why are you always there to catch me when I fall?" she asked softly. He smiled.

"The same reason you're always there to catch me. That's what friends are for." That wasn't why he was always there, and he knew it. She didn't though, and it was better that she didn't. She was quiet for a moment.

"Dav?" she asked again.

"Yeah?"

"This is great and all, but can we slow down and land? I'm going to be sick."

Dav laughed, and banked, looking for a good place to set down. An arc-rifle blast nearly took the holoskimmer's nose off. Raith had warned him this little jet would handle someone his size for about ten minutes and decent speeds before the microcells shut down to recharge for an hour, but one hit from an arc cannon would dissipate the craft instantly. And Dav was carrying more than just himself. He probably only had a couple of minutes of power right now even if they didn't get hit with an arc cannon.

Dav banked sharply to avoid a second blast as a Coalition cruiser raced past. He looked where the cruiser was heading and saw hundreds of ships, most Coalition, moving toward where a number of Sy'hli battle cruisers had just crashed. Dgehf's ship was visible as well, cruising down to try and defend the Sy'hli ships.

Dav couldn't believe Dgehf was still alive, considering the sudden loss of all of those Sy'hli cruisers. He didn't see any other loyalist craft. Dgehf was probably the only allied ship left in the air, and from the smoke trailing from it, that wouldn't be for much longer.

Dgehf's ship's guns were blazing like machine guns, flash after flash in rapid succession as they tore into the Coalition ships. Dav banked again as the small holographic readout on the front windshield told him another craft was coming in behind. Dav recognized it. Sandro.

No time for that, Dav thought as he saw Raith's escape pod come down to the left, several miles away. Better go join up with Raith, then they could go help Dgehf and his family get away from the masses of Coalition gathering. Sandro's ship banked and headed toward them.

Oh great, Dav thought to himself. That figures. Sandro's ship opened fire. He banked and rolled, Allie yelping and clinging tighter, face buried in his back. Several blasts were close enough that Dav felt a slight electric tingle as the arc cannon blasts ripped through the air just outside the holoskimmer.

Another few seconds and he'd reach Raith. He

couldn't see Raith, or his escape pod, through the thick jungle, but he could see the cloud of smoke. Raith would be fine, Dav assured himself. And once inside that jungle, Sandro couldn't easily fire at them, or spot them. He and Raith could make good time and get far away before Sandro could land and come after them.

Slowing slightly as he neared, he rolled over and around a few more arc blasts. And then the power on the holoskimmer gave out. Dav took a turn to yelp as he found himself with Allie suddenly moving through the air above the treetops without a craft.

Dav pulled Allie's arms off him and spun in her grip, wrapping his own arms tight around her as they dropped fast into the trees. He angled himself so that his back and head would hit anything they collided with, desperately trying to protect Allie.

They hit the treetops, Dav's body slamming into several and snapping them free. Branches and leaves whipped him fiercely as they fell, ripping through the foliage. Before they could lose much forward momentum, Dav's back and helmet slammed hard directly into a tall tree, Allie's body slamming hard into his chest. Even through the suit, Dav breath was forced out of his lungs in a rush, and he swore he felt something crack in his head. He didn't even remember hitting the ground.

# CHAPTER TWENTY ONE

# BETRAYAL

Allie woke slowly. One of these days, she'd make it a whole day without getting knocked unconscious, she mentally grumbled to herself. She looked around, and recognized her surroundings. Once again, she was in the jungles of Ayaran. Almost by reflex, she reached up to stroke Tic, more for her own comfort than anything else, but her little purple friend wasn't there.

She remembered now, Tic was aboard the Sy'hli battle cruiser with… Dav! The memory of her rescue by Dav and then falling through the trees snapped sharply back into her mind. Looking around, she spotted first Raith, leaning over her.

"Allie?" Raith asked, watching her closely. He had taken her helmet off, and he was holding a dermal regenerator and another device she didn't recognize.

"Yeah, I'm okay," she assured him, though she wasn't entirely sure of that. She felt sore, though not broken as far as she could tell. "Where's Dav?" she asked. Raith gestured, and Allie followed the movement to where Dav lay. He was still out, unmoving.

"Is he okay?" Allie asked. Raith hesitated, but nodded.

"Yeah, he'll be all right. He hit really hard though. I warned him about pushing that skimmer to top speed until we were sure of its microcell battery lifespan. Lucky it was the both of you. With only his weight to carry he'd have been going twice that fast. The impact probably would have killed him."

"You built that crazy piece of machinery?" Allie asked, though she already knew he had. Raith shrugged.

"For emergencies. Not much good for long travel, though honestly I think it's faster than I thought it would be. He could cover a lot of miles in a very short time, wait an hour for the recharge, then go again. Even if he just sat around for that hour, his average speed would be pretty good. Not as fast as if in a ship the whole time, but a whole lot faster than walking. I'm going to have to see if I can improve the battery cells and install an audible battery warning. There's a battery life indicator on the holographic display, but he must have missed it while he was busy dodging arc cannon fire."

Allie just stared at him. Raith paused and looked at her.

"What?" he asked. She shook her head.

"It's official," she said with a sigh. "All boys are completely insane." Raith gave her a cheeky grin.

"Took you long enough to figure that out," he said with a wink.

"Raith, if you two are down here, where's Tic?" she asked. Raith's expression dropped and Allie's heart went with it.

"The Sy'hli ships were sabotaged."

"What happened?" she asked, fear and a sick feeling in the pit of her stomach grew.

"We appeared right where we were supposed to after you Jumped us. I'll ask where you went in a moment. The Sy'hli ships' engines started exploding. None of the ships went up completely, but they were all, one by one, immobilized. With no engines, they fell. All of them."

"You two made it," she pointed out. "Where's Tic?"

"Right after the explosions started, Cade showed up," Raith explained. Allie felt her face go white. "He must have been the one to sabotage the ships. Anyway, I shot him and closed the door. He blew it open while Dav and I went for the maintenance tunnels to escape. Tic went after Cade. Cade caught up with us in the escape pod bay. I didn't see Tic."

"We have to find the ship," Allie said firmly. Raith nodded.

"Agreed. If Tic is okay though, she's probably already out in the jungle."

"Where's Dgehf?"

"Still fighting, last I saw. The only one of our guys still in the air. That was several minutes ago, though. He shot Cade out of the air, so that's something. Someone else showed up too, a huge, vicious-looking black ship. It's helping Dgehf, but I don't have any idea who it is. Sandro is flying around somewhere though. We need to get moving."

"What about Dav?"

"I can carry him," Raith said. Allie nodded and Raith helped her stand. He watched her closely, but she nodded to him that she was okay. He turned to Dav.

"No need," Dav said, sitting up slowly. Raith stepped over and helped him up.

"Dav!" Allie cried. As Dav turned to look at her, she could see that something was wrong. "What?" she asked at his dark expression.

Pain burst through the back of her neck. It felt like a flaming poker had been pressed against her skin. She screamed and jumped forward away from the source of the pain. Turning, she stared straight into the eyes of Preston. He wore a light suit of body armor, and held a strange device in one hand. A vicious grin was on his face. Allie pulled her hand back from her neck, which still burned. There was no blood.

"What did you do to me?" she demanded, angry. How had Preston even gotten here? Last she saw him, he was being escorted to the prison on Sy'hloran. He sure hadn't Jumped. She was the only one who could do that.

"Just a little injection. A rogellium cocktail we've been working on. Hurts, doesn't it?" the weasely man said with a sneer. She felt sick. Sicker than she already did from the virus, anyway. Reaching for the energies, nausea slammed into her gut so hard that she immediately curled over and vomited. Preston laughed.

Allie turned to look at her friends. Raith already had a gun out and leveled at Preston, watching Allie to see how she wanted to handle this.

"Raith!" she screamed, but it was too late. The stone Dav had picked up was the size of his own head, and he slammed it against the side of Raith's head hard enough that the solid stone shattered. Raith dropped, unmoving. Staring in complete shock at Dav, his eyes met hers and she knew. Those were not Dav's eyes.

"No…" she whispered. Preston laughed again, moving around to Dav's side, picking up Raith's gun and pointing it at her.

"Sorry, my little Starjumper," Dav, the Highlord, sneered. How such a beautiful face could suddenly be so ugly, Allie had no idea. Never had she seen more purely that beauty came from within as now, when she saw the evil infesting Dav through his eyes. She reached for the energies to push the infection out of him like she had with Tyren, and was overcome with another wave of nausea.

"Did I forget to mention? An injection of my rogellium cocktail will make you unable to Jump. Maybe forever," Preston said. "This is the first field trial." The Highlord's smile was every bit as predatory as it had been in Tyren's face.

"Now you have no help," the Highlord laughed. "Your Sy'hli friends have been blown out of the sky, your android has been decommissioned, Artus, Imber, and your mother are back on Sy'hloran all getting sicker by the moment, even your traitor Maruck friend has been shot down. And best of all, your boyfriend here now belongs to me. I have the Maruck, now the Sy'hli, Sandro, and Cade, both of whom are heading this way as we speak. And Preston, of course. He's proven quite useful."

Preston preened at the praise like a fat cat.

Allie looked back over her shoulder. If she could make it to the thick foliage a few feet away, she'd have a chance. Looking back to Preston and the Highlord, she knew there was no chance. Preston had the gun ready and trained on her, and in Dav's body, Allie wouldn't even make it those few feet before the Highlord caught her.

"Thank you, by the way, for knocking Dav out. I was taking control slowly, but that little happy accident gave me the chance I needed to lock his mind away for good. I won't make the same mistake I did with his brother."

"You won't succeed," she told him. He laughed.

"I already have. I could surrender to you right now, and within a few months the entire galaxy would be dead anyway. The infection is spreading on ships and wormholes faster than light itself through the galaxy. Now that we're here, the Dawn Virus is as well. It will already have passed through the wormhole to Pahrvic, and begun infecting the miners there."

"So why haven't you just killed me?" Allie asked, taking a slow step backward. The Highlord stepped forward, raising Dav's hands.

"Because I want to kill you with my bare hands."

He walked forward an instant before a roiling purple ball of crackling energy slammed into the ground beside him. The earth itself warped and cracked where the blast had hit, the shockwave blasting the Highlord, Allie, and Preston all backward. Allie landed softly on a bed of thick underbrush. The Highlord and Preston weren't so lucky, hitting the ground when they landed. Allie struggled to get untangled from the brush and get back to her feet.

The Highlord made it up first of course, and lunged for Allie. A rapid-fire series of ripples in the air flew forward, striking Dav's body in rapid succession and knocking him backward. Captain Abram and Spike ran into view.

"Captain!" Allie shouted as she made it to her feet.

"Go!" he shouted, pointing to one side. "Cade is coming! We can handle these two, and I think we can slow Sandro down. Dgehf is that way!"

"I can't leave you to Cade!"

"Don't be stupid, Spike can handle him! Go find Dgehf!" Allie looked to Spike, who gave her a cocky, lop-sided smile.

"Thank you," she said. A quick look to the still-unmoving Raith and she steeled herself. "Take care of Raith!"

"We've got him," Captain Abram said, as Spike tackled Preston who was just getting up. The Captain went for Dav, who was moving slowly. Allie ran.

Running through the jungle was a little like swimming through pudding, she thought as she shoved through another tangle of vines. The little glowing lizards were faded and dim, and had clustered together tightly, as if they were afraid of all the commotion in the jungle. She didn't blame them. Ships being shot down, Cade and Sandro running around, and who knew what else was going on all over this poor jungle.

The animal sounds she remembered had all gone completely silent, the purple sky above empty of any birds. Everything had gone silent and still.

"Dgehf!" she called into the jungle.

There was no reply, but she kept pushing on. Captain Abram had said Dgehf was this way. Dgehf may have landed, but considering he was the only ship out there on their side, except the big black one Raith had seen which was probably the Blackstar, he'd likely been shot down as well, as the Highlord had said.

"Dgehf!" Allie called again.

She fought back tears. Raith might be permanently damaged, Tic might be dead, Imber was sick and dying, and Dav was now infested with a parasite, and the only weapon they had against the parasite had been rendered powerless by Preston's injection. She could feel the rogellium running through her veins. Her head throbbed, but she didn't know if that was from the rogellium or the Dawn Virus. She looked down at her hand and could see her veins, glowing very faintly.

Looking around, she realized she was completely lost. Running in the jungle wasn't a good idea if you didn't know the terrain. She'd expected to find Dgehf by now. Something moved through the brush toward her.

Turning to look and grabbing the gun still miraculously at her side, she shouted in frustration at the futility of it all as C.A.D.E.-16 emerged. His clothing was gone, as was most of his artificial skin. What was left of his face was singed around the edges. Dgehf really had shot him out of the sky, she realized. Pity it hadn't killed him.

The sleek metal plating that covered his machinery like armor was scored and gouged in several places in patterns she recognized. Tic had also done some serious damage. The thought of Tic made her heart leap into her throat. She tightened her grip on the gun aimed at Cade.

"Where's Tic?" she asked.

"Who?" Cade asked as he paused.

"The jicund," Allie replied. Cade smiled.

"I'm afraid she went down with the ship. Don't worry though, she wasn't moving when I left her anyway, she probably didn't feel a thing."

Allie fired her shatter gun as fast as she possibly could in pure rage and frustration. It was hopeless, it all was she knew, but she would go down fighting. Cade didn't even bother dodging. The pulses hit Cade squarely, to Allie's surprise, peppering his chest and head. Cade barely twitched with each blast. She stopped firing and Cade straightened with a laugh.

"Come on, girl. I've upgraded and adapted my systems so many times that your toy gun there is useless. You can run if you want. That would make this more fun for a second or two."

Allie threw the gun at him, and Cade ducked by reflex. She almost grinned. Cade growled and stepped forward. Allie stood firm.

"Suit yourself," Cade said, "I'll just kill you right here." His arm came up, some strange weapon emerging from the shifting forearm plates. Allie braced herself, but stared Cade squarely in the eyes. After all she'd been through, she wasn't about to cower or scream. She wouldn't give him the satisfaction. Neither would Raith.

The young android shot out of the underbrush like a bullet, grabbing the weapon on Cade's arm, and tearing it off with the unique squeal of ripping metal. Cade slammed his other fist into Raith's face, knocking him back.

Allie saw the wound on the side of his head where Dav, the Highlord, had hit him. The artificial skin there had torn, leaving another patch of slightly dented metal visible. Raith hit and rolled, coming back up in a lunge at Cade.

"Allie, Jump!" he shouted.

"I can't!" she yelled back, running for her gun as the two androids struggled.

"Run!" he replied. She was getting tired of hearing that.

"No!" she argued, trying to get a shot at Cade. She knew it wouldn't help, but she couldn't just go running off again.

Another crashing sound came from the other direction, and a whistling, windy howl tore through the jungle. Sandro. This was getting ridiculous, Allie thought as she grit her teeth and turned to point her gun that direction. Movement came from the sides, away from the sound, and Allie almost fired until she recognized Dgehf and his family.

"Dgehf!" she cried in excitement. Then Sandro emerged from the brush, the tearing, lashing tentacles seeming everywhere at once. Allie fell backward as Dgehf leapt straight into the middle of the storm of slick, black whips. Dgehf's mate and son were right behind, and to her horror, so was Daghren, the little Maruck.

She fired madly into the tentacles, but couldn't even tell if it was doing any good. Raith and Cade crashed to the ground beside her, still struggling. She was again useless. Captain Abram and Spike ran into view.

"Dav's loose, that way!" the captain called.

Spike aimed her mighty Shane at the mass of tentacles, but the Maruck were everywhere, biting, clawing, tearing, ripping. Tentacles slashed at them, biting shallowly into their impossibly tough skin. The black acidic blood hissed on their fur, but didn't seem able to burn their skin.

Their roars and Sandro's howls were deafening. A small explosion knocked her off her feet As Cade got a shot off with one of his weapons. Allie hit the ground and rolled a few times before she was able to find her feet again. She was no good against Sandro or Cade, but maybe she could help reach Dav somewhere inside the Highlord's mental prison and he could help battle the Highlord from within.

Allie ran with Captain Abram after Dav, Spike still trying to get a shot off at Sandro, leaving Raith and her Maruck friends to battle the two most dangerous beings she knew of in the entire galaxy.

Allie followed right behind Captain Abram, and realized immediately that he wasn't human either. While his speed wasn't much better than she'd expect from a human, his strength was truly impressive as he tore through vines as thick as his torso and shoved small trees out of the way without apparent effort. He made a perfectly clear path for her to follow, though.

Minutes later, they emerged into a large clearing, the thick grass sloping down to the far side. Dav was almost across the clearing, running incredibly fast. What caught her attention though, was the army on the other side of the huge field. The army looked to be entirely Coalition troops. The Highlord was shouting something at them as he ran. The troops parted to let him past, and raised weapons at Allie and the captain. At least a hundred men stood across from them, all armed, weapons drawn.

The captain had a gun as well, but they stood no chance against a hundred men. Once again, Allie was useless. Without her Jumping, she was an ordinary thirteen year old human girl.

The treeline beside Allie suddenly moved, many small trees stepping forward. They weren't trees, she realized, they were the People of the Tree! Allie looked up into Ghier's eyes as he stepped up beside her.

"Hello, Allie Bennett," he said in his smooth, soft voice.

"Ghier!" she replied, excited to see him despite his betrayal during her last visit to this world.

"I am here to ask your forgiveness," he said, tone sorrowful.

"Now's not the time, Ghier," she said, looking pointedly at the troops even now running toward them across the field.

"Along with my forgiveness, I seek to aid you," Ghier said. "My people were quite angry when they learned what I had done, even though it was done to protect them. They were right of course. I was cowardly in not standing for what was right, but I feared for my people's safety. No more. We stand with you, Allie Bennett."

With that, Ghier turned and took one long step forward onto the grass. A line of two dozen of his people stepped up along with him from the treeline. As they stood, they literally planted their feet, roots burrowing deeply and hard into the ground. Allie watched in fascination. Captain Abram looked to her in astonishment and curiosity. Allie shrugged. She didn't know what was about to happen either. They were still very outnumbered.

The People of the Tree closed their eyes, and raised their faces to the purple sun. Reaching their arms out as though absorbing energy straight from the sun, they looked so peaceful and calm. Turning toward the troops who were almost in firing range, she saw something unlike anything she'd ever witnessed.

The ground began rolling and pitching under the men's feet like an angry ocean. The men were tossed about like leaves on a storm. Then the ground erupted, thick, vine-like roots bursting out by the hundreds, wrapping themselves around the charging men. Impossibly entangled, the roots began to still, along with the rolling earth below them.

A perfect path lay running down the center of the field through the men, now all lying tied up in roots on the ground. They shouted and struggled, but none seemed to be making any headway. Allie stepped slowly beside Ghier and gently touched his arm. He turned his green eyes down to her.

"What in the stars did you ever have to be afraid of?" she asked him. Ghier gave her an apologetic smile and shrugged.

"Burn the jungle, and our power is gone," he replied simply. She nodded, understanding.

"Ghier, I forgive you. There isn't much I wouldn't do to protect my friends and family, either. Thank you, for helping me." She looked across the field and saw the Highlord just under the trees, staring. He saw her looking and shouted something at her, but he was too far to make it out. He turned and ran into the jungle. "I have to go help my friend," she told him. He nodded. "You are more than forgiven." Ghier smiled warmly.

"Thank you, Allie Bennett."

"Thank you, Ghier," she said, then began running down the path the People had left open for her, Captain Abram by her side.

"Allie," the captain said as he ran beside her. She glanced up at him. "You have some very unusual, and very powerful friends." Allie smiled.

He was right. She had friends everywhere she'd gone. From Dgehf to Raith to the People, even to Captain Abram. They were all here to help her, risking their own lives for her. Even without her Jumping, she realized, she wasn't useless. Her kindness had built a virtual army of allies. She was a unifying force, bringing people together for a just cause. Katharine was right. A little kindness went a long way. Her smile slipped as she realized how many of those friends had given their lives for her, too.

She didn't know how Raith, Spike, or Dgehf's family was doing, but knew Cade was more than a match for Raith, and Sandro was more than a match for anything except maybe Spike's gun, Shane. Spike was with them, so maybe they stood a chance. Tic had crashed along with all of the Sy'hli. To be fair, she had helped them in their war by bringing them here, they hadn't come for her, but she still felt partly responsible.

Once more, she and the captain pushed into the jungle. It was thinner on this side of the field, and she wondered if they were nearing the edge of the jungle. They had to catch Dav, she knew. He would either be killed in the coming fight, or would succeed and would die in the plague anyway. But she had to make sure Dav was free.

The irony was that he had such a hard time believing that a parasite could so completely take over someone's mind. Now, he would understand. Perhaps she could free him and he could see his brother Tyren one last time before the plague overtook them all, and could see his brother in a more forgiving light.

Someone had to find a cure, she told herself. Someone had to. It couldn't end like that, or why were they even bothering to fight?

She fought because she couldn't give up, she knew. She never would, not until her very last breath. Allie wouldn't abandon her friends like that. She would help Dav. She had to.

# CHAPTER TWENTY TWO

# SHOWDOWN

Another heavy blow from Cade knocked Raith back, breaking his grip on the bigger android. He would lose this fight, he knew. It didn't matter though, if Allie was able to catch and rescue Dav.

He didn't know if she could, unable to channel the energies into him to purge him of the colony like she had with Tyren, but he had to give her the chance. Raith rolled to the side as Cade fired another weapon at him. The ground where he'd been laying exploded upward in a shower of dirt. He rolled to his feet and dove. Cade grabbed him and slammed him down.

Part of his mind was busily processing the outside information. Spike hadn't yet gotten a clean shot at either Cade or Sandro. Dgehf and his family were in rough shape, but all of them were still fighting, and the number of crushed, limp, and severed tentacles was testament to the fight they were putting up.

A ball of purple blasted past as Raith was thrown down, aiming for Cade. Cade dropped and rolled, the blast shredding through several trees beyond him in an explosive shower of splinters and leaves. Raith smashed his elbow into Cade's face as he got within range, using the leverage to roll the other way and back to his feet.

Cade was faster and was already leaping for him. One of Cade's many weapons snapped out and fired a moment before Cade reached him, tearing through Raith's flight suit, his artificial skin, and damaging his shoulder joint. The arm was still marginally functioning, but wouldn't be any good for fighting. Cade's advantage grew.

An odd roar reached Raith's ears, a sound like a hurricane tearing through a town. Whatever Dgehf's family had just done, they'd seriously hurt Sandro. He was surprised any of them were still alive. He knew a lot about the horrifying alien known as Sandro, all from data records of places and people he'd attacked and destroyed.

He also heard Spike growl in frustration as Cade once again slammed into Raith, removing her ability for a clean shot. This was not her kind of fight, he knew. With that gun, she belonged on a field overlooking the big battle, tearing massive holes in the enemy lines with that ridiculously over-powered gun.

"I don't know why you keep trying to fight me, Raith," Cade said. "I tear you apart every time. I beat you on Kobek, I beat you on Irifal, and I beat you on the Delta."

"Because someone has to fight you," Raith snarled

back.

"But you lose!" Cade said, slamming his knee into Raith's side, gripping him by the damaged arm. "Every single time!"

Raith felt one of his internal processors crack as his metal ribcage bent slightly. Cade slammed the knee into him again and the processor shattered. Raith's systems rerouted those system to an alternate processor.

"And yet somehow, I save people every time. Doesn't sound like a loss to me," Raith retorted.

He wrenched free and dropped to the ground as Spike shot over his head. Cade dove to the side and rolled back to his feet, and unleashed a barrage from his weapons systems that sent Spike diving for cover this time. Trees and bushes exploded in a line as Cade strafed the treeline she'd jumped into.

"That's your weakness," Cade snarled, turning his attention back to Raith, who had climbed to his feet.

He was moving slower, he knew. Many of his joints and systems had been damaged in the admittedly short fight. Raith hadn't managed to do any serious damage at all. Cade's armor plating was too strong.

"You care too much about these organics. Haven't you realized we're superior?" He fired at Spike again, who vanished once more into the brush, but not before she unleashed another huge purple blast from Shane. Cade dove to one side as the ball of energy ripped another hole in the wall of foliage.

"That's your weakness, Cade." Raith retorted, jumping in and slamming a lightning-fast kick to the android's chest. It didn't even dent. Raith stared.

"I've upgraded, Raith. I don't have any weaknesses."

"Says the guy with a shredded face," Raith threw back as Cade leapt on him again.

"I think I'm getting tired of toying with you, Raith."

Raith slammed his head into Cade's, aiming for a series of deep gouges Tic had left. The metal plating cracked right along the cuts. Cade rolled off of him.

I'm sorry, Allie, Raith thought to himself. Cade would destroy him in another few moments. Once he turned fully on Spike, she would die as well, with or without her huge gun. He couldn't see her at all, she may already have been killed by that last barrage. Dgehf's mate had been flung back into a tree and lay still for several long seconds before she pushed herself back to her feet. Sandro still seemed like a writhing nest of angry snakes as he flailed away at the other Maruck.

Even if they won by some miracle, the Dawn Virus would kill all of the organics anyway. Raith knew their odds of survival were astronomically low. He didn't know exactly how low, his processing was still being rerouted to a viable system, but he knew it was low enough that hope was pointless. He couldn't even shut down the nanovirus.

His secondary processing systems connected fully. Wait, he thought, he couldn't shut them down. He couldn't help it, he smiled as the idea hit him. Now he just needed to survive this fight. Spike appeared behind a shattered tree and fired at both Cade and Sandro. Cade dodged. Sandro didn't. Another terrible shrieking roar from Sandro, and Dgehf shoved a huge fist deep into the center of the writhing mass as the tentacles spasmed from Shane's blow.

In the distance, a huge rumbling, like an earthquake shook through the trees from the direction Allie had gone. Raith registered heavy vibration in the ground under his feet as Cade bent one of his arms back and slammed a fist into his face repeatedly.

Raith brought his heel down onto one of Cade's ankle joints, right where he knew the bearing attached. The bearing gave way and Cade stumbled backward, letting Raith go. Raith leapt up.

"Go help Allie and the captain!" Raith shouted to Spike. She hesitated, then left her shattered tree cover and ran past him toward the trees. Cade kicked him with the broken foot, sending him flying back. A fraction of a second afterward, he had an idea. It was yet another brilliant idea, if he did say so himself. He barely missed Spike as he flew backward, narrowly avoiding bringing her down with him. It was close enough, he knew.

Raith grabbed Allie's dropped gun as he landed within reach and fired. Cade didn't even dodge. The shatter gun's pulse struck him squarely in the chest. He didn't even flinch.

"That's your other weakness, Raith. Not enough upgrades," Cade smirked, leveling an armful of weapons at Raith. Raith raised his other hand and pressed the top button on the small device he'd stolen from Spike's belt as she ran past.

"What is tha…" Cade began. Then his system shut down. His body went rigid and he dropped face-first to the ground like a fallen tree.

Raith stood slowly, dusting himself off and scanning his damaged regions. He clipped the small device to his belt.

"Upgrade all you want, you outdated lump of tin. I'm still smarter than you," he said to the prone form. The captain may not have been willing to share that stunning technology, but Raith had no qualms about stealing it in a pinch. Or with a pinch, he thought with a grin.

He walked over to Cade and withdrew a small tool from his belt. After rolling the stiff android over, a few quick turns and he removed one of Cade's chest-plates. Reaching in, he shorted Cade's power supply. Deactivating the power supply like that was final, he knew. Cade's systems would be instantly erased, his circuits fried, and everything that was Cade was gone in a brief series of sparks.

Raith felt regret. Cade was the only other android that had survived the Infection, the only one to have fully integrated his emotional subroutine.

In a sense, Raith and Cade were two of a kind. With Cade gone, Raith was all that was left, anywhere in the galaxy, and his power cells had been so badly drained in the fighting, the system deteriorating at an increasing rate, that his systems calculated only three months left before he too became no more.

But if he could save his friends and get them back to Sy'hloran, he thought he could at least save the rest of them. It was untested, a wild and outlandish idea, but as his processors ran simulations, he calculated a twelve point five six eight percent chance of success. That was better than nothing, and he would fight, and die, to try it.

Turning to the battle between Dgehf's family and Sandro, he was stunned to see Dgehf's family, all of them, still fighting. Dgehf was so deep in the nest of tentacles that he was barely visible, but he was clearly still fighting.

Scanning the situation for a way he could help, he noted that the mass of tentacles didn't have a single point of origin. As he took a second to study it, he realized that the creature's tentacles all seemed to be clumped in groups, each leading to a point they branched off, that point leading to another point that also branched off.

The tentacles were all so long and moved so rapidly that it was difficult to tell, but Raith became certain they all eventually joined to a single central body. Probably where the thing's brain was. Before he could attempt to locate that singular mass, he realized Dgehf had come to the same conclusion.

The shrieking that suddenly emerged from the monstrous alien was one of pain, and panic. Panic of the type that only came from a being who believed himself immortal who had just discovered that he wasn't. The tentacles whipped around madly, flinging Dgehf's mate, his son, and his nephew back and making it impossible for them to wade back in.

Without warning, the tentacles all dove inward, the whole mess turning into a rippling, tightly-packed ball of black cord. Dgehf was nowhere to be seen. The ball of tentacles spasmed once, then twice, then the whole mass collapsed limply, like a dropped bowl of spaghetti noodles. From beneath the oozing, limp mass in the center, there was movement. Dgehf's family stepped forward as one, growling.

Tentacles moved, shoved aside by a huge, clawed fist. Dgehf stood slowly, painfully, from the middle of the disgusting heap. He was dripping black ichor, and clutched in his hands something blue that also dripped black ichor. Dgehf held it up and let out a victory roar so loud, so filled with the uniquely Maruck glory of victory, that Raith found himself cheering along. Dgehf's family took up the roar, and the five of them shouted their victory across the jungle.

Battered, bloody, torn, and dripping acidic slime, the family turned to Raith. Even the youngest was in rough shape, but Daghren, small as he was, was a true Maruck warrior and stood tall and proud beside his warrior family, victorious. Raith smiled as he looked at his friends.

"Let's go help Allie," he said. The group snarled their assent, ready for another fight, and as a pack they turned and charged into the forest along Allie's trail, Raith right behind them. Twelve point five six eight percent, Raith thought. It was enough.

# CHAPTER TWENTY THREE

# TIC

Tic crawled from the burning wreckage of the fallen Sy'hli battle cruiser, using her claws to rip through the metal panels she was buried beneath.

She had held the machine-man long enough, she hoped. The machine-boy and Allie's mate had to have made it to safety. Not yet Allie's mate, Tic corrected herself, but someday. Tic didn't understand why the two seemed to ignore it. Tic could see it. The machine-boy could see it. The glowing girl could see it. Everyone knew they belonged as mates, but Allie and her mate didn't seem to see it yet.

It didn't matter, Tic knew. If they survived, they would know. She chattered angrily as she felt the pain not only from being slammed against the bulkhead by the machine-man, but from the sickness inside of her. Everyone was sick, she knew. She could smell it long before she could see it.

Tic didn't understand much about sickness, but she knew that among her people it was rare, and always ended in death unless they could get them to the People of the Tree. Tic liked the People. They were of the jungle, like she was. They helped all things of the jungle, and the jicund were no exception. They harmed nothing, something that nothing else in the jungle could claim, except some of the plants. Not even all of the plants, though.

Emerging from the wreckage, Tic looked around. She couldn't suppress the chittering trill of excitement. She knew this place! To many other kinds of jungles she had gone with Allie, but at last she had come home. Taking a deep breath, thousands of scents touched her nose, her little mind immediately identifying all of them.

From that one breath, she knew precisely where she was in the jungle she called home. She also knew everything was in hiding, and there were many creatures around that did not belong here. Fire was everywhere, coming from many big sky-boats like the one Tic had crashed here in.

Smoke clouded the air and made the sky look murky, like the water in the swamps beyond the jungle edge. Tic had been there once, it was part of her adulthood ceremony. She didn't like it, it smelled wrong. She had returned with a tooth of the red bog beast however, one of the biggest any in her family tribe had ever seen, proving her strength and resilience to her people.

She had emerged without scars as well, something few could claim. Tic knew she'd gotten lucky, but it had still built her some notoriety among her people.

She claimed the name Tic that Allie, her sibling-bonded, had given her, but her people had another name for her. She was sad that Allie could not pronounce her real name, or understand jicund, but was happy with the name Allie had given her. Only Allie kept her own name in Tic's mind. She had her own names for everyone else in her own language.

Tic didn't know why Allie couldn't understand jicund, since she seemed to understand all of the other languages. Tic understood some, like a little Sy'hli, but her people couldn't pronounce most other spoken languages. They weren't equipped for it. That didn't mean she didn't understand. It didn't matter, Tic knew. Allie understood her well enough.

Tic took another series of sniffs. Several Sy'hli were also climbing out of the broken Sy'hli sky-boat. She was glad many had survived. Perhaps all had, she didn't know. The Sy'hli were interesting, and Allie's mate and his older sibling were good. Tic could smell that they were good.

Even the other sibling smelled good now. He didn't used to. He smelled the way Allie's mate had begun to smell. Tic knew his mind was sick too, just like his brother's had been. He was not as sick yet, but would be soon. She had just begun to smell it when they had gone onto the Sy'hli sky-boat.

Tic chittered unhappily. She could not smell Allie. She would find Allie and their friends. Racing from the wreckage, she launched herself into the treetops of her jungle. She had missed this place. The feel of the spongy tree branches beneath her feet was so comforting, so familiar. The sticky sap didn't stick to the jicund's fur or feet, like they did some other animals. It let them basically rule the treetops.

She practically flew, leaping from tree to tree and branch to branch, traveling much, much faster than Allie could have moved even over open ground. Ducking and twisting as she went, she dodged smaller branches. This was her home, and this was her playground.

Moving near the edge of the jungle, the smell of many, many men reached her sensitive nose. Changing course slightly, she reached the edge of the trees. There, she saw Allie's mate. His smell reeked of the mind-sickness. He was no longer good, Tic knew. She hissed softly.

He stood in front of a group of people so big, Tic couldn't begin to count them. They stood in ranks, far from the treeline, like the fields of grain the people of the nearby cities and towns planted. Among them were many, many of the beasts Allie called Maruck. Allie's mate was shouting to them, and they were listening. Tic could hear him. He was calling for war, calling for them to destroy his enemies, including the Starjumper. That was Allie, Tic knew. He said that together they would rule the galaxy once the Starjumper and the traitors of the Coalition had been destroyed. All of them, the Maruck and the men, were cheering.

This was very bad, Tic knew. All those men would hurt Allie and their friends. Allie's mate was no more. Tic didn't know if Allie could cure his mind-sickness the way she had with the older sibling, but she would have to help Allie to find out. Allie would be here, Tic knew. Allie had gone somewhere else, but she would be back here to help her friends. To help Allie, she would need help herself, Tic thought, and she knew just where to go.

Racing back into the jungle, she headed for the Place of Calling. She sped through the trees effortlessly. It would take a little while to get there, but it was worth the run. From the Place of Calling, she could summon the jicund. All of them.

Her people would help once they knew that their jungle was in danger. She just needed to explain to them which of the people were on their side, or Allie and all of her friends were in danger from them as well. When the jicund gathered for war, they took on the battle frenzy, a state of ferocity that Allie had seen several times since they had joined. If the jicund knew who was friendly however, they would leave those people be.

Tic almost felt bad for the army Allie's mate had gathered, though. They deserved it, she reminded herself. Bad people did bad things, and were hurting her home and threatening her friends. Tic would not permit that. She would just have to hurry.

She smelled Maruck. Allie's friends, she identified. She smelled her pack-mate the machine-boy, as well. He was good. There was something bad near them, as well however. Tic recognized it from the ship with the big man and the angry woman. The scent of the foul, tentacle creature set her fur standing up. She couldn't stop and help though. She could help more getting to the Place of Calling.

Faster, she told herself. Tic raced faster than she'd

ever run before. She blasted past a nest of the burrowing people so quickly that the big insects didn't even register her presence. She remembered fighting one of them to protect Allie, before they left home. They were fierce, but jicund were the fiercest animals on the planet. She didn't even slow.

It took several minutes, but she reached the Place of Calling. The huge volcanic peak rose abruptly out of the earth, walls steep and jagged. It hadn't erupted for countless generations, Tic knew, but she also knew that it was still alive. It spoke, from time to time, rumbling deep in the earth. The Place of Calling was at the top.

It didn't take long to get there at her speed. No other jicund were there. This didn't surprise Tic, it wasn't the season for the Gathering. The vast, cratered expanse of the Place of Calling was completely empty. She didn't waste time looking, though she'd only been to two Gatherings since she had achieved adulthood. Tic ran to the far edge, climbing the tall, sharp spire of stone along one rim that stood high above the others. This was the Place of Calling.

Taking a few deep steadying breaths, she reminded herself that it was okay for her to do this. Any jicund had the right to call the tribes if the emergency were serious enough, and this definitely qualified. It was something that had been done needlessly by a couple of younglings some time back as a prank. Their punishment had been severe enough that even Tic shivered now to think of it. This was worthy, she knew. It had to be done.

Tic began to sing. Singing was more of a ritual for the jicund, and was only done for very special occasions.

The melody she sang was high and long, the clear, whistle-pitch notes carrying from her great height far across the jungle. Within moments, she heard the song being picked up by other jicund far below. It would spread across the jungle at the speed of sound, she knew. And they would come.

She sang until she could hear the song ringing all around. A few changes to the end would tell them not to gather at the Place of Calling, but to the edge of the jungle, to the east. Tic would meet them there. Scampering back down, she ran across the summit to the side she'd climbed up. She would get down even faster than she got up.

Leaping out, she grabbed an outcrop of jagged stone, leaping almost immediately to another one much further down. In this fashion, she managed a controlled fall down the mountain. Leaping back into the trees, she headed once more for the edge of the jungle. She would give out a call when she got there, and tell the others where to meet with her. Her modified song had also told them to come in silence.

More minutes passed as she ran. She passed near the machine-boy and his Maruck friends. Relief struck her as she ran overhead and saw the Maruck and Raith all running through the jungle. There was no sign of the tentacle monster.

That was one of her pack who was okay at least. Now to get to Allie and have Allie help her cure Allie's mate, and then they could all go back and cure the glowing girl, and Tic's pack would be healthy and safe again. Tic didn't stop. She didn't have time.

She still didn't smell Allie, but knew she would come. Allie could appear from the air itself. It was magic beyond anything the jicund knew, but Tic was the only jicund special enough to ride with her when she traveled like that. That was because Allie and Tic were sibling-bonded, Tic knew. Very rare outside of the jicund family-tribes, but it did happen.

Minutes passed, and Tic reached a spot near the edge of the jungle. The troops in the fields below were beginning to move forward, toward the jungle. The destruction they caused would be terrible, almost as bad as the sky-boats falling from the sky. She dearly hoped none of her people had been harmed.

Tic sang a call to identify her position, and sat on a branch to wait.

The sun was setting, Allie realized as the jungle grew darker. That wasn't good, she knew. It would be dark under the heavy canopy of leaves and branches above much sooner than it would above the treetops.

Allie ran behind the captain, still chasing after Dav. He could outrun them both, and they both knew it. But he had to be running somewhere, and Captain Abram said he had a good idea where. Allie trusted him, and followed along as fast as she could move. Even without having to push through the brush, Captain Abram nearly outpaced her. He smashed through the brush like it wasn't even there.

The jungle was still eerily silent, but she could hear

ships cruising by overhead every so often. Of course, a lot of sound was probably covered by the big captain tearing through the jungle. He made enough noise that neither of them heard the approaching movement from one side.

A heavy form struck Allie from the side, heaving her easily off the ground, and plunged them both into the heavy brush on the other side of Captain Abram's trail. A hand clamped over her mouth before she could scream. Her abductor was moving quickly, and seemed quite adept at sliding around and through the underbrush.

Allie kicked and thrashed, trying to break free, but while she didn't think the figure was incredibly strong, it was easily stronger than she was. The figure ran, carrying her for some time before setting her down. She scrambled away, looking back. Preston stood there, grinning like a cat with a mouse.

"Thought you were rid of me? Not hardly. I didn't get where I am in the Highlord's ranks by being a fool. I am stronger, faster, and smarter than you seem to give me credit for."

"Why wouldn't you just kill me? You sure ramble on a lot," Allie said. She knew she was far enough by now that Captain Abram wouldn't hear her if she screamed. Not in this jungle. Preston sneered.

"You humiliated me, girl. For that, I think it will be more fun to play with my prey. Let you run while I track you, take you a piece at a time. You can try to run back to your big friend, if you like. You may not know this, but my people come from the jungle. Not this jungle of course, but enough like it for me to feel quite at home here. You'll be lost in seconds while I run circles around you."

Allie leapt at him, hoping to get a blow in with her strike gloves. Preston was right though, he was faster than she thought. He sidestepped easily, kicking her in the back as she passed. She stumbled and splashed into the mud, her cheek painfully striking a rock. Preston laughed cruelly.

"Not a good start. You'll live longer if you run," he said.

Allie climbed to her feet and wiped a trickle of blood from her face and looked at it. Glaring at Preston, she knew she was no match for him. He would never let her get a good shot in with the strike gloves, and she'd lost her gun. She had friends in the jungle, she knew, she just had to get to one of them before Preston caught her.

She turned and ran. Preston laughed behind her, the weasely man eager for the hunt. Pushing through the brush did not come naturally to her, and she felt branches and brambles slapping and slicing at her. She mentally thanked Raith again for the flight suit, as it saved her skin a thousand times in the first ten seconds. She kept her arms up to try and shield her face.

The blow came from seemingly nowhere as Preston struck her again from the side, knocking her into a shallow ravine. She rolled and hit the ground hard. She shook her head to try and clear it. She heard Preston laughing again as he disappeared into the jungle again.

Allie scrambled to her feet. He had been right. She had no idea which direction Captain Abram was. She'd run for ten seconds, been hit once, and was completely lost. This jungle just swallowed up any possible sense of direction she might have. Unlike Preston, she wasn't born to the jungle.

She got up and ran anyway. Pushing through the brush slowed her down dramatically, and it didn't help that her hands were getting more and more covered with the sticky sap from all the trees she kept barely avoiding.

Another blow from nowhere, striking her in the back of the head. She stumbled and splashed down onto her hands and knees in a shallow stream. This really was futile, she knew, but she had no options. She reached tentatively for the energies again, and the nausea welled up within her. Grabbing the energies, she vomited again. She let them go with a mental cry of anger and anguish that matched her vocal one.

There, deep in the back of her mind, she thought she heard a reply.

*"We come."*

# CHAPTER TWENTY FOUR

# FACE TO FACE

Allie ran for another minute, Preston appearing every few seconds. She had made it into a small clearing by a river. The river raged angrily, not a possible escape, Allie knew, though she might take it as a preferable death to Preston's hands. She lay on her back, scrambling toward the river backward as Preston stepped out into the open.

"I'm growing bored with this. Are you ready to die, Starjumper?" he sneered that last word. She had always seen him as weasely and weak. Standing there before her, he was small, he was slender, but he looked born to this environment. Without the robes his skinny frame now looked whipcord slender, his narrow little eyes glinting in the fading light.

"You'll die too, you know," she told him. "The Dawn Virus will kill all of us."

"The Highlord has promised me the cure."

"There is no cure. It was destroyed on the Helios."

"He shall save me," Preston said firmly. His faith in his master was admirable, but very poorly placed, Allie thought.

"The Highlord doesn't want to rule, he wants revenge against all life. His virus will kill everything, everyone, everywhere."

"I will rule at his side!" Preston shrieked. An odd, disjointed whooping began in the distance. The eerie howls rose and fell in sudden bursts, each cutting off just before another rose. Allie looked to the jungle where the sound came from and knew what was coming. She looked to Preston sadly.

"No," she said simply, "you won't."

Preston heard the howls as well, and looked back to the jungle, suddenly looking uncertain. They drew closer at a terrifying rate. As suddenly as they began, the whooping howls stopped. Moving slowly forward, in the darkness of the underbrush, eyes had begun to appear. They glowed an acidic yellow, all narrowed and hungry. There weren't many. There didn't need to be, Allie knew. Slowly, the bearers of the eyes moved into the fading light of the clearing.

Preston stumbled backward in a panic at the sight of the huge, dark, horned predators Allie knew as the Rrughn. Ydrahn was at their head. Allie could feel his thoughts. She could not dissuade him from his prey, and she didn't try. Preston had brought it to this. He looked back at Allie in a panic, and Allie slowly shook her head as she stood.

"I'm sorry, Preston." He broke, turned, and ran into

the jungle. The Rrughn took up their frightening howl, and gave chase, Jumping in seemingly random patterns as they pursued their prey.

Allie brushed herself off, touching a few new wounds on her face and neck. Brushing mud and debris from her flight suit, she wondered if she looked half as bad as she felt. Sick, battered, cut, and exhausted, she couldn't remember ever having felt this bad in her life. She stood in the clearing for a moment, deciding on her next course of action, when Ydrahn and another Rrughn reappeared.

*"Thank you, Ydrahn,"* Allie told him. She thought it was interesting that just speaking mind to mind with him didn't seem to make her sick like touching the energies did.

*"Speaker is like us. We protect our own,"* the Rrughn leader replied.

*"Is he...?"* Allie couldn't bring herself to say it. As awful as Preston was, it still pained her to know he was dead. So much wasted, she thought. Ydrahn pulled back his lips in a gruesome sneer, viciously sharp teeth glinting in the setting sun.

*"He is prey,"* Ydrahn said. Allie didn't argue. They had saved her life.

*"My pack is lost. Can you help?"* she asked. Ydrahn considered her.

*"You are broken,"* he said simply. She could feel the rogellium burning in her veins and knew what he was referring to.

*"I am poisoned,"* she said, doing her best growl to show her anger. Dav probably would have thought it

was cute, she thought. Ydrahn didn't take it that way. He growled himself, turning his amber gaze to the direction Preston had run.

*"You cannot go Between?"*

Allie shivered as he mentioned the Between. She knew it didn't mean what he thought it did, but it still brought to mind the recent memory of being lost, literally nowhere.

*"I cannot,"* she admitted.

She wasn't entirely sure what telling the Rrughn leader that would make him do, since he seemed to respect her because she could Jump, speak mind-to-mind like they did, and had a powerful weapon in the energies she could manipulate.

Ydrahn was not stupid, he was probably realizing at that precise moment that she had no weapons against them. She had no weapon, she could not Jump. Maybe he would decide she was prey. He considered her for a long moment, the other Rrughn sidling closer. She held his gaze with the fiercest, strongest gaze she could. Whether it helped, she had no idea, but Ydrahn's thoughts settled.

*"We will help,"* he replied. Allie barely suppressed a sigh of relief. The other Rrughn seemed disappointed, but stepped back.

*"Thank you. And thank you for coming. I didn't know you could travel this far,"* she told him. Ydrahn gave the mental equivalent of a shrug.

*"In the Between, there is no distance when my pack works together,"* he said. Maybe he understood it better than she gave him credit, she thought.

*"I need to find my pack,"* she said, *"especially the Sy'hli*

*boy I was with when we met."*

*"Ydrahn does not know 'Sy'hli'. Ydrahn knows boy. Rrughn can cure that poison,"* Ydrahn added, almost as an afterthought. Allie blinked. *"When you travel with us, the poison will… resist. Each step will leave more behind. There will be pain,"* he said, watching her closely again.

*"It must be done,"* she replied, holding strong to his gaze and showing no fear to him. This seemed to satisfy him. He sent a call to his pack, and they suddenly began appearing all around. Allie was grateful their fur was black and dark red, so she couldn't tell if any of them had blood on their long, slender muzzles.

*"Speaker is ready?"* Ydrahn asked.

Allie nodded, and the pack leapt at her. She knew what was happening as they swarmed her, but it was still terrifying. She felt the Jump begin, the slight hesitation in the flow of time, and the burning sensation of microscopic pieces of rogellium being torn almost physically from her body. Nausea swept over her as they Jumped again.

Another burning wave of agony coursed through her body as more of the rogellium was left behind. Another Jump, another wave of pain. When finally the Jumping stopped, Allie could barely stand. She reached out a hand and grabbed Ydrahn's fur to steady herself. Thankfully, it didn't seem to bother him. She straightened slowly as she caught her breath.

*"Thank you again,"* she said.

*"Boy is there,"* Ydrahn said, pointing with his long gaze toward what appeared to be the edge of the jungle.

Allie turned to follow his gaze. He was right. In the

grassy fields beyond the jungle, Dav marched, at the head of a wall of soldiers and Maruck. Loyalist ships swarmed the air above. Stepping forward, she reached for the energies. They responded smoothly, flowing with her will. She pushed them at Dav. They swirled harmlessly around him. Allie frowned and studied Dav.

This had worked with Tyren, she knew. It had weakened him. She reached her mind out, and felt... nothing. As far as the energies were concerned, Dav's body was a void. They couldn't enter it, his thoughts weren't part of their energy, he wasn't connected to the energies at all. How she hadn't felt that when she'd Jumped him here, she had no idea.

It did explain why jumping him hadn't harmed the parasites, though. He was locked in that strange empty place, secure behind some kind of... yes, some kind of shield. As she explored it with her thoughts, she could feel its surface. It was slick and smooth, and seemed to originate from within him. It made no sense to her, she'd never encountered anything like it, and knew Dav hadn't been like that before.

She couldn't push the parasite out if she couldn't get the energies inside of him, she knew. Her heart sank. She may not be able to help him. She still had to stop him, she knew.

Allie stepped forward, and into view at the edge of the clearing. The sun was setting in the distance, but it was much lighter here than under the canopy.

The Highlord stopped when he saw her and held up his hand. He looked surprised, but pleasantly so. Allie walked forward. The Rrughn stayed in the trees, she could feel them. This wasn't their fight, she would have told them to stay herself if the sight of Dav hadn't pulled her straight out into the open.

As she drew closer, the Highlord broke into a light run, the kind she'd seen Dav do a million times. Her throat tightened and she felt a lump rising. She wouldn't cry, she told herself. The troops stayed in place, awaiting their Highlord's command. She wouldn't cry.

The Highlord slowed as he neared and walked toward the fool girl.

"All alone, coming to confront my army," he exclaimed in genuine surprise, and more than a little satisfaction. After all of the setbacks, he'd still get the chance to kill her with his bare hands. "Your friends are falling all over this jungle, but here you are, confronting an army, all alone! You've given up, then?"

"Hardly!" came a shout from the trees. The Highlord watched as the beat-up, damaged old recon android came running out of the jungle and moved to stand beside the brat girl. He took her hand, a ridiculous gesture, he thought.

"We'll fight, Highlord," Raith said, "no matter the odds."

"You're still functioning?" the Highlord asked in mock surprise. Raith glared. "Okay, so one girl who can't Jump anymore and one slightly damaged robot. I'm surprised CA.D.E.-16 didn't tear you apart."

"Cade has been decommissioned," Raith said,

looking slightly smug. Well, that was a surprise, the Highlord thought to himself.

*They're smarter than you.* The Highlord twitched as the unexpected voice of Dav pushed into his consciousness. By all the stars, that boy's mind was strong! It had taken years before Tyren could speak to him. The Highlord shoved the voice down.

"It doesn't matter. Two of you cannot stand against my army."

"Forty two," called a deep voice. The mercenary captain the Highlord had hired to capture the girl, along with his sidekick lieutenant, and at least three dozen of his mercenaries came out from the treeline, all heavily armed.

"Goodness, whatever will I do? You betrayed me, Captain. Pity you'll have to die with the girl!" the Highlord exclaimed, enjoying that her entire entourage was showing up and he still had them all massively outnumbered. This was laughable.

*They're stronger than you,* the voice told him. The Highlord shoved the voice back, fighting to keep his smug expression on his face. Dav's voice wouldn't go away!

A huge Maruck came out of the treeline. It was the biggest Maruck the Highlord had ever seen. He was accompanied by two others, both near contenders for the biggest Maruck ever title. A fourth Maruck, a little bouncy one, came out as well. They moved up to join the ranks behind Allie. The Highlord took an involuntary step back.

"Four Maruck? I have four hundred!" The Highlord

snarled.

Dgehf stepped forward and flung something out into the field. It was black, slimy, and tentacled. Everyone there immediately recognized it. It was a piece of Sandro's body. Dgehf stood tall and roared. The roar literally shook the ground under their feet, and nearly deafened the Highlord. Dgehf lowered his head and stared down the field, straight at Klythe at the head of the Maruck ranks.

The Highlord looked back. The Maruck were muttering and shifting uncomfortably. Klythe looked genuinely afraid, and took an involuntary step back, almost bumping into the ranks behind him. Great. A coward Maruck, the Highlord thought bitterly. Looking back to Allie, he sighed dramatically.

"You can't win, Allie. All of these people, your friends, are going to die. I will let them go if you surrender now," the Highlord lied.

*They're better than you,* came Dav's voice. The Highlord slammed down into the voice, attempting to crush it. The tree line moved again, and a row of them seemed to walk out into the field. The People of the Tree, the Highlord knew. He'd thought he had them completely pacified. Ah well, there would be time later.

"I will burn this jungle to the ground!" he yelled at them. The insolence, the foolishness, coming out against him. He would see this whole jungle destroyed, he promised himself. There were perhaps thirty of the People, lining up at the tree line behind Allie.

"We will not let you," Allie said firmly.

She stood straight and proud. Despite her dirty,

battered appearance, in that moment she looked purely noble. He opened his mouth to throw a snide remark at Allie but was interrupted by an eerie howling from the trees. Walking slowly out from the trees, Jumping in a disconcerting pattern, a pack of Rrughn walked. The Highlord only even knew what those were thanks to some of the memories he'd ripped from Dav's mind. The knowledge did not reassure him. He still had plenty of numbers though, with ships coming in.

"If you insist, we'll kill all of your friends and then burn this jungle to the ground," the Highlord said softly. "I will kill everyone you love, everything you hold dear. I will murder your mother with my bare hands. Do you understand me? You have already lost. The Dawn Virus is the endgame. This is all just posturing."

Sy'hli began to flood out of the tree line, survivors of the sabotage Cade had inflicted, the Highlord assumed. There were a lot. Way too many, he began to realize as the kept coming out, forming ranks behind Allie.

The Highlord gestured angrily, and one of his commanders spoke quickly into his com in the distance. Seconds later, three heavy Coalition battle ships, all loyal to him, flew into view, lining up above his gathered army.

"You have nothing, Allie! Nothing I can't destroy!" Other ships began to gather, backing the Highlord. "Do you see?"

The girl looked at the ships calmly, then looked to the mercenary lieutenant and nodded. The woman pulled out a huge hand cannon, and touched a button on the side. The bar of light beside the trigger lit completely.

She leveled the cannon at the huge battle cruiser, and pulled the trigger.

The ball of energy that came from the end of the silvery gun was small, much smaller than the Highlord expected after that show. The dark purple ball flew forward incredibly fast, crackling and hissing. The air in its wake warped and bent so badly that the Highlord thought it might break.

When the little ball, smaller than Dav's head, struck the massive battle ship, there was a pulsing shockwave that radiated from the impact point. The shockwave went out some distance, encompassing half the ship, then suddenly contracted, ripping everything it had touched along with it, compressing it all into the dark purple energy ball at the center.

In a flash, half the massive battle ship was gone. Simply gone. Pieces of debris fell from the sky as the battle ship seemed to pause a moment before its one remaining engine gave out and the ship began to drop. His men beneath the huge battle cruiser began running madly for safety as the huge remains of the battle ship slammed into the ground.

The Highlord turned slowly back to look at the mercenary lieutenant. She looked… deeply happy. She turned her gaze on him, then slowly aimed her beloved Shane at another ship.

"Get back!" The Highlord shouted to the ships. The ships were way ahead of him and were already making panicked evasive maneuvers.

*Do you see?* Dav's voice came to him. *You built an army out of fear and threats of violence. She has built an army out of love and friendship. Your army might be bigger, but hers is stronger. The strong only follow those they respect. Nobody respects you, Highlord. Your greatest weapons have been destroyed. Preston is missing, Harelo betrayed you and is now in the care of the Sy'hli Empire. Cade has been deactivated, and Sandro is dead.*

"Shut up!" the Highlord screamed out loud. He saw the hope flare in Allie's eyes. It was too late. She knew Dav was still in there.

*And look there, in the distance. Even the Tchratchi come to fight at her side. Your fleet of traitor warships is already lost. Love, kindness, and respect will trump fear, force, and money, every… single… time.*

The Highlord looked where Dav pushed him. In the distance was a swarm. It could only be described as a swarm. The Tchratchi ships were only about a foot long, each probably only holding four or five of the tiny insectoids but there were thousands of them. Thousands of them, humming in at high velocity. They even sounded like a swarm, the Highlord thought in disgust and anger. The Highlord felt his victory slipping. Where they had come from, he had no idea.

He lashed out suddenly, kicking Raith backward. He turned and ran full speed toward his army, screaming for them to charge. His only hope was to push the battle into the trees. The Tchratchi respected nature far too much to fly their ships in blasting away in a jungle like this. His fleet was already gone, and he knew it.

The Tchratchi swarm drew close enough to open fire, and fire they did. Tiny bolts of purple energy, like miniscule versions of the huge blast from that crazy woman's hand cannon. There were thousands of little purple darts zinging through the air all at once, the air hissing and crackling in their wake.

Where they struck, devastation was unleashed. The swarm reached his ships and flowed through their ranks, leaving a raining trail of fiery ruin as they passed through his fleet at top speed.

His men, Maruck included, were already charging. They parted slightly to let him through. It would take only seconds for them to reach the enemy line, and plow it straight back into the jungle. Sy'hli soldiers or not, his soldiers still had them outnumbered and outgunned. He could still win.

He turned after making it through the line, and watched. Allie's forces remained still. She had a soft smile on her face and held one hand out, stilling her troops. She waited. What was she waiting for, he wondered? An instant before his men reached her and crushed her and the blasted android underfoot, he realized what she had been waiting for.

The thick, dense foliage high in the treetops erupted as something burst through the barrier and leapt with incredible speed and range to land directly down on his approaching men. It took him a moment to realize what was happening.

They were small, they were fluffy, and they were angry!

Hundreds, thousands of jicund came down on the heads of his front linemen like an angry hornet's nest. Their furious shrieks were deafening, even from here, and completely drowned out the terrified shrieks of his men. Even the Maruck were scrambling to get away, swatting and batting at hordes of tiny, purple demons.

They turned from a furry, purple rain into a wave of fanged fury in an instant as the last of them came down and literally covered his men. The jicund began rolling over his ranks like a swarm of locusts as they spread out onto the field. Allie's men had charged, the over-sized Maruck family lunging straight for the Maruck ranks, the biggest male seemingly without effort grabbing Klythe by the lower jaw and flinging him violently to the ground. The huge Maruck leapt on his fallen quarry, and the Highlord lost sight of him as the two armies collided full force and blended together into one huge, deafening clash.

The Sy'hli performed like the seasoned troops they were, breaking into strike teams and moving with maddening grace and speed through his men, firing, striking, taking down several men for each one of them.

The People of the Tree reached their hands to the sky, their feet to the earth below them, and the ground beneath his rear ranks burst upward, the very earth and plants themselves fighting against his men. His men couldn't even begin to battle the very ground beneath their feet, he thought in a panic. Vines and roots snaked around like tentacles, flinging and ensnaring his men everywhere he looked.

And through it all, the eerie shifting howl of the Rrughn as they simply appeared at random all over the battlefield, taking down his men and then vanishing again before anyone could even fire at them.

Dav was right, the Highlord realized. He

outnumbered his enemy, but they were stronger. This battle was lost. His fury reaching proportions beyond his capacity for reason, he spotted Allie. She stood back near the tree line. She wasn't a warrior. She had a gun in hand, but obviously didn't trust her own aim enough to try a shot into the boiling turmoil before her.

In his rage, he no longer heard Dav's voice. He no longer saw the troops. He saw only Allie. He would lose this battle, but he would kill the girl first. He broke into the terrifyingly fast run the Sy'hli were capable of, moving straight through the battlefield like a bullet.

The Highlord ducked, rolled, dodged and leapt around combatants as each group or individual waged their own war. He was completely untouched by the crossfire, and nobody, from either side, seemed willing to target him. Even the jicund left him completely alone.

Allie saw him. She didn't try to run, she didn't try to shoot at him. She lowered the gun and watched him approach. He could see the sadness in her eyes even from here. He would grab her, and crush the life from her.

A pair of battling Maruck flew past in front of him, blocking his view of the hated girl for an instant. When they passed, she was gone.

"No!" he screamed in outrage.

Looking madly about, he tried to figure out where she had gone. Turning around, she was there, right behind him. Faster than any human possibly could have reacted, the Highlord grabbed her with one hand around her throat and lifted her effortlessly off the ground.

"I'll kill you!" he snarled in outrage. She mouthed words to him, unable to get air past his choking grip. The hated girl used her hands not to pry him off of her, or even to attempt it, but just to help support her weight by gripping his wrist.

"Dav," her lips formed the words as she hung calmly. She wasn't even fighting back. What was she doing? "I love you."

The Highlord never saw it coming. At her words, Dav surged up in his mind like a raging hurricane, tearing through the Highlord's mental and physical holds in a raw torrent of emotion-fueled willpower that left the entire colony of parasites momentarily stunned.

The Highlord dropped Allie as he struggled against Dav's impossible mental strength. The young boy's willpower was beyond iron, beyond steel, and burned through the Highlord's defenses. It was unbreakable, unstoppable, and fueled by the love of the girl he cherished above all others. The Highlord felt his control of Dav's mind and body being slowly, steadily, inexorably, pushed back.

No, he thought to himself! All this way, he would not succumb now! He would see his victory and vengeance enacted! Pulling on reserves of hatred and bloodlust he didn't even know he had, he pushed Dav's mind back first one small bit, then another. His consciousness snapped back to the physical world as Allie, who had moved forward the instant he'd dropped her, kissed him.

The unexpected act alone stunned him, and Dav's mind shoved the Highlord's down. Through the touch of her lips, her breath into his, Allie poured the energies of the universe. Bypassing the energy shield in such a way, the energies flowed through Dav's body unhindered. Her hands on his face, she held him firmly, but gently.

The power of space itself filled him, burned him, purified him. Light blazed all around the pair with the sheer force of the energy she had drawn in, bright enough that everyone on the battlefield was stunned by its brilliance.

The Highlord screamed inside Dav's body, but Dav had full control of the body and he held Allie tightly to him. The energy went through Dav's body like a wall of fire, the Highlord's very essence obliterated in its passing. Dav felt the tiny energy shield in his lungs short out with a painful surge of energy. In seconds, it was over.

Slowly, the light faded around the pair as Allie released the energies, leaving the field awash in the deep violet glow of the nearly-set sun of Ayaran, just barely still peeking above the horizon. Allie did not release him though, her lips still pressed to his, though it had changed. Dav kissed her back, with all the gentleness he knew she deserved.

After a long moment, she pulled back. She looked into his eyes and smiled softly. There was no shyness there, no hesitation. She looked at Dav, and he felt the unfettered strength of her feelings for him. How he had never seen it before, he had no idea, but he would never let it go.

# CHAPTER TWENTY FIVE

# GRATITUDE

The battlefield was still and quiet, marred only by the hum of the Tchratchi ships now lining the edge of the field as they finished bringing the Highlord's fleet to the ground. Everyone, man and beast alike, was staring at the young pair.

After a moment, the warriors on the battlefield began to regain full awareness of their surroundings as the intensity of the moment wore off. The traitors loyal to the Highlord began to notice the Tchratchi, and slowly lowered weapons and raised their hands.

Dav and Allie both looked around, changing position to be side by side. Dav took her hand in his and held it firmly.

"Wow, you really made a mess," Dav said teasingly as he surveyed the damage.

"Hey, half of this is your army!" she accused.

"Not mine," he corrected, and she smiled.

"I'm actually really impressed you brought all this together," Dav admitted.

"What can I say, I'm just that awesome." Allie said.

"Can't argue with that," he said with a bright grin. Allie had missed that smile. She had thought for a time she'd never see it again.

"Allie!" Raith called as he jogged over. One arm hung loosely at his side, he had a big gash in the side of his forehead where the Highlord had struck him, a huge, scorched wound on his shoulder and upper chest through which she could see his machinery moving, and he displayed several smaller cuts, dents, and scrapes.

"Raith!" She cried, grabbing him in a tight hug. He hugged her back with one arm. "I'm so glad you made it! You look terrible!"

"You too," he replied playfully as he released her, not bothering to clarify which of her comments he was returning back to her. "Where in the stars did you go when we got dropped here?"

"Nowhere," she replied.

"Come on, you've got to tell us," Dav urged, joining in.

"No, seriously," she affirmed. "I went to nowhere, engaged in mental battle with the last surviving member of mankind's progenitor race, flung him into the plane Beyond the Between where the very reality of his being was probably torn apart, saved another lost Starjumper, lost not only in space, but in time, and tore through the barrier of the physical dimension to bring myself back to you. I missed slightly, thanks for catching me," she added to Dav with a playful smile. Dav and Raith looked at each other, then back to her.

"I'm almost sorry I asked," Raith mumbled, with his usual mischievous grin, somewhat marred by the damage to the synthetic skin on the side of his face.

The Sy'hli had already begun tying up their prisoners of war. The jicund were all gathering by the tree line. Allie felt a surge of sorrow at the sight of them until she realized that they wouldn't have come to her aid without…

"Tic!" she shouted, spotting her dear little purple friend.

Tic looked a bit banged up herself, but was in surprisingly good shape considering she'd been slammed about by a combat android, then dropped in an exploding space ship from the outer atmosphere and into the middle of a jungle. Tic leapt into her arms, and Allie hugged her tightly.

"Thank you for coming to help, and bringing your… family?" she asked, looking at the jicund.

They were all adorable, she thought. Their eyes were various shades of blue and purple, some minor variations in size and facial shape, but they all looked very similar. The biggest variation was in their purple color. They ran the range from the palest lavender to a deep purple so dark it was nearly black. Sitting in a huge horde like this, it was the most diverse collection of purples she had ever seen, probably ever. Allie knelt down and looked at the mass of jicund closer to their level. Some were clearly older, some younger, but she had no idea if any were juveniles.

"Thank you all," she told them. She didn't know

how much they understood, but if they did understand her even half as much as she thought Tic did, she wanted to be sure they knew her gratitude. "You saved a lot of my friends' lives today and stopped a very bad person from destroying a lot more lives. I'm so sorry about the jungle. I'll have the Sy'hli Empire let me bring a cleanup crew here as soon as possible to try and get the broken ships out, and help restore some of the damaged jungle."

The jicund chittered and chattered contentedly in response, and Allie laughed. For all she knew, they might even have understood her. Several even came up and touched her arm or hand before running back into the jungle. A slightly bigger, dark purple jicund came over to them both and began chittering rapidly at Tic. Tic chittered back. This went on for a moment, then Tic jumped down and pressed her forehead against the other jicund, who put one three-fingered hand around the back of Tic's head.

It was their version of a hug, Allie understood. She didn't know how she knew that, but it felt like a very affectionate gesture to her. The pair broke and the dark jicund vanished into the brush. Tic jumped back into Allie's arms, and scrambled to her shoulder.

"Allie," Captain Abram said, interrupting her as he approached, his men at his back and Spike at his side.

"Thank you, Captain," she said, wrapping her arms around the big man's waist. He laughed deeply and hugged her back.

"You're welcome. I am sorry for losing you in the jungle. I should have been watching more closely," he told her.

"It's okay," she replied. "Preston was raised in a jungle like this, you wouldn't have caught him in time. Besides, without that, I wouldn't have brought the Rrughn to help." She gestured to the pack, standing near the tree line. The others all gave them a very wide berth. Even the Maruck kept glancing nervously at them.

"Is that what you call those things?"

"That's what they call themselves," she corrected. "Spike? Wow. Just… wow." Spike grinned and patted Shane.

"I don't get to turn him up to full power often. That was fun. Thanks for giving me an excuse to let loose."

"How did you even get that thing?" Raith asked. "Tchratchi, if I'm not mistaken."

"You're not. And it's a long story for another time. One of them did me a favor a long time ago. I did him a bigger one in return, and he had this made for me to square us up. I still think I got the better end of the deal."

"I'll say," Raith said admiringly.

"Stay close," Allie told them. "I'm about to Jump a whole lot of people to Sy'hloran. I can bring your ship too, if you like, so we can have the Sy'hli Empire fix it for you."

"I'm sure that's just what they'd do," Captain Abram said with a cynical laugh.

"They will," Dav said firmly beside her.

"Are you really Sy'hli royalty?" Captain Abram asked. He recognized Dav from their kidnapping, so knew who Dav was supposed to be. Allie suspected he was just affirming that the boy really did have the right to make that kind of offer.

"Prince Davrelan, of House Tyr-Arda, of the royal family of the Sy'hli Empire," Dav replied. Captain Abram looked at Allie, who nodded. The Captain grinned.

"Well then, Your Highness, I certainly won't refuse your generous offer. The Blackstar took quite a beating up there, and it'll be a pretty penny to fix. Worth it, helping Allie, but it'll take a huge bite out of my savings, and nobody wants that," Captain Abram said with a wink to Spike. She glowered at him, but again Allie could see the light in her eyes when she looked at him. She suspected that money was one of Spike's most beloved things, next to Shane and Captain Abram.

"I need to get the Rrughn home," Allie said, noticing the Rrughn eyeing the other members of her army, "before they eat someone." The captain nodded and Allie, Dav, and Raith walked over to the Rrughn. Allie noticed with some satisfaction that Dav and Raith both kept a little bit of distance.

*"Thank you again, Ydrahn," she said to him. "That was not your fight, but you came to my aid anyway."*

*"Speaker is like the Rrughn,"* he said simply, as if that were enough explanation. For him, it was. Allie nodded.

*"Call for me if you need my help. I owe you one."* Allie said. Ydrahn gave a little whuff sound, that Allie took for a laugh.

*"Ydrahn shall. The birthing season was not long ago. Soon will be the pups' first hunt. Speaker can help with Skykillers. They fly thick when the pups hunt their first prey, we lose many each season."*

*"I will come,"* she said, though she hadn't expected

that Ydrahn would take her up on her offer at all, let alone so soon. Ydrahn turned, and with his pack ran along the tree line for a moment, then vanished.

Allie realized just how many different people had come to her aid and felt a swell of gratitude. All friends, all willing to risk themselves for her and her cause. She'd never felt more loved than she had in this moment. Of course, Dav's hand in hers helped that. She walked to Ghier.

"Ghier, I owe you so much," she said. Ghier shook his head.

"I cost you one battle. I helped you win another. If you have forgiven me and call me once again friend, we are even." Allie grinned and held out her hand. Ghier looked at it for a long moment, then held his out similarly. She took the hand and shook it.

"Deal," she said. Ghier smiled at the odd custom, and at her acceptance. "Next time though, just let me know you're in danger. I'll make some calls and we'll get it sorted out." She glanced around at all of her friends. Ghier laughed lightly.

"I underestimated you, Allie Bennett. A powerful ally you are, and I am glad you did not decide to become my enemy. It would have been justified."

"No, I couldn't hate you for trying to protect your people. Besides, you did the right thing in the end. That's what matters. I'm sorry about the jungle. I already promised the jicund we'd get a cleaning crew out here to clear as much wreckage, and repair as much damage as possible," she said. Ghier nodded, then hesitated.

"You... do not look well, Allie Bennett," Ghier said

cautiously, as though afraid he would offend her.

"I'm sick, Ghier," she said, looking at her hands. The glow was stronger in her veins and the burning, while tolerable, was constant. She bit back the lump in her throat. If she was this bad already, how was Imber?

"Perhaps I can help," Ghier said as he reached out and touched her forehead. He recoiled almost immediately as though bitten by a venomous serpent. "No, no I am sorry. That I cannot help." Allie nodded, unsurprised.

"That's okay, Ghier. Thanks for wanting to help."

"Thank you, Allie Bennett. You are a true friend to the People of the Tree. Please, come back and visit as well."

"I will," she promised.

Hugging Ghier, she then turned and headed to talk to Dgehf as the People vanished into the trees. The Sy'hli had finished tying their prisoners of war and had rounded them up into tidy rows. That would make it easy for her to Jump them all to Sy'hloran, she thought with a smile.

Dgehf and his family looked in worse shape than anyone, including Raith. The gashes and wounds they all carried were testament to their struggle with Sandro.

"Oh, Dgehf," she said, unsure how to proceed. "We need to get you back to Sy'hloran for some medical care."

"No need," Dgehf rumbled deeply. "Dgehf and family need ship. Maruck medical supplies there. Son trained. Son warrior." Dgehf looked proudly at his son. "This day, earn warrior mark. Allie witness ritual?" he asked. Allie nodded.

"Of course," she said, having no idea what to expect. This was rather abrupt, but she supposed that a warrior ritual would logically take place on the field of the great battle that earned the honorable status.

Dgehf's son's wounded chest puffed up with pride and surprise. Dgehf turned to his son, and began chanting in Maruck. With one long claw, etched a single, intricate band low on his son's tusks. Allie hadn't noticed before, but realized that Dgehf and Garenha both had them as well. They were subtle, but noticeable now that she was paying attention. Those were the only markings on Dgehf's tusks, though Garenha's were completely covered in etchings. They would probably be the only ones on his son's too, if Allie understood the tradition correctly.

"Dhoreg," Dgehf said. Allie realized it was the first time anyone had said the younger Maruck's name. "Day before, just Maruck. This day, warrior of our clan. Honor to you."

"And you," Dhoreg said, his voice nearly as deep as Dgehf's. Well that was simple, Allie thought.

"Daghren," Dgehf said moving to the youngest Maruck, who looked both confused, and all at once incredibly excited.

"Dgehf, no," Garenha argued. "Daghren cub!"

"No," Dgehf said gently, "Daghren warrior. Battle by my side, your side, Dhoreg's side. See there?" Dgehf said, holding up Daghren's chin. A vicious gash, still covered in black ichor ran along the side of the little Maruck's neck. "And there?" Dgehf added, pointing to another huge gash down his arm. It was shallow, all the wounds on the mighty Maruck were, but it looked excruciating. Daghren didn't flinch as Dgehf touched it. Daghren had just as many wounds as the bigger Maruck.

"Garenha see," she replied, still looking uncertain about this.

"Warrior earned," Dgehf said firmly, but gently. He turned to Daghren. "Daghren fight. Daghren fight strong, fight fast. Daghren brave, not run from terrible foe. Daghren charge with family and find victory. Daghren warrior."

With that, Dgehf etched the mark into the young Maruck's tusks. Daghren could barely contain himself, and began jumping excitedly around and grunting in enthusiasm as soon as Dgehf was done. Dgehf chuckled, a low, resonating sound.

"Allie warrior," Dgehf said with a toothy grin her way. "Want mark?" he held up one vicious claw, longer than her longest finger.

"Um," she said, stepping back and raising her hands. "That's okay, thanks though. I'm fresh out of tusks." Dav, Raith, and Dgehf all laughed. "Can I at least Jump you back to your ship? Save you the walk."

"Yes," Dgehf said. "Thank you, Allie friend."

"Okay, let me go talk to the Tchratchi, and we can go."

Dgehf nodded, and Allie turned to the Tchratchi line. One of the little ships landed, and a small Tchratchi warrior came out in full battle gear. It was impressive, she thought. It would be terrifying if he were more than two inches tall, but even so she knew the little insectoid was more than a match for her.

"Starjumper has done well," the Tchratchi said in his own language. She clicked and scratched back in perfect Tchratchi, elbowing Dav when he threatened to crack a smile.

"Thank you. Your timing was flawless, and your execution even more so. The Tchratchi are every bit as formidable as I had heard."

"Your words are generous," the Tchratchi replied. "The Starjumper will continue to help bring peace back to the galaxy." Allie caught the tone. It was not a request.

"I will," she promised. "In any way I can." The Tchratchi nodded, satisfied. It looked around at the prisoners and all the Sy'hli."

"You require transportation?" it asked.

"No, thank you," she replied. "I can handle it."

The Tchratchi regarded her carefully for a long moment, then nodded and went back into the small ship. The ship lifted again, and the Tchratchi swarm as one launched into the sky, humming as they rolled and spun together, looking very much like a swarm of giant, angry bees, and they were gone. Allie took a deep breath and looked at her friends. She didn't feel so well. Now that the rush of battle had worn off, she suddenly felt very drained, and her body ached all over. Sick people should not be running around like this.

"Okay," she said to Dav and Raith. "Let's get our Maruck friends back to their ship for some first aid, then we can come back here and bring everyone back to Sy'hloran." The pair nodded, and she headed for Dgehf and his family.

"Daghren   warrior!"   Daghren   said   proudly,

thumping his chest and grinning to show off his warrior mark.

"You certainly are," she said with a laugh. "Mighty and powerful, and brave! Just like your uncle," she said. Daghren's grin spread clear across his face.

"Allie ready?" Dgehf asked. Allie nodded.

"Are you?"

He nodded and his family gathered closer. He reached to touch her, but realized he was still covered in Sandro's blood, which he knew to be caustic to her.

"It's okay," she reassured him. "I don't need to touch you for this." Dgehf looked surprised, but nodded.

"It will be good to get back to the ship. Garenha gave birth this morning," he said in Maruck. Allie about choked on her astonishment.

"What?" she asked, stunned.

"Just this morning. A female," he explained.

"Where is the baby?" Allie asked, horrified at both the baby left alone, and Garenha having given birth that morning, and battling that evening.

"On our ship," he replied. "Not ideal," he said, giving her an apologetic look. "No choice." Allie looked to Garenha. The woman looked war-torn and exhausted, her black eyes dull and weary.

"Garenha, I can't tell you how much I respect your strength," Allie said. Garenha nodded with a smile.

"Thank you, you have shown great bravery and strength as well. I am sorry, for misjudging you when first we met." Allie smiled.

"That's okay. Like the Tchratchi, it's easy to underestimate someone this little." Garenha nodded and smiled.

"I shall not make that mistake again," the noble Maruck warrior replied.

"Shall we take you to your baby?" Allie asked.

At this, finally, Garenha's eyes sparkled. Allie was filled with warmth at that reaction. Maruck may be a fierce species, but there was love there, and kindness. Allie had hope that they would be able to ally with the Maruck in the future. They would be powerful allies, and fierce friends, all the more so if Dgehf regained leadership.

Allie reached her mind out, embracing the energies. They flowed through her, pure and unobstructed by rogellium or outside interference. She felt like a fish being returned to the water after a frightening stint on dry land. This was her element.

She wrapped her mind around the Maruck family, Dav, and Raith, and sent her mind to touch Dgehf's ship. She found the docking bay easily, since she'd been there before, and Jumped. The transition was instantaneous, and as smooth as walking through a doorway. This, she knew, was how Jumping was supposed to feel.

"We can bring your ship to Sy'hloran," Allie told them when they had landed. "They'll repair it for you."

"No," Dgehf said, shaking his head. "Much bad blood between Sy'hli and Maruck. Will rebuild, but not in one day. My ship will fly well enough to get us somewhere safe. I can repair myself."

"Are you sure?" Dav asked. "Your family are friends to the Sy'hli royal family. None would threaten you there."

"Thank you, Dav friend, but Dgehf's family must heal. We will visit soon, if Dav friend accepts?"

"Of course!" Dav said. "Honored guests of the prince."

Dgehf smiled and clapped Dav on the back. Deghf's hand more than engulfed Dav's entire back, and the blow caused Dav to stumble. It probably would have killed Allie, she thought with a wince.

"We'll leave you in peace then," Allie said. "Goodbye, Dgehf."

"Wait," said Garenha. She looked a little uncomfortable for the first time Allie had ever seen, as though she was suddenly uncertain about the reaction to what she was about to say. "Would you like… to meet the new cub?"

Another first, Allie could barely contain a girlish squeal. A brand new baby Maruck? How could she possibly say no to that?

"Oh yes, Garenha, I would love that very much!"

Garenha gestured for them to follow. The group moved through the ship, to a room near the center. Opening the door, they went inside. In what could only be described as an iron basinet, a small figure wrapped in soft leather squirmed.

Allie moved forward beside Garenha, and peered inside. Within the little cradle was possibly the cutest little beast Allie had ever seen. The tiny face that peered up at her with midnight-black, sparkling eyes was so full of fuzzy brown fur, that all she could see was the two little black eyes, and a little black nose.

Garenha scooped the infant Maruck out of the cradle

and held her low so Allie could see. The baby Maruck opened its mouth and let out a soft, smooth purring noise. Its little mouth had a full set of short, dog-like teeth.

One little hand worked its way free, stubby little fingers reaching for Allie. Allie looked to Garenha, who nodded. Allie held out her two fingers. The little Maruck was the size of a small human child and could easily grip her two fingers in its over-sized hand. The baby grabbed her fingers and squeezed. Allie gasped, immediately prying her hand free of the baby's vice-like grip.

"I think she got your strength," Allie said to Garenha, cradling her bruised fingers as she finally pried them free. Garenha chuckled and nodded. Dav and Raith watched the little Maruck squirm.

"Full set of teeth at birth, huh?" Dav asked.

Dgehf nodded. "No baby food for you, then," he said, poking a finger playfully at the fur ball. The baby stretched and yawned. Dav gently stroked the baby's fur, then stepped back. Raith looked at the infant.

"I've seen pictures. And videos," Raith said, "but this is different. She's beautiful."

"Thank you," Garenha said softly, and Allie got another glimpse of the woman inside the warrior. Maruck weren't that different from us, she decided. Some good ones, some bad ones, but people nonetheless.

"She must feed," Dgehf said softly.

"Thank you," Allie said to Garenha, allowing Dgehf to gently shoo them out of the room. Dgehf and Daghren followed them. In the passageway, Allie touched Dgehf's arm carefully in one of the few uninjured spots. He appeared to have scraped off most of the black ichor, though some still stuck to his fur. She just didn't want to cause him pain by touching one of the wounds.

"Thank you Dgehf, you're a great friend."

"Allie is a great friend too," the huge Maruck rumbled, his massive hand, capable of crushing Allie in one fist, resting with incredible gentleness on her back.

"Call me if you need anything, or want to visit," Allie told him. "I can be to you, or have you to us in a flash."

"Dgehf will call. Thank you, Allie friend."

"Goodbye, Dgehf. Goodbye Daghren!" she said to the excitable little Maruck. He pounced on her in a hug, squeezing too tight. She gasped.

"Gently, gently!" Dav shouted in alarm, prying Daghren's arms off of her. Allie sucked in a breath. A hissing sound reached her and she realized his hug had rubbed some of Sandro's caustic blood on her suit. Dav reacted fast, grabbing handfuls of dirt and rubbing them onto the ichor. How he knew that would help, Allie had no idea, but it did. The hissing stopped almost instantly.

Daghren looked extremely embarrassed.

"Daghren sorry."

"It's okay, thank you for the hug. We'll see you soon, okay?"

"Okay. Daghren sorry," the little Maruck said. Allie laughed.

"I know, I'm okay," she assured him, hugging him again to reassure the poor cub, careful not to touch any of the black patches. He hugged her back with exaggerated gentleness.

"All right, we need to get some prisoners back to Sy'hloran, and see how Imber is doing." Dgehf and Daghren nodded.

With only half a thought and seemingly no effort, she took her friends back to the battlefield. The Sy'hli were ready and waiting, guarding the prisoners. Captain Abram and his men were helping.

Now came the moment she'd been dreading. She looked at Tic on her shoulder and reached up, bringing Tic into her arms. Gently, she kissed Tic's furry head. Tic's little ears twitched and she chirped in question.

"This is your home, Tic. You can go home again. All the bugs you can eat, and a nice comfy jungle to call home." Allie knew she couldn't take Tic away again. Tic chittered, almost angrily back at Allie.

"Your family is here," Allie protested, not understanding Tic's speech, but reading the tone perfectly. Tic looked back at the jungle and chirped sadly, then looked back to Allie. "I can't make you go," she said, "we both know that." Tic chittered, sounding satisfied.

"But I want you to know I won't be mad if you want to stay here. This is your home." Tic whistled once, sharply, and climbed firmly back to Allie's shoulder, where she gripped tight enough that it was not quite painful, but made a clear point. Tic had made her decision. She would stay with Allie. Allie laughed, mostly in relief.

"Okay, okay. You can stay with me. We'll come back and visit though, okay?" she said. Tic chirped happily. Allie noticed Dav watching her strangely. "What?" she asked.

"Sometimes, that little critter worries me," Dav said. Tic let out a contented purr, and reached out to tug on Dav's hair. "Hey now!" Tic chittered and let him go. Allie grinned.

"That'll teach you to pick on a girl," she said. Dav sighed melodramatically, making Allie giggle.

"Everyone ready?" Raith called out.

They got nods from mercenary and Sy'hli soldier alike. The number of captives was impressive. Allie knew she could do it though. Mentally, she reached out. This was a little harder, though still not as hard as jumping a hundred Sy'hli warships.

Allie wove her mental net around all of the men and women present, and around the Blackstar many miles away in the jungle.

"Hey, Captain Ahab," Dav called suddenly, "I want my Interceptor back!" Captain Abram burst into laughter as Allie Jumped them all to Sy'hloran.

# CHAPTER TWENTY SIX

# SACRIFICE

They all landed neatly on one of the huge prison platforms, to the absolute panic of the Sy'hloran prison guards. Only the obvious traitor prisoners and the huge number of Sy'hli strike troops calmed them before they started shooting. Even one of the big battle cruisers had moved into position when they appeared. A prison captain ran out to them, approaching one of the Sy'hli ship captains. They began speaking rapidly. Allie moved over to them.

"Don't worry Captain, our security is the best in the galaxy."

"Oh yeah?" Allie snapped. "Then how did Preston, the Highlord's right-hand man, get out of here?"

"Young lady, that was not this prison, and it took a fully-functional combat android to get him out. I didn't even know there were any of those left operating. And I'll thank you to show some respe…"

"Hold your tongue, Captain," the ship's captain interrupted sternly. "This is the Starjumper and Prince Davrelan." The prison captain paled slightly and he bowed.

"I beg your pardon. I should have known when you all arrived so suddenly," the man said, stumbling over his words. And that, Allie knew, was why he wasn't a ship captain.

"Think nothing of it," Dav said grandly. "Just be sure that these prisoners are secured immediately. Watch the Maruck, they can be a little… nasty. As for my friends," Dav gestured to the mercenaries and their captain who had already moved over to the Blackstar that Allie had not only Jumped along with them, but had moved nearby, "make sure that they are taken to the palace guest quarters, and their ship into the royal docking bay where it is to be repaired immediately."

"Yes, Your Highness," both captains said and bowed. Allie walked with him as he turned and strode away, Raith along with them.

"Now that that's taken care of, let's get ourselves to Imber and see how she's doing."

"Yes, Your Highness," Allie said bowing deeply.

"Stop that!" Dav said with a laugh.

There was no laughter when Allie Jumped the trio to the infirmary. Imber looked terrible. The glow covered her entire body now, her veins and heirlines showing brightest of all. She was still unconscious. Dav looked to the doctor at the console by Imber's bed.

"No breaks, Your Highness. We still can't stop the virus," the doctor said. Allie noticed the doctor had a faint glow in her eyes as well. None of them would last much longer.

"Why did we go through all of that?" Dav asked softly, eyes back on Imber. "All that fighting, all that struggle to save lives, and in the end, we're all going to die anyway? What's the point?" he finished, his tone growing angry.

"Actually," Raith interrupted, "I had a few ideas to try."

"Anything good?" Dav asked, suddenly hopeful again. Allie tried to keep her own hope in check. Imber probably wouldn't last another day.

"We'll find out pretty quickly," Raith replied. "I'll need some time in here with her though. Alone. And access to that equipment." Raith pointed at the top-of-the-line Sy'hli lab equipment set up on one side of the room. The doctor opened his mouth to protest, but one look from Dav and it shut with an audible click.

"Of course," said the doctor, bowing and walking out of the room.

Dav walked over to Imber, and gently touched her hand. He leaned down and kissed her cheek and whispered in her ear.

"Hang in there. We're still here." Dav stood and left. Allie squeezed her friend's hand as well.

"Can you do this with one arm?" she asked Raith before leaving. He nodded.

"Yes, it's mostly simulations and some programming. Besides, I can use it a little," he told her, lifting the arm and moving the fingers. They looked a little imprecise in their movements, but they moved. She nodded, and headed for the door.

"Good luck," she said as the door closed behind her.

Raith immediately went to work. He had only enough time for one shot at this. Imber's vitals were already unstable, he could see that much on the readout above her bed.

Quickly he grabbed one of the samples of her blood from the table. Everyone else had been moved out of this room, so there were a couple of empty beds beside the table they'd set up the mobile lab on. He moved to the equipment and hurriedly prepared the sample for study.

The entire plan hinged on one key factor. The nanobots had to have been built the way he suspected they had been, or this wouldn't work at all. Even if they had been, he still had a worryingly small chance of success. His estimations gave Imber less than eight hours until her organs shut down on her.

This would take six hours, at least, he knew. He was racing the clock from the moment he'd seen her and the condition she was in. Quickly he scanned the sample, growing frustrated as he waited for the scanner to work. It was amazing that something that took precisely the same amount of time, every time, to the nanosecond, seemed to take infinitely longer when you were in a hurry.

Done. He grabbed the datapad with the readout and began scanning thousands of pages of data gleaned from the five second scan. It took him another five seconds to scroll through all the pages, his processors taking in every bit of data at a glance.

The results were inconclusive. The system wasn't refined enough for the data he needed. The Highlord probably had the only machines capable of this kind of work back on the Helios. That made this harder, but not impossible. He could still attempt his idea, but it was a gamble as to whether or not it would work at all. If they were built the way he suspected, then he had a chance. A small chance, but a chance. If they were not, he would waste the next six hours, and every living thing in the galaxy, starting with Imber, would die.

He moved to her bedside, pulling over the chair. He took her hand in his good one, resting his wounded one over hers. Raith looked at the girl on the bed. She was more to him than a friend. He knew that, had known for some time. It was impossible, though.

He had very little time left, whichever way this experiment turned out. If he succeeded, she would live a long, and hopefully happy life, finding love, raising a family, continuing to be a huge asset to her friends, the Sy'hli royal family, and to the Starjumper… If he failed, she would be dead in hours, and he would go around the same time.

Even if he succeeded, he would be gone. Even if he weren't gone, it wouldn't have worked, he knew. He was a machine, she was a biological. All of his emotions and thoughts were a result of his programming. It didn't matter to him, though. He loved her just the same. He loved her smile, he loved her laugh, he loved the way she talked to him like a person. Not many people in this galaxy did that. He loved Allie and Dav for that too, but with Imber there was something more.

With Imber, he forgot that he was a machine. He was able to suspend that part of his mind, and just be with her. She made him laugh, she made him feel that his existence, such as it was, had real purpose. With her, he felt alive.

Reaching up to his face, he was surprised to find his cheeks were wet. He was built with tear ducts, to aid in his emulation of a young human boy, but he hadn't activated them. None of it mattered. He would do his best to save her, and Allie and Dav, everyone. And when it was over, he would have succeeded, or he would have failed. Either way, he would be gone. He wouldn't even know if it worked until after he was gone.

Standing, he leaned down low over Imber's luminescent form, and gently kissed her lips. The most alive he had ever felt, in the hours before his death. He appreciated the irony. Straightening with resolve, he moved to the console beside her bed, touching the control pad and began his work. Whether he succeeded or failed, he would die trying.

Many hours had passed, and Allie was concerned. She knew Imber didn't have long, but she also knew that if Raith was still in there, he was dedicating every bit of processing power he had into attempting his cure, whatever it was.

She sat now, in the waiting room beyond the

infirmary, with Dav beside her, holding her hand. She appreciated his strength, but she could see his pain and worry as well. She couldn't see any glow in the backs of his eyes like she could in almost everyone else's now. Allie knew it would only be a matter of time, though.

Unless Raith succeeded. Allie could think of a lot of ways to bet your life, but gambling on whether Raith could pull off a crazy last minute stunt was one of the most reliable ways to walk away unscathed.

Allie had said as much to Dav, who had laughed and agreed. Android or not, that boy had ridiculously good luck. Raith would argue that it was skill, not luck. Allie suspected it was a healthy dose of both.

Artus and Morgan had come, but both had other obligations they couldn't get away from. Imber's father was in another room, just as ill as Imber. Many of the Shaian on Sy'hloran were nearing their final moments, and many other races were falling too ill to work.

Tyren had come by as well, and while Dav had fervently told him that he understood now exactly what Tyren had gone through, Tyren had gracefully bowed out. He had come only to share his hopes for her recovery, and then went to post his vigil alone, to bear a burden of grief and guilt he felt he carried due to the Highlord's actions.

As firmly as Dav had believed Tyren held guilt for what had been done before becoming infected himself, Tyren held a similar belief that part of the burden was his, for not breaking free himself and ending it. When people started to die… if, Allie corrected herself, if people started to die, Tyren felt that part of that was his weight to carry.

She still had faith in Raith, though. If anyone could save them, it was him. And if even he couldn't, then in the end, the Highlord would have won. She couldn't bear that thought, so insisted to herself and Dav that Raith would solve it. He could do more research in an hour than a regular doctor could in days. Raith had been back there for almost six hours now, he had the equivalent of weeks of research and simulations run already, Allie knew.

The door opened, and both Allie and Dav shot to their feet. Raith stepped out. He hadn't taken the time to clean up and get some healing done like the rest of them. If anything, he looked worse now than when he'd gone in. His eyes were slightly dull, like his processing power was still elsewhere.

He stood for a moment, silent. Allie looked beyond to where Imber lay and gasped. There was no glow. Running to Imber's bedside, she panicked, thinking Imber had passed away. On the contrary, Imber looked much better. The glow was gone, she was breathing deeply and in a state of deep sleep. Her skin had some color, and she looked almost healthy.

"I took the liberty to..." Raith paused like he'd forgotten what he was about to say. Allie looked to him. That was odd, he never forgot. Anything, unless he'd programmed it out of his memory core. "The liberty to use some of the medical equipment to help her regenerate some, now that the deterioration has stopped."

Raith sounded tired, Allie realized. He never

sounded tired, either. Clasping Imber's hand in relief, she went to Raith. He was walking, very slowly, to the door leading to the big gardens outside. She and Dav followed. Walking to a big open grassy area in the middle, he looked up at the sky.

"Good," he said slowly, as if to himself, "lots of light." He seemed to be taking a lot of effort to speak, Allie observed with concern.

"You cured her?" she asked. Raith looked to her and nodded.

"Yes, I found a way to cure her. To cure everyone."

"Raith, that's great!" Allie shouted. Dav was watching Raith with worry on his face.

"How long?" Dav asked. Raith looked at Dav, and smiled. It was a ghost of his old mischievous grin, but Allie could still see the spark there.

"Can't get anything by you," Raith said with a chuckle. "I actually have a few weeks left," he replied.

"What?" Allie asked, confused. Raith continued.

"But I need that for the cure."

Allie had no idea what he was talking about, but Dav seemed to get it. Dav nodded slowly, bit his lower lip in a gesture Allie had never seen from him, then stepped forward and put his arms around his friend. Raith return the hug tightly with his one good arm.

"Allie," Raith said when Dav had let him go. Why did this suddenly feel like a funeral, Allie wondered, a pit growing in her stomach.

"What's going on, Raith?" she asked. Raith stepped over to her.

"Allie, you're my first and very best friend. I owe

you… everything. My freedom, my friendships with Imber, Dav, even Artus and Morgan. I owe you the only happiness I've ever known."

"Raith, you're scaring me," she said, voice cracking.

"Don't be scared. You don't have to be scared of anything, anymore. The plague will be lifted from this world by dawn, and all other worlds in a few days. It will be cured so fast that there won't be a single casualty. Not one living soul. The Highlord is destroyed, the traitors to the true Coalition are now being hunted by the Sy'hli and Tchratchi, and to top it off, you're in love with a prince. Life doesn't get any better," he gave her a half grin.

"But what about you?" she asked, beginning to admit to herself what Raith and Dav's actions were telling her.

"Allie, I'm reprogramming the nanovirus to reprogram the other nanobots. I pulled them all out of Imber, and am reprogramming them right now. I need to release them, so they can ride the light and the wormholes and reprogram all the nanobots. It works fast, you'll see. This whole world will be cured by dawn."

"They're in you?" she asked, not understanding. He smiled softly.

"A robo-boy carrying a robo-virus. Makes sense, right?"

"So what does that mean for you?"

"I need to release them fast, and with a lot of light. I'm going to overload my power core."

"Raith, no!" Allie cried. "Can't you just pull them out of everyone?"

"One person at a time at four hours a piece? I

wouldn't even get through this palace before the rest of the galaxy was dead. Like I said, fast and with a lot of light."

"But Raith, you can't do that!" she said, fighting back the tears.

"I have to. It's totally safe for you, it's just light. Besides, I only have a couple of weeks left before my power core runs out anyway. This way I'm able to save the galaxy while I go."

"Raith," Allie said, unsure what else to say. He was right, as always. The tears fell freely down her cheeks.

"Allie, you'll be great. The galaxy is already a safer place than when you came into it, thanks to you and our friends. Dav, Imber, and Tic will take care of you, and you'll take care of them. All the tough stuff is over, you don't need me anymore anyway." Allie stepped forward and put her arms tightly around him, pressing her face into his neck.

"We'll always need you," she said into his collar. He hugged her with his one good arm.

"The reprogramming is done. I have to go," he said after a long moment. Allie sniffled and let him go. She stepped back. Raith reached up and scratched Tic behind the ears. For once, Tic didn't purr or trill. "Hey, take care of these guys for me, would you?" he asked. Tic chirped a soft assent. Raith leaned forward and kissed Allie's cheek tenderly.

"Take care of Imber. She won't take this well when she wakes up, and will need a good friend to help her through it. Thanks for everything, Allie. You're the best friend I ever had. And I've had the best time of my life since I met you guys." Raith flashed his trademark grin, his eyes sparkling. He really was done with the nanobots, she knew. His eyes were bright and focused.

Allie stepped back with Dav, holding his hand tightly. Raith moved a few more feet away, then turned around to face them. He held one hand up in a casual wave, then closed his eyes. For a long moment, nothing happened. Then Raith began to glow. Not like the glow in her own veins from the virus, but a warm, bright glow all over.

She felt the warmth from the light as it built in intensity. As the light grew, Raith's features became indistinct, lost in the brilliant glow. Small particles of brighter light began to shoot out from his body, like tiny stars, she thought. One struck her, but she didn't feel anything. The radius of his light stretched out across the gardens now, long beams arcing away into the sky.

Raith was too bright to look at now, and Allie was forced to look away. She looked at Dav, who watched in typical determined fashion. The light shone off the tears on his own cheeks. He squeezed her hand reassuringly, but didn't look away. She tried to look at him, but couldn't take the intensity of the light.

Her eyes went to the doorway of the infirmary waiting room, not far away. Imber stood, leaning against the doorframe for support, her face ashen and her hand covering her mouth in horror and grief. Tears poured down her face.

Before Allie could go to her, the light was gone. Allie looked back, and there was no sign of Raith. No sign he'd ever been there at all. She felt better though, she realized.

Looking down at her hands, she watched as the glow visibly faded, faded until it was completely gone. Raith had been right, the cure did work fast.

Imber's sob pulled her eyes back up. She ran to her friend and embraced her. Imber clung to her like Allie was her only support, physically and emotionally. Raith was right about that, too. She was going to need a good friend to help her through this.

At the end of it all, Raith had been the one to save the galaxy. Not the Starjumper, not the Coalition, not even the Tchratchi. In the same instant, she had watched the salvation of the galaxy cure the greatest plague the galaxy had ever known, and she had lost one of her dearest friends.

In either case, the galaxy would never be the same.

# EPILOGUE

# SALVATION

Allie closed the last clasp on the intricate, elegant dress she now wore. It was a design unlike anything she'd ever seen and was at once delicate and other-worldly. She had never even seen anything quite as beautiful, let alone dreamed of wearing something like this.

Months had passed since the battle on Ayaran. The Tchratchi had come in the trillions and were even now sweeping the galaxy. Peace in this quadrant had come almost overnight once the full strength of the Tchratchi swarm had been turned to bear on the forces trying to bring chaos and pain.

Even the Coalition opposed to the Sy'hli had become very compliant once the first fleet of Hgrundewa had been annihilated in less than thirty seconds. Artus and Dav had been working hard to reassure the Coalition that domination was not on the Sy'hli agenda and after months of diplomatic meetings and visits off-world, the Coalition was once more working together to further the unity and well-being of mankind in all its forms. Once it was truly clear the Sy'hli did not mean to attempt to dominate the galaxy again, even those most aggressively opposed to the Sy'hli had at least reached a stage of steady truce. Sinara's arrival had helped with that as well, though Allie knew the Tchratchi presence had made a huge difference in everyone's feelings of aggression.

The behavior of all of the Coalition, firm ally and otherwise alike, had come to resemble that of a field of mice trying to go about their business with a huge pack of well-fed wolves hanging around. They all knew the Tchratchi had no intention of harming anyone who meant no harm to others, but it was still more than a little intimidating knowing that the swarm could readily kill them all if they decided to. Allie wasn't worried. She understood the Tchratchi.

They were a peaceful race at their core, and while not exactly benevolent, they weren't hostile either. They had their section of space and were happy staying to themselves, as long as the rest of the galaxy kept its struggles from spilling into their territory and threatening their way of life. Even the Highlord had understood that to an extent, right up until the release of his virus, which he believed would end all life, including the Tchratchi. The Highlord would have succeeded too, if Raith hadn't sacrificed himself for the rest of them.

Allie's throat tightened at the thought of her friend. His death had hit them all hard, and only the close support of Artus, Dav, Allie, Imber, Tic, Morgan, and even Tyren, had held all of them up against the pressing weight of their grief. Dav, Artus, and Tyren had become close, like Artus and Tyren used to be, from what Allie understood. Tyren recognized that his presence diplomatically would cause more harm than good, so he kept mostly to himself around the palace and avoided the emissaries and ambassadors of the other races.

Allie had seen him with his brothers though, and even Dav showed by his actions that he had completely forgiven his eldest brother. This was a relief not only to Artus and Tyren, but to Allie as well. Having found himself in the same position Tyren had been in obviously changed Dav's perspective. Tyren himself had opened up a great deal, the grief that had threatened to overwhelm him due to the guilt he felt at even unwillingly having participated in the release of the virus and the end of the galaxy had vanished the moment Raith's cure had taken effect and he knew that not one more person would lose their lives as a result of the Highlord's evil.

Tyren had expressed more than once his admiration and respect for Dav having been able to beat the parasitic colony, as Tyren had been unable to do. Having no siblings, Allie didn't quite understand the bond the brothers shared, but once Dav's feelings of resentment and anger had vanished and Tyren's guilt had calmed, the trio had come together to support, encourage, comfort, and rebuild one another in a way that made her envy the brothers.

The eldest of the House of Tyr'Arda may not have

been involved actively in the diplomatic goals and leadership of the Sy'hli anymore, but behind the scenes he and his brothers had many long conversations about the state of the galaxy and the council.

Tyren had a sharp mind and a keen insight into the political motivations of the various people of the Coalition, and many of the specific emissaries as well. Dav had told Allie more than once they couldn't have come so far so fast without his help.

Allie looked at herself in the mirror. Her mother had done her hair, but Dav had chosen the dress for her. She had asked him to, not knowing what was fashionable in the Sy'hli court. He'd done a brilliant job. Her breath caught as she gazed at her reflection. For the first time, she felt she might actually fit in with the events of the day, looking like she belonged next to Dav during Artus' coronation as the Emperor of the Sy'hli.

More than that, Allie was to be inducted into the Order of the Silver Star by her mother and Sinara. It was to be a huge ceremony, following the even more grand coronation. They had decided the ceremonies would be done together, allowing everyone to attend both.

Allie and Morgan were about to Jump back to Earth to bring Katharine back to Sy'hloran. They had spent a week back on Earth after the battle at Ayaran, reuniting with her adoptive mother, and Morgan's dearest friend. The reunion had been tearful, for all parties, and only the presence of Tic and Allie's demonstration of Jumping had helped Katharine overcome her complete disbelief of everything they told her.

In the end, she had agreed to come with Allie and

Morgan back to Sy'hloran to live, on the condition that Allie bring them all back to Earth often to visit friends, family, and for the occasional cheeseburger or pizza. Katharine was still astonished that they could come back anytime for a random treat, to catch an Earth movie, or do any of the normal, ordinary things they used to. Even more incredible, it would take less time to travel from across the galaxy than it would have to have driven downtown before.

Katharine had asked for a couple of months to prepare, get her things in order, and come to grips with such an amazing life change. Allie and Morgan had gladly granted it, but today was the day Allie would go back to bring Katharine to her new home on an alien world, where she would watch her best friend induct her adopted daughter into an ancient and powerful order of guardians and protectors.

Dav had even said he would make Katharine the emissary to Earth and the human race. Sadly they wouldn't know anything about it, but Katharine would be given the unique opportunity to represent her entire species in front of a galactic Coalition to ensure they were looked after and left to develop and evolve in peace. Katharine would be finishing getting ready for the coronation and induction ceremonies as well, wearing a traditional Earth formal gown. Allie hoped she wore the green one. Katharine had always looked regal in the green dress on the rare chance she'd had to wear it.

Allie left her room, Tic once more on her shoulder and purring like a happy kitten. She wanted to go see Imber and make sure she would be ready for the ceremony. Imber had strongly spoken for Artus with her father and the Queen, and gained a great deal of political ground for the new Emperor and representative of the Sy'hli Empire on the Coalition Council.

It had taken the brothers some time to decide that was how things should be. While it was the right way according to tradition for the next eldest to take the crown, Artus was convinced Dav would do a better job. Tyren was out of the question for obvious reasons, and he had already abdicated any claim to the throne. They had argued about it for weeks before Tyren had finally stepped in and pointed out the obvious.

Not only would the people respond better if things were done according to tradition, but Dav's natural knack for politics and diplomacy, coupled with his incredibly quick mind, charismatic personality, and unbendable will made him a perfect choice for a diplomatic emissary.

Artus would rule from Sy'hloran, handling the Council with the help of Morgan as representative of the Order of the Silver Star. Dav, with Allie's aid, would travel on diplomatic missions to other worlds, meeting with other people both in and outside the Coalition.

Allie's translating abilities would be invaluable, as would her ability to move them anywhere they needed to go instantaneously. They could travel across the galaxy in the morning after breakfast, spend all day helping others and negotiating with other races to further peace and harmony in the galaxy, and Allie could Jump them back home in time for dinner. Of course some longer trips would be required, but they would waste no time in traveling.

Dav was actually a little disappointed about that, but Captain Abram, true to his word, had brought back the Peacekeeper, and Dav could fly it just for fun now. Allie could bring it along with them anywhere they went as well, so he could play in other systems as well.

They were stuck bringing along a virtual army of Sy'hli Royal Guards as well of course, at both Morgan and Artus' insistence, but that was to be expected. Allie felt another pang of loss as she thought of how perfect Raith and Imber would be as bodyguards as well.

Ambassador Oren wouldn't let Imber travel anywhere he wasn't, and expressly forbade her from going on diplomatic missions with the Starjumper and the Sy'hli Prince. Allie considered it lucky enough they were even still allowed to be friends with her.

Although these days, Imber wasn't doing too well, and was obsessing about some project. Nobody knew what it was, but it had brought life back to Imber's eyes, so nobody pushed too hard. She'd taken Raith's death harder than any of them, and the knowledge that he'd not have lasted much longer anyway due to his failing power core didn't seem to help her at all. She was always so distant and quiet lately. Imber spoke when you talked to her, but she didn't engage with others like she used to.

Imber had been spending more and more time in her private workshop lately, and Allie had more than once Jumped her to other worlds or space stations to acquire parts Allie couldn't even pronounce, but that Imber insisted were incredibly rare and critical to the project.

Allie would check on Imber, then go meet up with

her mother. They would go get Katharine, then return in time for the beginning of the ceremony. Walking down the hall, she rounded a corner and saw Dav just coming the other direction. She froze.

He looked absolutely incredible. His hair had been gently styled into something that was halfway between the usual, carefully wild style he preferred, and the precisely crafted, noble style both his brothers were wearing these days. His high boots, sharply-cut pants, and royal blue jacket trimmed in silver made him look every bit the young prince, the color of the jacket making his already-striking eyes look so brilliant they were almost luminescent.

It took her a long moment to realize Dav had frozen as well and was looking at her with an expression that probably resembled the one she currently wore. They must have looked like a couple of idiots, she thought, blushing as she glanced down and smiled. Dav flashed his perfect grin as she looked up at him again. He moved forward.

"Allie, wow," he said, "you look… perfect." Her blush deepened.

"Thanks. I feel kind of silly, but…"

"Don't," he said simply, reaching out and taking her hand.

"Thanks," she said again. "You look great, too. A proper prince," she added. He laughed lightly.

"Yeah, well. I still feel like the kid down the block. These formal outfits make me feel a little ridiculous."

"Don't," she replied with a grin.

He shook his head with a smile. Artus and Tyren

weren't the only ones who had grown closer to Dav over the last few months. Simply knowing without doubt how the other felt had opened up levels to their connection neither knew had existed. She loved him, she knew, and seemed to love him more every time he looked at her with those incredible eyes. In those eyes was her entire existence, and they threatened to swallow her whole any time she looked at them too long. And Dav was prone to staring. She gave him a nudge with her elbow as she held his hand firmly. Allie started walking again, toward Imber's room just a few doors down the hall.

"Checking on Imber?" he asked. She nodded.

"I'm worried about her. I haven't seen her all day, and she was a little… intense last night. She said she was almost finished with that project, but I wanted to make sure she was ready for the ceremonies before I go get Katharine." Dav nodded.

"I was heading to find you. I figured you'd want to check up on her," Dav said. "I hope she finishes soon, I'm starting to worry too."

"She'll be okay," Allie said as they reached Imber's door. Allie touched the control panel by the door and sent a notice signal to let Imber know she was there.

Imber raised the magnification goggles from her head and wiped at her brow. Months, she had been working on this project, and was minutes away from completing the greatest work she had ever attempted. She had been shipping in obscure parts for months, even having to custom build some of her own. Nobody in the galaxy had ever done this before, had ever attempted what she was going to attempt.

Her family and friends were worried about her, Allie and Dav kept trying to get her to come out with them, and stop shutting herself away. Her father and uncle, and even her great aunt the Queen had been unable to convince her to quit obsessing over this project. None of them even knew what this machine would do, could do.

Since Raith's death, and she did consider it a death, she had been unable to bring herself to even get up in the morning, until an idea struck her. A tremendous, galaxy-altering idea. If this worked, so many things would be different, so many things would be better.

She pulled the goggles back down and leaned in close. The circuitry on this processor was incredibly complex, and she had to keep pausing to check the old diagrams she'd managed to dig up, her holographic display by the workbench showing the intricate detail of the systems in as fine a magnification as she could hope. She only wished these goggles were as precise.

They helped, but she still felt like she was trying to thread a tiny needle with the tiniest thread while wearing a pair of heavy welding gloves. The microscopic welder in her hand flared in a tiny burst, then again. One more circuit complete.

Spinning around on the wheeled chair, she grabbed the alloy-coated heavy cable. Leaning back over the work, she pulled the goggles back off. The cable had fifty tiny wires bound inside it, and each had to be attached to the exact right place. She had less than a nanometer's variance or the whole project would fail.

She didn't like to think about it, but the project could actually explode when she attempted to power it up once she finished this wiring. A small flashing light on her readout told her someone was ringing her doorbell. She ignored it, fusing the first two wires into place. She moved as fast as she could without risking a sacrifice in the quality of her work. She couldn't afford to sacrifice any of her precision, for anything.

"Hold on!" she shouted, fusing more wires into place.

"Imber?" the readout on her display transcribed the voice beyond the door. It was Allie, she knew. Allie had said she'd come by today, to check on her. If she'd only come ten minutes later, Imber grumbled to herself.

"Just a minute!" she called back.

A few more wires, and she could connect the primary power coupling. Then, she'd upload the data from the small scanner she had managed to rescue, then connect the final injector, and the system would power on. Or explode. No, she thought. This has to work.

It had taken her some time to find that specific scanner. She'd lost her tools on the Interceptor ages ago, and it wasn't until Dav had gotten the Peacekeeper back from Captain Abram, who had already sold it, that she learned her tools had been sold by the person who bought the Peacekeeper.

Captain Abram had been invaluable in tracking it down. She owed him a lot. Without that scanner, none of this would work. The light flashed. Allie was ringing her doorbell again.

"Hang on, I'm almost done!" she shouted, her excitement and anxiety about this pushing its way into her voice.

"Imber, are you okay?" the readout transcribed.

"Great, just give me a few more minutes!"

The last of the wires was fused into place. She pulled out another device and did a quick circuit check. Everything lit up, the circuit was successfully in place on the processor, and drawing power correctly from the system. A success.

She connected the primary power coupling, holding her breath. This was the part where an explosion was most likely, though it could also happen when she plugged in the last power injector. Risky? Absolutely. Was it worth it? Imber didn't hesitate for a moment to insist that it was.

She connected the scanner and switched it from echo mode to backup restore. If anyone else had used this since she lost it, this wouldn't work. It had to have the original backup in place from those many months ago when she'd last used it. She waited several minutes while the little backup system downloaded to the data core.

"Imber?" came the transcription. Allie was probably getting worried. Imber felt bad, but she was literally moments away from seeing if she was brilliant, or if she was dead.

The workshop door would withstand the blast, she knew. Allie would be fine if things went badly, as long as Imber didn't let her in too soon. The little echo system flashed that it was complete. She removed the device, sealed a few open panels, and then picked up the last power injector. This was the moment, she knew.

Imber was almost afraid to plug it in. This project was the only thing keeping her going, the only reason she still had to try and interact with the world. If this failed… If this failed, she'd be dead anyway, and it wouldn't matter. And if it worked…

That was enough. Imber plugged in the power injector. She heard the faint hum as the power core routed its power through the injector system and the couplings, and into the system components for the first time.

There was no explosion. Imber let a breath out she didn't realize she'd been holding this time. The internal systems were powering up quickly, in the correct order. Only the first power cycle would be this slow, she knew. The components needed to warm up.

The door behind her opened. Imber didn't even notice. Allie and Dav walked in behind her a few steps, then stopped cold when they saw what was on the table before her. Allie's hand went to her mouth in shock.

"Imber. What are you doing?" Dav asked softy, tone filled with concern, and a strong tinge of concern.

"Imber, this isn't possible," Allie gasped.

Imber didn't respond. She was watching, intensely, for one specific thing. The power hit the processor, and the processing system began to warm up. This was it. Her gaze snapped up as the processor completed its warmup. Her heart pounded in her chest. She almost couldn't take another second, and then it happened.

The clear, new eyes opened, and locked with Imber's. And Raith smiled.

# ABOUT THE AUTHOR

Christopher Bailey lives in Washington state with his amazing wife, happily raising their first child. Working professionally with children for more than twelve years has helped him develop a fondness for children's literature, and a frustration for the lack of good stories for older children that are completely family-friendly.

Inspired by an argument between two children in the school where he worked, he decided to write his first novel, "Starjumper Legacy: The Crystal Key". In answer to that argument, magic and science are one and the same, only divided by level of understanding. The real truth is that both exist in our world today if you only take the time to look closely enough.

With over a dozen more novels already in the works, including a children's chapter book series about superheroes, he looks forward to the chance to publish many more stories yet to come and hopes his readers enjoy reading his stories as much as he enjoys writing them. The adventure continues...